RUBY'S WAR

In the autumn of 1942, fifteen year old Ruby is collected from her aunt's guesthouse by her grandfather. She is taken to live with him in a village in industrial Lancashire, where a few days after her arrival a number of US Quartermaster Truck Companies of black troops take over a nearby camp. Before long tension rises between the newly arrived troops and the locals, many of whom still have embedded racial prejudices. As the town becomes divided, Ruby and her friends must struggle with adolescence, illicit love, dangerous friendships and the difficulty of doing what is right in a chaotic and unfair world.

RUBY'S WAR

RUBY'S WAR

by

Johanna Winard

Magna Large Print Books
Long Preston, North Yorkshire,
BD23 4ND, England.

British Library Cataloguing in Publication Data.

Winard, Johanna
Ruby Parker.

A catalogue record of this book is
available from the British Library

ISBN   978-0-7505-3990-6

First published in Great Britain by Allison & Busby in 2014

Copyright © 2014 by Johanna Winard

Cover illustration © Jayne Szekely by arrangement with
Arcangel Images

The moral right of the author is hereby asserted in accordance with
the Copyright, Designs and Patents Act, 1988

Published in Large Print 2014 by arrangement with
Allison & Busby Ltd.

Magna Large Print is an imprint of Library Magna Books Ltd.

Printed and bound in Great Britain by
T.J. (International) Ltd., Cornwall, PL28 8RW

*In memory of Private William Crossland
who was killed during the real Battle of
Bamber Bridge on the 24th June 1943*

CHAPTER ONE

Ruby left the guest house and turned down the familiar street of cramped boarding houses. As she neared the school, the squeals and yells of the children in the playground replaced the sound of bickering gulls. She hurried across the main road and waited at the edge of the girls' yard, until Mavis left the skipping game and came over to speak to her.

'Are you coming to help with the infants?' she asked, taking in Ruby's gymslip and turquoise jumper.

Ruby shook her head. 'I'm going to the cobbler's to collect some shoes for one of the guests. I could come back this way. When you come out, we could walk home together.'

'I can't,' Mavis said, rubbing her turned-up nose with the back of her hand. 'I'm going for my lesson. My mum's paying for me to go to Miss Sumner for shorthand and typing. When I leave, I'm going to work in the newspaper offices with my Auntie Barbara.'

A decaying, Victorian glass-topped canopy sheltered the row of shops opposite the school. The cobbler's little shop was squeezed in at the end next to the barber. She opened the door, the brass bell tinkled and Mr Bentham looked up at her over his glasses. The shop smelt of leather, glue and pipe tobacco. When Ruby handed him the ticket, he put down his pipe and went along the rough wooden racks at the back of the counter, mumbling to himself and inspecting the numbers chalked on the soles of the shoes.

'Crawford, Crawford. Here we are, a resole. Hand-stitched,' Mr Bentham said, lowering his voice, as if telling her a secret. 'Very nice.'

Ruby walked back home up another street of identical boarding houses to Everdeane, her uncle's guest house. Halfway along, as the smell of the salty air grew stronger and the clamour of the gulls rippled down the narrow street, she slowed her pace. In a shady alleyway between the blocks of houses, someone had chalked a hopscotch on the ground. Ruby tucked the shoes under her arm and hopped from square to square. The game wasn't much fun to play alone, and after a couple of tries, she wandered back up the prom towards the guest house.

Ruby stood at the bottom of the stairs, unsure if she should take the shoes up to Mr Crawford's room or leave them on the hall table, as if they were a telegram or a letter. The house was quiet, except for the sound of muffled voices – one high and two much deeper ones – coming from the kitchen. The sound made her tingle. Abandoning the shoes by the elephant's foot umbrella stand, she edged towards the kitchen door. She recognised Auntie Ethel's voice and Uncle Walt's. The third, a softer voice, she was sure could only belong to her dad. In the dark corridor Ruby pulled up her ankle socks, tugged down the hem of her gymslip and with a trembling hand opened the door.

When she saw who was sitting at the table with Uncle Walt and Auntie Ethel, she was afraid. The three adults were leaning forwards, as if waiting for someone to take a turn in a game of cards, but there were no cards on the worn oilcloth. The air was heavy, thickened with secrets. As she waited by the door for them to notice her, Ruby's stomach did the kind of tickle and flop it did on fairground rides. Then her Auntie Ethel looked up.

'Your granddad's going to take you for a stroll along the prom, Ruby,' she said.

Granddad got up slowly and began buttoning his long brown mac. 'Train back is at half past four,' he said.

'Then you'd best hurry,' Auntie replied, getting up from the table and straightening her overall with her bony fingers.

No one smiled, and as Ruby followed her grand-dad down the dimly lit hall, her knees began to wobble. He waited for her at the foot of the worn stone steps, leaning on the white balustrade near the gate. The sign hanging above his head read: 'Everdeane Select Guest House. Proprietor Mr W. A. O'Kane.' Granddad's wiry, pepper-coloured hair was lifting in the salt breeze. He tugged his cap out of his pocket and put it on. When she reached the bottom step, he strode ahead of her across the road to the promenade, where Tommy Wright and two other boys from her school were playing football. The tide was in. The sea was gentle. Its soft, silky grey ripples calmed her.

'I thought it was Dad. When I heard you, I thought he'd come. Do you think he knows about

13

Mum?' she asked, nibbling the end of one dark-red pigtail.

'No, Ruby, love. He'd have come, or written, at least. Thinks the world of you.'

It wasn't bad news; she'd been afraid he was going to say he wasn't coming back. But instead, he'd said, 'He thinks the world of you.' He was alive. He'd be coming for her. She grinned at Granddad, and when Tommy Wright's mucky ball caught her in the middle of the back, she laughed and kicked it back to him.

'Thanks, Ruby,' he shouted.

'That's not a bad shot,' Granddad said approvingly. 'Are the lads from your school?'

'All three of them. Two are evacuees. It's their turn to go in the mornings this week. The one that kicked the ball is Tommy Wright. He was in my class. He tells everybody he's fifteen, but he's not. He's fourteen and a half. He was always getting the cane. When we had gas mask practice, he pretended to choke and he made his mask do this rude noise. Last time, the teacher caught him.'

'Sounds like your dad. I remember his teacher collaring me one day and saying he'd upset old Miss Garvey. Every time she'd bent down, him or his mate made this farting sound with their hands, and she got that upset.'

They giggled, and for a moment, Ruby felt that it was going to be all right. Auntie Ethel always said neither her dad nor her granddad had ever grown up. That's why he could see the joke and why he would have arrived at Everdeane on a whim. Other grown-ups wouldn't have turned up unannounced, unless they'd come with bad news.

14

But Granddad might have come just because he'd fancied a ride out on the train and wanted to buy some cockles for his tea.

'This is where I last saw Dad,' she said. 'He was standing right here. He'd had a late night and he was watching us on the beach. We were digging sand, filling sandbags. It was too hard for most of us. There were lots of people helping, not just kids from our school; a lot of men were helping as well.'

'Bet he didn't.'

She laughed and waved her hands. 'You know what he's like. "My hands, Ruby, love. I've got to look after my hands." He just stood there watching the rest of us.'

'Always the same excuse,' Granddad said, taking a packet of five Woodbines from his pocket. 'Can't do any real work, it would spoil his piano hands.'

For a few minutes, they watched the gulls bobbing on the quiet water. Then he took out a cigarette.

'Ruby, love,' he said, turning away to light it. 'Now your mum's gone, I think it's best you come and live with me.'

'I can't,' she said squinting up at him. 'Auntie needs me here. We're full all the time now. It's not like before. It doesn't go quiet in winter any more. Not now all the government people have been moved up here to work. We're full all the time.'

'Auntie Ethel thinks it's a good idea. I'm ... well... I'm your closest relative.'

'Well, tell her you don't mind.'

'It's the room... I think they want the room. It's like you said, all these government departments are sending all their pen-pushers up here, so there's money to be made, even out of that little box room of yours.'

Ruby felt her cheeks begin to burn. She turned away and looked down at the waves. She tasted salt in her mouth and swallowed. Then a coldness – as familiar as the chill wind from the sea – curled around her.

'I'm sure you've been a good lass ... but ... anyway. That's why she sent for me. There's a train back in half an hour,' he said, leaving the sea wall and heading back over to Everdeane. 'We've got to pick your case up.'

'Dad thinks I'm here,' she whispered to the silky waves. 'He'll come here looking for me.'

Her small case was in the porch. Through the leaded light in the front door, she could see the wavy shapes of her aunt and uncle moving towards them. Auntie Ethel opened the door and pushed another battered suitcase out on to the step. She was wearing her apron and Pearl's fox-fur stole around her neck.

'Your mother's things are in here. I've taken nothing for myself, except this,' she said, stroking the fox's paw. 'It's no use to you, and she was my sister and well... Most of it's evening wear, but I know you're handy with a needle, so perhaps they'll come in. Here's her ration book,' she said, handing the small blue book to Granddad. 'Now, you be a good girl, Ruby.'

The fur stole had been a present from her father. He'd arrived on Christmas morning with presents for them both, a pretty dress for her and the fox fur for her mother. On the same visit, he'd taken

16

them out for tea. There'd been a band playing, and when he'd got up to dance with her mother, everyone in the room had watched them. She'd felt proud because they'd looked so glamorous.

Auntie Ethel went back down the hall, the grinning fox over her narrow shoulder. Uncle Walt watched her go, and when the kitchen door closed, he handed Ruby her mother's music case.

'This is yours,' he said, stroking the soft chestnut leather. 'It belonged to Pearl. Her musical arrangements. Some your dad did for her.'

'Best get going,' Granddad said. 'We'll have to take our time with these cases.'

He picked up her mother's case. As he began to carry it down the steps, Uncle Walt pressed a ten-shilling note into her hand, before slipping back inside the house.

The train was quite full. She waited on the platform with the cases until Granddad found a carriage with two empty seats. Ruby sat by the window with her back to the engine. In the west, the sky was silver-grey tinged with a delicate flush of orange, as though the colour of the gentle, silky water had been caught up by the dying sun. The idea comforted her and the dark chill began to lift. As the train began to move she fixed her gaze on the sunset, until the sky darkened and the guard called for all the blinds to be pulled down.

The compartment was crowded and dimly lit. Ruby hugged the music case to her chest, sniffing its familiar leather smell. The rough moquette seats made her legs feel itchy, and she tried to pull her school mac down to protect her bare legs. She gazed at the sepia photographs of Loch Katrine above the seats opposite, forced her tears back into her aching throat and tried to ignore her prickly legs.

The blue light made the other passengers appear indistinct. Her grandfather's head seemed pale and insubstantial, as though at any moment it might float free from his body. In the semi-darkness an American soldier hugged a pretty blonde, whose left hand lay like a starfish on the chest of his uniform, displaying a glittering new wedding ring. Snuggling close to the young man, the girl explained to the other passengers, a middle-aged couple and a lady in a brown suit and polished brogues, that they had been on honeymoon and her new husband was due back at his base the next day.

'What a coincidence,' the older woman said. 'We've been to a wedding ourselves. My cousin's daughter. Her young man is in the navy. We were hoping our sons could get leave. They're both in the RAF. Dick, my eldest, has been in since 1940. He's a radio operator. My younger boy, Christopher, was called up at the beginning of the year.'

'You must be very proud of your boys,' the lady in the brown suit said. 'I don't know what we should have done without the RAF. My family is from London. They were bombed out in 1940. This will be the first time I've visited them in their new place. My job was moved up here away from the conflict. I was told I needed to get the London train from Preston.'

'The next train should leave in about twenty minutes,' Granddad said, consulting his fob watch. 'You've plenty of time.'

'Have you been on holiday?' the lady asked.

'No,' Granddad said, shifting uneasily in his seat. 'I've been to collect my granddaughter. She's been helping out at her aunt's guest house.'

The train rolled to a halt and the engine hissed.

'I hope they tell us when we arrive at the stations,' the middle-aged woman said. 'You can't tell if we are waiting for a signal, or if we're at a station. They said when they moved the signs from the platforms that there would be someone to call out the name of the stations, but there isn't.'

'We travelled up from Preston during the day,' her husband added. 'They didn't do it then. This lady wanted to get off at Kirkham and she missed her stop. We can't even see out now, so how are we to know?'

'Well, we'll not miss Preston,' Granddad said. 'It's a big station. I know it well. I worked there for years.'

When they arrived at Preston station, the American soldier helped them out of the train with their luggage. The platform was full of British soldiers who were boarding a waiting train. Ruby struggled through the crowd, dodging kitbags and trying to keep Granddad's tall figure in view.

'Excuse me, love,' one of the soldiers said as Ruby struggled by with her case. 'Can you post this?' he asked, handing her a crumpled envelope. The soldier wore a greatcoat and his eyes were red and bleary. He put down his kitbag and handed her two pennies. 'I haven't been able to get a stamp,' he said.

'What's the matter, son?' Granddad asked.

'I was asking this young lass if she could post

19

this for me. It's to let my girl know where I am.'

The train began to make steam and the weight of men on the platform forced the young soldier forwards. He hitched his bag on his shoulder, and as he was carried away, he looked back through the crowd towards Ruby and her granddad.

'Don't worry, son. We'll see it gets sent,' Granddad called, but his voice was lost amongst the sound of slamming doors and the hiss of escaping steam.

Their second train was much smaller and the carriage was empty. After barely ten minutes, they arrived at a deserted station. It was a clear night, and she could make out a steep, shrub-covered spoil bank behind the opposite platform. The air smelt of coal smoke, and Ruby could hear traffic crossing the railway bridge above her. She shivered and put down her suitcase next to the empty ticket office.

Steep wooden steps led from the station's platform on to the railway bridge. At the top, Granddad put down the larger case. She could hear his chest rattle, as his whole body bent to the task of filling his lungs with the thick, damp air.

'This bridge is the highest point round here,' he said between gasps. 'On a good day you can see for miles.'

Ruby was about to ask if she would be able to see Blackpool Tower, when the darkness around them filled with the yowling of injured animals. She shuddered. They sounded very near.

'Did they make you jump?' Granddad laughed. 'It's only the engines in the shunting yards. You'll get used to them soon enough. Other side of this bridge, there's big sheds for trains. Goods trains. Massive things.'

The road was busy. Beams from the narrow headlights of a blacked-out bus appeared suddenly at the top of the bridge. When the updraught from the double-decker hit them, it made her blink and press as close as she could to the rough wood fence.

'Now watch yourself,' Granddad said. 'The footpath's narrow over these two bridges. Not too bad when we get down the other side. Have you a torch?'

'I have one at home ... at Auntie's,' she said.

Ruby followed her grandfather down the first bridge and up to the top of a second one. Below her the silver tangle of railway lines clattered, the straining engines spat and the sound of their wailing filled the night.

At the foot of the second bridge, there was a row of blacked-out shops on one side of the road. On the opposite side, she could see a large, white public house, a line of white cottages, followed by a short string of terraced villas and then a longer terrace of smaller houses. As they walked by the shops, Ruby found it hard to see but she made out the darkened windows of a butcher's shop, a newsagent, and then the broad, dome-shaped door of a church hall. Between them, she glimpsed narrow side streets, each with a line of the same squat houses. Her grandfather turned down one of the streets. Points of light bounced towards them from the torches of passers-by, who called out 'good neet' into the blackness.

Granddad rapped sharply on one of the front

doors and pushed it open. She followed him, stumbling down the two steps into a small room. There was a table in the centre with a gas mantle hissing softly above it. The shadows above the gaslight hid the face of a woman standing by the table. All Ruby could see was her old-fashioned black blouse and the equally black brooch at the collar.

'Who's this?' the woman asked, as her grand-dad put down the big suitcase.

'This is our Will's little lass,' he said. 'Ruby, love, this is your Auntie Maud. Always makes a fuss of your dad, does Maud. She's not seen you since you were a babby.'

'Humph,' Auntie Maud said, taking a seat at the table. 'I thought she was with her mother's people.'

'Well, Ethel thinks she'd be better here,' Grand-dad said, sitting down next to her.

'Oh, does she,' Auntie Maud said, opening the newspaper that was lying on the table.

The room fell silent. Now that the woman was seated, Ruby could see that she had round glasses and the same sharp nose as Granddad. Gazing into the shadows beyond the gas mantle's yellow light, she could make out a heavy dresser with an oval photo frame on top and a full-length photo-graph of a young man in uniform hanging on the wall above it. She wondered if the young man might be her grandfather. The only other piece of furniture was a single bed, partly hidden by a curtain that hung from the ceiling. There was a huge white shape under the counterpane.

'That's your Uncle Joe, Ruby,' Granddad said,

22

taking off his cap and nodding towards the figure on the bed. 'He's not well,' Granddad added. 'He needs someone to...'

'He's got someone,' Auntie Maud snapped.

Getting up from the table, Maud hobbled over to the hearth and filled a small white teapot from the kettle. They watched as she made her way slowly over to the bed, pushed back the curtain and put the spout of the lidless teapot into Uncle Joe's mouth.

'So you'd best take this lass home. And if your fancy woman don't like it, then she knows what she can do. If she does clear off, 'appen the little lass can manage for thee.'

'Just for a couple of nights. She'd be a good help.'

'Not for an hour. No. I know you too well, our Henry.'

'What do you say, Joe?'

Uncle Joe had the same thin nose as Auntie Maud and Granddad, but the rest of him was very white and fat. He made Ruby think of a young gull, so when he turned his bloated form towards them and fixed them with a bright black eye, she almost expected him to open his mouth and squawk.

'You never mind what Joe thinks,' Auntie Maud said. 'You just get that lass home.'

Then Maud sat down with her back towards them, and all Ruby could see was her aunt's fine grey hair, plaited and rolled into a tight bun at the nape of her neck. The room was silent again, except for the rustle of the thin newspaper as Auntie Maud turned the page. Then the clock on the mantelpiece began to stir, making first a grating sound as though it was clearing its dry throat, before commencing its uncertain chime. On the opposite side of the table, Granddad's shoulders appeared to shrink, making his mac look much too big for his narrow frame. It was seven o'clock. Ruby remembered that she hadn't eaten since breakfast at seven-thirty, and as though reacting to a signal, on the final stroke her stomach began to rumble. The chimes were also a signal to Granddad who, as the clock fell silent, made for the door.

Ruby followed him outside. In the blackout, the houses appeared to be so close together that she wondered if it would be hard for even the brightest sunlight to force its way down into the cobbled street. When they reached the main road, Granddad crossed over and made for the public house. Blackout material had been used to cover the glass in the door, but the name, The Railway Inn, had been cut out of the blind and the letters covered with a translucent mauve fabric. Through the dim shapes in the blind, she could see sleeves and shoulders pushed up against the door of the crowded bar.

'We'd best go round to the back,' Granddad muttered, turning into the narrow alleyway and capturing a soldier and his giggling girlfriend in the beam from his torch.

'Clear off, you dirty buggers,' he shouted. 'I've a young lass here.'

Ruby wanted to tell him not to worry on her account – she'd lived in a guest house since she was nine and was used to courting couples. But Granddad had disappeared, and she was left to struggle with her suitcase in the dark. Then she heard a door open and music spilt out into the night.

'Come on, Ruby, love,' Granddad called. 'Where are you?'

She headed towards the sound and a strong, warm hand took hers, guiding her into a narrow passageway that smelt of cigarette smoke and stale beer.

'This here's Johnny Finlay, Johnny Fin,' her granddad said, nodding towards the large man standing next to him.

Johnny Finlay, who was over six foot five, bent down, put his huge hands on his knees and smiled. 'Nice to meet you. Is that your music case?'

Johnny Finlay wasn't a handsome man; there wasn't even one hair on his wide bony skull, his nose was flat with a funny bump in the middle and his front teeth were missing. If she'd been alone, Ruby was sure she would have screamed with fright.

'Oh, she's got all her parents' musical talent,' Granddad said. 'Now, Ruby, you wait here with the cases. Me and Johnny have a bloke to see.'

When he opened the door to the brightly lit bar, she heard someone call his name. Then Johnny Fin gave her a friendly wave and followed him. Ruby sat down on an empty beer crate. Since her mother's death, whenever Auntie Ethel had given her a dull job to do, or when she'd finished her schoolwork before the other children, Ruby would slide back to the time before Pearl's accident, and as there was nothing of interest in the hallway, she closed her eyes.

She was back at Everdeane. It was winter, and all the visitors had gone. She was with her mother in the guest bedroom they'd shared out of season. Sometimes in the early evening, they would sit together in the large bay window to watch the setting sun. Then, if she'd a booking at one of the clubs in town, her mother would sit down in front of the mirror, put on her make-up and become Pearl Barton, nightclub singer. Ruby had loved those times. Her mother would laugh and sing and talk about the club or the theatre where she was going to perform and how she might get asked back to sing again.

Ruby could smell her perfume, hear her excited giggles and the distant, tinkling music carried down the prom on the sea breeze. She felt someone shake her by the shoulder, smelt Pearl's face powder and opened her eyes. For a moment she thought the woman in the dimly lit hallway was her mother, but she wasn't as pretty.

'What are you doin' here?' the woman asked. 'Are you all right, love?'

The woman wore a glittery top and had blonde hair set in finger waves and, although she wasn't as pretty as her mother, when she smiled Ruby could tell that she was kind.

'It's all right, Vera,' a voice called from the doorway. 'She's with Henry. I think he's trying to get up a bit of Dutch courage before he takes her home. It's his granddaughter.'

'Dutch courage? And you're letting him?'

'Best keep out of it.'

'You can just go and tell him now, Bert Lyons, it's more than your licence is worth to have a child in your pub.'

'She's not doin' any harm.'

'I know that, you soft bugger. The poor kid's sat on her own in the dark, while he gets drunk. You tell him you're not serving him, and he's taking her home, now.'

Ruby followed her grandfather back through the yard to the front of the pub. This time, he didn't seem to notice the couple cuddling in the dark. They walked back along the main road, past the row of white cottages, the darkened houses and the blacked-out shops and church hall on the opposite side. When the rows of houses ended, the footpath narrowed and the air became colder.

'Be careful,' Granddad said. 'Here. Hold on to the belt of my coat. This bridge over the river is narrow. It's not far now.'

As they edged their way up the little humped-back bridge, Ruby could hear the running water. They were almost at the top when the sound of a bus engine broke through the inky silence. The tiny slits of light from its headlamps sprang up in front of them, and her granddad pushed Ruby in close to the rough stone parapet.

'Bloody fool,' he shouted. 'Fancy coming over at that speed in the blackout.'

At the bottom of the bridge they turned off the main road. Above them, the moon slid out from behind the clouds. They'd turned into a narrow lane with a single row of cottages on the opposite corner. Granddad didn't cross over but walked up the lane between the tall hedgerows until they came to a single white stone cottage.

'Here we are,' he said, fastening up the belt on

27

his mac. 'You hungry?'

When he opened the front door someone screamed. A blonde-haired girl, wearing nothing but salmon-pink French knickers, was standing in the centre of a white sheet, her arms wrapped across her naked breasts. For a moment there was silence, and Ruby felt the warm air from the room swirl against her cold legs. Then the door behind the girl burst open, and a fat woman charged at them.

'Don't just bloody stand there, get out!' she shouted and slammed the front door.

'Shall I go round the back, Jenny, love?' Grand-dad called through the letter box.

When there was no reply, he took out his cigarettes and squatted on his haunches. Clouds began to cover the moon and the darkness crept towards them, stealing up from the gate along the narrow garden. He pulled up his collar to light a match, and then all she could see was the tip of his cigarette, pulsing slowly with each inhalation. Ruby squeezed her music case tightly and swallowed hard. When he'd finished, he knocked on the door again. This time it swung open.

The fat woman's cross face appeared from behind a swell of white cotton sheet. 'Will you shut that door,' she said, shaking and folding the fabric.

Then, with the folded sheet under one arm, she began collecting pieces of fine tweed cloth that were scattered on the furniture and the floor. Depending on the way it caught the light, the fabric was either a soft lilac or violet in colour. One of the pieces, a sleeve, lolled on the back of an easy chair by the open fire, another hung over

28

a wooden chair next to the table, and still more were piled on the tabletop, where they clashed with the red crushed-velvet cover. The plump woman moved easily, bending to scoop up each piece of fabric, folding each one as she moved on to take up the next one. With each movement, her crystal drop earrings glittered icily.

Ruby shivered. In front of the range was a large brass fender with boxes for holding kindling built into its two corners. She would have loved to sit on the padded top of one of the brass boxes and stretch out her fingers to the coal fire, but thought it was better to stay by the door, until she was invited to sit down.

'I offered to go round the back, Jenny, love.'

'What, an' walk in on our Sadie again, when she's in the scullery havin' a wash?'

The plump woman scooped up the pieces of a paper pattern that were lying on the floor, and as she settled down in an easy chair to fold them, there was a knock at the front door.

The blonde girl, now fully dressed, hurried in from the scullery. 'I'll get it,' she said. 'It's only Lou.'

She opened the front door to a dark-haired girl of about her own age.

'Oh, is this my suit?' the girl asked, picking up a stray scrap of fabric from the flagged floor.

'I was hoping to have it tacked up by now, and you could have tried it on,' the woman replied. 'I was pinning it on our Sadie, but we was interrupted.'

'Who's this?' Lou asked, smiling at Ruby.

'This is Ruby,' Granddad said. 'She's my son's

daughter. Lives with her aunt, since she lost her mum. I've been over there to sort out some family business and thought I'd bring her home with me for a few days. She can stay in her dad's old room.'

'Ahh,' the blonde girl cooed. 'That'll be nice. Nice to meet you, love. I'm Sadie and this is Lou.'

'Hello, love,' Lou said. 'Haven't you got lovely eyes.'

Outside, a horn tooted loudly, and the two young women checked their make-up in the mirror.

'That's our lift,' Sadie said. 'See you later. Don't wait up.'

'I don't know what Jack's mother will think when she sees a Yank calling for her son's intended,' Granddad said, as the sound of the engine died away. 'Blackout or no blackout, she misses nothing.'

'What Sadie does is no business of yours, Henry,' the woman said.

Granddad bent down and picked up a delicate piece of paper pattern from the pegged rug.

'I was wondering,' he said, handing the piece to the woman. 'Since Ruby will be staying here, would it be fitting for her to call you Grandma, Grandma Jenny? If you wouldn't object?'

'Well, it's more respectful than Jenny,' the woman said, and smiled slightly as she took the tissue paper from his outstretched hand. 'I suppose she'll need feeding as well.'

Granddad winked at Ruby and began unbuttoning his mac. 'Take your coat off, Ruby,' he said, 'and we'll hang it here. Then I'll get the tablecloth. Is it in the dresser drawer, Jenny?'

'It's not Sunday,' Jenny said, handing him a newspaper, which he opened out and spread over the velvet cloth.

'Ruby and me will set the table,' he said. 'Leave that to us. I'm sure she knows how to set a table.'

'Let's hope so,' Jenny replied, getting up from the chair. 'The plates are in the bottom of the oven in the range. Use the cloth on the rail to carry them, and make sure you put it back. Knives and forks are in the right-hand drawer,' she said, pointing to the dresser by the kitchen door. 'I'll go and cut the bread.'

When Ruby pulled open the oven door, the smell of stew bubbling in the large brown pot made her feel dizzy. Granddad, who had taken off his jacket and his stiff collar, took a seat at the table, and as she set out the knives and forks, he did his secret grin and winked again.

'Here. Put this on the table,' Grandma Jenny said, coming back from the kitchen with a plate of bread. 'I'll bring the stew. No doubt it's dry by now.'

'Grandma Jenny is a very good cook, Ruby,' Granddad said.

Jenny carried the steaming pot to the table. When she took off the lid, the rich smell filled the room.

'Not too bad,' she declared, spooning out the deep-brown stew on to the plates and tucking the tea towel in the waistband of her apron.

The food was warm and comforting. The meat was tasty, although Ruby didn't recognise the

31

strong, dark flesh. She squashed the soft, waxy potatoes into the viscous gravy and let the taste of the sweet carrots fill her mouth.

'Now, that was worth waiting for,' Granddad smiled, when they'd dabbed up every last drop and their plates were clean and dry. 'Wouldn't you say so, Ruby, love?'

'Well it took you long enough to get home to it,' Jenny said, 'and via the pub, by the smell of you.'

'It was the train. It was delayed,' he said, avoiding Ruby's eye. 'The station was that busy, soldiers, all kinds. Ruby was getting knocked here and there. So I took her into the station bar to wait. All that luggage and rushing about, the lass could have been knocked off the platform. Might there be any pudding left?' he asked.

'You can't expect to have decent food served up at the drop of a hat,' Jenny said, surveying the empty plates. 'You're lucky there's anything left. Was there Yanks at Preston?' she asked. 'Our Sadie says there's a rumour that the Yanks are sending black GIs up here.'

'No, they was ours. We had some black lads in France last time. They was Yanks. Nice enough lads, from what I could see. Jenny, love,' he said, winking at Ruby, 'did I see you coring apples this morning?'

'It's more than you deserve,' she replied, heading over to the oven again.

The fat apples were filled with dried fruit, made soft and full with fragrant apple juice. At Everdeane, when baked apples were the pudding, there was much less fruit packed inside, and the visitors had been forced to use their individual sugar rations to make the tart flesh edible.

Once she'd eaten her apple, Ruby began to feel sleepy. It was only a holiday. A few days, he'd said. They just needed her room for a bit. She yawned. If they'd told her sooner, she could have been packed and waiting for Granddad when he'd arrived.

Jenny brought a large brown teapot over to the table and collected the dishes. Instead of drinking from his cup, Granddad tipped the tea into his saucer and began to sip it. Ruby expected Jenny to complain. Auntie Ethel would never have allowed it. No wonder she hadn't offered him a cup of tea. But Jenny didn't say anything. Instead, she opened up the white sheet again, and after pinning part of it across her wobbly bosom, began tacking the pieces of the suit together.

When they'd arrived, Jenny's face had been pink and angry. Now, as she sat by the fireside, her wide doughy face looked tired.

'If I'd known you were bringin' her home, I'd have aired the bed,' she said, slowly drawing her needle in and out through the fabric. 'There's a brick warming in the bottom of the oven. She can have that. I'd put it in for me, but as you're home, you can warm my feet.'

'You don't worry, Jenny,' Granddad said, getting up from the table and picking up the small case. 'I'll take her up.' He handed Ruby the brick wrapped in a piece of old sheet. 'Come on, Ruby, love. Let's get you to bed.'

'Is that all she's been sent with?' Jenny asked, eyeing the small brown case.

Ruby didn't hear the reply and followed him

33

through the kitchen and up the stairs. Granddad put the brick into the bed and set the case down near the door.

'I'll leave the landing door open just a bit. You can close it once you've got undressed,' he said. 'There's no light in here. I'll fix one up in the morning.'

'The other case, Granddad,' she said sleepily. 'Is it...'

'Sleep tight,' he said, giving her a beery kiss. 'It'll be okay, you'll see. Her bark's worse than her bite.'

Ruby was too sleepy to find her nightclothes. Instead, she put her gymslip and school blouse on the cane chair by the bed and crept under the chilly sheets. The brick quickly warmed the top half of the mattress. Then she edged it down until she could curl up with the brick, parcelled in its thick layer of wrapping, a few inches from her feet. Her eyes closed, and telling herself that it was only a holiday, Ruby drifted away from the small, damp room.

CHAPTER TWO

When she opened her eyes, Ruby remembered Pearl's suitcase. She sat up, but except for a thin line of light showing under the door, it was dark and she couldn't see anything. The cold stung her bare arms, and she wriggled down again under the covers. Her toes probed the frayed sheet around the brick, but no warmth came through the wrapping. She stuck out a hand and was groping in the darkness, feeling for her socks among the muddle of clothes she'd left on the cane chair, when she heard angry voices coming from the kitchen. Pulling her hand back inside the safety of the blankets, Ruby listened. She thought it must be Granddad and Jenny, but she couldn't be sure. Then she heard footsteps; someone walked along the landing and then back again. She slid further into her blanket cocoon and waited. The door opened slowly and a pale-grey light filled the room.

'You awake?' Sadie whispered.

Sadie wore a dark overcoat over her nightdress and carried a white enamel potty. She placed the naked toes of one foot on the lino and in two hops landed beside her on the bed.

'Blimey, it's cold in here,' she said. 'I've brought you this. It's a bit small, but it will have to do.'

Ruby sat up and pulled on her school blouse. The chamber pot was worn and dented and had a thin blue line around the rim.

'I was fifteen in February,' she said, 'I don't...'

'Well it's either this or go outside,' Sadie said.

'The bathroom...'

'Bathroom? There's no bathroom, just the lavvy in the yard,' she replied, unclipping the blackout curtain and pointing to a small red-brick outhouse with a rough wooden door. 'It's down there. You wouldn't get me out there in the dark. It's bad enough in the day, with Monty to contend with.'

'Monty?'

'Henry's bloody cockerel.'

As if he'd heard his name, somewhere in the

yard Monty began to crow.

'That's him,' Sadie said. 'When you go, don't forget to take the long brush by the back door. If he comes for you, belt him with it. He's a bugger for pecking your legs. He ruined a pair of my nylons last week.'

The voices from the kitchen grew louder, and Ruby scrambled out of bed and pulled on her crumpled gymslip.

'Don't worry about them,' Sadie said, settling down on the bed and pulling out a pack of Lucky Strikes from her pocket. 'They're always at it. Ever since we moved in here, it's been the same.'

Ruby sat on the cane chair and gazed around the room. Apart from the old chair and the single bed, the only other piece of furniture was a small wooden bookcase. There were no curtains, except the blackout curtain Sadie had taken down, and the only thing covering the floor was a piece of cracked lino. She found it hard to believe that this had ever been her father's bedroom. Her father loved luxury and style. He always wore nice suits and, although she couldn't remember it, her mother had said that when they were on tour they'd stayed in the most wonderful hotels.

'Looks like all these were your dad's books,' Sadie said, tipping her head to one side to read the titles. 'They're adventures mostly. I like romances. This room's not up to much, is it? You've not even got anywhere to hang your clothes.'

'I haven't got many,' Ruby said, nodding towards the small brown case. 'I'm only staying for...'

Sadie looked up and smiled. 'What's in the case?' she asked.

36

'My clothes and things.'

'Not that one. The big one he left under the window in the garden. Last night, my friend was just walking me to the door and we fell over it. I could have broken my neck. I got him to carry it inside. She'd have found out about it, anyway. That's what they're rowing about now.'

Earlier when she'd woken up and remembered the case, Ruby knew in her heart that what Granddad had told her on the prom was true, but when the door opened and the big suitcase wasn't in the room or on the landing, she'd begun to believe that she really might just be staying for a holiday.

'What happened?' Sadie asked. 'Did you have a row with your auntie?'

'No. It's the room. They want the room. But last night Granddad said ... I was only...'

'Do you want a hankie?'

Ruby shook her head and stared hard at the books on the shelf. Her mother had once told her that when she was about to go on stage, to take her mind off her fears, she would count the lights around the mirror in her dressing room or the pots of make-up on her dressing table. Now, Ruby counted her father's books and tried to forget the ache in her throat.

'Look, I'll go and talk to her,' Sadie said. 'It's not you she's mad with. It's him, for lying to her.'

They heard a door slam, and Sadie knelt up and looked out of the window.

'That's him off down the garden to feed his birds,' she said. 'I'll go down and see her. Give me a few minutes, and then come down.'

As Sadie slid off the bed, the weak morning

sunlight broke into the chilly room, warming her curls to the colour of Tate & Lyle syrup. When she'd gone, Ruby made the bed, pushed the potty underneath and put her suitcase on top of the white counterpane. Then she counted one elephant, two elephant, until she got to one hundred and Sadie called her name.

The big, dented suitcase stood in the middle of the kitchen's flagged floor. Its sides were covered with labels from the seaside hotels where her parents had worked in the summer seasons before her father left.

'I should have known, when they sent her wearing that gymslip,' Jenny said. 'I should have known he was lying. I mean, who'd send a child on holiday wearing school clothes?'

Sadie, who was wetting a comb under the tap, winked and turned back to the mirror. She'd changed into a pair of brown tweed trousers and a cream jumper and had metal clips and rollers in her hair. After adding a final roller, she twisted a scarf into a turban around her head and grinned.

'You hungry?' she asked. 'Come on, we'll have some breakfast.'

Ruby followed her into the living room. There was a loaf and a jar of home-made blackberry jam on the table.

'Cut us a couple of slices,' Sadie said, picking up the teapot from the hearth. 'That's the last of the jam, so don't put too much on, and there's no sugar.'

In the daylight the living room looked smaller. On the wall opposite the table, a large six-sided brass-framed mirror decorated with a pattern of

38

ivy leaves hung above a sideboard. Through the mirror, she could see the reflection of the garden, the lane and the fields on the other side.

The tea was warm, but tasted stewed. At Everdeane her mother had made pobs for breakfast. Each morning, she'd buttered slices of day-old bread, cut them into little squares, soaked them in warm milk and sprinkled sugar on the top. Sometimes, if she'd managed to get extra sugar on the black market, the topping was brown and would be crunchy. After she was killed, Uncle Walt sometimes made them, but if Auntie Ethel was in the kitchen, he didn't use much sugar.

When Jenny came in, she sat at the table and nibbled at the leftover crumbs on the breadboard. Granddad, whose clogs clattered in the silence, came in a few minutes later and began poking the fire noisily.

'Do you want me to get some veg for dinner, Jenny, love?' he asked. 'Jack's mother will be here. What should I get?'

'Get what's ready, Henry,' she replied, 'but remember we've another mouth to feed now.'

Granddad didn't answer, but hurried over to the coats hanging by the front door, and as though he was a stage magician, produced Ruby's blue ration book from his overcoat pocket.

'There'll be more coupons,' he said. 'Ethel gave me her book.'

Jenny, who had just dipped a tiny crust into the jam jar, held out her hand for the book, and Granddad clip-clopped across the flagged floor and laid it in her hand.

'Come on, Ruby,' he said, 'get your coat. You

can help me get the veg for dinner.'

Granddad took an old jacket and a muffler from behind the kitchen door and led the way across the yard. The garden at the back of the cottage was bounded by a hawthorn hedge. The field on the other side sloped down to the stream and then rose up again and continued along the back of the terraced houses that faced on to the main road. An Anderson shelter stood on the ground near to the toilet, with old marrow plants still growing on top. Beyond that there was a chicken run, and then a shed and a pigeon coop. A double row of fruit bushes stood in front of the pigeon cabin, and a substantial vegetable plot ran down the side of the cottage to the lane and another neatly clipped hawthorn hedge. In addition to vegetables, there were also two apple trees and an old, twisted pear tree by the gate. In the smaller front garden, Ruby could see crowns of rhubarb, clumps of herbs and the green tops of onions peeping out of every available space.

Granddad opened the shed and took out an old basket and a fork. 'Here,' he said. 'I'll show you how to lift the spuds and carrots.'

He stuck the fork into the ground and the ferny tops of the carrots trembled and fell. He lifted one up by the green top and shook it, gently brushing the soil from the skin with his thumb.

'Look at that,' he said, rubbing the dark, crumbly soil between his fingers. 'Beautiful. We have the river down there to thank. All this was once flooded. Not many round here have such lovely stuff as this to work with.'

The door to the chicken run was open and the

birds scratched and pecked around in the veg patch, dipping under the green leaves and stirring up the soft tilth with their scaly feet.

'Love it out here they do,' Granddad said. 'Plenty of grubs and beetles. Do all the gardening for me, do this lot, and give me eggs as a thank you. Look. Here's our general. He's coming to have a look at you, Ruby. Now then, me lad,' he said, as the large cockerel strutted down a row of beetroot tops towards them. 'He's a grand chap, is Monty,' Granddad said, as the bird cocked his head to one side and eyed him cynically. 'He'll stand no messing from these lasses.'

As Ruby took the fork and felt the earth yield under the metal, Monty positioned himself at her side, holding one vicious claw in the air, and when she lifted a potato plant, the cockerel darted forwards, the swiftness of his movements making her flinch. Each time the fork disturbed the dark soil, she was forced to pause – bare legs purple with cold – as the cockerel stabbed at the desperate worms around her feet.

When she carried the basket of vegetables into the kitchen, the large suitcase had gone, and Sadie was dancing with an imaginary partner in the centre of the tiny room.

'Come on, Ruby,' she called, as she and her grandfather took off their shoes by the kitchen door. 'I'll teach you this dance. Look. Follow me,' she said, twirling to a dance tune on the radio. 'This is how the Americans dance. There was this new band on last night. They were ever so good.'

'You'd best get on with them potatoes, Sadie,' her mother said. 'I'm nearly ready for them to go

41

in. Then get changed, before you go and fetch Jack's mother.'

'I don't want to go too early, Ma,' Sadie said, wrinkling her nose, 'or she'll have me taking that flippin' dog for a walk again.'

'You promised Jack you'd look after it,' Granddad said, washing his hands in the sink.

Jenny, who was mixing pastry on the drop-down flap of a tall, cream-painted cupboard, looked over her shoulder.

'You can get some wood in, that coal's rubbish,' she said. 'Ruby, you can empty out the veg, and get that dirty basket off the draining board.'

Ruby took the basket by its dilapidated handles and tipped the potatoes into the sink, and Granddad shuffled obediently out of the back door. He looked older and smaller than the granddad who'd been waiting in the kitchen at Everdeane the previous day; it was as though that granddad had been hung up in the wardrobe, along with his dark suit and starched white collar.

Ruby ran cold water into the sink and scrubbed the carrots carefully. On the opposite side of the room, Jenny began to roll out the pastry. Her bottom was so big that it pulled her skirt up, making it show the dimples on the backs of her knees.

'Shall I start peeling the potatoes?' Ruby asked.

Jenny waddled over and inspected the vegetables in the sink. 'Aye,' she said, 'they're not big enough for roasters. Them carrots need to be sliced for boiling, as well.'

By twelve o'clock the food was ready, the fire in the living room was crackling and the newspaper

42

on the table had been replaced with a white tablecloth embroidered with Tudor roses and butterflies.

Although she only lived in one of the cottages on the opposite side of the lane, Mrs Lathom arrived wearing a neat, grey, fitted coat and a cloche hat made of black felt. As Sadie took her coat and hat, she patted her taut, faded curls into place. Then putting her head on one side, she surveyed the room, taking in each detail, including the child in the crumpled gymslip.

Granddad, who had been sent upstairs to change out of his shabby trousers, was sitting at the table with his back to the fire reading the newspaper. When her beady eye fell on him, he coughed and, with a great show of rustling and folding the paper, stood up.

'Na then, Nellie,' he said, taking the newspaper and dropping it on the easy chair.

'Henry,' Mrs Lathom said, her long neck bending to inspect the crockery set out on the table.

'Sit down, Nellie,' Jenny said, as she bustled in carrying the dinner plates.

'I'll sit near the fire, if I may,' Mrs Lathom said, slipping into the seat where Granddad had been sitting. 'I'm suffering something awful with my neuralgia. The doctor said I mustn't go out, not even to Mass. But I told him I must go. I'll offer my suffering up to the Sacred Heart for the safe return of my boy, I told him.'

Granddad took the seat nearest to the door, and Sadie, who had changed into a Fair Isle sweater and a modest tweed skirt, sat next to their visitor.

Mrs Lathom fell on to the food, and it wasn't until the plates had been collected and the room was beginning to fill with the subtle perfume of spiced plums, that she turned her unblinking attention on Ruby.

'And who's this?' she asked.

'This is our Will's girl,' Granddad said.

'Was it you arriving that caused all that noise last night?' Mrs Lathom asked. 'When I heard that engine stop outside, I thought they were coming to tell me bad news. It took me hours to get off again.'

After several minutes, during which time everyone at the table applied themselves to the golden pastry and the sweet, luscious filling, Granddad said, 'Aye, you might have heard us, Nellie. Train was late. We got held up. Troop trains. All of 'em full. This young soldier, as was getting on one of them trains, he stops us and asked us to post a letter. I think it's to his girl. He gave Ruby the money for the stamp to post it for him. Have you still got that letter, Ruby?'

'Oh, that's romantic,' Sadie said. 'Where is it now?'

'It's in my music case,' Ruby said. 'Can we go and post it, Granddad?'

'No letter from my lad,' Nellie said. 'Sadie's as upset as I am. Only news we've had was a note to say he was fine and a photo of him in tropical kit. It was a sign. He was letting us know they was sending him to the tropics. No wonder I'm suffering, and that dog's pining.'

'I could tell Ruby where the postbox is,' Sadie said. 'She could take Bess with her. Bet you'd like that, Ruby?'

'Our Bess wouldn't go with a stranger,' Nellie said, eyeing Ruby's unruly plaits and grubby blouse.

'Bess is friendly enough and she's a quiet dog. Let her try,' Sadie said. 'I'm working. It's dark now, when I get home. Jack wouldn't have thought of that when he asked me to take her out. Tea?' she asked, looking around the table. 'You stay there, Ma, I'll get it.'

'Well that's true,' Nellie Lathom said. 'I don't suppose my boy would have left me, if he'd known that I would have been on my own and having to cope with that dog all this time.'

'Well that's settled, then,' Granddad said. 'Ruby can go back with you and take Bess out. You go the way we walked last night, Ruby. Bess will take you. She's walked that way hundreds of times, and there's a stamp machine outside the post office. So you can post that letter.'

When Sadie returned with the teapot, the talk was of the war and the comings and goings of the American troops stationed nearby. Mrs Lathom, who was the kind of person who quickly lost interest in any topic when she was not a central participant, decided it was time to leave.

'Here's my rations,' she said, opening her bag and placing a twist of tea and one of sugar on the table. 'I haven't much. They don't consider those of us who have our loved ones fighting, but I'll pay my way. Now, if this child's going to take the dog out, she'd best come with me. Then I could pop back and show Sadie that new pattern I've got for socks.'

45

Ruby collected the soldier's letter from her room and followed Mrs Lathom to her front door. Bess was a black spaniel with intelligent eyes who, leaving her mistress without a backward glance, led the way to the main road. Once there, she turned in the direction that Ruby had walked with her granddad the night before.

In the daylight, the shops and the church hall looked smaller, and the pub that had been so warm and welcoming in the blackout was closed. Everything was still. As they climbed the railway bridges, Ruby could see a row of poplar trees in the distance, and behind them, way out to the west, the banks of cloud building, bubbling up over the Irish Sea. On the other side of the bridges, there was a second pub and another row of blacked-out shops, including a post office with a stamp machine and a postbox. She took the letter addressed to Miss Maggie Joy Blunt out of her pocket, added the stamps and dropped it in the box.

As they wandered on, Ruby imagined Maggie Joy coming down the stairs and finding the letter on the mat. She could picture the wedding and herself as guest of honour, dressed in lilac organdie, throwing orange blossom over the happy bride and groom.

Bess trotted by the Co-op and another pub with a war memorial outside. Then, with her tail wagging, she turned on to a recreation ground. A boy of about seven was kicking a football, and an older girl, in a dark coat and brightly coloured pixie hood, pushed a smaller boy on a wooden swing horse. Bess barked, and the children looked up.

'Is that Jack Lathom's dog?' the girl asked. 'What you doing with it?'

'I'm taking her out for Mrs Lathom,' Ruby said, as Bess dragged her over to the swing. 'She lives near my granddad.'

'Have you been evacuated?' the girl asked.

'No. I've come to stay with my granddad for a bit, but I usually live with my auntie.'

'Where's your mum and dad?' the older boy asked.

'Shut up, our Jimmy,' the girl said, 'that's rude.'

'My mum died in an accident,' Ruby said, bending down to stroke the dog.

'Throw her a stick,' the boy said. 'Jack used to.'

'I've not to let her off the lead.'

'Was she hit by a bomb?' the girl asked, climbing on to the swing with the smaller child and adjusting his grey balaclava.

'No. It was an accident in the blackout. She was hit by a taxi.'

'We saw a bomber,' Jimmy said, pointing over the rows of terraced houses. 'He come swooping over here. Right over the rec. You could see the Jerry pilot inside. He comes right over here and then he turned and headed over to the railway lines and the factory. Then there was this bang, and he'd killed some folk on Ward Street. Twenty-five. One kid was killed on his way to buy some toffees.'

Contemplating this particularly cruel injustice, the children gazed silently over the rooftops.

'Are you coming to our school?' the girl asked. 'It's over there by the church.'

'I don't know,' Ruby said. 'I only got here last

47

night, and I'm fifteen, but I sometimes helped with the little ones at my school.'

'You can have a swing,' the girl said, lifting her little brother off the swing horse. 'You could put Bess on your knee. She'd like that.'

The children took turns to hold the dog on the swing, and Bess, who appeared to be enjoying the novel experience, smiled broadly.

'Have you ever tasted ice-cream cake?' Jimmy asked, sticking out his bright-red knees to take Bess's weight. 'We have. The Yanks give us a party, 'cos our dad's in the war. They come and collected us in trucks and took us to the base. We're going again at Christmas. We're all getting a present from Father Christmas. He's coming there to see us. He's an American. I bet you didn't know that.'

The girls grinned at each other over the younger child's head, and Ruby was about to ask the girl her name, when she jumped off the swing and picked up the smaller boy.

'We'll have to go,' she said. 'Jack sometimes took Bess down by the churchyard, and then up the road. If you keep on going, you'll come to a crossroads. Turn right, go up to the next crossroads and turn right again. Then go up that road, until you come to the river. You'll be able to see the Lathom's cottage from there.'

As she watched the children go, Ruby pushed her cold fingers deep in her pockets and felt the raw wind on her cheeks. The rec was deserted, except for the hens clucking in their run on the other side of the field. She turned and headed back to the road. On one side, there was a newsagent and a butcher, and on the opposite side, there was a row of terraced houses with a clog shop at one end and a chemist shop at the other. As the main road spooled out into the distance, she could see more shops, a petrol pump and at the edge of the village, rows of privet hedges and larger houses.

Bess trotted by the blacked-out shops, until they were almost opposite the turning between the chemist shop and a white pub. There was no traffic on the road, and all the house doors were shut tight against the cold, grey afternoon. Ruby walked along, until she could see up the road the girl had pointed out. There were two larger terraced houses facing the crossroads. In one, the curtains had been drawn right back. A lady with a pale face sat in the window, and as they walked by, she raised her frail hand and waved.

Bess crossed the main road and walked purpose-fully by a small whitewashed chip shop that was squashed in between the pub's yard and a row of terraced houses. At the end of the row of houses, she trotted by the church and into a small wood at the back of the churchyard the girl had men-tioned. Once inside the wood, she put her head down and snuffled through the deep, dry leaves, drawing Ruby further into the shelter of the little copse. It was clear that this part of the walk was going to take some time, and Ruby found a seat on a bare oak branch low enough for her feet to touch the ground. As the dog rummaged around her, a thick warm smell of autumn rose up from the earth. Bess's tail went on busily wagging until she found a stick. Then sitting down with her discovery in her mouth, she looked quizzically at Ruby. When she didn't move, the dog dropped it at her feet and leant her silky warmth against Ruby's knees.

It was the gentle friendliness, as though they had always been pals, that brought the tears. Ruby rested her cheek on the dog's bony head and rubbed her gauzy soft ears. For a while, inside the green house of rhododendrons and laurels, Bess allowed herself to be hugged, kindly licking each tear as it dripped from Ruby's chin, before tactfully placing the stick on her lap.

'All right,' she said, wiping her eyes on the sleeve of her mac, 'you show me where, and don't run off, or we'll never get to come again.'

Bess led the way through the copse and on to a field at the back of the church. When Ruby slipped off her lead, the dog did two excited circuits of the uncut grass before returning to wait expectantly by her stick. Ruby had little experience of dogs – they were not permitted at Everdeane – but she'd watched as people walked their pets on the sands, and threw the stick as far as she could across the field. When the dog returned and she took hold of the stick again, there was a great deal of growling and wrestling. Then Bess dropped it but continued to guard her prize, growling softly when Ruby tried to pick it up. Eventually, to indicate the first part of the game could begin again, she suddenly sat down and looked up hopefully at Ruby, who threw the stick once more. They played happily, until the long, wet grass soaked into Ruby's socks and made her shiver. The pale-grey sky was growing darker, and the next time the dog raced

50

back with her prize, Ruby clipped the lead back on to her collar.

The road from the church to the crossroads was edged with an orderly border of semi-detached houses, daintily curved street lamps and a number of short avenues, each with its own identical row of dwellings in the same red-brick and pebble-dash.

At the first avenue, a woman with a smart new pram turned the corner, and a railwayman who was peddling by on a heavy, black bike waved to her.

'How's babby, Mrs Smith?' he shouted, as his bike squeaked by.

'Oh, she's grand now, thanks,' the woman said. 'Her chest's much better.'

The woman smiled at Ruby and bent down to pat Bess. She wore a fitted brown coat and a round crocheted cap embroidered with a daisy chain on the crown of her light brown hair.

'Look, Kathleen, a doggy,' she said.

A beautiful, dark-eyed baby looked around the pram's hood, pointed a pink-mittened hand at Bess and made a gurgling sound.

'Doggy,' the woman said, beaming with pride. 'That's right, love, it's a doggy. She's just started talking,' she said to Ruby. 'It's the first time she's been out in three weeks. She's been really poorly.'

At the crossroads, Bess turned by a decrepit wooden garage with a charabanc parked beside it and headed towards a railway bridge. The land around was flat, with little to break up the long hedges, except for a couple of stands of trees, a few scattered cottages and a large house partly hidden

51

by trees. The nameplate on the gate read: Doctor H. Grey MD. The house looked older than the smaller ones along the main road and had high windows and a handsome porch built of pale stone.

In between investigations, the dog kept up a steady pace, and Ruby found that if she shifted the lead from hand to hand, holding it in one and keeping the other in her pocket, she could manage to stay quite warm.

When they reached the river and were in sight of the cottages again, Ruby dawdled. She picked up a leaf and dropped it from the stone bridge into the shallows, imagining it riding the rippling water, until it met a much larger river travelling west. After a while, Bess became restless and they wandered to the end of the lane. For a moment, before she turned the corner, when her view of the cottages was still partly obscured by the trees and hedgerows, Ruby's heart lifted. It was a familiar sensation: after her mother had died, each time she'd arrived back from school or from an errand, and sometimes just before turning on to the prom, she would suddenly feel sure that her father would be at Everdeane waiting for her. Yesterday, when she'd heard Granddad's voice, she'd felt the same involuntary optimism. It was a delusion that reason and experience couldn't crush, and now it had followed her to Granddad's cottage. Ruby quickened her pace, expecting some sort of sign that he'd arrived at the cottage to collect her. At the gate she hesitated, gazing at the blank windows, hoping to see some hint that her father was already there. Hiding Bess's beloved stick under a bush, she ran up the path and pushed open the door.

Mrs Lathom was nodding by the open fire, a half-knitted sock for a deserving soldier unfinished on her lap, and Granddad was reading the newspaper. He looked up and smiled.

'That fresh air has given you some colour,' he said. 'Take the dog round to the back door. I'll get some water for her, and we'll use the old towel under the sink to wipe her paws. Then you can help Grandma and Sadie to make the tea.'

The disappointment sank quickly; it was an accustomed sensation and didn't last. By the time she'd finished helping her granddad rub Bess's muddy paws, the feeling had been replaced by the hope that there would soon be a letter from her father asking her to go to him.

'There's stewed plums in that pan,' Jenny said, handing Ruby a china bowl, 'you can put them in here. I've made some cream. It should have thickened up by now, though I'd almost run out of vanilla essence to flavour it. It's in a mixing bowl in the scullery. If it's thickened, pour it into that glass jug on the top shelf of the kitchenette. Be careful, mind, that's my best jug.'

When Ruby returned with the mock cream, Jenny was carrying a white enamel dish from the meat safe over to the kitchenette. The contents were covered with a plate and a flat iron had been balanced on top. Jenny put the dish on the flap of the kitchenette, took the iron off the plate, carefully inverted the metal dish, and tapped the bottom with the tip of the flat iron. Then she gently lifted the dish to reveal a wobbling mass of clear jelly with fragments of pale meat suspended inside.

'This brawn's set lovely, if I do say so myself,' she said. 'I was lucky to get a whole sheep's head.'

Years ago, when she and her parents once stayed at Everdeane as guests, there'd been brawn for tea. Ruby hadn't been able to look at the wobbling mess on her plate. She'd been afraid that Auntie Ethel would be cross, but her mother had winked and slithered the foul stuff on to her father's plate. Then they'd giggled so much that her dad said they'd nearly given the game away.

The pressed-brawn sandwiches were to be eaten with pickled onions and beetroot. When she took her first bite, Ruby felt her stomach begin to rebel. She tried not to look at the glutinous substance oozing out from between the slices of bread, and Bess, sensing that Ruby needed her help, quickly settled to the task of delicately licking the gluey stuff from her fingers.

Unlike her, Mrs Lathom, Granddad and Jenny were all munching happily, but Sadie only nibbled at her sandwich and refused the pickled onions.

'No thanks,' she said. 'Me and Lou's been invited to a farewell do at the Railway.'

'I'd forgotten about that,' Granddad said. 'Some of the Yanks from the base are leaving. Should be a good do. Hal and his mate asked me to call in for one last game of darts. I said I might call in to wish them all the best. Why don't you come, Jenny?'

'How can I?' Jenny said. 'I've still got the washing to put to soak.'

'Oh, leave the washing for once. It'd be nice to give him and his mate a good send off. Very generous, they've been. A bit loud, but grand blokes. Hope the next lot's as friendly. You could come with us as well, Nellie.'

'Well, I've got the doctor's shirts to put to soak, Yanks or no Yanks,' Jenny said, collecting the empty plates.

'Ruby can do them shirts and these pots,' he said, handing his granddaughter his empty plate. 'Go and get that dish of plums and the cream for us, Ruby, love. She can manage the washing-up, and you can show her what to do with the shirts.'

The dish of spiced fruit was waiting on the kitchenette, along with a set of five smaller matching dishes. Each was decorated with a repeating pattern of soft fruits in red, yellow and purple. Ruby took in the dishes, collected the heavy glass jug of mock cream and put the teapot to warm in the hearth.

'I've always thought these dishes were lovely,' Nellie said, taking a bowl of fruit from Jenny. 'I remember how your poor Lucy loved them, Henry. They were a wedding present from her side of the family, weren't they? They look expensive. But I don't recognise this,' she said, pouring the mock cream from the glass jug. 'Lucy had a lovely cream jug. Is this one new? It's the war, I suppose, you can't get the quality.'

'You want a cup of tea, Ma?' Sadie asked. 'Look, Ruby's warmed the pot.'

'Oh, that would be nice,' Nellie said. 'Then I'll take Bess home, before we go out.'

The tea was drunk in silence by everyone, except Mrs Lathom, who gave them a detailed account of her medical complaints. When she'd left,

Jenny went upstairs, the sound of the bedroom door slamming behind her startling Granddad, who'd just poured his second cup of tea into his saucer and was gently blowing on it.

'Come on, Ruby,' Sadie said, rolling her eyes towards the ceiling and collecting the dishes from the table, 'we'll take this stuff through and wash up.'

'Aye, good lass,' Granddad said, abandoning his saucer of tea and hurrying towards the stairs. 'I'd best get my collar and tie on.'

When the sound of angry voices from the room above grew louder, Sadie switched on the radio and sang along, as they carried the pots through to the kitchen.

'Put that lot on the draining board, and I'll show you what you have to do with the shirts,' she said, leading the way to the small brick scullery off the kitchen. 'These are the doctor's shirts, so be careful,' Sadie said, pulling a shirt from a pile of clothes in a washing basket. 'Before they're soaked with the rest of the wash, you rub the collars and cuffs with that yellow soap over on the windowsill. Then, they go in the dolly tub. It's easy, but make sure you rub them well. Now, I'll get the hot water for the washing-up.'

On the wall next to the sink, hanging by a wooden handle, was a small mesh box with thin slivers of soap inside. When Sadie had poured in hot water from the kettle and topped it up with cold from the tap, Ruby took the box down and whisked it through the water until suds appeared on the surface. Then she began washing the dishes, and Sadie unhooked the small shaving mirror that hung above the sink and began to apply her make-up.

'Do you think this jumper's too plain?' she asked, eyeing herself critically through the little mirror. 'I mean, we are only going to the Railway. Hal doesn't call them jumpers. He says sweaters. I was wearing my white silk one when I first met him. When we was dancing, he says, "Gee, I like your sweater." I love the way they talk.'

'Is he your boyfriend?'

'No, he isn't,' Sadie said, pausing her lipstick in mid application, 'I was being friendly, that's all. I mean, Hal's too old for me for a start. He's thirty. They come to dances in town and ask us back to dances at the base. Anyway, Jack's... Well, we don't know when we'll see him next, when he'll be back.'

By the time Ruby had finished the pots, the house was quiet again. Granddad came downstairs wearing his collar and tie and looking quite cheery. He wandered around the kitchen humming to himself, jangling the coins in his pockets and inspecting their handiwork. Jenny appeared a few minutes later. She had long earrings swinging from her ears. The red and white stones matched those in the necklace sparkling on the expanse of flesh above her low-cut, black blouse.

'You look nice, Ma,' Sadie said. 'I'll just get my coat.'

'Bring my fur jacket down will you, love,' Jenny called after her. 'I think it might be chilly.'

As Jenny looked around the kitchen, noting the pile of clean pots and the empty flap of the kitchenette, the red and white stones chopped the air.

57

'What's she done with the rest of that brawn?' she asked.

Granddad looked over at Ruby and followed her gaze to the meat safe.

'It's in here, see,' he said, opening the wire mesh door to display the remaining brawn quivering on its plate. 'And Sadie's been showing her how to do the laundry.'

Jenny patted the row of stiff, yellow curls along her forehead and frowned.

'He's very particular is Doctor Grey. Well, at least, his wife is. She'd best make sure they're really well rubbed and she'll have to check for any missing buttons. There's spare ones in a box, and the cotton's in a toffee tin in the dresser.'

'Don't worry, Ma,' Sadie said, handing her mother an off-white coat of baby-seal skin. 'I'll get the box and the cotton.'

'You can shut that radio off as well,' Jenny said, shrugging on the coat and heading towards the living-room door, 'radio batteries are scarce.'

Hal pulled up the collar of his coat and started the jeep. Since he'd arrived in England, a lid of grey cloud had been clamped permanently over the whole island. As far as he could see, there was no corner of the entire place that wasn't damp. He sighed, stared out at the slick, dark road and watched his buddy Clayton jog over from his quarters.

'Lieutenant Roach reckons it's much warmer in the south,' Clayton said, as he climbed in beside him. 'Says the place is altogether different. No industry, for a start. Fishing, mainly, and farming.

Less people altogether.'

'Well that could be good, or not so good,' Hal said, lighting his cigar. 'I mean, there might not be enough women to go round. Or if they're country girls, and not like the tramps around here... But then, a uniform goes a long way with a simple country gal.'

'You'd best watch your mouth, now. Who you calling names? Not that nice Sadie you've been hankering after?'

Hal stared gloomily out at the darkening streets. Since he'd met her at the dance in town, Sadie had been on his mind. She was so pretty and had seemed just as sassy as the others. Yet, Sadie had managed to outfox him every time. She loved to dance, and her legs... Well, those were film star legs. He sighed. Sadie, for all her cute green eyes, was a flirt and a cock-teaser.

'I'm sick of Sadie and her ways,' he said. 'She says she don't have a boyfriend, and then she says she's promised to an army guy. She's a tease and she knows it.'

'She's no innocent, ain't Sadie. I've heard–'

'We know what you've heard. Well I don't buy it.'

'You sayin' if you can't crack it, nobody can?'

'I'm sayin' she don't play fair. The others know the score. If they want nylons ... well...'

'We know,' Clayton laughed, 'it's one before an' one after. So why we goin' to see her?'

'Seein' her's just a perk. I'm on business. You and me's goin' to say our goodbyes to the locals. Good relations an' all that. And I've got some business.'

'You're a grabbing bastard. You don't need the money.'

'If I don't, someone else will,' he said, swinging the jeep around a tight corner on the road out of the camp, making the cases of whisky and gin in the back tinkle. 'And I'll need money to entertain those nice southern girls.'

When Henry opened the pub door and pushed aside the thick curtain, the two Yanks were already handing out drinks and Johnny Fin was playing the piano. The women followed him through the low-slung clouds of cigarette smoke and he found them a table by the fire in the pub's lounge. The Yank sergeant brought over a pint of beer for him and a sherry for Jenny. When he was introduced to Nellie, he smiled bashfully.

'It's a pleasure to meet you, ma'am,' he said. 'I've heard such a lot about your son from Sadie. He sounds a real wonderful guy.'

Nellie flushed with pride and, as most women did, immediately fell for his handsome, open face and guileless charm. She shyly accepted a sherry, and Hal was able to draw Sadie away from the group, explaining that she had promised to sing for them on his last night.

'Sadie, you goin' to miss me at all?' he asked, when they were out of earshot.

'I'll miss all you boys,' she said, sipping the gin and tonic he'd bought her.

'All of us, equally?' he asked, trying to put his arm around her waist.

'We'll all miss you, Hal,' she said, removing his arm. 'Mum and Henry were ever so grateful for

60

that tinned stuff you gave us, and I know that–'

'Kiss me,' he said, pressing her against the wall.

'Don't, not here,' Sadie said, wriggling free of his grasp. 'Jack's mother...'

'Well, come outside.'

'I thought you wanted a song,' she said, smiling at him over her shoulder, as she headed for the group around the piano.

He didn't follow. Instead, he joined Clayton at the corner of the bar, where his light eyes flicked constantly around the crowded room and back to Sadie, who was chatting to Johnny Fin and the landlady by the old upright piano.

'What's up with Hal?' Johnny Fin asked.

'He's really sweet on you,' Vera, the landlady, said as she picked up the empties from the piano's scuffed lid. 'It's his last night. You don't know when your luck's in, you don't.'

'We'll all miss him,' Johnny Fin said, with a toothless, gummy grin.

'Wouldn't hurt you to give him a cuddle,' Vera said, before heading back to the bar.

The first time Sadie had seen Hal at a dance in town she'd been taken by his big-boned good looks. In the shabby dance hall, his strong white teeth, wide shoulders and thick sun-bleached hair looked completely out of place, as though a movie star had stepped down from the screen and asked her to dance. Yet, Sadie soon found that he'd none of the easy-going manner of many of the other GIs she'd met.

She gazed over at the bar where Hal had a crowd of locals around him. All the women – no matter how young or old – fell for him. Everybody loved him. The little kids and the old folk saw his broad smile and his strength. He made them feel safe. Hal drew people to him and he was desperate for everyone to like him. Hal wanted to charm everyone. It didn't matter who it was: it could be the priest who wanted help sorting out a children's party, or one of the old folk who was short of coal, or someone needing a lift to the hospital. Hal would be there listening politely, and they would hang on his every word. It was the only time he looked relaxed; the only time the coldness left his eyes.

'He'll get over it,' Sadie said. 'Look, he's over there now chatting, buying another round.'

Vera didn't reply. Holding a cluster of pint glasses in each hand, she went back over to the bar where Sadie saw Clay take her arm. Clay was Hal's shadow, following him everywhere. When he caught her watching them, he smiled and whispered something in Vera's ear.

'Another lot of knock-off, no doubt,' Johnny said, squinting at the pair through the smoke from his cigarette.

'Come and help us would you, Sadie, love?' Vera called, opening the flap on the bar to let Clay through. 'Hal's brought some food for later.'

Hal smiled self-consciously at the group around the bar, and took a second round of drinks over to Henry's table.

'I was wondering,' he said, putting the tray of drinks down. 'If the ladies would excuse us, could we have one last game of darts?'

'It would be my pleasure, lad,' Henry said.

Over time, the coating of nicotine on the vault's

cream walls had turned into sticky, brown rivulets. The tables were stained, and the battered chairs – rubbed to a dull sheen by the movements of numerous backsides – were ancient. A domino school of older local men had colonised the tables next to the listless fire, others were hunched over games of cards and a small group of GIs were sipping beer and playing a friendly game of darts.

As Hal and Henry walked in, the landlady and Sadie began handing plates of ham, bread and pickles over the bar.

'I'm leavin' tomorrow,' he said, smiling broadly. 'So as this is my last night here, I thought we could have something to eat and drink, and a last game of darts.'

'We'll all be sad to see you go, lad,' one of the elderly domino players said, to a general mutter of agreement from the other drinkers.

'Who's this new lot coming in?' another asked, accepting one of the plates of sandwiches.

'Well, not all of us are moving,' Hal said, 'but there'll be some changes. There's another camp opening down the road. It's for Quartermaster Truck Companies. Not supposed to say how many,' he said and winked. 'You should see that place.'

'Nice?' Henry asked.

'Naw. It's a dump.'

'Not for you Yanks, then?' someone else asked.

'Black guys,' Hal said, blowing the smoke of his fat cigar in the direction of the younger group of GIs at the dartboard.

'Black? Black soldiers?' Bert Lyons, the land-lord, asked.

Hal's pale eyes hardened. 'Yep. But they're not over here to fight. They don't fight. Can't trust a black with a gun.'

Hal gazed around the room, and the group of GIs playing darts became watchful.

'So, this is my last night here. My last chance to beat Henry at darts,' he said, smiling broadly.

'Well, if they don't fight, how come they're over here?' Henry asked.

'They just back up the real GIs. Maintain trucks, fetch and carry. More trouble than they're worth most of 'em, I'd say.'

'I've never seen one, except on the pictures,' Bert Lyons said.

'Lou's boyfriend has,' Sadie said, handing out the plates of food to the domino players. 'He's in the merchant navy. He's seen 'em on ships, and in Africa. I reckon there's good and bad in everybody.'

'Got to be very carefully handled,' Hal said, ignoring her comment. 'Problem is, you can't never trust 'em. Don't know what they might do.'

'Best to keep clear,' one of the elderly domino players agreed, sucking on a silver-skinned pickle.

'Can't do that if they're here,' his companion pointed out.

'Well, you'll have to be awful careful,' Hal said, with a concerned look at his audience. 'I can't understand why you've never had the posters.'

'Posters?'

'Yep, you know, the government puts up warning posters when there's a danger, or sayin' how to treat foreigners.'

'Never seen anything like that,' Bert Lyons said.

64

'Well, it's lucky that I called in. I mean, a lot of it ain't their fault. It's like any creature, you've gotta learn how best to handle them. One thing you must never do, because it causes embarrassment, is to ask them to sit down...' he said, pausing for a moment, savouring the attention of the men in the shabby, little vault. 'Tails. They got tails.'

'Never. I've never heard of that,' Vera said.

'Well, it's not something that's mentioned. Very sensitive. Our government don't like it brought up. Especially not, well if you'll pardon me, with another country's citizens. We like to keep it to ourselves. But, these poor guys will soon be here, so it's best you know. You see,' Hal said, offering Henry a cigar, 'if you'll pardon me bein' frank, you and me, us white folks, our tails dropped off long ago. But black folks ... well, they still have one. Only a small one.'

'But it don't drop off?' asked one of the elderly drinkers.

'No, sir, and you see it makes it hard for them to sit like we do. And I know you wouldn't like to upset the poor guys. Can't understand your government not having given you this information. What I'm saying, sir,' Hal said, turning to Bert Lyons, who was leaning on the bar, 'if these guys come in here, it's kinder not to ask them to sit down. You see unless they get stirred up, they're simply happy fellows, and it would upset them. They'd sit to be polite, but, you see, it would be very painful with a tail. Then there's the food,' Hal added.

'Do they have special food, like?' Vera asked.

65

'No. They eat same as us, but when they get hungry...' Hal paused and gazed around again at his audience. 'Well, I don't want to say this, because I know you'll think I'm exaggerating, and it ain't commonly talked about, but they bark. Not a loud bark, like a hound. It's a sort of growl at the back of the throat. Something between a whimper and a growl. It's part of the way they're brought up. It's to tell their mammies where they are, an' that they're hungry. They don't sit down to meals, you see. At home, their mammies would go out and give them their food outside. It's just a different way of doing things.'

The vault fell silent. Mouths munched appreciatively on slices of thick pink ham enclosed in soft white bread, but most of all, relished the generous lashings of salty golden butter. In the lull after all the customers had been served with the food, Sadie felt a cold draught, as the air from the quietly closing vault door brushed her legs; the younger GIs had left unnoticed, their half-finished drinks on the table beside the abandoned dartboard.

'They're real nice folk, mostly,' Hal continued, picking up the darts. 'My pappie was real fond of 'em. Where I'm from, folk know to be careful. They're like children, you see, an' it's unfair on them to get them excited.'

'It doesn't seem right to have them come to war,' Vera said.

'Well, like I say, ma'am, they're only helpin' us real soldiers out. They can be trained. We been trainin' 'em in the South for years. Oh, we sure do know all about training black folks. But if you hear this, well it's not a bark exactly, more kind of a mooing sound, then it's best to watch out, 'cos when they're hungry they can sometimes get real snappy.'

CHAPTER THREE

When she woke, Ruby heard someone lifting the back-door latch. The sharp metal clack was followed by the sound of her granddad coughing and then a rasping noise, as the edge of the toilet door caught on the stone flags. She sat up, pulled on her vest and jumper, and with her legs tucked under the blanket, unhooked the blackout curtain.

The frost had made a feathery pattern on the inside of the window, and Ruby used her thumbnail to scrape away two holes to see through. Everything was still. Instead of yesterday's grey clouds, there was a clear turquoise sky, yet a low mist hid the fields and the stream. By contrast, the garden was in dazzling sunlight. All the vegetables were covered with a thin coating of frost, and the leaves of the old marrow plants on the Anderson shelter had been turned into silver twine.

The cold made her fingers sting, so she snuggled down again, hugging them under her armpits. Ruby lay for a while, her feet tucked under her nightdress, watching her warm breath quickly turn to plumes of dragon smoke in the freezing room. Then closing her eyes, she tried to imagine the clear sky outside was really over the sea and she was back in the bedroom she'd shared with her mother. But instead of the sound of her mother breathing softly in her sleep, Ruby heard her grandfather's clogs clattering back across the flags and thudding on the stairs.

'Don't be long, lass,' he called, gently pushing at the open bedroom door. 'I've brought you the big case. Your mum's things ... that Ethel gave you. I know there's not much room in here, but I'd keep it by you.'

In the living room, Jenny was coaxing heat from the few remaining embers of last night's fire.

'There's some tea in't pot,' she said.

She handed Ruby the teapot from the fender. Then, unhooking the shovel and brush from the brass stand in the hearth, she began cleaning the old-fashioned fireplace. From her seat at the table, Ruby watched Jenny, her large bottom encased in a floral overall, rock vigorously from side to side. At Everdeane all the old fireplaces had been replaced by smart modern ones – cream tiles in the guest's lounge and pink in all the best bedrooms.

'Cut yourself a slice of bread,' Grandma Jenny said. 'When you've had that, you'd best have a good wash. Have you got some other clothes?' she asked, using the chair to pull herself up from the floor.

'I don't know,' Ruby said. 'Auntie Ethel packed my things.'

Taking out a tin from her overall pocket, Grandma Jenny sat down heavily on the chair next to her and began to roll a cigarette.

'You'll have the rest of your school things. That can't be your only gymslip,' she said, licking the fragile cigarette paper and carefully lighting the end.

'I've left school. I've been helping Auntie and Uncle. Before that, I'd only been going part-time because of the evacuees from Manchester.'

'Well, we'd best look,' Jenny said, getting up from the table. 'You're only going to be here for a while. Not long ... just until we get things sorted out. I can't have you under my feet all day. We'll go to the school and see if you can go there until...'

'I go back to Everdeane?'

'Most likely. Is that what you want?'

Ruby nodded. 'My dad will be coming for me, expecting me to be there.'

Jenny nipped the end of her cigarette and got up from the table. 'Let's have a look at this case they sent you with,' she said.

The small suitcase revealed a change of underwear, a second gymslip, a navy-blue cardigan, a green-and-black tartan kilt, a green jumper and matching cardigan, two pairs of plain white socks and one lacy pair, and two red tartan hair ribbons. Ruby gazed at the pile of clothes and wondered if she should say that the gymslip was too short.

'She hasn't sent any of my summer things, because I'll be going back before then,' she said.

Jenny didn't reply, but nodded in the direction of the large case. 'What's in there?'

'They're Mum's things.'

When Jenny tipped the clothes on to the bed, the little room filled with Pearl's perfume.

'Well, a lot of good these are,' she said, lifting up a beaded silk slip.

69

Underneath the mound of silk and glitter, they found the black velvet dress Ruby had worn for her mother's funeral and a pair of patent leather shoes. There was also a pair of black woollen gloves and matching beret that she didn't recognise, along with a half-completed scarf her mother had once tried to make for her father.

'These'll do,' Jenny said, picking up the gymslip and the green jumper from the bed. 'You can wash in the kitchen. Use my hairbrush and put them ribbons in as well.'

Ruby ran cold water into the sink, barred the back door and undressed. When the living-room door opened, she held her rumpled clothes tight against her naked body. Jenny bustled in, carrying a kettle full of hot water.

'Tha's got nowt I haven't seen afore,' she snapped, pouring the water from the sooty kettle into the sink. 'Now, hurry up.'

Ruby obeyed, rubbing the coarse flannel over her body, reddening the delicate flesh already mottled with shame and embarrassment. Before her mother had died, she couldn't wait to grow up. In their bedroom at Everdeane, when she'd watched Pearl dressing to go out for the evening, she'd loved to try on her evening dresses and use her powder and lipstick. Sometimes, if her mother was in a good mood, she'd help her to put on the make-up. On those nights, they would stand together in front of the long mirror, and Pearl would hug her and say they could be mistaken for sisters. Then she'd died. Now Ruby didn't want to grow up; she wanted to slip back to the dark winter afternoon before the accident, and before her

70

body began to sprout hair and breasts.

By the time she was dressed, Jenny had changed out of her overall and was wearing a black coat with a fur collar and a bright-red hat. The hat was perched just above the row of yellow kiss-curls and skewered into place by a large hatpin in the shape of a bird.

'We'll go by the lane,' Jenny said, locking the front door behind them. 'Here, give me your arm. I thought this stuff would have cleared by now.'

The sky was still a clear pale blue, but beneath it, the early mist covering the fields had thickened into a milky fog. Ruby shivered and pulled on her newly discovered gloves. There was no sign of the hens; even Monty the cockerel was quiet. Instead of turning towards the main road as Ruby had expected, Jenny headed up the lane.

Despite the mist Ruby recognised most of the landmarks from her journey back from the village the day before. Close to the cottage the surrounding fields belonging to the farm were separated from the lane by a stout wooden fence. Beyond the fence, the mist had spun a dense web around the trunks and lower branches of the silent trees at the edge of the field, and fine tendrils had penetrated the neatly clipped hedge that pressed against it.

As they walked towards the stone bridge, Ruby heard footsteps rustling the frost-stiffened leaves. She imagined German paratroopers creeping along the other side of the neatly clipped hawthorns and was sure she felt Jenny's hand tighten on her arm. Then a basket appeared on top of the hedge, and an imperious female voice boomed out from the fog.

'I say, there. Take my basket would you, whilst I negotiate the fence.'

A large lady, wearing a tweed hat over her trailing grey hair, clambered on to the second highest rung on the old gate. She was dressed in a pair of men's corduroy trousers and an old, torn jacket. After a great deal of panting, she threw a muddy leg over and climbed down.

'How do you do,' she gasped. 'I'm Iris Bland. I live down the lane at the end cottage.'

'Next to Nellie Lathom?' Jenny asked.

'Is she the lady with the adorable little spaniel? I'm afraid I don't know her. I've only just arrived. My things are coming later today. I thought I'd explore. Do you live nearby?'

'I ... I live at the white cottage on this side of the lane with my daughter.'

'Ah, then we're neighbours,' the woman said, taking off the shapeless hat and rubbing her purple face. 'You seem to have quite a flair for gardening. How delightful. I've discovered some fungi, but I suppose you're an expert on wild foods. There's much less mist once you get out of the dip.'

'I'm glad to hear it,' Jenny said. 'We're walking into the village.'

'It shouldn't interfere with your plans,' the woman called. 'Lovely to have met you.'

'Wonder why somebody that posh is renting one of John Bardley's old cottages,' Jenny said, as they watched Iris Bland stumping off up the lane. 'I bet she's come out of the way of the bombing. Or she's been bombed out.'

'She might be a spy.'

72

'Oh aye, and what's she spying at in Bardley's field?'

'She could be sending messages to her leader.'

'She'll be meeting her maker, if she eats them things in her basket. They looked like toadstools. You never know, she might want some washing or cleaning done. Though she doesn't look like she has much. Mind you, you can never tell with some posh folk.'

The old woman was right; once they reached the little stone bridge, the fog disappeared. In the sunlight, the lane looked so much prettier than it had when she'd walked along it the day before. On both sides, the hedgerows stretched into the distance, their glittering line broken only by the occasional stand of trees or an isolated cottage. Between the white lacy branches of one small coppice, she could see an old mansion and wondered how she'd missed it yesterday.

'Who lives there?' she asked.

'It's been empty a good while. I've heard it's going to be turned into a hospital, once they open the Second Front.'

In the early morning sunshine, the curtains of spiders' webs hanging from the iron gates appeared to have been stitched together with thousands of tiny glass beads. The tightly closed gates made Ruby think of the opening stage set of *Sleeping Beauty*, when Pearl had played the fairy godmother at the Theatre Royal. She'd gone to watch the panto with her father. From her place in the darkened stalls, Ruby had listened to the audience applause as the curtain went up, revealing the gates to the enchanted castle and her mother dressed in a beautiful ballet dress.

At the end of the lane, before they turned down the road of small, pebble-dashed semis she'd walked along with Bess, they came to the large house with the nameplate on the gate.

'It's his shirts we're washing,' Jenny said. 'He's very good about your granddad's medicine. He knows he was gassed, so he doesn't charge as much for it. He worked in one of the army hospitals as a young man. He knows what it was like. But you'd best not get ill. We can't expect him to take you on for free as well.'

The school was next to the church and consisted of two single-storey buildings. The smaller one was made of red brick, and the other was of older smoke-blackened brick and had tall windows.

'That's the church hall and the infant school,' Jenny said, as they walked by the red-brick building and across the playground. 'The older children are in this other place. Before the church was built, it was a chapel. Now, keep your mouth shut, unless you're spoken to,' Jenny warned, as they came to the heavy wooden door at the end of the old chapel, 'and don't say anything about being here for a holiday.'

They stood together inside a small, square hallway. Through an open door, Ruby could see a table piled with papers and books. Near the door were two battered easy chairs; one had a coat over the back, and the other had a large handbag and a packet of ten Player's cigarettes on the arm.

'Looks like where the teachers have their tea,' Jenny said.

The other door was closed. Jenny put her ear to

it and listened.

'That's one of the classrooms,' she said, as the sound of muffled chanting escaped through the stout door. 'We'll have to wait here until they've finished. It can't be long off dinnertime. I think they're saying their prayers.'

In the chilly entrance hall, Ruby tugged nervously at the hem of her short gymslip. She hoped that the teacher would put her in the same class as the girl she'd met on the swings. If she had a friend, then staying at Granddad's might not be so bad: she would be at school all day, and at weekends she and the girl could take Bess for walks, so Jenny couldn't say she was in the way.

After a few minutes, a serious-looking boy with thick glasses came out of the classroom carrying a handbell.

'Is your teacher in there?' Jenny asked. 'Will you tell her I want to see her?'

The boy went back inside. When the classroom door opened again, a tall lady with wiry, marmalade-coloured hair followed him into the hallway.

'Can I help you?' she said. 'I'm Miss Conway.'

Miss Conway wore a custard-coloured blouse buttoned to the neck. An oval lattice-work brooch of dull, silver-grey metal sat between the points of the collar. She was what Ruby's Auntie Ethel would have called 'a good class of guest'. Above the sound of closing desk lids and excited voices, Jenny explained that she'd brought Ruby to start at school that day.

The teacher didn't reply but led the way to the front of the classroom. A large, brown desk stood on the top of a plinth. Miss Conway climbed the three steps and gazed around.

The room fell silent. There were about fifty children in the class, some sitting in pairs at heavy iron-legged desks, others behind long tables arranged around the walls. They were all between thirteen and fifteen. The girls wore jumpers or cardigans in different colours and styles; none of them wore gymslips. The younger boys wore grey, green or black pullovers, and most of the older boys wore jackets. Ruby could see the girl from the recreation ground sitting in the middle row next to a pretty girl with curly hair. The girl from the swings and the pretty girl smiled and whispered together as if they were best friends. Miss Conway brought a thick leather strap down sharply on the desk, making the exercise books dance and ending the quiet hum of chattering voices. Then with a nod to the child nearest to the door, she dismissed her class.

Once the children had filed out, the teacher took her seat, picked up a smart fountain pen, peered at them over her half-moon glasses and asked for Ruby's age and full name.

'Her mother's dead, you see,' Jenny explained. 'So she's come to stop with me and my ... husband for a while. He's her grandfather. Nothing's settled, you see.'

Jenny's lie made Ruby's cheeks begin to tingle and she stared at the parquet floor. In the next-door classroom, chairs scraped and feet scuffled. Then the door in the wooden partition separating the two classrooms opened. A small boy wearing wellingtons and an oversized jacket came in, carrying an unsteady pile of exercise books. As the door closed behind him, the thin partition shuddered.

Miss Conway winced. 'Quietly please, Edmund,' she said.

For a moment the small boy froze. Then, realising there was no escape, he moved gingerly forwards – wellingtons squeaking – towards the front desk, where he dropped his burden and fled.

From the shelf behind her desk, Miss Conway selected a book – *Lives of the Saints* – and chose two pages for Ruby to read aloud. They were about the life of Saint Catherine. Then she asked her to take two shillings and sixpence from a pound.

'She seems to have been quite adequately trained,' she said, gazing at the piles of inky books on her desk. 'If she's fifteen, she is able to start work.'

Ruby looked up at the tall windows and listened to the sound of the children in the playground. She wondered if the girl from the swings and the pretty girl with the dark curls were out there, or if they spent their dinnertime helping with the younger children, as she and Mavis used to do.

Miss Conway got down from her desk and motioned for them to follow her to the door.

'We have over fifty pupils in each class and very few books or paper,' she said. 'Since she is a Catholic, I suggest she could join us each morning for prayers and catechism, but I'm afraid I can't offer her a place. If she were a younger child, possibly.'

Miss Conway left them in the little hallway. Ruby followed Jenny back across the playground. This time Jenny didn't take her arm. Instead, her tiny feet hurried on ahead towards the village. Ruby followed, past the recreation ground, the war memorial and the Co-op. When they reached the Railway Inn, Jenny's pace slowed.

'I'll have to have a little drop of something for my nerves,' she said, dabbing her face with her hankie.

But when she discovered Granddad and Johnny Fin sitting side by side in the vault, Jenny's nerves were shaken even more.

'Next time you want your dirty work doing,' she shouted across the bar, 'you do it yourself. You should have seen how that old bugger looked me up and down, and then she said she'd had enough schoolin', so there's no place for her.'

Bert Lyons, the landlord, smiled and gave Ruby a wink. 'Well, if the little lass is so clever,' he said, handing Jenny a port and lemon, 'perhaps they should have given her a job helping out in the school.'

'Sounds like they could do with the help,' Vera, his wife, said, pouring herself a drink and offering Jenny a cigarette. 'From what I've heard, there's only three lady teachers for the whole lot of them. And they've had to come out of retirement because of the war.'

Granddad looked across hopefully from the vault, but Jenny ignored the remarks and went to sit by the fire.

'Well, she's certainly a likely lass,' Johnny Fin said, following Jenny into the best room and setting a tray of drinks on the table.

'You didn't see this woman,' Jenny said, finishing her first glass of port and accepting a second one from the tray. 'Send her every day for prayers, but she'll not be able to stay.' Jenny shook her head and took a sip from the second glass.

Johnny Fin lifted his half glass of beer to his lips. Then, placing the glass delicately on the table, he suddenly twitched violently, and Jenny had to grab the table to save the drinks from spilling.

'Send her every day?' Jenny said again, ignoring the twitches. 'I told the old bitch what she could do with her prayers and her schoolin'. I gave her a right mouthful, I can tell you.'

For a moment Johnny's whole frame became rigid and he made a short sobbing sound through his nose. Then his body relaxed again. He lifted his glass of beer to his lips and smiled across the room at Ruby.

'Here,' he said, taking a glass of pink liquid from the tray. 'Come and sit over here, love. Try this. Bet you'll not have tasted anything like it.'

Ruby took a sip and felt the syrup-sweet liquid pop and fizz in her mouth. It tasted of tinned cherries, followed by a sudden hint of bitterness.

'It's cherryade,' Johnny said. 'It's what the children drink in America. They put ice cream in it. I bet that tastes nice.'

In the dark pub lounge, the pink liquid was glossy. Ruby didn't want to drink it all at once. She looked into the glass and watched it sparkle, as the little bubbles chased each other up the side. Then with every sip, with each delicious eruption on her tongue, she tried to imagine the wonder of ice cream and cherryade.

'Come on,' Johnny Fin said, nodding toward

the upright piano in the corner. 'Your grandpa says you've got your dad's musical talents. Have you got a lot of music in that case of yours? Shame you've not brought it. Let's see if I can find something for us to play.'

'The music in the case is mostly the arrangements for my mum's songs. I used to play for her, and I can pick up tunes from the radio.'

They sat side by side on the stool. Ruby played the songs that were her mother's favourites and Johnny joined in. She was surprised by his capable playing and by his rich tenor voice. As Johnny's gnarled fingers followed her lead on the keyboard, the teacher's meanness, her disappointment that the girl from the recreation ground had a friend and her fear at Jenny's anger all began to dissolve. It was, Ruby decided, a funny school, if the kids were still learning catechism at their age; she could say hers from beginning to end.

'You fancy a bit of dinner, love?' the landlord asked, waddling over to the piano to bring Johnny another half-pint of beer. 'There's quite a bit of stuff left from that do last night. You fancy a nice bit of ham, Johnny?'

'Have you been listening to this?' Johnny asked. 'Lovely touch. She's a natural, if ever I heard one. I bet that teacher never got as far as hearing you play. Bert'll give you a job in here.'

Bert Lyons shook his head. 'She's too young,' he said, and went over to lock the front door and switch the lights off. 'Vera wouldn't have it, and a pub's not the place for a kiddie.'

As she and Johnny were playing, Ruby noticed that her granddad was still in the vault. From time

80

to time, she saw him look out over the top of the bar, as though he were peering from a trench. It wasn't until Vera had handed round plates of left-over ham and slices of bread, that he slipped cautiously into the best room. The sight of the food had helped Jenny's temper, and soon she and Granddad were sitting together, drinking and laughing, with the landlord and his wife. As the afternoon wore on, Granddad came over to the piano, his railwayman's cap tipped on the back of his head, and took out his mouth organ. Johnny Fin got out his spoons, and they played the songs from their days in the trenches. They were all singing 'It's a Long Way to Tipperary' when there was a deep rumbling sound and the bottles on the shelves behind the bar began to shake.

'It's an air raid,' Jenny wailed.

'No,' Bert said, sliding back the bolts on the front door, 'it's on the street outside.'

Through the top half of the frosted-glass window, Ruby could see trucks rolling slowly over the railway bridge and snaking back into the distance as far as she could see.

'It's the Yanks,' Johnny shouted. 'Another lot of Yanks have arrived.'

On the road outside, the head of the convoy was forced to a halt by a group of women who had left the queue outside the butcher's and were now hugging the two American officers in the back of the leading jeep.

'Take it easy now, ladies,' protested the sergeant, who was trying to drive the vehicle.

On both sides of the street, people were coming out of their houses cheering and waving. In the shunting yards the engines' hooters were sounded in welcome. Men reached up to shake the hands of the soldiers on the trucks, and the women kissed the ones they could reach. Mr Benson, the ARP warden, cycled along the pavement waving a Union Jack, and groups of small boys ran alongside the slow-moving trucks shouting, 'Give us some gum, chum.'

The little group in front of the pub stared up at the faces of the black soldiers in the trucks.

'All right, lads,' Granddad shouted. 'Nice to see you. You come to help us knock Jerry's block off?'

'Call in anytime,' Bert shouted, pointing at the sign over his pub. 'The name's Bert Lyons. I'm landlord here, and the first drinks are on me.'

'What are you sayin', Bert Lyons?' Vera hissed. 'Hal said—'

'Aye, he said a lot of things. Do they look like they can't sit down to you? They're customers like any others and there's nothing wrong with a full pub, whatever colour the folk are.'

Con Hartley gazed out from the cab of the lorry at the fat, red-faced man outside the pub.

'What's he say?' he asked Wes, the driver.

'He wants us to call at his pub for a drink. He says the first one's on him.'

Con grinned and shook his head. 'You'd think we'd won this war already,' he said.

A couple of days earlier when their ship had docked, Con hadn't been sure what to expect. The only things he knew about England came from the cinema. In his hometown of Detroit the newsreels had shown bomb sites, people walking to work with rolled umbrellas and shops with signs outside that read: 'Business as usual'. On the ship coming over, they'd shown them English films about men in uniform who'd talked about 'the Hun' and smoked pipes, and women in floaty dresses who drank tea from tiny cups in gardens full of roses. The destruction caused by the enemy bombing of Liverpool was the first he'd seen. But it wasn't the devastation that had surprised him so much as the shabbily dressed white people lining the streets, the rows of cramped houses and the hundreds of grubby kids begging for chocolate and gum. He picked up some more gum and threw it out for the children.

'Thanks, mister,' a small boy shouted.

Con waved, pulled up his collar and shivered. The countryside was green and pretty, but it was also damp and cold. It had been a long day. They'd heard that the camp they were heading for was new and had been built especially for them. He rolled his head and stretched the muscles in his neck. He was ready for a shower, some hot food and then a good sleep between soft blankets in a warm, dry hut.

CHAPTER FOUR

Once the convoy had left the village they made better progress. The light was fading, and the deepening twilight drained the colour from the surrounding farmland. Behind a stand of slender trees, Con could see the grey sky slashed with bitter orange. By the time the trucks reached a second village it was almost dark and the streets were empty. A line of Military Police in jeeps directed the Quartermaster Truck Company off the main road and into the camp. The convoy drew up in front of a US flag hanging disconsolately from a pole, and the men on the trucks gazed around in silence at the motley assortment of broken-down huts.

Once inside their hut, Con could feel his buddies' resentment crackle between the patched, water-stained walls. No one spoke as they unpacked their gear; they all knew that white soldiers would not have been housed in such a shabby collection of buildings. Con lay down on his bed. Wes was the only one of them that he knew well. He looked over, but Wes had his back to him. Wes was the nearest to him in age, and the only one who knew that he'd lied about his own age and enlisted using doctored papers. That was only a few months ago, but it could have been a lifetime away.

Con rolled on to his side and curled up, putting his arm under his head to shield his nose from the reek of mildewed bedding. As a child, he'd been protected from racism. In his school there was a mix, black and white. The white kids were the children of the Jews, Syrians and Armenians who owned shops in Paradise Valley. Segregation was there. He knew about it; his grandma was from the South. But it didn't touch his life, until he joined the army. In the US Army it wasn't possible to ignore it. Where Con slept, where he

84

ate, where he could go for recreation, were all regulated by his colour.

He looked around the hut. On the ship over, he'd watched each of the guys deal with the humiliation in his own way. Bo Little, who was the eldest in their group, burned with a barely suppressed fury. He'd got a reputation for his quick temper, and Con had learnt to stay away from him when he was angry. Michael Holt, Bo's closest buddy, shared his feelings, but Holt's anger burned more slowly. Holt read a lot, he knew how to argue his corner, but he stayed out of the way of any trouble. The other guys were from the South and had plenty of practice hiding their resentment, but from their tight shoulder muscles and the way they avoided looking each other in the eye, Con knew they felt this slight as deeply as the other men.

He looked out of the ill-fitting window. The cloud had come in low and was covering the stars. When he was unhappy and couldn't sleep, Con recalled the poems his grandma had taught him when he was a small boy. He closed his eyes and drifted away to the gentle rhythm of her voice reciting one of her favourite bits of Shakespeare.

That night Ruby lay in bed and wondered if Jenny might make Granddad send her back to Everdeane. For a moment, just before she fell asleep, she began to believe that it might happen and that Auntie Ethel would have no option but to agree. Ruby smiled, imagining walking down the prom to meet Mavis from school, but then Auntie Ethel's face with its thin mouth floated into her mind.

'It's as likely as a seagull singing "Roll out the Barrel",' she told the empty room.

Next morning Grandma Jenny looked very pale. She was standing by the cooker with a red headscarf over her hair. Underneath it, Ruby could see the row of steel clips holding the curls flat against her forehead. Jenny lit a cigarette. The outline of the lipstick she'd worn yesterday was still around her mouth. After inhaling a couple of times, she coughed and spat into the sink.

As quietly as she could, Ruby took the plates from the kitchenette, set the table in the living room and poked the fire. Then she took the padded lids off the brass boxes on the corners of the fender. One contained old newspapers and the other had thin sticks inside for kindling. She blew on the ashes and fed the still-live coals with thin scraps of wood and knots of paper. Once the flames strengthened, she carefully built a pyramid from the precious nuggets of coal. When she heard Granddad's clogs on the stairs, she picked up the kettle from the hearth and took it into the kitchen.

Granddad was leaning against the meat safe. The buttons on his vest were open, and under the frost of white hairs, his mottled chest shuddered.

'Give him a minute, love,' Jenny said, taking the kettle from her. 'He'll be better when he's had a drink. You take the bread through and I'll get his medicine.'

Ruby sat by the fire listening to each gasp, willing every breath to be easier than the last. Then Jenny bustled in carrying the teapot.

'He's going outside,' she said. 'He'll not be

long. Cut him two slices, and one for you.'

About twenty minutes later Granddad came into the living room dressed in his railwayman's waistcoat. His breathing was back to normal, but he moved unsteadily, as though he'd been walking all night. After one silent cup of tea, he picked up a slice of bread and smiled.

'What Jenny says is right, Ruby, love,' he said. 'There's no point in trailing to school every day, just to read a book.'

'They're taking on at the mill,' Jenny said, pouring herself another cup of tea. 'I'm going to see if I can get on. You'll be better off staying here and helping out. Trailing backwards and forward, just for a bit of religion, is a daft idea. You can always read your catechism here.'

'Helping out here,' Granddad said, doing up the silver buttons on his waistcoat, 'is better training for a lass than reading that stuff. You'll pick up all sorts from Jenny. How to do the doctor's shirts, and a bit of cooking. What do you say?'

'I help Auntie at Everdeane,' Ruby said. 'When I go back I can–'

'That's settled then,' he said, getting up and reaching for his white muffler. 'You can start with the doctor's washing.'

Jenny laughed and shook her head. 'How come things allus work out your way?' she asked.

Granddad put on his railwayman's jacket and cap. 'There'll be a bit more all round,' he said. 'There's Ruby's ration book, and if she does the doctor's shirts... I'm off, Ruby, love. Boiler's lit and the water's ready,' he called, as he closed the door.

'Is your dad as cheeky as him?' Jenny asked, as they watched Granddad tip his cap on to the back of his head and set off down the path whistling.

The washing was done in the small brick scullery off the kitchen. Jenny put the shirts into the tub and began pressing and twisting the handles of the posser, forcing the hot soapy water through the clothes, until it oozed, then squirted and finally poured squelching and glugging through the holes in the round copper plunger. When she was out of breath, she rested on the posser's wooden handle.

'It's hard work,' she said, wiping the steam from her face. 'Here, you have a go, until I've washed up. Then we'll see how you got on.'

Ruby took the posser and pushed down.

'Try not to splash and get it all over yourself,' Jenny said. 'The water's supposed to stay in the tub.'

When Jenny came back, she took the pair of wooden tongs from their hook on the wall and pulled a couple of shirts out of the tub. Her glasses were quickly covered in steam and she had to take them off to inspect the shirts.

'Them's clean enough,' she said. 'Now, use the tongs to get them out and put 'em in these buckets, and then rinse them in the kitchen sink. Then they come back in here to the mangle. Have you used one before?'

Ruby nodded. 'I've used Auntie's. Me and Uncle Walt used to do it. I know how to starch as well, and how to do the Dolly Blue.'

'Once you've got them out of the way, put the next lot in. That's all our stuff, but there's no use wasting hot water. I should be back by then. I've

88

made up the starch, but you say you know how to do it, and how to use Dolly Blue?'

Ruby nodded, and although Jenny had tried to hide it, she knew she was impressed.

'Your dinner, some cold potatoes and pickled beetroot, is on the kitchenette,' Jenny said, using Granddad's shaving mirror to apply a layer of lipstick to the faded outline sketched around her mouth and pulling the clips from her row of stiff curls. 'Keep your eye on that fire. I should be back soon.'

As Ruby worked, carrying buckets of clean shirts through to the sink, the smell of warm soapy clothes gradually filled the kitchen. The dripping buckets made a dark path across the floor, from the dolly tub in the scullery to the sink and back again to the mangle.

As she waited for the sink to fill with cold water, Ruby stretched up to look at herself in the shaving mirror hanging above it. Her face looked pink and tendrils of dark-red curls stuck to her cheeks. She didn't look like her mother, who had brown eyes and pale blonde hair. Her dad once told her that she'd got her blue eyes and red curls from his mother, Lucy, who had died when he was seventeen.

She looked out at the clear sunny morning. Monty was scratching in the yard, and the clattering and hooting from the engine sheds filled the air. The hawthorn hedge along the bottom of the garden sparkled with hoar frost, and the roofs of the houses in the distance glittered. She wondered if her father had stood here looking out of this window, thinking about his mother, and if he'd felt the same dull ache in his chest. She plunged her hands into the icy water, moving the dull ache briefly to her fingers.

By ten o'clock she was dipping the little muslin bag of Dolly Blue into the water, swirling it by its wooden peg and lifting it out again, before cupping her hands, dipping and testing the colour, until the mixture had turned the water blue. As she was sinking the last of the shirts into the sky-blue water, she heard shrieking. Ruby put down the damp shirt and listened. It wasn't the metallic howl of the rails that she'd heard on the bridges. She thought it might be Bess and hurried to the front door.

Across the lane, Mrs Bland and a plump grey-haired postman were holding Mrs Lathom up by the arms. They were standing by her garden gate, and between each deep inhalation, Nellie Lathom threw back her head and wailed. Ruby hurried over to ask if she could help. Each explosive sound only ended when Nellie's teeth slipped down, forcing her to gasp and close her mouth. Ruby thought of a difficult toddler whose tantrum was being controlled by its parents, but then she felt ashamed and looked away. There was a letter on the path. She picked it up.

'She's had a bit of bad news,' the postman said, as Mrs Lathom gathered her strength again. 'Her lad's been taken prisoner. Sometimes folk are relieved, you know, missus,' the postman said. 'They're feared that they've been killed.'

This did not reassure poor Nellie, who groaned and sank to the ground with her head on her breast.

'Can you walk, my dear?' Mrs Bland asked, pulling the taller woman up. 'Put your arm around me. That's right. Now, my good man, if you'll assist me to the door of my cottage, we won't delay you further.'

As they struggled to help the distraught woman down the lane to the end cottage, Mrs Bland turned to Ruby. 'I wonder, my dear,' she said. 'Could you help? Would you check my neighbour's house? Make sure the fireguard is up and check there's nothing on the stove. Then if you would close the door. I'm going to take my neighbour into my house. She's had rather a shock. So, if you would bring the door key there.'

Inside the neat cottage, Ruby found Bess looking out from under the table. When she bent down to rub her chin, she felt the poor dog tremble.

'It's all right, Bess,' she said, as the dog sniffed tentatively at her hands. 'Don't worry. I'll come back for you.'

Mrs Bland's tiny cottage was packed with boxes and trunks. Large pieces of furniture stood in a huddle in the centre of the room. Mrs Bland appeared between two large cupboards and smiled.

'Thank you, my dear. I thought tincture of valerian would be helpful,' she said, waving a small brown bottle in her hand.

Ruby squeezed between the furniture. Mrs Lathom was sitting in a chair wrapped in a cream blanket edged with frayed blue satin. A single bed was propped against the wall, and the room was very chilly. Ruby shivered. Her sleeves were wet, and the soapy water on the front of her gymslip had soaked through to her skin.

'I'm going to make tea,' Mrs Bland said, heading for the kitchen door. 'I thought we might need smelling salts, but I think she'll be all right. If she does feel faint, dear, put her head between her knees.'

After a few minutes, Mrs Lathom noticed Ruby standing by the chair and began to groan.

'Oh, poor Sadie. You'll have to tell her my boy's a prisoner of the Japs. Oh, my poor boy. Sadie, where is she? She'll be heartbroken.'

'She's at work,' Ruby said, hoping that Mrs Bland would come back quickly. 'There's no one in but me.'

'Here we are,' Mrs Bland said, carrying a silver tray with a matching silver teapot, milk jug and sugar basin. 'Hot, sweet tea. Thank you, my dear,' she said. 'I think we can cope now.'

'Shall I take Bess?' Ruby asked. 'She's frightened.'

After some reluctance, Mrs Lathom agreed that she could take the spaniel home with her, and Ruby found it easy to encourage the dog out from under the table.

Once they were back at the cottage, Ruby left Bess sitting on the rug by the fire and went to peg the shirts on the line. When she came back, the dog was still trembling, and Ruby wondered if Bess should have a blanket as well. She built up the fire, putting on the tiniest pieces of coal from the scuttle, and shared out the cold potatoes between them. Bess ate her share greedily, but when Ruby offered her a small slice of beetroot, the vinegar made her sneeze. She would have liked to listen to Workers' Playtime, but it didn't seem right after such bad news. Instead, she filled the kettle and tried to think...

When Jenny opened the front door half an hour later, she looked flushed and pleased with herself. Then she saw Bess sitting by the glowing fire and the edges of her red mouth fell. Ruby poured the water into the waiting teapot and explained about the letter.

At the news of Jack's imprisonment, Jenny crumpled on to a chair, and Bess slithered under the table.

'Such a nice steady lad,' Jenny said. 'Such good prospects, his uncle having the garage and coach business.'

When Jenny had finished her tea, she lit a cigarette and pulled a bottle of brandy from the dresser.

'You're sitting here and that water's going cold,' she said. 'You've got the rest of our stuff to do yet. Then you'd best start tea. I'm going to see how Nellie is. There's potatoes in the pantry. Do enough for three. Our Sadie's at work. Then pull some carrots, and there's cold ham in the meat safe. Slice it thin, mind.'

At the end of their first day in the new camp, Bo suggested that they take the landlord of the Railway up on his offer of a free pint.

'Do you think this landlord is for real?' Wes asked, as he and Con followed Bo and Holt to the bus stop.

Con shrugged. 'Well, he sounded friendly. In fact, the whole lot of them looked real glad to see us.'

He peered into the gloom. Bo and Holt were

barely visible. The only things he could see clearly were the white markings that edged the sidewalk, and he wished the other guys would slow down.

There was a crowd of men waiting at the bus stop. Their cigarettes bobbed as they spoke. He found the accent unfamiliar and had to listen carefully.

'Where you off to, lads?' one of them called.

When Wes explained that they were going for a drink, there was laughter.

'Lucky buggers,' a voice said. 'We're on our way to a twelve-hour shift. That's if the bloody bus ever comes.'

In the light from their torches, the men shuffled and chatted. Under their flat caps their faces looked gaunt and they smelt strongly of a chemical; an acid, he thought.

'Aye, twelve hours filling bombs to drop on Adolf,' another one said. 'Look out, here's the bus.'

The men clattered up the stairs. Con climbed on board and hesitated on the footplate. He wasn't sure if he should follow the men in their long, greasy macs up the stairs, or if he was supposed to go downstairs. The inside of the bus was almost dark, lit only by an eerie blue glow. The white people in the seats nearest the door gazed at him.

'Here, come and sit down, love,' a large woman on the side bench seat called. 'There's room for all of you, if I move this basket.'

'Thank you kindly, ma'am,' he muttered, and sat down next to the woman.

'Can I hold your basket for you, ma'am?' Bo

asked, taking the seat next to Con.

'Oh, no thanks,' the woman said. 'It's not heavy. I've been taking some things for my daughter. She's in hospital.'

The windows of the bus had been taped over, and Con was beginning to wonder how they would know when they'd arrived at the pub, when the conductress came down from the top deck.

'Where you off to, lads?' she asked.

'We'd like to go to the pub called the Railway Inn, please, miss,' Bo said.

'You off for a drink?' she asked. 'That's thrupp'nce each, lads, please.'

Each man fumbled in the darkness with the unfamiliar money. The girl shone her torch on their hands, taking three large brown coins out from each soldier. As she picked through the coins in his cupped palms, Con noticed that her red fingernails were chipped and her hands were grubby. It was hard to see her face, but he could make out a cap perched on top of a mass of dark hair. In the half-light her curls took on a strange bluish tinge. As the girl was punching out their tickets, the bus swayed and she grabbed the rail.

'Nearly had me on your knee there,' she laughed. 'I'll give you a shout when we get to the Railway.'

'Here, never mind him,' an old man on a nearby seat shouted. 'Come and sit on my knee.'

'You're not as good-looking, Walter,' the woman with the basket said, and Con could hear the girl chuckle and the other passengers' good-natured laughter around him in the darkness.

'Here we are,' the conductress shouted, from the middle of the bus. 'The next one's yours.'

As the dark shape moved off, they heard the hissing and clanking from the railway siding.

'I guess it must be over here,' Holt said. 'I saw the sidings just before the landlord shouted.'

'That's right,' Bo said, 'they were blowing their hooters.'

Con followed the sound of his friends' voices. These people with their shabby clothes and funny accents might stare, but he thought they meant to be friendly. He'd found them hard to understand, but the white men at the bus stop and the conductress called them all 'lads' not 'boys' and there was warmth in their tone, not contempt.

'Do you reckon anybody can sit where they want here?' Wes asked, as they reached the pub door.

By the time Granddad arrived home from work, Ruby had washed all the clothes and put them on the line. Jenny didn't come home for tea, so she and Granddad ate alone and listened to the news on the radio. When she'd cleared away the pots, Granddad spread his newspaper out on the table and settled down to read before he went on fire-watching duty at the church.

'Looks like our lads have given Jerry a beating again,' he called to her in the kitchen. 'That's the idea. If we keep hitting their factories like this, it's bound to hurt production. It says it were a main centre for their engineering that was hit. Made parts for aircraft, warships, heavy guns, all sorts.'

Ruby put the food she'd made for him on the table. It wasn't much, but by stretching out two thin slices of ham and some onion she'd managed to fill the sandwiches for his breakfast, together with a couple of twists of tea and sugar so that he could make a warm drink in the chilly sacristy.

'It's me and Johnny on at the church tonight,' he said, taking his coat from its hook near the door and squashing the carefully made sandwiches into the pocket. 'It's not too bad. You can usually get your head down. Only trouble is, Johnny snores. Sounds like an old engine. The other night, I was well away. He wakened me up. Reckoned he could see a ghost. Turned out, it was the reflection from the sanctuary light. It reflects on the wooden panels at the back of the altar, see. Johnny swore it was moving. I said I'd meet him at the Railway for one first. You'll be all right on your own here, love? I don't know how long Jenny will be across the way, and Sadie's working until late. Then she'll probably go to Lou's. She's going to be upset, no doubt.'

'Can Bess stay here?' she asked.

'I suppose so, but watch she doesn't upset Monty if you take her outside. I don't want him upset. Or the hens. They can be put off laying, see.'

When Granddad had gone, she took Bess into the yard. She couldn't hear any sounds from the cottages down the lane, and she thought that Mrs Lathom would be exhausted after so much sobbing and Jenny might be helping her to bed.

When her mother died Ruby didn't cry. She'd had the odd feeling that she was floating above everything, looking down on herself. She didn't cry when Auntie Ethel moved her out of the room she'd shared with her mother and into the box room, or when Ethel had thrown all her mother's stage make-up away. She didn't cry at the funeral, when her mother's friends from the theatre hugged her and left her face sticky with lipstick kisses. Then weeks later her teacher had read her class a story called *Black Beauty*, about a horse that was treated cruelly. When they read about the horse's death quite a lot of girls cried, but Ruby couldn't stop. In the end, the teacher took her into the office, and the caretaker made her a cup of tea.

Ruby tried to imagine what Jack was like. She wondered if he was handsome. She'd thought the soldier on Preston station was quite handsome and imagined Maggie Joy sitting in her sunny bedroom stroking the creased envelope. She wondered if she should have written on the back to explain to Maggie Joy how her soldier boyfriend had given her the letter at the railway station.

Ruby could hear Bess snuffling in the garden and followed her. On the other side of the lane, she could see the dark outline of Bardley's farm and the illegal slivers of light leaking through the gaps in the milking parlour's wooden door. The sky was clear. It was a night that would be good for the bombers. Then the hens in the shed began clucking, and she called softly for Bess and went back inside.

Bo pushed open the pub door and the others followed. The air was warm and smelt of beer and cigarettes. When his customers fell silent, the portly landlord, who was reading a newspaper on the bar, looked up and reached for one of the glass tankards hanging above his head.

'Now, lads,' he said with a smile, 'the first pints are on me.'

On the other side of the bar, a row of men in overalls and railway workers' uniforms stared over at them, as the landlord took down five glass tankards hanging above his head and pumped each one full of pale golden beer. For a moment, the five pint glasses stood on the bar. Then the landlord handed one to each of them, before taking the final one for himself.

'Your good health, sir,' Bo said raising his glass to the landlord.

'And yours too, son,' replied the landlord.

The beer was the colour of honey but tasted bitter. Con found the sensation of warm beer in his mouth unpleasant. He tried to avoid meeting the eyes of the silent men on the opposite side of the bar and forced the bitter liquid down. Bo was the first one to put his pint glass back on the bar, and with relief, Con did the same.

'That's a mighty nice drink, sir,' Bo said, wiping a line of white froth from his pencil-slim moustache.

'Aye, we like to think so,' replied the landlord. 'Cheers.'

'Aye, cheers,' called the men on the opposite side of the bar, suddenly nodding and smiling as Con put the glass to his lips again.

The room on their side of the bar was in semi-darkness, lit only by the wall lights and the blazing coal fire. An elderly couple with sunken faces sat at one side of the fire, and on the other side of the hearth, a British soldier and a plump light-haired girl whispered together. The only other customer was a lone man in a raincoat, sitting under one of the wall lights reading a newspaper. By contrast, the opposite side of the bar was full of customers. They were, Con noticed, all men. Some sat at the bar, others at tables playing cards and three more, a fat clergyman and two men in caps and mufflers, threw arrows at a bullseye on the wall.

'You ever played darts, son?' an elderly man at his elbow asked.

Con smiled shyly. 'No, sir,' he said.

'Well, don't get Henry to show you how,' the landlord laughed. 'He can't play for toffee.'

The old man, who wore a porter's cap set at a jaunty angle, pulled a face, and the men on the opposite side of the bar chuckled.

'You settled in at the new camp?' he asked, as the landlord refilled his glass.

Remembering the humiliation of the night before, Con looked down at his feet, unsure what to say.

'I was in the last lot. Me and Johnny Fin, here,' the old man said, nodding in the direction of another old man who'd just walked in the bar.

The second man smiled and extended a large hand. When Con took it, the man's face suddenly contorted in a series of twitches, as though he'd been electrocuted.

'N-n-nice t-to m-m-meet you,' he stuttered.

'Here you are, Johnny,' the man in the porter's hat said, handing his friend a pint.

To Con's surprise, when he was handed the drink, the man's twitches stopped and he walked steadily over to the piano.

'I'm Henry,' the old man said, shaking each of their hands in turn, 'Henry Barton.'

'My father was there, as well,' Con said. 'In

100

France. He came out of it okay, but his friend was shot. Sniper.'

'It was the gas that got me,' Henry said. 'Johnny, there, carried me for miles on his back. Wouldn't be here, if it wasn't for him. Any of you lads play?' he asked, nodding over to the piano.

'Wes does,' Con said. 'Come on, Wes, when's the last chance you got to play?'

'Move over, Johnny,' Henry shouted. 'Let's see what this lad can do.'

The landlord leant over the bar and grinned at the three other soldiers.

'If the rest of you lads are interested,' he said, nodding over to the fat priest who was grinning at them from the other side of the bar, 'Father O'Flynn wants to know if you'd like to learn how to play darts. You'll be all right with him,' he said, winking at them. 'He's had some of the Yanks playing like champions in no time.'

'Except that Hal and his mate,' one of the old men wearing mufflers called, as Bo and Holt made their way through to the other side of the bar, and Con followed Wes over to the piano. 'They couldn't play for toffee.'

'You play as well, son?' Henry asked Con.

'Me? No sir, I don't.'

'He can sing, though,' Wes said with a wink.

'Only in church, and my grandma said I make a bullfrog sound tuneful.'

As Wes played and Johnny sang, Henry told Con about the time he and his old friend Johnny had spent as soldiers.

'The last lot did for poor Johnny's career,' he said, accepting the pint of beer Con brought him

101

from the bar. 'As a young man he was the prize-fighter "Gentleman" Johnny Finlay. You might have heard of him. Fought all over the world.'

'Is the ... twitch ... from the war?'

'Oh no, that's the boxing. Punch-drunk,' Henry said, pointing to his own head. 'Odd thing is, you'll notice when it gets busy, he waits on tables and collects glasses. Lives over the shop, so to speak, and helps out around the place. When he carries a tray of drinks, or piles of empties, he's as steady as a rock, but the rest of the time... Doesn't seem to bother him when he's playing, neither. No. He reckoned he'd seen so much killing in the war, he never fancied the fight game after. Mind you, by then he was too old, anyway.'

Towards the end of the evening, at Henry's suggestion, Con switched to mild and found it far pleasanter.

'We're off fire-watching. Thought we'd get a few down us first,' Henry said. 'Me and Johnny is calling for fish and chips before we go on duty. If you're hungry, we'll introduce you to another treat, now you've got your taste for the beer.'

From the outside, there was no hint of what kind of place the small building was. The old man opened the door and they stepped down into a small, dimly lit room. A queue of people waited in a line that ran along the bare, light-green walls and doubled back on itself in front of the wooden counter. Behind the counter, a man in a white apron stood over a shiny, green range and lowered wire baskets of pale sliced potato into the bubbling fat. His assistant, a small, bent woman with sparse black hair curled around her heavily made-up

102

face, wrapped up the food in white paper, and then into newspaper bundles.

As they edged to the head of the queue, Con was able to watch the rest of the customers through a mirror set into the back of the range. Nearly all the people waiting in line looked grey and tired. From their dress, the men in overalls or long greasy macs, and many of the women in trousers with headscarves tied around their heads in a turban style, he guessed that most of them were shift workers on their way home. There wasn't the same banter as there had been on the bus, or in the pub. But when a customer, a bony-faced man with frayed cuffs, caught Wes studying the unfamiliar brown coins that he was counting out into the hand of the bent woman, the man nodded shyly and then called 'good neet' to them as he slipped out into the darkness.

Con watched the bent woman who, despite her awkward gait, moved briskly, scooping up the fish and fries. When they reached the front of the queue, she looked at him.

'Yes, sir,' she said. 'What would you like?'

Con's eyes met Bo's in the mirror. His throat felt dry as, in the silence, the woman's face creased into a ghoulish smile.

'Fish and chips six times,' Henry said at last.

'Do you want salt and vinegar?' the lady asked.

As Con nodded dumbly for all of them, a voice from the back of the queue called, 'Can you make that seven times, love?'

Henry turned and smiled. 'Hello Sadie, love. I'm glad you're here. We'll just get served and I'll introduce you.'

103

The girl grinning across at them had an almond-shaped face, with a delicate tapering chin, green eyes that slanted upwards at the corners and perfect, white teeth.

'This is Sadie,' Henry said, when Con stumbled out into the darkness.

'Nice to meet you,' she said, as someone handed him a bundle in hot newspaper. 'Now come on, eat your chips or they'll get cold. I'm starving. There's nothing like chips and fish after a long shift. You off fire-watching, Da?'

'Aye,' Henry said in between mouthfuls. 'I've just thought, these lads will need somebody to show them how to get back to their camp. Can you manage on your own, Johnny, whilst I show them the way?'

'No need,' Sadie said. 'I'll walk them part of the way. I'm calling in on Lou on my way home. Just let me finish these chips.'

The group wandered along until they reached a school. Then Henry and Johnny said goodnight and walked up through the playground.

'Them was lovely,' Sadie said. 'Can you see that building?' she asked, pointing towards a single-storey building just visible through the gloom. 'Well that's the church hall where we have the dances.'

She led them down a quiet suburban lane, pointing out shops, asking where they were from, laughing and chatting with them as easily as if it was something that she did every day.

Con walked a few steps behind. He could hear her laughing, and Bo, in his deep growl, asking her about Henry and her job. The hot food had warmed him, but as he followed them, Con felt the damp air creep inside his clothes and a chill rippled through him.

The sky was clear and the moonlight lit up the wet road in front of them, making it shine. In every garden wet leaves glistened and dripped. He thought of home and the summer heat and wondered if he would ever feel dry and warm again. Then he heard the guys giggling with Sadie about some joke, and the sound of her tinkling laughter made him smile. When they came to a crossroads she stopped. 'I go this way,' she said. 'You keep straight on and you'll come to the camp.'

'Will you be all right?' Bo asked. 'Should we see you home?'

'No. No thanks. I'm fine from here. But thanks for asking. I'm calling in on my friend; she only lives a couple of houses down. Listen, if you can get passes for Saturday, why don't you come to the dance at the church hall?'

They watched her until she disappeared. It was too dark for Con to make out the others' faces.

Then Holt laughed softly, 'Ain't she the prettiest thing you ever saw?'

'And she asked me to the dance,' Bo said.

'Us,' Con said. 'She asked us all to the dance.'

'But she's...' Wes whispered.

'What?' Bo growled. 'She's what?'

'You know what,' Wes said. 'You wouldn't go to meet a white girl. At home...'

'We're not at home, and she asked me...'

'Us.'

'She probably wants you to sing. They got groups goin' round all the churches singing.

105

Everybody likes to hear happy, singin' black folks,' Holt said. 'I told her I got prizes for dancing. She's–'

'No you ain't.'

'I do so. I got a prize in high school.'

'You're lying, man. You're no better mover than me.'

'I am so. I'll show you. May I have this dance?' Holt asked and grabbed Bo's arm.

'Get off me. You lied to that little white girl. You said...' Bo tried to wrestle him, and when Holt broke free, he chased him along the road. 'I'm gonna make you sorry.'

'You can't dance as good as me. An' you can't run as fast.'

'Yes, I can. Bet you didn't tell her you was married? You're a disgrace.'

'Can you believe this place?' Wes said, as they watched Bo chase Holt down the lane. 'These people ... white people. Dressed like poor folk, all of 'em...'

'Might be, but they're friendly. Talk funny too, but they're good people.'

'Folk here might be shabby,' Wes said, offering Con a cigarette, 'but they still white and the people on the bus, the old guy and the landlord...'

'The woman in the shop ... she called me "sir".'

'I know...' Wes grinned. 'Never thought I'd hear that. Like you said, folks here ... they're different. Got to give you that.'

They caught up with Bo and Holt, who'd grown tired of wrestling. Wes tried again to persuade Bo that to dream of dancing with a pretty white girl was crazy, but he refused to be discouraged and began to sing. He continued to sing as they walked the rest of the way down the lane and up the main street, his deep, rich voice rising in the night air, followed by Wes's lighter tenor. As they neared the turning to the base, a jeep swung out and blocked the road.

'Hey, you. You, boy,' one of the MPs in the jeep shouted. 'Quit that racket.'

But Bo sang louder, and the others joined Wes's sweet tenor, lifting their voices to follow the harmony.

'I said quit that,' the furious MP bellowed. 'You ignoring me, boy?'

Bo stopped, balled his hands into fists and headed towards the jeep. The others fell silent. Then the bedroom window of one of the terrace houses across the street suddenly rattled and snapped open. A large woman stuck her head out.

'Who you tellin' to shut up? It's you that wants to stop yellin'. You're in England now, love. You carry on. It sounds lovely. It's him as wants to shut up.'

'Aye,' called a small man, whose shiny head was just visible around the side of his wife's heavy body, 'you 'ave a sing if you want, lad. It's very nice.'

'And you in the white hat,' the woman shouted, 'can keep the bloody noise down.'

CHAPTER FIVE

'Here, put this in your purse,' Jenny said, opening the chest of drawers and taking a half-crown from an old tin. 'If you see a queue, doesn't matter what shop, or what's being sold, just join it. Just get what you can. I can allus swap it.'

Ruby blushed, guiltily pushing the silver coin down beside the ten-shilling note her Uncle Walt had given her.

'I'll write down my Co-op number for you. They'll not serve you without it. Oh, and I'm registered at the butcher's near the Co-op, so if you see a queue outside the other one, Bamford's, don't bother. They'll not serve you there.'

Jenny took a piece of brown paper from the drawer, unfolded it carefully and began to parcel up the doctor's freshly laundered washing. As she did, the afternoon sunlight caught the smooth contours of the newly pressed cloth and the runnels of sweat webbing her tired face. She'd spent the whole morning testing each flat iron Ruby had brought from the fire, judging the heat needed to press the dampened fabric and bending every muscle to ease each pleat on the doctor's dress shirts. Now she unfastened a loop of twine, tugged it out across her apron front and measured the length against the parcel. When it was neatly fastened, she patted it.

'Now, that's ready,' she said, and stood back to

admire her handiwork.

The parcel's bulk made it difficult to carry. Ruby tried holding it by the loop in the string but the sides puckered, so she carried it in front of her, balanced on her outstretched forearms. She decided to take the main road. The air was clear and the cloudless sky a deep, pure blue. A light breeze ruffled the fading leaves, and the late-autumn sunlight made them shimmer.

At the gate of the doctor's house she met an elderly man carrying a bunch of orange flowers.

'Now, young lady,' he said. 'Is that parcel for the doctor?'

The man's moss-green cap shaded his eyes and his windowpane check shirt was held up around the elbows by two broad elastic bands.

'I've brought the doctor's laundry,' she said. 'I was told to go around to the kitchen door and ask for Mrs Alice Watts.'

'Well, I can help you there,' the man said. 'I know the lady well.'

She followed him through the gate, their feet crunching out of time on the white gravel. The drive was edged with slick-leafed rhododendrons and shielded from the road by tall trees, whose thick foliage made the house appear gloomy.

'I know you were told to go round to the kitchen door,' the man said, 'but on this occasion you can follow me through the front. I'm Dick Watts, by the way. Alice is my wife, and I know for a fact that there's no one at home.'

The house was made of the same red brick as the smaller ones along the main road. Ivy clung to the walls and climbed on top of the porch, softening the building's sharp angles. Inside the narrow entrance hall the lower part of the walls were covered with plain green tiles, interspersed with some depicting exotic flowers, each labelled with its botanical name. Above the tiling, the walls were papered in an equally dull green stripe. A large wooden hatstand took up almost half of the space, and on the wall opposite, there was an enormous barometer in a similar type of shiny, dark wood.

Mr Watts tapped the glass. 'Ah, the pressure is rising,' he said. 'Now, I've got to take these flowers into the sitting room and then I'll show you where you leave your parcel. I shouldn't be a minute.'

The vestibule opened into a spacious hall. Facing the door, a broad staircase twisted and then climbed out of sight. Behind it, a wall made of individual panes of pale green and yellow glass rose up as far as she could see. The effect was to flood the building with light; even the crosses of tape on each pane didn't spoil the feeling of space. The dappled light from the window fell on to the stairs, making the pattern of tangled roots and leaves in the carpet appear to move, as though the trees behind the windows were creeping indoors.

'Wait here,' Mr Watts said, heading towards a set of double doors on her right.

When he slipped silently behind the doors, Ruby felt the house settle around her. Somewhere deep inside the building she heard a clock's pulse. A bowl of white roses stood on a table in the centre of the room. Their perfume, mingled with the tang of sun-heated old varnish and floor polish, filled the hall. Every wall was hung with pictures, but it was the portrait next to the sitting-room door that

110

caught her attention. Ruby crept closer. The subject, a beautiful woman in a pale-blue suit and matching cloche hat, gazed down at her. She was admiring the delicate fingers resting on the rim of a small table, when a door behind her opened. Ruby felt something thud into her, pushing her forwards with such force that the parcel left her hands. As it skittered across the red-tiled floor, a large dog bounded after it.

'No!' Ruby yelled, grabbing the parcel and holding it out of the dog's reach.

When she held the package higher, the dog, pleased with the game, danced around and yapped excitedly, jumping and snapping at the prize. She was rescued by a stout, white-haired woman in an apron.

'Get down, Rover,' she said, dragging the young dog away by his collar.

Then the sitting-room door opened, and the lady in the portrait walked out, followed by Mr Watts.

'Are you all right, dear?' the woman from the picture asked. 'You're a naughty boy, Rover. He's just a puppy, you see, and rather too playful.'

At the sound of his name, Rover leapt towards his mistress, scattering the papers she was carrying.

'I'll take him, madam,' the plump lady said.

'Would you, Alice?' she replied. 'Now look what you've done, you bad dog. I'll never get these in order again.'

Once the dog had been dragged away, Ruby put her parcel on the first step of the staircase and began to help Mr Watts and the lady to pick up the papers. Some of them were covered in neat, italic handwriting and the rest of it was sheet music.

'Oh dear,' the lady said, 'I'll never get them sorted out. I don't know anything about notation. Do either of you have any ideas? Mr Watts?'

'The writing has little numbers in the corner of the pages,' Ruby said. 'I think they follow on, and the music ... it has words ... I know the songs.'

'She's right,' the lady laughed. 'Clever girl. How stupid of me not to see. I'm glad you were here,' she smiled, as Ruby put the sheets in order. 'I'd have been lost without you. Goodness, did that naughty dog scratch your face? Mr Watts will take you to the kitchen and get Alice to put something on it. Then you must come back and see me before you go.'

'Missus says to put something on her face,' Mr Watts said, dropping the parcel on the table. 'She's brought the doctor's laundry.'

Mrs Watts rinsed her hands and dried them on her apron.

'And whose idea was it to come in by the front door?'

'I didn't know the missus was in, and you said you'd gone to Bamford's for the meat.'

'That was hours ago,' his wife said, and smiled at Ruby. 'Sit down, pet,' she said. 'Let's look what that stupid dog has done.'

When Mrs Watts lifted her chin, Ruby could smell fresh herbs and washing soap on her hands.

'It doesn't look like much harm has been done. We'll just bathe it with soap and water, and I've some cream as will soothe it.'

'There's iodine in the cupboard,' Mr Watts offered.

'What, and make her face smart? No. Delicate skin shouldn't have iodine on it,' Mrs Watts said, filling a bowl with soap and water. 'Make yourself useful and put the kettle on,' she said to her husband. 'We'll have a cup of tea, when I've done this.'

Mr Watts took the kettle and filled it. 'Missus wants to see her again before she goes,' he said. 'I took her the chrysanths. She doesn't want 'em. Says they're too hot, or something. Says to take 'em for the altar at the church.'

'Too hot, indeed. Whatever next,' his wife tutted. 'When you've put that kettle on, you can unpack that washing, or they'll be creased again.'

Once Ruby's cheek was bathed, Mrs Watts poured the tea and offered her a biscuit.

'They're my own recipe,' she said, 'oats and butter I call them, but it's a while since there was any butter in them. What's your name, dear?'

'My granddad's...'

'Oh, I know who you are, dear. You're the picture of Lucy, your grandma. Same lovely eyes and the same hair.' Mrs Watts smiled and took a sip of her tea. 'She was older than me, but I can remember her. She must have been about twenty at the time. Such a beauty. Ask Dick, here. He'll tell you.'

'Oh, she was indeed,' Dick Watts said. 'Tall, like you. I knew who you were, when I saw you at the gate. Are you visiting?'

'I've come to stay with my granddad. I've never seen a picture of her.'

113

'Well you could be twins,' he said.

'You still haven't said what your name is,' Alice Watts said, offering her another biscuit.

'I'm Ruby. My dad picked it because my mum is ... was called Pearl.'

'Well, it's very pretty. I'm Alice and this is Dick. If you're coming regular for the washing, use the back door.'

'I'm to ask if there's any more shirts to go back,' Ruby said.

'Well there's a problem there. Some of the doctor's collars want turning, and I haven't got time, us being short-staffed, and the missus, bless her heart, is no needlewoman.'

'I know how,' Ruby said. 'I've done my uncle's.'

'I don't know. They're good shirts and hard to come by. Tell you what, you can do one of Dick's old ones, and if it's suitable, I'll consider it. Now, I'll take you through to see Mrs Grey, and remember next time, come to the back door.'

Mrs Grey was sitting in an easy chair reading a magazine. She looked older than her portrait, but no less beautiful. Her hair was pale, almost white, and brushed back from her high forehead. She had finely shaped eyebrows arched above her generous, velvety lashes and brilliant blue eyes. When she smiled, Ruby felt as if it was just for her.

'You look better already, dear,' she said, perching her cigarette on the edge of a scalloped glass ashtray. 'Tell me, do you play?'

'Yes, madam,' Ruby said, glancing at Mrs Watts to check if this form of address was appropriate. 'My father arranged music for my mother to sing, and I played for her when she worked on new pieces. She was working on that song.'

'So you can play popular songs? How wonderful. What a find,' Mrs Grey said, getting up from her seat.

The large room had two enormous windows overlooking the lawns at the back of the house. Under the largest one was a baby grand piano with a dark-red shawl spread across the top. Mrs Grey opened the lid.

'Could you play something for me?' she asked. 'Something from memory?'

Ruby took off her mac and sat down at the piano. Mrs Grey returned to her seat and motioned to Mrs Watts to join her. Ruby didn't feel nervous; she loved to play. When her hands touched the keys, she always felt at home. She played 'The Last Rose of Summer', a song that she knew just fitted the lovely room. The instrument was tuned perfectly and at the end of the piece, her audience applauded.

'My, how wonderful,' Mrs Grey smiled. 'She's very good, isn't she, Alice?'

'She is indeed, madam, and she's a handy girl as well. She's going to turn a collar for me, and if it's satisfactory, she'll do Doctor Grey's shirts.'

'That's wonderful. Doctor Grey's shirts are getting so worn, and they're impossible to replace. Now...'

'Ruby,' Mrs Watts supplied.

'Now, Ruby, do you think you could play for my guests? I've invited some people... Oh Alice, I haven't told you, have I? I met Mrs Prendergast in town and ... well, I just felt we all needed 'cheering up.'

'The help, madam... Mabel finishes at the end of the week.'

'Yes, yes she does. Ruby, do you think you could help? If you could...'

'She's not trained, madam,' Mrs Watts said, getting to her feet and straightening her apron.

'We'll keep it simple. Just simple food. Mr Watts can help to serve. Ruby can help you, and then play for us. When you come next week, dear, bring your music. We'll choose something for you to play before dinner, and then you can help in the kitchen.'

When Ruby left the house, the shadows were lengthening. She hugged the old shirt to her as she walked back to the cottage. On her way to Doctor Grey's, she'd taken the long way round through the village, hoping to see the girl from the swings. Now, instead of walking home the short way by the lane, Ruby took the long way back to the cottage again. This time, with her mind full of the lovely room and its piano, she imagined herself sitting at the baby grand, with the Greys' guests, handsome men and their elegant wives, standing by the window, listening to her play.

Con took Sadie into his arms. As they danced, he felt her hair brushing against his chin. The music was soft, romantic and yet oddly distant; it was as though he and Sadie had left the church hall and the rest of the dancers behind them. He looked down at the curve of her smooth, apple-pink cheek, and she lifted her face for him to kiss. Her mouth tasted sweet, and he drew her closer. She looked up at him, smiled her pretty smile, and slipped her arms around his neck. Con couldn't believe that this beautiful white girl had chosen to dance with him. He wasn't much used to girls, and the only time he'd danced before was at his school dance, but his feet knew the steps and were moving perfectly in time to the music. He wasn't sure what to do next. He hoped she'd lift her head again and invite him to kiss her. For now, he was happy just to have her in his arms. Every other guy he knew would be jealous. He smiled and dipped his chin, hoping to catch the feel of her soft hair and inhale its perfume. Instead, her hair felt scratchy and the smell of it made him squirm. Con put out his hand to push her away and heard a yell.

'Will you let go of my foot,' Wes shouted.

Con sat up. It was dark and cold, and he could hear a rustly sound that he knew he should recognise.

'What you doing?' Wes asked.

Con gazed around, his eyes gradually growing accustomed to the blackness.

'I thought we were at a dance,' he said.

'Well, we ain't. We're in the back of a truck. It's dark and I'm tired. Now, settle down. The guy on the dock gate said they'll start loading again as soon as it gets light.'

Earlier that evening, along with the rest of the disappointed drivers, they'd wandered into the streets around Liverpool's docks looking for a meal and a bed for the night. They'd found a pub near the dockside selling bowls of stew that Wes identified as mutton. After a drink of brown ale to

117

wash away the taste of the grease from his mouth, Con had headed back to the truck. His body was too long to stretch out comfortably in the cab, so he'd climbed into the back, using his jacket as a pillow.

Con shuddered as a chill mist coming in from the Irish Sea slithered over the cobbled wharves. He wanted a warm drink, but all the bars around the port were silent. He wanted a cigarette, but the blackout around the harbour was total and any breach would bring the patrol running. Somewhere in the streets around the docks a dog barked, a cab door slammed and footsteps rang in the silence. Above him there was a clear sky; one bright star was shining over the sea. Moonlight glinted, silvering the sides of the anchored ships.

As he listened to the suck and slap of the water against the quay, Con recalled the day he'd gone with his father to the river to watch the Liberty ships carrying iron and coal to the factories and sailing back out again loaded with jeeps, trucks and tanks. To comfort his nagging homesickness he curled his long legs into his chest, holding on to his body's warmth. He wondered if the stuff they'd be loading in the morning might be parts for B-24 Liberator bombers made at the plant at Willow Run. Then he closed his eyes, and for a few hours he was back home in Detroit.

It was almost mid morning by the time the trucks were loaded. Once their papers were checked, they drove out from the docks and bought hot pies and bottles of cold tea from a woman outside the gates. The damp mist had lifted and above the city the sky was cloudless. The bright autumn sunshine lasted all day. Con enjoyed the journey through the miles of changing countryside, marvelling at the tiny houses hunched against the broad sky. Wes was in a good mood as well: he'd spent most of the night playing cards with the other guys in the waiting convoy, and most of the time on their way from the port to the airbase working out different ways to spend his winnings. It was late afternoon before the trucks were unloaded and cleared to leave the airbase, but as they headed back towards the camp, his mood darkened.

'Not that we'll get to spend much any time soon,' he said.

The week before, after the MPs reported them for swearing, lewd singing and waking civilians, Bo had insisted that they went to see Captain O'Donal together. It hadn't done any good. All they'd got from the captain was a lecture on them being visitors in someone else's country, while the MP smirked at them over his shoulder.

The trouble was that, although Captain O'Donal was a decent guy, he was weak. If he'd been alone there wouldn't have been a problem, and they would have got their passes, but Captain O'Donal always buckled if the MPs got involved. So instead of going to the dance they'd been in-vited to, the four of them had been confined to the camp.

'You can spend it on some girl. I bet there'll be another dance this Saturday for sure. In fact, I heard some of the guys say so.'

'I reckon we should stay well clear of these white girls. They're trouble. If that girl hadn't been so

119

friendly, then Bo wouldn't have been singin' and we wouldn't have lost our passes.'

'You know what,' Con said, 'you sound like that MP. "You boys git too excitable around white women."'

'I'm sayin' they're trouble.'

'It's not them that's trouble. It's that cracker MP. He hates us. He'll do anything he can to–'

'Exactly, so why give him the excuse?'

'All Bo was doing was singing. That guy didn't know it was because of some white girl.'

'What do you think he'd have done if he had?'

'It doesn't matter. It's not up to him. Like Captain O'Donal says, we're in someone else's country, and it's not like back home. The folks here like us. They want to make us welcome. Trouble is, the MPs and the rest of them.'

'That MP's a redneck and that's for sure. You got to be careful with them guys. Bo's crazy if he thinks they'll back off.'

'That's the trouble with the army, too many rednecks and not enough black officers. Bo said that when he was training, he was at Camp Robinson, Little Rock.'

'Now, that is real Deep South, that place.'

'He said that they wouldn't serve black soldiers with liquor in the stores. He heard that this one time, some white soldier said to the store owner, "Well these guys come from the same place we do, so serve them, or take the stuff you sold us back." So the storekeeper took the drink back, but then he must've rung the cops, because the cops arrived and turned the white soldier's car over.'

'Then what happened?'

'Next day, the whole lot of them gets extra marching, or something, and the town's off limits for the whole camp.'

'That's what I mean. The army's not on our side. You shouldn't listen to Bo. He's a hothead, an' he doesn't know the South like I do. I'd say them guys was lucky...'

'Hold up... Isn't that the old guy from the pub? Look, on the railway bridge... Slow down.'

Henry was sitting with his back against the bridge's sooty bricks, a half-filled sack of stolen coke between his trembling legs.

'I'm just havin' a rest. The climb from the station's got to me,' he said, bending forwards with his hands on his knees, forcing air between his spittle-flecked lips.

The tall, red-haired girl standing next to him put the brown paper parcel she was carrying on the floor and tried to lift the misshapen sack, but it hardly cleared the ground. Then gradually, like a rusty pocket-knife, the old man began to straighten and his breathing slowed.

'I had Johnny to help me last time, and we borrowed Mrs Feeney's pram, but she said we left it mucky.'

'Where do you want to go?' Con asked, leaping down from the truck and picking up the sack in one hand.

'That's very good of you lads. Am I glad to see you. It's not but a hop and a jump.'

When the soldier looked puzzled, Ruby laughed. 'He means it's not far,' she said, 'just over the humped-backed bridge and down the first lane you come to. It's the white cottage on the left.'

Outside the stone cottage, Con opened the tailgate and helped the old man down.

'I'll take your sack in for you,' he said. 'Just tell me where it goes.'

'This is very kind of you, son,' Henry replied. 'This is my granddaughter, Ruby, by the way,' he said, nodding towards the girl standing on the edge of the truck.

'Pleased to meet you,' Con said. 'Can I help you down?' The girl blushed as she took his hands, and when he lifted her down, her bones felt as fragile as a bird's.

'This here's Jenny,' the old man said, nodding towards a plump woman in an apron who was standing at the cottage door. 'I've got a bit of coal, Jenny, love. These lads have been good enough to give me a lift home with it. Put the kettle on for us, will you. We're just takin' it round the back.'

Jenny wiped her wet hands on her apron and smiled. 'Nice to meet you, I'm sure,' she said.

When Henry took them inside the cottage, Con felt the top of his head brushing the low ceiling. In comparison to his mother's kitchen, there were few cupboards and there was no refrigerator. The only piece of equipment he could see was a sparkling white cooker, but the pans sitting on top looked so old he was sure his mother would have thrown them out, or given them to the church for the children's summer camping trips. The living room was just as small and shabby: the mismatched chairs looked worn, and the only other pieces of furniture were a table and an ancient dresser.

'Sit yourselves down, lads,' the old man said,

indicating the seats at the table.

The old lady brought in a tray with teacups and a plate of small cakes that had been made by sandwiching some kind of yellowish cream between two crackers. The girl followed her, carrying a large brown teapot inside a woolly cover. It looked far too heavy for her narrow wrists, but when Con reached and took the clumsy pot from her, she blushed and hurried back to the kitchen. If she was Sadie's sister, they were very different: Sadie was small and curvy, but the younger girl was tall, gawky, all arms and legs, and she didn't have Sadie's sense of fun either.

The old man poured out the tea and offered them one of the small cakes.

'Will you tell Sadie we're real sorry we missed the dance,' Con said, trying to nibble the cake that fractured into tiny pieces as he bit into it, 'we couldn't get passes.'

'Well that's a shame,' the old man said, carefully collecting up each crumb of shattered biscuit from his waistcoat. 'I know she looked for you. Tell you what, why don't you come to the pub again on Friday? Sadie will be there.'

When she discovered that Jack had been taken prisoner, Sadie hadn't cried. In fact she didn't do very much, except sit by the fire drinking Granddad's brandy and listening to Jenny's story about Mrs Lathom and how upset she'd been. After their second drink, Jenny had tried to persuade her to go round and see Mrs Lathom on her own, but Sadie said it was best left until the next day. But the next night she'd sulked and said she wasn't going, until Jenny agreed to go with her. That was a few days ago, and now Ruby could hear her getting ready to go out with Lou to a dance in the next village where the black soldiers had their camp.

'Be a love and help me with this hook,' she said, bursting into the little back bedroom. 'Lou's going to be here any minute.'

Her dress was green satin with a pattern of flowers and leaves. When she moved, the bias-cut skirt swayed, and the light caught the different textures woven into the silky fabric. It had a sweetheart neckline, short sleeves trimmed with black velvet bows and the belt buckle was velvet as well.

'Blimey this floor's cold,' she said hopping from one foot to the other. 'Hang on a minute.'

When she came back, Sadie was carrying a rug with a picture of a cottage on it.

'Here,' she said, spreading it on the floor. 'Your feet won't get as cold when you get out of bed.'

'Are you going to meet the Americans who came here?'

'We'll most likely bump into them. I said we'd probably see them later.'

'Did you go dancing with him ... with Jack?'

'Jack wasn't my boyfriend. It's Ma and his mother who thought that would be a good idea. I used to dance with him sometimes at the church dances ... not that he was much of a dancer.'

'Mrs Lathom said—'

'She said a lot of things. Before he went, I promised Jack we'd look out for Nellie and that I'd write to him, that's all. Jack cared a lot more about football and a few pints than he did about

124

any girl.'

Later, when the door closed and Lou and Sadie's laughter had faded down the lane, Ruby sat on her bed to admire her new rug. It was a half-moon shape, and although the backing was ripped, when it was on the floor it looked okay. The cottage had four windows and roses climbed around the door. There was a thatched roof, and in the foreground, flowers – lupins, she thought – in pink, yellow and blue. The sky was blue as well, with a couple of clouds and two black 'V' shapes to stand for birds. Ruby imagined that Maggie Joy lived in the cottage and that her soldier boyfriend would come up the light sandy-brown path and knock at the door. When Maggie Joy opened it, they would stand there kissing under the roses.

She took off her shoes and padded over the springy surface to the bookcase. The shelves had been painted black but in places it was worn and showed the pale wood underneath. Ruby took the books from the shelves and piled them on the floor. Then she wiped the dust away with her hands and began to sort the books into alphabetical order.

Her father's books were mainly adventure stories – attacks on desert forts, journeys through the jungle to find lost treasure, or spy stories from the last war – with soft covers and wavy pages. There were also a couple of books of folk tales that she couldn't imagine he'd ever read. These books had gilt lettering on the spine and a tree picked out in gilt on the front and back. At the beginning of each new story, there was a picture; some of them were of witches or goblins and others of princesses and castles. The only other book, a copy of *Great Expectations,* had 'Happy Christmas from Uncle Joe and Auntie Maud' written inside in curly black letters.

When she'd finished sorting the books, Ruby wiped the dust on the inside of her gymslip, and taking one of the books of folk tales, curled up on the bed with her feet under the counterpane.

CHAPTER SIX

A week later, Ruby returned with the work-shirt washed and pressed and with a very neatly turned collar, and Mrs Watts allowed her to work on the doctor's shirts. By early November, she'd also played for Mrs Grey's guests at two of her fund-raising afternoon teas. These occasions – to raise funds to provide a free buffet for servicemen arriving at the town's railway station – did not attract the elegant ladies and gentlemen Ruby had hoped to see. Instead, the invited guests were mainly the wives of local businessmen, but there were also some town councillors, the vicar and Father O'Flynn.

Before the afternoon tea was served, the guests perched on an assortment of garden chairs in the entrance hall to hear a talk. The first one – How to Remodel Your Hat – was given by Mrs Prendergast who, according to Alice, stuck her nose in where it wasn't wanted and liked to organise things, just as long as she wasn't doing the work.

The second – My Time in Egypt and The Holy Land – was a lantern show by Major Southworth who organised the Home Guard.

Ruby helped Alice prepare the tiny sandwiches and individual fruit tarts, and Dick set out the chairs. Then after the talk – as the guests chatted, and Mrs Grey encouraged them to buy raffle tickets for a jar of bottled fruit – she played the piano. Towards five o'clock, Mrs Grey announced the winner of the raffle and everyone began collecting their coats, leaving donations in a collection box discreetly placed near the front door. When the guests had left, Dick carried the chairs back to the summer house, and Ruby helped to clear away. The extra work created by the fundraising made Alice Watts cross, and the contents of the basket that Mrs Grey had brought through to the kitchen didn't help.

'Look at this,' Alice said, tipping the sorry twists of tea and sugar and pieces of margarine no bigger than Ruby's thumbnail on to the table. 'Supposed to bring part of their own rations to help with the makings for the fundraising tea. Wouldn't even care if it was quality tea they left, but it isn't; it's just sweepings. Then she'll be complaining the doctor's tea is weak, and there'll be no bottled fruit left when it comes to Christmas, but she'll expect a good table just the same.'

By the time Mr Watts came back from clearing the hall, Alice had finished her grumbling. There was a plate of sandwiches on the kitchen table, filled with the same carefully made lentil paste flavoured with herbs or with rabbit meat that had been served to the guests, along with a small fruit tart for each of them and a pot of tea. Mr Watts munched contentedly at his sandwich and winked at Ruby.

'Nothing's too good for the working classes,' he said.

When Ruby arrived home after the fundraising tea the black GIs, Con and Wes, were there along with their friends, Bo and Holt. Since the day Con and Wes had helped them carry the coke home, they'd become regular visitors. Wes and Granddad were mending the pigeon cabin; Con was throwing a ball for Bess on the field next to the river; Bo, the best-looking one, was teaching Sadie and Jenny a new set of dance moves in the kitchen, and on the other side of the lane, Holt was helping Mr Bardley mend his tractor. It was clear that life at the camp was not to their liking, and they took any opportunity they could to get out. Everyone in the village liked the black GIs from the new camp, because they were friendly, and when they were invited for a meal, they brought gifts of tea and sugar and offered to help out by doing odd jobs. The luxuries the four GIs brought to the cottage made Jenny very happy, and in exchange, Jenny got Ruby to do the soldiers' washing, and they often had meals there as well.

'Mrs Grey wants me to play at their dinner party next week,' she said. 'I told her I had to ask you first.'

'She can't go dressed like that, Ma,' Sadie said, untangling herself from Bo. 'She'll have to have something proper for a thing like that.'

The radio was playing dance band music and Bo began trying to show Jenny how to dance.

'Don't look at your feet, Ma,' he said. 'Just follow me. Try it again. Ready? One, two, three and then feet together.'

'I'll never get it,' Jenny laughed. 'I'm like a carthorse.'

'No you're not,' Bo said, effortlessly spinning her around. 'You're the next Ginger Rogers. You've just got to go with the music.'

'Stop that now,' Jenny squealed with delight, 'I'll never be able to see to make Henry's tea at this rate.'

Ruby took the parcel of washing into the scullery.

'Is there another fundraising do next week, Ruby?' Jenny called, her face pink with the excitement of dancing.

'No. They're having this dinner party next week instead. On the fifth. I told her I'd let her know, if you said it was all right for me to go.'

'On the fifth?'

'It's to celebrate Bonfire Night. Mr Watts says they're having an indoor firework display.'

'Indoor fireworks?' Sadie said. 'They should have invited the kiddies for that. Me and Bo are trying to get a party up for them in the hall. Games and such. We could do with them fireworks. You can't go dressed like that. You'd need something better to wear, and it's short notice to start making you something.'

The problem of what to wear for Mrs Grey's fundraising teas had been quite easily sorted out by letting down the hem of her gymslip and adding another piece of fabric of almost matching black to the hem. The sleeves of her blouse were lengthened by letting in a contrasting band above the cuff, and they'd found some dark-blue check to extend the sleeves and the hem of her mac. The whole project had taken them the best part of a week, and it was difficult to see how a dress could be created in three days.

'I've got a black velvet—'

'Never mind that now,' Jenny said. 'Bo, love, you go and see what Wes and Henry are up to, and tell them tea's almost ready, and Ruby, get your jacket off and set the table.'

In addition to the luxury of sugar and tea that the GIs brought in payment for having their washing done, they also kept the family well supplied with meat. Tonight there was a leg of pork served with Henry's potatoes, roasted and crispy from the fat, but soft and fluffy inside, and the last of the windfall apples had been used for the sauce.

'Holt says he's staying to help finish the tractor and then he'll eat with John and Marge,' Bo said. 'Don't worry, I'll eat his.'

'I've no doubt you would,' Jenny chuckled.

'Wes reckons he can find me some paint for the pigeon cabin, now we've mended it,' Henry said, when they'd settled down to eat the meal.

'Can't see what the point of that is, Da,' Sadie said. 'It's wasting paint. You've no pigeons.'

Henry looked around the table. 'Ah, but I will have. I'm going to apply for a licence. The Voluntary Pigeon Service it's called. You get issued with a permit, and that entitles you to buy seed.'

When Sadie giggled, Granddad looked cross. 'It's not a joke. Wes is going to fetch some paint next week. Very useful creatures, are pigeons.

Very intelligent.'

'Tasty too,' Jenny said. 'Though, the meat's a bit dark.'

'Will you shut up, Ma,' Sadie grinned. 'You're putting poor Con off his food. This isn't pigeon, love. Take no notice. This is the leg of pork Bo got for us.'

'The lad can tell the difference. Can't you, love?'

'I'll give you an instance of how valuable a bird a pigeon can be in wartime,' Henry said, ignoring the growing hilarity around the table. 'When Liverpool was bombed, the telephone exchange was hit. They couldn't send for help, see. So they used pigeons. Messages tied to their legs, asking for extra appliances for the docks and more Civil Defence workers. And do you know, those birds arrived two hours before the telephones was repaired. Now they want to use them behind enemy lines. You can't trace a pigeon like you can a radio operator.'

'No, they'll eat the bloody things instead,' Jenny laughed. 'Someone's havin' you on, like they was about these lads barking when they was hungry. Come on, lads, let's have your plates. There's a nice fruit pie waiting in the kitchen.'

'Don't you be too sure, Jenny,' Wes said. 'Look at Bo, there. If he don't get Holt's share as well as his own, I reckon he'll be howlin' any minute.'

'That was just a typical white trick,' Bo said, 'tryin' to set folks against us before we even got here.'

'Well, it didn't work,' Sadie said. 'We didn't much care for the lot before; too loud and stuck-up for our liking. Always talking down to everybody and sayin' how everything's much better over there.'

'Hear about two of our guys goin' in a bar near the camp?' Bo said, handing round cigarettes. 'The girl behind the bar asked if they were Negroes, an' they thought they might not get served, after all these stories that's been goin' around. So they says, "No, ma'am, we're Red Indians."'

When everyone started laughing, Jenny said, 'What did she do?'

'Haw, she just served 'em. It's not you folks that's the problem. It's our own army. They don't treat the black man fair.'

'Well, at least here,' Henry said, 'everyone's treated the same.'

'The same? The same?' Jenny said. 'Then how come I do the doctor's washing and his missus sits around givin' talks?'

'We all have the same rations, though,' Ruby said.

'Oh aye, we do. How come they have fires in all their rooms in that big house?'

'It'll all change after the war,' Henry said. 'You'll see. Everything will be shared out. There'll be no paying to go to doctors. If there's two kiddies ill, you'll not have to decide which you can afford to pay the doctor to see. There'll be pensions as well for all the old folk. So folk like our Maud won't have to struggle. The working man will be able to hold his head up. There'll be no bosses telling us what to do. We'll all have a say.'

'Give us your plates, lads,' Jenny said. 'The only way to get Henry off his soapbox is to feed him my fruit pie.'

When the meal was over Ruby cleared away, and Con helped her carry the dishes into the kitchen. Of the four GIs they'd befriended, Con was her favourite; he was quieter than the others, not so much fun as Bo, but he loved Bess almost as much as she did.

'You didn't say much,' she said, as they stacked the dishes. 'Don't you like it here as much as the others?'

Con poured the hot water from the kettle into the sink and rolled up his shirtsleeves. He picked up the small mesh box by its wooden handle and whisked it in the water, until the slivers of soap inside made the warm water froth.

'It's not that simple,' he said, as he began washing the dishes.

'Are you homesick?'

'No. Well, yes. It's the camp... The guys ... well a lot of the time the guys are real unhappy. Like Bo says, we're not treated right and ... well, our captain's a good guy, but some of the others they hate us just for the colour of our skin.'

'What colour's the captain?'

'There are no black guys in charge.'

'I thought you were all black.'

'There's some black sergeants. Some of them are okay, but some are out for themselves.'

'Well, we all like you ... the locals, I mean.'

'I ain't so sure,' he said, swishing the mesh box under the water again. 'Mrs Lathom ain't too keen.'

'Why? What's she said?'

'It's nothing really. It was when I took Bess

133

back tonight. I just said she was getting used to me, and she said Bess was her son's dog. Then she went on about him being a POW and Sadie being his girl. She said she wasn't sure he'd want someone like me taking his dog out, 'cause when he left, he'd asked Sadie to look after Bess... It was just the way–'

'Take no notice. She's like that with me as well. She didn't want me taking her out either. She's a right old bugger.'

'Buuggur,' he laughed, trying to imitate her flat northern vowels. 'She's a right old boogger.'

'None of your cheek,' Ruby said, splashing him with the bubbles. 'You get them plates clean and behave.'

From the living room, they could hear Sadie's giggles above the rest of the laughter, as Bo landed a punchline to one of his stories.

'Is it true, though? Con asked, looking at Ruby's reflection through the window. 'Does she have... Is she...?'

The cold November wind blew at the back door, making the latch rattle. Ruby picked up the dried dishes and began stacking them noisily in the kitchenette.

'Is Jack Lathom her boyfriend?' she said, finishing his question for him. 'You'd best ask her, if you're that interested.'

When the pots were cleared away, Ruby went upstairs and opened her mother's suitcase. The black velvet dress was wrapped in brittle paper. She took it into Sadie's room and tried it on in front of the dressing table mirror. Although the dress was less than a year old, the hem of the full

134

skirt was now almost six inches above her knees. It had been bought for her to wear at her mother's funeral. At first, when the question of what she should wear to the funeral was discussed, she'd imagined selecting an outfit from one of the dress shops in Lytham where she and her mother had often window-shopped. Instead, she was taken to a poky house in one of the backstreets, where the narrow hallway smelt spicy and unfamiliar. Her Auntie Ethel had clutched her handbag tightly under her arm as the thin, foreign-looking woman who'd answered the door showed them into the dark front room. A heavy curtain concealed a bed piled high with assorted blankets. She'd measured Ruby and then brought in a piece of black cloth to be inspected. Her aunt refused to give the woman any money until the dress was finished, and when they returned a few days later, she'd tugged at the seams until she was happy that the garment was sound. When the woman came back with the dress packed in its layers of brittle paper, she'd left the door at the end of the hall open. Black eyes stared out of the semi-darkness, and a naked child, who'd gazed out curiously from the doorway, was dragged back into the room. As they'd hurried away, Ruby remembered her auntie muttering something about bloody Jews.

She sat on the bed and inspected the unknown craftswoman's skill. The seams were bound with silk, each buttonhole hand-stitched and each stitch a perfect match. If the dress had been a painting, the skill of its creator would have been applauded. At first, she'd hated the idea of the handmade dress, but on the day of the funeral,

135

when she slipped it on, Ruby had felt special, as though the funeral was part of a film and she was the star. She'd enjoyed the fuss, the attention, but afterwards, when the dress was folded away, the horror crept up on her; her foolish, sweet mother had gone. Then she began to feel annoyed: it was typical of silly, flighty Pearl to step out in front of a taxi in the blackout and leave her. Then came the half-remembered arguments, the times she'd made her mother cry. How Ruby wished she hadn't sulked when her mother had left her alone in the evenings, and that she'd pretended to be pleased by the little presents of sweets and cheap trinkets Pearl brought back to make amends.

'Is that the dress you got for the funeral?' Sadie asked, eyeing her sympathetically through the door. 'Mum sent me up to see how you was getting on. She's set on you keeping this job. You haven't half grown. Quite the young lady,' she said, giving Ruby's arm a squeeze. 'You'll have to start wearing a bra. Don't look like that. You can't stop nature. If you're going to play for these posh folk, they'll expect you to dress the part.' Sadie sat on the floor and inspected the hem on the dress. 'We can lengthen the skirt and put a new top on. I've a blouse I don't wear that will do, pale blue and black. We can unpick this at the waist. It would look funny wearing an evening frock and no bra. At this rate, you'll still be wearing these bloody gymslips when you're sixty.'

'Who do you like best?' Ruby asked, struggling out of the dress. 'Bo or Con?'

'Con's a nice lad,' Sadie said, lifting her hair up and gazing in the mirror, 'but he's just a kid. Bo said he lied about his age to get in the army.'

Michael Holt was waiting by the farm gate, his cigarette a dancing pin of light in the blackness. He'd been reluctant to leave the fireside with the sleepy cats and the nodding farmer and his wife. Since they arrived in England, his feeling of resentment against the army had deepened. The only place Holt felt safe was at the farm. He would have liked to stay there in the barn, working on the tractor, listening as John moved among the slow, easy weight of the cows in the byre next door. At the camp there was a feeling of threat and violence. The men were packed in close together with nothing to occupy them and told to look busy, but most of the time there was nothing for them to do, so they lazed around and took their anger out on each other over stupid grievances. And when the trucks were sent out, they were often sent to pick up stuff that hadn't arrived and could spend days waiting for things that didn't come, or had been delivered to the wrong place. They could have been training. None of them had been given much basic weapons practice. The guys who'd done basic training with him were only ever issued with wooden guns. And it wasn't as though there weren't any weapons in the camp, but the rumour was that the captain had orders not to issue them unless the Germans landed.

Holt climbed on to the top rung of the wooden gate, his cigarette cupped protectively in his hand, and sat down. The damp autumn air felt raw and he shivered. He could hear the clatter of the railway points in the distance, then the click of

Henry's front door, followed by the sound of chuckling and whispered conversation. He put out his cigarette, and settled the metal engine part he hoped to replace into the pocket of his tunic for safe keeping, contenting himself with the idea that he would be able to get something to replace the worn part at the camp. Holt loved engines and was happiest when he was solving a problem, repairing a fault, or finding a solution. He'd spent the whole day stripping down John Bardley's tractor, kneeling in the empty barn, cleaning, testing and tinkering. Parts for the old tractor were impossible to find, and John Bardley had crouched at his side, his mild, worried eyes following each step of the process. The Bardleys, Marge and John, put their faith in his assurances that he could fix the engine. They treated him with respect, and Marge welcomed him into her kitchen, feeding him, listening to his stories of home and calling him 'son' so naturally that it made him want to weep.

Holt fell in behind his buddies, his boots in time with theirs, until their laughter subsided and they all tramped along in silence, each with his own thoughts, each reluctant to return to the camp and the indignities the army meted out to the black soldiers.

'You got that old tractor fixed, Holt?' Bo asked.

'Nope, but I think I know where I can get a part. Going to see the sergeant in charge of the workshops.'

'I heard they're sayin' too many passes have been handed out.'

'No point keepin' us in, when there's no work. Could give us battlefield training, if they weren't

138

so jumpy.'

'Black GIs with guns? Lieutenant Roach won't wear that.'

'Then they'll say we're no good for fighting. It's them that's afraid who we might want to fight,' Holt said.

'They reckon there's more coming next week.'

'There's going to be trouble. All these guys and nothing to do.'

'They should be happy we're keepin' ourselves busy. Holt, you know the words to "Swing Low, Sweet Chariot"? I mean, all the way through?'

'No, why?'

'I promised Sadie I'd sing something at her friend's wedding,' Bo said.

'Wedding? You never sung in church.'

'Sure, I did. I sung as a little boy.'

'One minute you're shouting about how the army's treating us and handing out newspapers,' Con said over his shoulder. 'Next minute–'

'Who asked you?'

'I'm just saying.'

'Well don't. Mind your own business.'

'Do you know she has a boyfriend who's a POW?'

'Who?'

'Sadie, you know who.'

'No, she ain't. He's just a friend. Now mind your own business. You're just a kid. You keep out of it or–'

'What about "Deep River"?' Wes suggested.

Con dropped back and listened to the two men softly crooning.

'Take no notice of Bo,' Holt said. 'He don't

mean no harm. Always been the same. Any pretty girl can lead old Bo round by the nose. And anyway, none of these girls are as pretty as the black girls back home.'

The next day Bo and Con stayed out of each other's way. In the camp, Bo was well known and admired because he spoke his mind. As other soldiers arrived, he passed around copies of *The People's Voice* and other black newspapers. Bo had contacts. The papers argued that the army was ill-treating the black soldiers and called for an end to segregated units. Bo set up meetings. Con had been to some of them. Bo explained the arguments, but sometimes his papers and his discussions helped to stoke the resentment, creating ripples of impotent anger that, from what Con could see, just made things worse.

At some meetings he got the guys who'd come from the Southern states to tell what had happened to them. Con knew about the South. His grandma had come north after she'd married, but she'd always thought of it as her home. Today, a guy was telling a tale about a group of black soldiers that had been taken out of one of the training camps in the South and made to work in the fields for a white senator. Con sat on the edge of the crowd and listened to the soldier sitting next to Bo.

'...and when we complained,' the soldier said, 'the colonel sent armed MPs to make sure we carried out his orders.'

The atmosphere made Con edgy, and when Wes suggested he help to find some wood for one of Henry's projects, he was happy to slip away.

Their luck was in; they found a pile of rough-sawn timber and a driver who was leaving for the port with an empty truck. He helped them load it and agreed to drop it off at the cottage.

When they arrived next day, Henry was delighted with the uneven lengths of timber.

'Just do me fine, lads,' he said. 'We'll have a brew, and then measure up. I've promised the old girl at the end cottage I'll knock up some shelves for her. Should be worth a couple of pints.'

The whole ground floor of Mrs Bland's cottage was little bigger than a single garage and almost as dark and cheerless. Con, whose bedroom at home in Detroit was larger than the living room in Henry's cottage, gazed around in amazement. The old lady smiled at them over the tea chests stacked four high in the tiny room.

'I've drawn this to indicate where I would like you to put the shelves,' she said handing Henry a sketch.

He took the paper and tilted his cap on to the back of his head.

'Looks like there's one on every wall, missus,' he said.

'That's right, and then I would like some in my bedroom. I thought if I used the empty chests for my clothes, the rest of the wall space would hold a considerable amount.'

'We'll have to carry some outside to make room to work.'

'Oh, they mustn't get damp.' Mrs Bland patted the tea chest's coarse wood. 'They've suffered enough already with smoke and then water...'

'It'll be fine, missus,' Henry soothed, 'weather's

141

set fair, and we'll bring 'em back in before we go.'

They worked steadily, measuring, cutting and nailing. Henry proved to be an almost instinctual craftsman, first studying the space thoughtfully, riddling and sucking his teeth, before marking the wood to show them where to saw. He was rarely out in his calculations, and by late afternoon, they'd fixed the wooden batons on both sides of the chimney and shelving had been constructed from floor to ceiling on the opposite wall.

'We'll just sweep up in here, missus,' he said, 'and then bring them boxes back in. There's enough shelves there for you to start unpacking some of them books. That should keep you busy for a couple of days. I'll come back later and nail the rest of the shelves in place. Then the next time these lads get a pass out, we'll have a look at the upstairs.'

'If we take a look now,' Wes said, 'I'd know how much timber to get.'

'Make it soon, will you lad,' Henry said, following Mrs Bland up the stairs. 'I need something to keep me out of Jenny's way. The place is full of women and sewing. They were all stitching away when I left, finishing a frock for our Ruby. And then there's stuff for this wedding all over the place as well.'

The house had one bedroom and a tiny space at the top of the stairs. The only furniture upstairs was a single bed. When he heard the door of Henry's cottage slam, Con walked over to the window and bent down to peer through.

'Is Sadie going to work today?' he asked.

'No, she's helping Ruby to get ready, and Lou's

there as well with her chap. That'll be Ruby off to the doctor's,' Henry said, as Ruby hurried by wearing a headscarf to cover her newly curled hair.

Henry gazed around the tiny room. 'You want shelves on all these walls?' he asked, consulting the sketch.

'Yes, I'll have my bed in the centre, and then a couple more shelves on the landing. Do you think you can get enough wood?'

Wes nodded. 'We got stacks of the stuff. We just need to fix a pass out and get the load dropped off.'

'Will you listen to that,' Henry said, ducking his head to look through the window. 'He's got the bugger going.'

On the opposite side of the road, they could see John Bardley walking behind the tractor Holt was proudly driving down the track from the farm.

'Good lad!' Henry shouted, as the GIs ran out of the cottage to cheer Holt's success. 'Good lad.'

'Tell you what, Henry,' John Bardley said, 'this chap is a bloody magician when it comes to engines. I'd have never believed it. We'd be lost without this old girl.'

The sound of the men clapping and cheering brought Jenny, Sadie, Lou and her fiancé, Frank, out of the cottage in time to see Holt stand up and wave from the tractor to acknowledge the applause. Then to show the revival of the old tractor wasn't a fluke, Holt rode it down the lane to the stone bridge. As he headed back towards the cottages, a jeep turned in from the main road and drove towards them. Two MPs stared out, taking in the little group standing on the pavement and the black soldier on the tractor. The jeep drew up, and a fat, pink-faced sergeant climbed out, walked towards the idling machine and stood in front of it with his hand up.

'You stop that engine now, boy,' he shouted.

The sound of the tractor died and the lane fell silent. In the distance the points in the shunting yards clattered and in the hawthorn hedge behind the cottages a blackbird began to sing.

Holt sat on the machine, his body rigid, his face an expressionless mask.

'Now get down here quick and tell me what you're doin' on this thing,' the MP said, as if speaking to a naughty child.

'What's up, lads?' Henry called cheerily. 'There's no trouble here.'

'There's no problem here,' John Bardley added. 'Young Michael has been giving me a hand. There's no trouble.'

'Begging your pardon, sir,' the MP said, glancing at the two elderly men on the pavement, 'this here soldier is under arrest.'

'Arrest?' Wes gasped. 'Arrest? What for?'

The MP ignored the question. 'Get down and give me a hand here,' he called to the jeep's driver. 'Let's hope you boys all got passes, or the rest of you are in trouble as well.'

Con's fingers trembled as he felt in his pocket for his pass.

'What you arresting them for?' Frank asked. 'They're here 'cos they've been invited.'

Without looking around to see who had spoken, the MP unbuttoned his holster and growled, 'Get down, boy, like you was told.'

'Now just a minute,' John Bardley said, his face flushed with anger, as he stepped into the road and placed his hand on the tractor's wheel. 'This tractor is mine. Don't you order him to get down off my tractor.'

'This man is in public and out of uniform, sir. It is against army–'

'This man has been grafting all day mending my bloody tractor. Why in hell's name would he do it in his uniform! There's no need for this. That's my tractor, and this soldier has been helping me.'

The driver, who had been checking the black GIs' passes, unclipped his holster and walked over to the farmer.

'Back off, guy,' he said softly.

When Mrs Bland – who had come out to check on her precious books – saw the MP pull out his gun, she strode over to join the white-faced farmer.

'You're on English soil,' she said. 'We don't use guns against people here. This gentleman has explained why this young man is not in uniform. Now, any more nonsense and I shall write to your superiors.'

'Aye, we're all witnesses,' Frank called. 'If our police come, you'll be in trouble. Your lads were in trouble in Liverpool last week for waving guns around.'

The fat MP didn't flinch, but refastened the clip on his holster and nodded to the second MP who did the same. Then the two men walked over to the jeep, and the pink-faced sergeant looked around the silent group, his eyes resting for a moment on the faces of each of the three black GIs, before he climbed back inside and the jeep sped away.

Ruby stood in the doctor's kitchen and wriggled uncomfortably: it was the first time she'd worn suspenders, and the contraption tugging the delicate stockings tightly against her thighs felt constraining, yet too fragile for its purpose. She'd tried walking around the cottage wearing the unfamiliar underwear, but the apparatus still felt unstable.

'Well, you do look a picture,' Alice Watts said. 'You'll have to be careful you don't get marks on that frock. Use my overall. It's behind the door.'

'I've brought a pair of shoes to wear as well,' Ruby said, pulling a pair of Sadie's shoes out of her bag. 'They're a bit big.'

'Well, push some paper inside. Your hair's nice too. Nice touch with those hairslides. You look grown up with it down.'

The hairstyle had been Sadie's idea. Ruby was going to plait it and wind it around her head but Sadie and Lou, who was visiting with her fiancé, had decided that it should be curled. Ruby had tried to argue that Frank wouldn't want to sit there and wait, but he'd just smiled and winked at her. She'd spent most of the afternoon getting ready. First, they'd washed her hair, then put it in curlers and then used the curling tongs, until the smell of singed hair filled the cottage. When her hair was finished, Sadie had helped her put on her newly altered dress and said how nice she looked.

Ruby pulled on the faded overall and sat down next to Alice, who was preparing the vegetables

146

for the evening meal.

'Now, madam wants you to play at the start of the evening when the guests are arriving,' she said. 'Himself will open the door and do coats and the doctor will do the drinks. Then you can help in here. Once they're in the dining room, Dick has to get the fireworks ready in the hall. Fireworks inside. I don't know where she got the idea. She wants them to go off when the pudding's being served. It's to be decorated with these little sparkly things. She hopes her guests will think that's all there is. Then we pull open the door and whoosh! All the fireworks go off in the hall.'

'Lou and Sadie did my hair for me,' Ruby said, dragging the colander into the centre of the large wooden table and taking out the last of the carrots for peeling. 'Lou and her fiancé have come to visit.'

'Is he nice?'

Ruby smiled, thinking of Frank's rosy cheeks and black curls. 'He's happy just to be with Lou. He must be, because he's spent most of his leave listening to nothing but talk about buttonholes, hymns and wedding breakfasts.'

Just before seven, Mrs Grey came into the kitchen to check on the progress of the meal.

'Goodness, Ruby,' she said. 'I thought Alice had brought in another young lady to help. How grown-up you look.'

'Quite lovely, she is, madam. Stand up, dear. Take off the overall and show Mrs Grey your dress.'

'It's quite charming,' Mrs Grey smiled. 'She's such a find, isn't she, Alice?'

Ruby's cheeks turned a gentle pearly rose, and Mrs Grey had to agree that her new acquisition was indeed quite lovely.

'Now, come and let me introduce you to Doctor Grey. I've told him how clever you are.'

In the sitting room the heavy brocade curtains had been closed. Two men wearing evening dress stood by the open fire. Each one was holding a crystal tumbler.

'Darling, I want you to meet Ruby,' she said. 'Ruby, this is Doctor Grey. You remember, dear, I told you how well Ruby plays for my little gatherings, and she's such a help to Alice.'

From her weeks spent mending and washing his shirts, Ruby knew that the doctor must be a large man with a thick neck and broad shoulders, but what she hadn't expected was that he would be short, barely five feet tall. Doctor Grey, who had been standing with his back towards them, put his tumbler on the white marble mantelpiece and turned around. He had silver hair, and in profile, his handsome head reminded her of the plaster bust of a Roman emperor that she'd seen in the prop room at the Theatre Royal.

'My wife has told me how helpful you have been and I'm looking forward to hearing you play,' he said, as Mrs Grey bent slightly and draped her slender arm around his shoulder.

'Doctor Grey and I would like you to play when our guests arrive, but I suppose Alice has told you this. Now, I'd like you to come and look at the way the dining room has been set out. It will help, if I need you to set out the table for me. Not tonight, of course, but we will be doing quite a bit of entertaining at Christmas and the New Year.'

'Am I not to be introduced?' the other man asked, stepping forward and taking Ruby's hand.

'This is my brother, Ruby, Mr Rollo. It's thanks to Ruby, Rollo dear, that your music score arrived in order and not in an awful pickle.'

Rollo was tall and had his sister's dazzling blue eyes and high forehead, but his hair was dark and slick with pomade. He would have been handsome, but his protruding front teeth pushed out his sensitive mouth into a fretful pout. When he took her hand, Ruby glanced down at her red rough skin in his smooth fingers, and was suddenly conscious of the home-made dress and borrowed shoes.

'I'm glad you were here,' he said, 'to save the day.'

'Come on, Ruby,' his sister said. 'We need to check the table settings.'

The dining room was on the opposite side of the hall and looked out on to the gloomy front garden. The heavy curtains were black and gold, a theme that was echoed in the intricate floral wallpaper. The china was white, edged with bands of black and gold. The place settings were more complex than the ones used for the guests at Everdeane. Ruby didn't say that she'd been taught how to lay a table, but listened politely as Mrs Grey explained where each piece of cutlery should go. Then she was asked to reset one of the places, and when Mrs Grey praised her for her quick fingers, it made her blush.

There were twelve guests for dinner. Two of the ladies were younger and prettier than the ones

149

that came to the afternoon teas, but not as lovely as Mrs Grey, who had changed into an acid-green silk dress that showed off her long, graceful back. Her only pieces of jewellery were the discreet diamond studs in her ears and a diamond ring that flashed in the candlelight.

As Ruby played, she watched the guests arrive. They behaved as if they were characters in a film and called each other 'darling'. They said things like, 'Darling, how wonderful', and 'I love your dress, darling'. Doctor Grey poured out the drinks, and Mr Watts took their coats. One of the guests was Captain Edward O'Donal, who was in charge of the newly arrived truck companies at the nearby camp. Mrs Grey took him by the arm and introduced him to some of the other guests. Then another American arrived with Mr and Mrs Prendergast. He was called Captain Leary. She hadn't seen any of the other guests before, except for Mrs Grey's brother and Father O'Flynn, and she didn't hear their names. The handsomest man, except for Doctor Grey – who was too short to be really handsome – was Captain O'Donal, who reminded her a little of Rhett Butler in *Gone with the Wind*.

Once all the guests had arrived, Mrs Grey led them into the dining room. This was Ruby's sign to leave the piano and go to help in the kitchen. Alice looked very hot. She was cross with Mr Watts, who was already dressed in the suit he wore for serving the guests, and was getting in her way.

'At last,' she said. 'Look, Ruby's here. They've gone in. That soup's going to be cold. Ruby, you go and help, and don't forget, serve from the left.'

The soup was oxtail. As it was being served, Mrs

150

Grey explained to the two Americans who Guy Fawkes was, and that before the war there would have been bonfires. Ruby noticed that, as he listened intently to the story, Captain O'Donal's dark eyes reflected the flames from the candles. Doctor Grey smiled adoringly at his wife, and when Father O'Flynn pretended to be shocked and said that as a good Catholic she should have been on the side of poor Guy Fawkes, everyone laughed.

Alice had told her to leave the dining-room door open, so that they could find out when the diners were ready for the second course.

'We'll give them twenty minutes,' she said. 'Bring the trolley and the vegetable dishes from the pantry. Then go and stand by the door. Listen for the clattering to stop, or for them all to start talking.'

The main course was mock goose: a savoury dish made mainly with layers of lentils and onion. Alice pulled it out of the oven and prodded it.

'This was his idea,' she said. 'He didn't want his guests to think he was getting any extra, or anything on the black market. Rack of lamb would have been so much nicer. I've had to use all my onions and all the apples to make a sauce. There's no taste to it, if you don't put other things with it. He wanted roast potatoes. What does he imagine I have to roast them in, I'd like to know. There's no meat. There's no goose, so there's no goose fat.'

When the soup plates had been collected, Mr Watts carried in the 'goose' and put it on the plates for Ruby to serve. Then he followed her with the dishes of potatoes and vegetables, waiting for each of the guests to help themselves. When she had served the 'goose' Ruby went back to the trolley for the sauce and gravy.

'I wonder, Captain,' Mrs Grey said, as Ruby served him with apple sauce and gravy, 'if you could help me with my latest project.'

'Well I'll do anything I can, ma'am,' he said, as Ruby served the apple sauce.

'Oh, call me Diana, please.'

The captain coloured slightly, and Ruby almost caught Mrs Prendergast's shoulder with the gravy boat. Diana was the perfect name. Diana Grey.

'I've already enlisted Mrs Prendergast's help and some of the other ladies. We are hoping to organise cultural tours around the local factories. We thought art. A touring exhibition of paintings would be just the thing. And when Mr Prendergast told me you were in charge of the newly arrived truck companies...'

'It's such a shame,' Mrs Prendergast said from the opposite side of the captain, 'there are so many collections that are in storage. It would be a way to allow people to see them. Not the most valuable, of course. An opportunity to educate...'

'I'd be happy to help, if I can.'

'We also thought, if it was successful, of trying to get an orchestra, or at least a small group, a quartet or a trio,' Mrs Prendergast added.

'Edward could probably help you there as well, ma'am,' Captain Leary said. 'Our black soldiers sing really well. Very musical.'

'Well, that would be a wonderful idea,' she said, 'if your men aren't too busy.'

'Since the new GIs arrived they've made themselves very popular,' Father O'Flynn said. 'They come to our church dances. The other GIs seem to keep more to the camp. They invite the local people there, but they don't come to our social events very much. Can we expect the soldiers from your camp to be organising dances for our young people, Captain O'Donal?'

'I, well... We don't have the facilities... And the American clubs...'

'The clubs are quite a way out of the village, but I know the youngsters have always looked forward to their visits there and—'

'The clubs are white only, sir,' Captain O'Donal said.

Ruby noticed Captain Leary shift uneasily in his chair. As she moved on to Doctor Grey, he smiled at her and helped himself to the apple sauce.

'Is that not rather inappropriate at this moment in history?' he asked, putting the sauce back on the tray and motioning to Ruby that she could move on to the next diner, a young lady with bulging eyes and dark hair. 'After all, your men are here to join with us in fighting... And the war is surely a rejection of Hitler's racial theories.'

Mrs Grey, who was sitting opposite her husband, looked up, and Ruby saw the little fold between her eyebrows deepen.

'Thank you, Mr Watts,' she said. 'You can leave the rest of the vegetables and the sauce. We'll help ourselves.'

Ruby moved on to Rollo, the last person to be served. He waved her away and turned to his sister.

'Did I tell you what the latest fashion is in town?'

153

he asked. 'All the fellows are having the collars of their shirts changed. You know, pinstriped collars on a checked shirt, that sort of thing. Apparently, some fellows have done it for the war effort, because it saves cloth, I suppose. But now it's caught on as a style.'

As she slipped out of the door, Ruby was pleased to see that Mrs Grey was smiling again.

The dessert was stewed pears and plums. Mr Watts had taken off his jacket and was beating the mock cream that was to go on the top.

'If them things have to stand up in it,' Alice said, nodding to the thin fireworks on the table, 'it's got to be stiff. You'd best take it in yourself, Dick. I don't want Ruby getting sparks on her dress.'

'I've the rest of the fireworks to do,' he complained.

The trolley had been wheeled back in and now had a bucket of sand with fireworks – Roman candles and silver fountains – stuck in the top.

'Ruby can push the trolley in the hall and then you can light it. I don't know why he lets her do these daft things. Thirty-five if she's a day and behaves like a spoilt child. We've worked for the doctor and his mother for years. Haven't we, Dick? Never had all this,' Alice said, waving the dishcloth in the direction of the trolley. 'I don't know what his dear mother would make of it. Indoor fireworks. It's a disgrace. Prendergast is here as well. Anyone else who did this, and he'd be after fining them.'

'He asked him last week, when they was coming back from a meeting. Prendergast said it would be all right, as the trees would hide any light.'

When the dessert was ready, the cream held the fireworks in place. Then Mr Watts put on his gardening gloves and carried the tray into the hall, where Alice lit each little sparkler.

'Get them things put out as soon as you can. I don't want marks on the linen,' she said.

Almost as soon as they were lit, the little fireworks began to fizz and tiny sparks burst into life. Ruby opened the dining-room doors and everyone cheered them. She helped Mr Watts to serve the fruit in small crystal dishes and then they slipped out, closing the doors behind them. Mr Watts lit the larger fireworks on the trolley, and as the coloured balls of light escaped from the Roman candles, he pulled the door open again to squeals of surprise from the young ladies, followed by applause from the other guests. She and Alice watched the bubbles of colour from the kitchen door. Ruby was pleased that Mrs Grey's guests were impressed by the show, but she agreed with Sadie that the children would have enjoyed them more.

'You ever been to a bonfire, dear?' Alice asked.

Ruby could remember the noise of the fireworks. She'd been afraid. She remembered her father holding her and the smell of bay rum on his hair.

'Once, when I was small. I felt sorry for the guy. There were Catherine wheels and rockets, but I remember the treacle toffee the best.'

'Before the war, there was always a big bonfire on the rec. The children spent weeks collecting the wood.'

155

A fountain of stars followed the balls of light. Ruby's feet hurt in the ill-fitting shoes; she would have loved to have sat alone in the silent, dark hall and cooled her feet on the red tiles.

When the meal was over, she played again and Mr Watts served coffee and drinks. Mr Prendergast, Doctor Grey and the two American captains sat in the easy chairs near the piano.

'Ike's policy is segregated but equal treatment,' Captain Leary was explaining.

'It can't be that equal,' Doctor Grey said, opening his tobacco pouch and offering it to Captain Leary who shook his head. 'Prendergast tells me our hospitals have been told they must have separate lavatories, if not separate wards, for black and white troops.'

'It's what our men expect, sir,' Captain O'Donal said.

'And a separate blood bank,' Mr Prendergast added. 'Cleanliness, I suppose. Can't expect these chaps to be clean.'

Doctor Grey scraped out his pipe bowl and emptied the contents in the shell ashtray. 'What nonsense you do talk, Prendergast,' he said, tamping the tobacco in the pipe bowl. 'It's simple prejudice and nothing more.'

'I don't think the army would go to the trouble, if it was just that. The black man, I believe, is a simpler, less sophisticated sort of chap.'

'A history lesson for you, Prendergast. Captain O'Donal should know this one,' Doctor Grey said, lighting his pipe and raising a quizzical eyebrow towards his guest. 'A countryman of yours. A pioneer who developed blood plasma banks.

156

Do you know who?'

Captain O'Donal lit his cigarette and smiled nervously. 'I'm afraid I don't...'

'Charles R. Drew is the chap's name, Captain. Charles R. Drew, a black man.'

Ruby looked over at Mrs Grey and was relieved to see she and her brother were busily organising a game of cards. Later, when the guests were all involved in the game, Mrs Grey signalled with a nod in her direction that she could go. The darkened hall smelt of smoke, and the dining room was empty. It was late, she felt sleepy and hoped that Alice and Dick would have done the washing-up. When she opened the kitchen door, her granddad was sitting with Mr and Mrs Watts at the table.

'Here's Ruby now, Henry,' Mrs Watts said, getting up from the table. 'Off you go with your grandpa, love. Here you are, Henry,' she said, taking a small parcel from the draining board, 'just a bit of something for Maud and poor Joe.'

Granddad, who was dunking an oat biscuit in his tea, looked up and smiled. 'That's kind of you, Alice,' he said. 'Very kind.'

Outside the air was damp. On the drive, the leaves stuck to her shoes, and Ruby pushed her hands deep inside her pockets. As they reached the gate, Granddad tapped the parcel under his coat.

'We'll put this on Maud's doorstep on our way home,' he said. 'No need to mention it to Jenny, though.'

'Did you come to see Doctor Grey, or Mr Watts?' she asked.

'No. Ruby, love, I came to pick you up. I've been for a drink with Johnny.'

157

Ruby put up her collar, as Diana Grey might do, and imagined that her old mac was the cream coat she'd seen hanging on the stand in the hall. Then she slipped on the scarf to protect her new hairdo.

'You don't need to do that,' she said, taking his arm. 'I have a torch now. I bought it with my wages.'

CHAPTER SEVEN

'Ruby, you'll have to come in with me,' Sadie said, consulting the list she'd written on the back of a paper bag, 'and then Frank's brother can have your room.'

'He might not want to come here. He might feel shy with us.'

'Oh, he'll be all right. Arthur's fourteen. Frank's mum and dad are staying at Lou's; his sister and her husband and two kids are with Lou's auntie on Mercer Road; Charlie is across the road in Jack's room; Frank will be in the pub with Johnny.'

'It should be Charlie, as best man, doing all this organising,' Jenny said. 'And move all them papers off that table. Ruby, why have you put that table-cloth on? Get it off now. I've this hot pie in my hand.'

'We always have a cloth on the table at Mrs Grey's.'

'Well you're not there now. It's just making

washing. And she wouldn't have a cloth on if she was havin' to wash and dry the bloody things herself. Hurry up. This pie's hot,' she said, as Ruby grabbed the tablecloth, and Granddad spread out the newspaper. 'Now off you go and get the plates. I don't know what she's been doing,' Jenny said, when Ruby had disappeared into the kitchen. 'I've been at work, and she's been here all day and hasn't even set the table.'

Sadie got up, took the knives and forks from the table drawer and began setting places on the table. 'She was helping me and she's done the washing and made the tea,' she said, nodding towards the rabbit pie now sitting in the centre of the table, topped with a pastry crust that was decorated with a circle of pastry leaves. 'There's a lot to do before the weekend. Charlie's in Liverpool, so there's things he can't do, and I am maid of honour.'

'Ah, that looks good,' Granddad said, as Jenny began to serve. 'It's one of my favourites.'

For a while they ate in silence; the rabbit meat inside the large earthenware dish was little more than flavouring to the potatoes and dried peas, but on a cold November night, the pie was warm and filling.

'Charlie's only coming up the night before. He's seeing his brother off. He's in the Royal Navy. He's just joined up, and their dad's not best pleased, them all being in the Merchant. Lou and Frank have sorted most of it out. It's the flowers that's the problem.'

'Well if you will go and get married in the middle of November,' Jenny grumbled.

'There's the buttonholes and the table to

decorate, as well as the altar and the bouquets, and it's too early for Christmas decorations.'

'Alice uses dried flowers and leaves with berries,' Ruby said. 'Mrs Grey said they were charming.'

'Did she now?' Sadie said, eating the last piece of rabbit meat from her plate. 'Charming.'

'She has them in the hall.'

'Oh, well that's all right, then.'

'It's bloody easier than trying to make silk ones,' Jenny said.

'Auntie Maud's got some. White and pink silk roses. They're under a glass globe thing on her dresser. I saw them last ... week...'

Jenny, who had been scraping up the remaining gravy from her plate with a lump of bread, looked up and glared.

'And when did you see her last week?'

The piece of pastry in Ruby's mouth dried, and Granddad got up from the table.

'I'll just go and cover that motorbike up. Young Michael's taken a real fancy to it,' he said. 'Got most of that rust off. Don't want it getting damp. Might as well check on the hens as well.'

'Have you two girls left that washing out?' Jenny snapped, as Granddad scuttled out. 'If you've finished your tea, be quick and bring it in. It's never going to dry.'

It was so cold in the yard that the shirts on the washing line had frozen. The arms were twisted up as though pleading for help, and in the twilight they looked almost human. Ruby took one down and stood it on the cobbled yard.

'Now's your chance to get yourself a fella, Ruby,'

Sadie laughed. 'Get yourself a partner,' she said, dropping the washing basket on the ground. 'Which one do you fancy?'

'I don't want to leave anybody out,' Ruby said, shaking the line so that the stiff limbs twitched and jerked. 'Look, now they're all having a dance.'

On his way back down the garden, Henry caught sight of the icy jig in the light from the kitchen door and dropped the white enamel bucket he was carrying.

'What the hell are you doing? It's after blackout and you can see that bloody light for miles. Stop buggering about the pair of you and get inside,' he shouted, snatching up the bucket and slamming the kitchen door behind him.

'Grumpy old sod,' Sadie sniggered. 'Come on, Ruby, let's get this lot inside and have a brew.'

Granddad was sitting by the fire, and Ruby noticed that his hands were shaking. She sat on the seat of the kindling box to get a better look. He wasn't coughing as he sometimes did, but as he stared into the fire, his face was ash pale. Jenny didn't look up, but switched on the radio and took out her knitting, resting her puffy feet up on the brass fender. They drank the tea Sadie had poured for each of them, and by the time they'd cleared the table, he was dozing in the chair.

'You've a long face,' Sadie said, as they began the washing-up. 'What's the matter? Henry can be a grumpy old bugger sometimes, take no notice. And Mum's just tired. She'd forgotten how hard it is in the factory. She'll get used to it. Give her a couple of weeks.'

'I think he's mad with me. He told me not to mention us going to see Maud and I forgot. If she asks, I'll say I went on my own. Or I can say I saw her in the street and she asked me to go on an errand. Alice Watts gave us food for them – Maud and Joe. The first time we left it on the step, but the next time, we knocked at the door ... and he said not to tell and...'

'Oh for goodness' sake, you just let it slip. It's his fault. He should have just told her. Here, give me a lift hanging up these shirts. Lou will be here in a minute.'

'Why doesn't she like him going to see Maud and Joe?'

'It's a long tale. Maud, well she's his sister, and when Mum... Well, you can't have two women in the same house.'

'Did Maud live here?'

'No, he lived there. After your dad left home, he gave up the cottage and moved in with Maud. It suited them both at the time. This place belongs to Mr Bardley, like the other cottages do. All the furniture belongs to him as well, except the cooker. Mum insisted on them getting that before she moved in. He'd still kept the garden on. The couple who rented it after him were old and didn't want the trouble.'

'Then what happened?'

'Well he was courting Mum, and when he found out it was up for rent, he asked Mum and me to move back in here with him. You see, the wife had died and the old chap couldn't manage on his own. He went to the Little Sisters, I think. When she found out, Maud wasn't too happy.

162

Mum wasn't that keen on moving in here either, but she'd not much choice. Hang on, I can hear him.' When he opened the kitchen door, Henry's sparse hair was rumpled and he was yawning, but the colour had returned to his face.

'Oh, I'm glad you've got them clothes put up to dry,' he said, smoothing down his limp shirt-sleeves. 'Lou and Frank have just arrived.'

By the time Ruby had dried her hands on the tea cloth and followed Sadie into the living room, Lou was standing by the open front door.

'Frank wants to know if you want to go with him for a pint, Mr Barton,' she called. 'He's by the gate. He says you'll want to escape from all this talk of weddings like he does.'

'No thanks, love. Tell him thanks all the same. I've had a bit of a shock,' Henry said, going back to his seat and folding up his newspaper.

'A shock?' Jenny asked. 'Who's given you a shock?'

'These two daft buggers,' he said. 'Messing about in the yard. In that light... I thought for a moment... They was jiggin' an' twistin'. They looked... It took me by surprise, that's all. Hang on, love. I'll just have a word with Frank before he goes.'

'If you're not going out, you stay in here in the warm,' Lou said. 'I'm walking Frank to the end of the lane. I'll tell him you're a bit off colour.'

'Messing about they were. I thought... Supposed to be a blackout as well. Next thing, the ARP warden will be round. I'm going off to bed out of the way.'

'Ruby, take that newspaper off the table,' Jenny

163

hissed, 'and then take your granddad a drop of brandy.'

When Lou reappeared, Sadie had taken her paper bag lists out of the table drawer and was smoothing them out on the red velvet cloth.

'A couple of the girls at work have promised tins of salmon,' Lou said, sitting next to her. 'We've got some bottled fruit from Auntie Eileen towards the trifle, and Mum's made the fruit cake. It's not big, but she's hiring a cardboard one from the confectioner's for show. She wanted me to have a sponge, but I want a fruit cake, and we've managed to save enough dried fruit and eggs from our rations.'

'How is he?' Jenny asked, when Ruby came back downstairs.

'He says he's staying up there now. He's not coming down and not to wake him at supper time.'

'That's so he doesn't have to explain himself.'

'Here's the parachute silk my mum's dyed,' Lou said, pulling a parcel out of her basket. 'I've kept some for my trousseau, but that should be enough for a blouse for you, Sadie.'

'That's enough. Look, Ma. That's plenty, and it's come up nice.'

'There's that much to buy. The trouble is, my mother's a widow. She's not much money, and you don't get any extra coupons for weddings.'

'We'll have to see what else people can let us have,' Sadie said. 'Let's compare lists of who we've asked. We don't want to ask the same folk.'

Ruby sat by the fire making roses from scraps of silk, and Sadie and Lou went on talking of nothing but food and weddings until it was bedtime.

Con was also tired of the wedding, but for a different reason: Bo. Bo had taken the invitation to sing very seriously. It was true that he could sing, but not half so well as Wes, who was his tutor. The problem hadn't been helped by Sadie and Lou, who'd changed their minds about the sort of song they should sing. First, Sadie said they should sing 'Old Man River', and then Lou decided it should be 'Swing Low, Sweet Chariot'. Now, just days before the wedding, Lou's mother wanted a hymn that everyone could sing instead. He could hear them now trying out 'The Lord Is My Shepherd', but from what he could hear, it didn't suit Bo's voice.

'Reckon you'd best let Wes sing it on his own, Bo. Or else get some of the other guys to help out.'

Bo threw himself on his bed. 'Like you? You gonna sing?'

'I didn't say I could sing.'

'You can't sing an' you're not much of a soldier either. You almost crapped yourself when that MP went for Holt. If I was him, I'd not want a little boy like you watching my back.'

'What would you have done?'

'I'd–'

'Come on, guys. We got this to do. Come on, Bo. You can do it. It's not hard, and Con, you go and find yourself some place...'

'I'm going,' he said, getting up from his bed and heading for the door.

'Bo, lay off.'

'Me?'

165

Wes looked nervously at the older man. 'You promised to sing. You told her you could,' he smiled. 'So let's get on. Con's right. We'd best sing together.'

'I didn't know she'd...'

'What?' Wes grinned, sensing that Bo was calming down. 'Take you up on your offer? Look, it's going to be okay. We'll sing together. Your voice is fine. It's just you can't stay in tune. But I'll be there. You can follow me, like we're doin' now. Then after the first verse, the rest of them will be singing. Con did the right thing at Henry's. We all did. You weren't there. There was nothin' you could have done. Those guys were spoilin' to shoot someone.'

Before Bo could answer, the door opened. A black sergeant they hadn't seen before walked in. Both men stood to attention.

'Stand easy, guys,' he said. 'Captain will be introducing me to you men later. I'm doing an unofficial tour around on my own. I'm Sergeant Mayfield.'

The new sergeant was a small, muscular man in his late twenties. When they had introduced themselves, he sat down and smiled.

'Like I say, this is unofficial. Rumour is, you guys would be the ones to ask about an incident with an MP.'

'The singing...? The singing incident?' Bo asked.

'No. It was a gun. The MP pulled a gun? The word is it wasn't reported. You report it, soldier?'

'The ... well, even the black sergeants want a quiet life,' Wes said. 'So there's no good reporting it here, Sarge.'

'Well, I don't agree with you there. Intrusion into local customs is what I'd call it. Army don't want to offend the Limeys, and no English policeman would carry a gun. You're helping them by keepin' the whole thing covered up. Is that what you want?'

'No. The locals weren't happy and they–'

'I know you're right, some of our own folk only want a quiet life. I'm not one of them. You guys watch yourselves, but I want you to know I'm on your side. I hear you have organised some meetings. I'd like to attend, if that's okay. By the way,' Sergeant Mayfield smiled. 'Did I hear you singing? Army likes nice, happy singing black guys. You think about that?'

'We're singing at a wedding of a friend,' Bo said. 'A girl we met; it's at her friend's wedding, and her folks... Well, we get on real well with them. They're like us. They made us feel welcome.'

'The English don't have segregation, but it don't mean they aren't prejudiced. The other thing we need to do is get something going here for the guys. There's a bad feeling to this place. I want some ideas. Education, sports ... baseball, maybe. Or basketball,' he said, smiling up at Wes. 'You got the build, son. You play?'

'I played in high school.'

'It's up to us to show them there's no difference, black or white,' Bo said.

'Let's hope we get the chance, soldier. What we really want is to change the way things are back home. After this war, we need to make sure that the black man should be respected in his own country.'

On Wednesday the long spell of sharp autumn days came to an end, and for the rest of the week the kitchen, scullery and living room were full of damp clothes. Mrs Grey had a chill and she'd cancelled the afternoon fundraising tea. None of the GIs called, and the evenings were filled with Jenny and Granddad snoring and the clatter of the sewing machine in Sadie's room.

On Friday some of the washing was still too damp to iron, and by late morning it was clear that the rain had set in for the day. Ruby built up the fire, hanging the still-wet shirts over the fireguard, and then began cutting up the potatoes for the hotpot. It was when she was looking for the ointment, after cutting her finger on the knife, that she found an old eyepatch and remembered Mrs Prendergast's lecture about remodelling hats. In it, she'd used an old eyepatch of her husband's to show how – with the help of stiffened buckram, velvet and reused feathers – it was possible to make a very stylish hat.

The eyepatch Ruby had found was pink, but she was determined not to let that put her off. In Sadie's room, she rescued scraps of parachute silk, bits of the lilac fabric left over from Lou's costume and a remnant of old net curtain, donated by a neighbour, that had been used to recover a hat for Lou to wear. Ruby got to work, cutting, stitching and sticking. Getting the veil to hang just right, tucking and easing the fabric in place, fixing the tiny bows of silk to cover the joins between the net and the eyepatch, were the hardest parts, and by the time she had finished

Sadie and Jenny were almost due home.

'You're looking pleased with yourself,' Jenny said, eyeing the washing that Ruby had hastily moved into the kitchen. 'That fire's a bit low. You'd best put that hotpot in the oven, if them potatoes are ever going to brown.'

After tea, Ruby went to her room, pinned up her hair and slipped the thin elastic into place.

'Close your eyes,' she shouted. 'You too, Granddad.'

'Whose is it?' Sadie asked, as Ruby paraded in front of them. 'Was it your...?'

'I made it,' she said. 'It was Mrs Prendergast's talk that gave me the idea. It's an eyepatch. I found it in the drawer.'

'Blimey,' Jenny said and got up to admire the confection. 'It just might work.'

'If I have my hair pinned up,' Sadie said, taking the hat from her and perching it on her own head. 'It's almost too nice. I don't want to outdo the bride, do I? Lou's going to be really pleased. She's right clever, isn't she, Ma?'

'She is, unless we need an eyepatch.'

Sadie giggled, turned her head and lifted up her hair to admire the effect. 'Oh go on, Ma,' she said. 'That thing must have been in there for ages.'

On the day before the wedding a thick fog clogged the streets. It clung to Ruby's clothes and made the curls she'd carefully teased in place around her face droop and turn into a damp frizz. In the silent lane, the air tasted of smoke and coal dust. Even at midday, women were bumping into each other's baskets, and as she walked through the village to

Lou's house, Ruby could see torches waving in the gloom.

She spent most of the day at Lou's, helping her mother to cook and to clean the neat, little house. By early afternoon the kitchen table and the pantry were full of small sponge cakes, sitting in golden rows on wire trays, waiting for a topping of mock cream or a dab of precious icing. Mrs Halliwell, an anxious red-faced widow, took in the contents of the table and pantry shelves, including the dark fruit cake and the trifle.

'It looks a poor show,' she said. 'My neighbour's coming to help with the sandwiches in the morning, but I'll have to be up by five to get it all finished before the wedding. We'll all need to be up, if everybody is to be ready on time. Then, I suppose we'll all be taking Communion, so there's no need to make breakfast. I was thinking we could have fish and chips for tea tonight. Our Lou said to eat them out of the papers to save washing-up. Though I don't like to, really, but I need the plates for some of the food tomorrow, but then I'm worried what Frank's people will think. Then they might be late with this fog, and you can't keep chips and fish warm.'

Ruby was just about to offer to stretch out the rabbit meat she was planning to use for tea, when Granddad hurried down the Halliwells' backyard and knocked at the kitchen door.

'It's really bad down the line,' he said, wiping his feet and taking off his cap. 'The trains are going to be delayed. Don't know what time Frank and his folk will arrive. Is Lou here?'

'No,' Mrs Halliwell said, her pale eyes filling

170

with tears. 'Her and Sadie were on early shifts, and then they were going to pick up the cardboard cake we've hired from the shop. I don't know what's keeping them.'

'Don't worry. Frank's not going to miss his own wedding. If he can dodge the U-boats, he can find his way here in the fog. Ruby, on your way back, go and tell Nellie that Frank's best man's going to be late.'

'I don't know why she couldn't have married a local boy,' Nellie Lathom said, when Ruby knocked on her front door. 'He's a very nice-looking lad, but we don't know the family.'

Ruby was about to ask if she could take Bess home with her for the rest of the afternoon, but Nellie, who was a reluctant host to Charlie, Frank's best man, closed the front door. There was no sign of the hens in the garden at the cottage, and when she opened the back door, the kitchen felt cold and damp. As she was taking off her coat, she heard voices coming from above her head. Her heart began to thump. Ruby crept to the bottom of the stairs. She heard someone crying and a floorboard creaked. Silently, she began to climb up, hesitating on each step, her heart drumming.

'Don't worry, love,' she heard Sadie whisper. 'We'll sort it out. Let's look in that suitcase. Drag it from under the bed. There's got to be something in there we can use.'

Lou's voice sounded thick with tears. 'We've no time to do it,' she said. 'It won't dry in time.'

Ruby edged up on to the next step. Above her, she heard the floorboards creak again and then a scraping as something was pulled across the floor.

The door to Sadie's room was closed, but when she got to the landing, she could see that her own room was open. Lou and Sadie were kneeling in front of her mother's suitcase. Pearl's dresses spilt out around them, and Sadie had a pair of scissors in her hand.

'There's plenty of things in here we can use,' she said.

'No!' Ruby shouted, pushing the two women aside and snatching up a beaded dress. 'No, there aren't,' she said, holding the dress close.

'We're looking for something to cover the marks,' Sadie said, pointing to the mock wedding cake on Ruby's bed and the greasy brown stains across the side of the bottom tier.

'They're not spare. No.'

'We've had a go at painting it with Henry's whitewash.'

Lou sat back on her heels and rubbed her tear-stained face. 'It won't dry in time,' she said.

'No.'

Sadie picked up a white cocktail dress edged with a border of sequins. 'We thought we could use these.'

'No.'

'We can stick–'

'No. Paint it. It will dry.'

Sadie got up, holding the dress in one hand and the scissors in the other. 'It won't, love,' she said. 'We can't paint it all. It won't dry.'

'It will. Get off,' Ruby said, snatching at the dress.

'Ruby, love.'

'I won't let you,' she shouted, wrapping her arms

172

around Pearl's precious clothes. 'Leave them alone.'

Banging the door shut behind them, they left her sitting on the floor hugging Pearl's precious dresses. Later, Ruby got up and stood in the centre of the room, looking out at the grey afternoon, with nowhere to run, nowhere to go, and when she heard unfamiliar footsteps on the stairs, her stomach twitched like a trapped fish.

'Ruby, you in there?' Con had to bend his head to get through the doorway.

'We've come for the cake,' he said, nodding towards the bed.

The bottom of the cake was square. Under the greasy brown stain the cardboard had become wavy. Lou was right: the paint hadn't dried.

'They're all at Lou's. You okay?'

'They wanted the beads...'

'That's a real pretty dress,' Wes said, following Con into the room.

'It was my mum's. It was one of the dresses she wore when she sang... The night she died ... she wore her black one. If she'd worn this...'

'You're shivering,' Con said, taking off his battledress tunic. 'Here, put this on.'

Ruby allowed him to put her thin arms inside the jacket and stood silently in the centre of the tiny room, the gorgeous dresses glittering around her. Con looked helplessly at Wes, hoping he would know what to do; after all, Wes had a sister.

'I'm going downstairs to make us a fire,' Wes said. 'It's pretty cold in here.'

Con sat on the bed and picked up the cake. The discoloured white paper was lifting away from

173

the cardboard.

'They've got some white powder Lou's mom takes for her stomach. They're gonna make it into a white paste... You want help folding this stuff?'

Ruby ran her finger over the sequins, lifting them up, separating them with her fingernail. They were as delicate as fish scales.

'When my grandma died, my mom wouldn't let anyone touch her things. I got her book with me. It was her favourite, and I'd punch any guy who touched it. It's Shakespeare, *Twelfth Night*, so I guess there's not much danger of that. I don't think old Bo's gonna fight me for it.'

Ruby smiled. 'They're mine... You see... They were just taking them, cutting them off.'

'Can they go back on?'

'I'll want them back. If they put them on the cake, I'll...'

'You do what you want. You decide.'

'They should have asked.'

'I know.'

'The fire's going good,' Wes said from the door. 'You want somethin' to eat?'

'Jenny,' Ruby said. 'I've not made her any tea.'

'We'll get fish 'n' chips for us all. Come on, it's real cold up here. Come and get warm.'

When they followed Wes down the stairs, Nellie was waiting in the kitchen.

'I've come to see if there's any news,' she said. 'That young man's not arrived. The pie I've made is dried up. I've had to give it to the dog.'

'They're due on the next train, Henry says. I'm going for some fish 'n' chips. We'll get enough for him and you, ma'am,' Wes said. 'Did I tell you,

174

Ruby? We've got some tinned apricots for the party. Lou's mom was real pleased.'

'Well, in that case, I'll not disturb you,' Nellie said. 'Your granddad's still at work, I suppose, Ruby?'

When Wes left, they worked steadily. As Ruby snipped the sequins, Con used a pinhead to put the tiniest spot of Granddad's glue on each one. Ruby watched him. She liked the way he carefully pressed each silver disc on to the wobbly surface of the damp cardboard.

By the time Sadie got back to the cottage, Ruby was in bed and the cake, sparkling with its new frosting of sequins, was standing in the middle of the table.

'Tell you what,' Sadie said, as she climbed into bed next to Ruby. 'Frank's brother is a funny little kid. Well, not little. In fact, he's big for fourteen.'

Ruby felt Sadie's weight next to her and the warmth of her breath on her neck in the darkness.

'Lou says thanks,' she whispered. 'She's... Well, thanks.'

On the morning of Lou's wedding, the weather was damp and sulky. There was barely enough grey daylight in the church to allow the congregation to appreciate Lou's lilac suit or Sadie's jaunty new hat. Ruby shivered. The cold was making her feel hungry. At Everdeane they didn't go to church, and on Mondays, when the teacher asked the class to put up their hands if they'd attended Mass, she'd always crossed her fingers and put up her hand along with the rest of the children.

Once Lou had reached the altar, Ruby couldn't see her. She was sitting in the second bench next to Arthur, Frank's younger brother, who was wearing his navy school mac and school scarf. He was dark like Frank, but not so handsome. The rest of his family was in the front row. His mother, Grace, who was small and thin, had started crying as soon as the service began. His father, Jacky, looked like Frank and wore the same uniform, but he was fatter and his face was red. Next to them was his sister, Lydia, with her husband and two little girls.

Lou's mother had decided that they must have a nuptial Mass, and now the smell of incense was beginning to make Ruby feel sick. She was wearing Sadie's red coat and felt in the pocket for a hankie; it smelt of Sadie's perfume. She hadn't wanted to wear the coat, because the colour clashed with her hair. She'd planned to wear a scarf over her auburn curls, but earlier that morning when everyone was getting ready, Jenny had brought her own red hat downstairs and insisted that she put it on. Then Sadie said she could wear Jenny's black funeral hat instead, with a blue hair ribbon tacked over the black silk. She'd worked quickly to fix the light-blue ribbon in place, and by the time everyone else was ready to leave the hat was finished, but Jenny was still cross.

When they'd arrived at the church, together with Nellie and Charlie, Bo and some other soldiers were waiting outside. During the service, the whole choir had sung 'The Lord Is My Shepherd' and everyone joined in. Now Frank and Lou were in the sacristy signing the register, and Bo and the other soldiers were singing 'Deep River'. It was hard to tell which voice was Bo's, but on the high notes the rich sound rippled, lifting, soaring over their heads, and Frank's mother started crying again.

When Bo arrived at the church he'd felt nervous. He'd wanted a cigarette, but Wes didn't agree.

'Think of your voice,' he said. 'You don't smoke just before you sing.'

Bo put his cigarettes away and looked around at the four other guys who were going to sing with them. It wasn't what he'd planned. A couple of weeks before the wedding, Wes had arrived at the hut with these new guys, southerners, who sung in a gospel choir in their church back home, and explained that they'd agreed to sing if he paid them. They'd argued, but in the end, he'd accepted that Wes was right. The problem was that the camp was getting busier; there was less time hanging around between jobs, and so they'd less time to work on the songs. Inside the church, their voices sounded better than they'd ever done in the hut at the camp, but when the time came to sing without the rest of the congregation, Sadie was in the sacristy with Lou and her new husband, so he didn't even know if she'd heard them.

As the church emptied, they were surrounded by people complimenting them on their singing, and he spotted Holt's small, wiry frame at the edge of the crowd.

'Did it sound okay?' he asked, pushing his way through the onlookers.

'It sounded just fine,' he said.

'You don't sound that sure.'

'I'm sure. It was fine.'

'Then what's the matter with you? You don't look so happy.'

'I was thinking of the last time I heard that hymn. I was at church with Arleen.'

Bo sighed and put his hand on Holt's shoulder. 'You had a letter?' he asked, but Holt shook his head and his broad face clouded.

'Nope. I guess the post ain't the first thing they're thinking of sending over here,' he said. 'I heard there's bags of the stuff all stored up, waiting to be sorted.'

'Army's going to take a while to send our mail on. It'll just be another week or so. Now we're in the camp, the stuff will catch up with us.'

Holt grinned and nodded towards Sadie, who was heading their way. 'Hi, there,' he said. 'Did you hear?'

'Yes, it was lovely. I could tell your voice above the others,' she said, smiling up at Bo.

Holt's grin widened as, beside him, Wes shook his head. But Bo didn't care: Sadie was happy.

They followed the rest of the wedding guests through the village. Everyone came out of the shops to cheer: the butcher stood on the doorstep and waved his straw boater; the cobbler stood outside, waving his cap and smiling; the chemist and his assistant applauded and the girls at the Co-op came out to clap and cheer as the wedding party walked by. Bo could see that the southerners looked tense, and he winked at Wes and Holt. The first day, when the trucks had rolled through the village, they'd felt the same, but now being among

178

white folk was beginning to feel normal.

The little house was crowded. The tables were piled with food, and once the southern guys had been introduced to the bride and groom and given plates of food, they began to relax and smile.

'This is how it should be at home,' Bo said, 'everyone mixing, not different.'

'Come on, lads,' Frank's father said, handing out glasses. 'Will you join me in a toast? This here is the best Irish whiskey money can buy. Here's to my boy and his lovely young bride, and here's to you lads. The singing was beautiful. My heart was fit to burst.'

When they'd all drunk to the bride and groom, Frank's father filled their glasses again.

'Think you'd best eat up and go,' Holt whispered to Bo. 'One or two more and he'll ask you to sing. Then what you gonna do?' Holt winked at the rest of the choir. 'Think we'll stay and dance with these nice ladies, but you'd best go before Sadie finds out you can't sing half as pretty as she thinks you do.'

Bo grinned. He didn't get riled. He didn't care. What Holt didn't know was that last night he'd asked Sadie out, and she'd said yes. They were going to the movies in town, and he was so happy he felt he could have done anything.

When everyone had eaten, the dining table was folded down, the carpet rolled up, the chairs pushed against the wall and the neighbour's piano rolled in from next door.

'You children go out of the way,' Lou's mother said. 'Ruby, take Arthur and Lydia's little ones upstairs. You can take some cakes and cordial.'

Ruby was angry. Arthur was younger, still a schoolboy, and Frank's nieces were only seven and nine. She wasn't sure what to do to amuse them; for a while they played hide-and-seek, but the only places to hide were under the bed or behind the curtains and in the wardrobe.

'It would be better if it was night and we could play ghosts,' Arthur said.

Next, they played 'I spy', ate the cakes and drank the cordial. Then the girls played with Lou's make-up, and Arthur tried to do jumps and cartwheels on the bed, but he wasn't much good at it. When the girls spilt Lou's face powder on the dressing table, Ruby made them stop, and Shirley, the eldest one, began to stamp her feet and threaten to cry. To avoid trouble with the adults, she let them have turns bouncing on the bed until they felt sick and wanted their mother. Arthur volunteered to take them downstairs, and Ruby hoped that now the youngsters were back with their parents she and Arthur could join the party.

'Do you want a drink?' he asked, when he came back. 'It's turnip wine.'

'Why can't we go back down now the kids have gone?'

'It's always the same,' he said, settling himself on the floor by Lou's bed. 'We've lots of parties at our house, and I'm always sent upstairs.'

'Well, I'm not a kid,' Ruby said, smoothing down her dress. 'I'm fifteen and I'm working.'

Arthur pulled the cork out of the bottle and poured the pale yellow liquid into their cordial glasses.

'Have you ever tasted wine?' he asked. 'I've got a cigarette as well.'

The wine smelt of rotting vegetables and tasted sour.

'That's quite good,' he said, sucking in his fat cheeks. Then he lit the cigarette and handed it to Ruby. 'You can have the first puff,' he said.

Ruby took the cigarette and lifted her chin as she'd seen Mrs Grey do. The burning sensation was a shock. When she'd watched Mrs Grey breathing in the smoke from her thin, black cigarette holder, she'd imagined that it would feel smooth and cool in her mouth. She fought the desire to cough and her eyes began to water. Arthur took the cigarette back and inhaled between sips of wine.

'I don't work. I'm at the grammar school,' he said. 'I've done war work, though. We did the names on the ration books. I could have done yours. We got the job because we can write neatly, you see.'

'We filled sandbags,' Ruby said, 'where I lived before. We filled hundreds of them.'

'When I leave school, I'm going in the Merchant Navy. I'm going to sail from Liverpool to Canada. It's dangerous work. Air cover can only reach so far, and then you're on your own. You always know if you're in for it; if it's a good swell and a clear night with a full moon, then Jerry can spot you. A Royal Navy escort,' he said, placing a line of biscuits in a defensive formation on the lino, 'is there to pick up men from sunken ships, but it's still dangerous. Forty ships sunk every month in the Atlantic, they say.'

181

'Is that what Frank does, on the merchant ships that go to Canada?'

'Mmm, they carry wood and metal mostly.'

'He must be brave. Poor Lou...'

Ruby was watching the biscuits sailing bravely over the lino when Arthur suddenly bent forward and kissed her on the lips. She yelled and slapped his face, her hand jarring against the side of his head, and the sound echoed above the dance music. Arthur bent forward holding his cheek.

'Bugger off,' Ruby said, jumping to her feet and scattering the biscuits.

'What's the matter? You shared my cigarette,' Arthur said, almost in tears.

'What's that got to do with it?'

'Well, our lips have touched. My lips have been where yours have on the paper. So that's like a kiss.'

Ruby was about to lift her hand again, when Lou appeared at the bedroom door.

'You two all right up here?' she asked. 'Come and help me get my case down will you, young Arthur? Mr Watts has arrived in the doctor's car to take us to the station. Why don't you both come down and see us off? We'll be going in a minute.'

When they went downstairs, Arthur's mother and father were waiting.

'Oh, there you are,' his mother said, dabbing a tear from her eye. 'I hope you don't mind us sending for our Arthur to come down, Ruby. I wanted him to be with us to wave his brother off. He said you wanted to stay up there and play, but I didn't think you'd mind.'

Doctor Grey's car, trimmed with bandages tied

182

into bows, and with 'Just married' written in pink letters on a card in the back window, was waiting by the front door.

'Thanks for looking after Arthur, Ruby,' Frank said, as they waved the couple off. 'You're such a good girl.'

'If anyone wants to complain about the improper use of petrol,' Dick Watts called through the open car window, 'you can tell them, I happen to be on my way to the junction to collect vital medical supplies for the doctor.'

As the car drove away, everyone in the street came out of their houses to cheer and wave. Once the car had gone, all the neighbours and their children joined the party. Sadie organised party games for everybody and Ruby, Arthur Frank's nieces and all the neighbours' children were allowed to join in. After a few games of 'pass the parcel' and 'musical chairs', Ruby was bored and she went to sit at the piano with Johnny Fin.

'Do you want to play for the next game?' he asked. 'I need to get another drink.'

Ruby played for another couple of games of 'musical chairs' and then everyone had a break for more food and drinks.

'I'll take over, if you like,' Johnny said, lining up bottles of stout on top of the piano. 'Young Arthur looks a bit left out. Look, he's sitting over there on his own. I'll play a couple of tunes, and you can go and dance with him.'

'No thanks,' she said. 'I'll play instead.'

'Or we could both join the party. Look, young Con's on his own. I've found an old bloke who knows all about that motorbike him and Michael

183

are talking about repairing and I want to have a chat ... arrange for them to meet. I can get Wes to play for a bit.'

'No. I'd rather stay here. Where's Granddad?'

'He's over there with Jenny.'

Granddad was holding on to a chair with one hand and on to Jenny with the other; they reminded her of a picture of Jack Sprat and his wife in a nursery rhyme book.

'Is he all right?' she asked, shuffling through the music to find a different song to play.

'Well, he's had a few,' Johnny said. 'No doubt he'll suffer for it in the morning. We all will.'

'No. I mean is he ill?'

'Well, the gas hurt his lungs, you know that. But Jenny sees to it that he eats well.'

'The other night there were some frozen shirts on the line, and he turned white when he saw them. We were making them dance for a joke... He wouldn't say what was the matter.'

'I don't know, love. We never talk about... Well, it doesn't do... Don't worry, pet. It's nothing you did. Now, come on, what about you and me havin' a dance? Let's get young Wes over here to play for a while.'

CHAPTER EIGHT

The rain tapped on the sides of the hut. The thirty or so men who had crowded inside perched on the beds, smoking and chatting amiably. It was so cold that Bo could see his own breath.

'Listen up,' he said. 'Sergeant Mayfield might be joining us. I guess all you guys will have seen him by now.'

The men around him shifted, and he noticed one or two of the younger ones looking nervously towards the door.

'Any of you men got a problem with that?' he asked.

'Some of the guys think he might be listening for ... well, for the captain,' Wes said, searching the faces of the men around him for their agreement.

'If he comes, what's he going to report?' Bo asked, as Holt began handing out copies of the *Michigan Chronicle* to the guys near the front of the group. 'We're only swapping newspapers and discussing things that concern us.'

Around the crowded hut, there were murmurs of agreement. Bo hadn't planned to organise meetings; they had begun as a way of passing around newspapers. Then he'd discovered that many of the men from the South found reading hard, so he began reading out articles. Gradually more of the men had taken to bringing things they'd read; so now, as well as swapping papers, a lot of the guys stayed to smoke, to talk and to listen. Sometimes there was a discussion about what they'd read, and other times it was just one of the guys who'd heard something and wanted to tell the others about it. Over the weeks, Bo had watched the faces of the men as they listened and he began to learn how to draw out the points from their conversations, so that everybody got to have their say.

'Then let's say something does get back,' Holt said. 'What they gonna do? It's not political.'

'Could be,' one of the southerners from the choir said. 'Officers won't be too happy if they hear about it.'

Bo knew that the guy who'd spoken up struggled with reading and he didn't want to knock his objection down. Now they'd got some confidence many of the southerners, who'd felt themselves at a disadvantage because of their poor education, would ask for points to be clarified and added their own experiences to the debate, knowing that he wouldn't allow them to be made fools of.

'Tell you what we do,' he said. 'We watch our mouths for the first few meetings and see if it gets back. Test him out. The guy's a sergeant, and we don't know his background. In the meantime, we'll ask around, find out what we can about him.'

When Sergeant Mayfield arrived he was true to his word, sitting with the rest of them and listening to the discussion about the lack of black officers. It wasn't until Bo invited questions that he stood up to say his piece.

'Some of you men may not know what we did in World War One. If you like,' he said, catching Bo's eye, 'next time, I'll tell you about some of the brave black men who fought in that conflict. The reason there's no black officers now is that in 1940 they put out an army policy statement restricting them from regular army units. Black officers could only be assigned to National Guard units. It meant they only needed a few guys. It meant that, when the government did decide black men had to be employed on a proportional basis, but in segregated units, most black outfits went short and had to be staffed with white officers.' Sergeant Mayfield's neck muscles bulged, he bounced on his toes and looked around the men in the hut. 'So what we need are the men with the right qualifications to apply to become officers. Then we can have our black lieutenants.'

'How about it, Bo?' one of the men shouted, and the hut erupted into cheers.

When the men had begun shouting their approval, Wes saw Con head for the hut door. He was still sore that Sadie was going on a date with Bo. The other guys had tried to sympathise. He was just a kid, after all. But he'd despised their sympathy, and Bo's attempt not to make too big a thing of it had just made it worse.

'Don't know why they just don't make the guy captain. Guy like that don't need no... He don't need no officer training.'

'She's only said she'll go to the pictures with him,' Wes said.

'So what? She's just as stupid as the guys in there. You're all taken in by good ole Bo. Even that sergeant.'

'Take no notice. Come into town with the rest

of us.'

Con lit a cigarette, handed one to Wes and grinned.

'You want to hear yourself sometimes. You sound like one of my mom's magazines: "Dear Lonely Heart, The girl of your dreams has gone off with a knucklehead. Take no notice. Get yourself a new hairdo instead." Come on, Auntie Wes, what should I do? Get my hair fixed? Have my nails done?'

'We could take a look at one of the dances in town.'

'Plenty more fish in the sea, is there, Auntie Wes?'

'Okay, we could go with the rest of them to a movie.'

'Yep, all of us with Bo and his new girl. Hope it's not a sad film. I might just cry.' Con sagged at the knees and dropped his head on his friend's shoulder.

'We'll try one of the other picture houses,' Wes said, disentangling himself from Con's embrace. 'We're picking up a crowd of locals and taking them in on the truck. We don't have to go to the same movie. There's twenty different picture houses in town. I reckon we should try a dance; we could go to a dance in town, instead of the one in the village. There's lots of girls in town.'

'And why would you and Holt want to do that?' Con asked, stubbing out his cigarette. 'Holt's married, and you have a girl.'

'So what? It doesn't mean anything. We can still go and dance and have a good time. Come on, you're in England. Who knows what will... There's

188

lots of pretty girls and... Well, the war. Who knows what's goin'–'

'We're a truck company. What will happen is that I'll be stuck driving trucks and never get to fight. The girls want to dance with heroes, not a truck driver.'

Wes sighed and tried to keep his patience. 'What's wrong with driving a truck? The war will be over one day and you can go back and–'

'I know, and be a truck driver or a mechanic.'

'Things will be better for black people.'

'Will they? They didn't change after World War One and guys fought then. We're not even going to get the chance to fight...'

Wes stubbed out his cigarette. 'Meeting's breaking up. Come on,' he said, 'there's a card game I've got to go to. At least it will take your mind off Bo.'

Bo and Sadie didn't go into town on the truck with the rest of them, because Bo wanted her all to himself. But his plans almost fell apart when she forgot her gas mask and they missed the early train. He didn't mind the wait on the dark platform, or the two hours in the queue to get into the movie, as long as he had Sadie holding on to his arm. In fact, he was sorry when the queue eventually edged forward into the brightly lit foyer, and she didn't need to snuggle so close up to him against the cold and damp. As the crowd was distilled from the blacked-out street into the foyer, Bo watched the people around him lift their faces, eager for the opulence of the highly polished marble pillars, gilded walls and glittering lights. At his side, Sadie adjusted her cute little hat in one of the gilt wall mirrors and he had to admit they made a handsome couple.

'Wonder where the rest of them are going? Don't seem to be here,' Sadie said, as they settled into their seats at the front of the circle.

Bo didn't answer, but gave her the box of chocolates he'd brought for her and sat back blissfully, taking in the crimson and gold interior and listening to the chatter around him. When the organ played he joined in the singsong, following the bouncing ball on the screen, and when the lights finally dimmed and Sadie slipped her hand into his, there was no happier man in the whole US army.

Con went into town on the truck with Wes and Holt. They'd stopped in the village to collect a group of local girls, including Lou and Ruby, four older couples on a night out and some local men on leave. The girls and the older folk had headed for the movies, but Con followed Wes and some of the other guys through the dark, crowded streets to the dance hall. The dimly lit entrance reminded Con of a church porch or a public library. A large woman with a painted face and thick glasses sat behind a small table just inside the door.

When they tried to pay, she squinted up at them. 'It's okay, love,' she said, nodding towards a set of double doors, 'servicemen get in free.'

On the other side of the doors, the air was sticky. At the far end of the room, above the grey haze of cigarette smoke and the shuffling crowd, Con could see the heads of the musicians. He followed

Wes, squeezing between the rows of seats lining the wall and the closely packed couples on the dance floor. Around the bar, where orders and drinks were being passed good-naturedly from the front to the back of the crowd, the crush was even deeper. Con wished he hadn't come. His uniform felt hot, and when the beer arrived, it was warm and unpleasantly sweet. Then the music stopped and the bandleader, a small, elderly man in a white jacket, walked to the front of the stage and waved his baton.

'Ladies and gentlemen,' he called, 'I would like you to welcome our American allies.'

There was a trumpet blast, a spotlight fixed on Wes's goofy-toothed grin and to the sound of 'The Star-Spangled Banner' the whole dance hall began to stamp and cheer.

As the music faded, a plump dark-haired girl with the yellow-stained face of a munitions worker touched Con's arm.

'Hello, I'm Rita,' she said, 'and this is my friend Sylvia.'

'Hello girls,' Wes said. 'My name is Wes and this is Con. Would you like to dance?'

Sylvia, who had a thin face and long, uneven teeth, giggled and took Wes's proffered arm. When Con felt Wes dig him in the ribs, he took hold of the plump girl by the elbow and steered her towards the dance floor. He had only ever danced once before, except with his mom's sister at parties, but it didn't matter because the floor was so crowded they barely moved.

'Is she paying you?' Jenny asked.

'I don't know,' Ruby said. 'I don't think so. It's for the school.'

'And why should we help them? That stuck-up cow of a teacher didn't help us.'

'It's for the little ones; the infants. We all have to do our bit.'

Jenny put down the mixing spoon and glared. 'Do your bit? You can do your bit here, washing her husband's shirts. And if madam wants to do her bit, she can wash 'em her bloody self. And you,' she said, taking up the spoon again and mixing vigorously, 'can get a job in the factory.'

Ruby gripped the handle of her basket. 'I'll have to go now, she's expecting me. I have to meet her and Mrs Prendergast at the house at one. If I let her down, she might not give me any work over Christmas. I mean, she might not want me to help at the house. Alice already wants her niece to have the job there instead of me.'

'Well next time, have the bloody sense to ask if you're being paid. You're wearing them good shoes as well. Take them off.'

'I wanted to look nice.'

'Nice? You're being asked to skivvy for nothing. Why do you have to look nice? Go and put them old ones on.'

Back in her room, Ruby pulled off the shoes Sadie had given her and hid them at the bottom of her basket. Then she waited by the window until she could see Granddad on his way down the garden from the pigeon cabin. Once he was in sight, she crept to the top of the stairs and listened for his arrival at the back door, hoping that the sight of his dirty clogs on the clean flag floor would distract Jenny's attention long enough for her to slip out unnoticed.

'Mrs Grey's waiting,' Alice said, as Ruby changed out of her old shoes in the pantry. 'Said to tell you to go through when you arrived. Going with her to the school to wrap presents, I hear. If you've got some spare time, I could use it. Never mind wrapping presents. The older girls could do that. Always did in my day.'

The infant class was held in the red-brick building that also doubled as the church hall. When they arrived, Miss Conway was in the process of drilling the children who were taking part in the Nativity play. One group of infants were angels and the other shepherds. The pretty, dark-haired girl, wrapped in a blue shawl, was playing Mary, and the serious boy, who'd answered the door when Jenny had taken her to see Miss Conway, was Joseph. The girl from the rec, most of the other children from her class and the rest of the infants were in a ragged semicircle around the dusty upright piano. Ruby guessed that they must be the choir. When the children saw there were visitors at the door, they began to whisper and giggle. Miss Conway, who hadn't heard the door open, walloped the thick strap on the piano's open lid, sending an angry thrum shuddering through the instrument that made Ruby wince and the children fall silent. Then the girl from the rec whispered to her that they had visitors. The teacher looked at them crossly over her glasses, but when she recognised Mrs Grey, she smiled.

Ruby's job was to cut oblongs of used Christmas wrapping paper and stick it on to the lids and sides of shoeboxes to hide the labels. There were fifty boxes, one for each infant. Ruby had hoped to be able to watch the rehearsal, but the paste was thin and most of the paper, from a bundle donated by parishioners, tore so easily that she could only listen to Mary telling the angel – the girl from the rec – that she would be the mother of Jesus.

Mrs Prendergast and Mrs Grey were sitting together at a small table next to hers. Mrs Grey was sorting through a collection of donated toys and sweets, before wrapping each small gift in paper or rolling it in cotton wool and placing it in a pile of gifts for boys or for girls. Mrs Prendergast then packed these into the boxes that Ruby had covered. She put each completed box in a stack, one for boys and one for girls. Then Douglas, a very thin evacuee boy with a bad cough, who was sitting at the table nearest the radiator, wrote out the labels from the school register and stuck them to the boxes.

When Miss Conway told the girl from the rec – whose name was Pauline – to go and put her wings on before they tried the speech again, Ruby listened to Mrs Prendergast and Mrs Grey instead.

'I think we need to take charge, before things get out of hand,' Mrs Prendergast said. 'I've heard that the camp is already attracting a certain kind of interest.'

'I know... Well, what I mean is, one's heard that sort of thing goes on,' Mrs Grey said, holding up a small knitted doll. 'We know that these places exist in towns ... in some areas. But not around here, surely?'

'My husband was told by someone of rank in

the police that it's happening in his area. It was only a matter of weeks before women of a certain type were actually coming out of the nearby towns and hanging around the camp. Some very young girls too. It's unfortunate. Their parents are working long hours on essential war work, and these girls are running wild.'

'Do you think we could include some ball bearings in with the marbles?' Mrs Grey asked. 'I mean, I don't think it would be considered unpatriotic. I haven't got them from a factory or anything. Mr Watts had them in his workshop. There must be at least two hundred. He told me he's had them for years. Do you think the little boys would be disappointed if some of them weren't real marbles?'

'On one occasion,' Mrs Prendergast said, tucking more paper inside a shoebox, 'two young girls were actually caught inside the camp. And the men had only been there a matter of weeks.'

Ruby was just beginning to take an interest in the conversation, when Pauline walked back on to the stage wearing a large pair of lopsided wings. When her friend giggled, Miss Conway forgot about the visitors and yelled furiously at the two girls, making the doctor's wife spill the ball bearings on to the floor. As they bounced and rolled, the shepherds and angels broke ranks to chase them. By the time they were all collected, Miss Conway had declared an end to the rehearsal and sent the children out to play.

'I wonder, Ruby, dear,' Mrs Grey said, once the children had left, 'could you help with a small party for some of the American officers?'

'Not a party, Diana. I was thinking something a little more...'

'Yes. Just a little get-together. A chat. An informal meeting ... over tea...'

'An informal meeting to coordinate the organisation of entertainment and welfare ... that sort of thing. With your WRVS hat on, so to speak.'

'I'll get Alice to make a few cakes. We don't need you to play, Ruby. I just need you to come and help out.'

'Don't drink all that brandy,' Jenny said. 'That's for the cake.'

Granddad, who was sitting in the armchair, coughed. 'Just a drop for my chest, Jenny, love.'

'It's cold in here, Ma,' Sadie said. 'If you're thinking of putting the cake in this oven, we'll need more coal on, and we can't all have brandy.'

'Can't do that,' Henry replied. 'Don't you read the paper? Output per miner's gone down, and the coal ration's being cut.'

'You said, with Ruby here, we'd get extra units. Me an' Lou're freezing. I waited ages for a bus from work, and in the end we had to get a lift on this open lorry. I've not been warm since.'

'If you two are cold, you can grate some of these carrots for the cake. I've usually got all my Christmas baking done well before now.'

'My fault, Ma,' Lou said, 'with the extra stuff for the wedding.'

'I'm not complaining, love. Bo brought us some dried fruit, and I got some on the black market.'

'Seems like years ago. I can't see his face. I keep trying to imagine him and I can't.'

196

'When did his ship leave?'

'Four days ago. I should be grateful, I suppose. At least he's not "on the pool". Some get sent back as soon as their ship docks. They've no say; they can send them anywhere, and they have to go. At least he's with the same captain and he says he's a good bloke.'

'Well that's something, at least. Sadie, why don't you make Lou a cup of tea? Then you can both give me a hand with the cake.'

'They don't care about them. It's all the Royal Navy. They don't care about anybody else. Merchant seamen know their safety doesn't count,' Lou sniffled. 'There was some on the train, filthy and smelling of engine oil. Been picked up from an open boat. Lost everything. Only had the clothes they stood up in. Looked like they'd never slept for weeks.'

'Well, at least they got home,' Sadie said, pouring hot water into the teapot.

Ruby, who was checking the dried fruit in the colander for stalks, remembered the soldiers arriving from Dunkirk sitting in the front room at Everdeane, silently accepting cups of tea and sandwiches, and gazing out at the waves.

'Wes doesn't like the sea,' she said. 'After the ship coming over here, he said he never wants to go on a ship again. He's afraid of being hit by a sub and drowning. He said–'

'How long does it take to sort through a bit of fruit?' Jenny snapped.

'Stalingrad's holding,' Granddad said over his paper. 'The Russians know how to deal with Jerry. Wouldn't like to be there in winter. They know how to deal with Jerry all right, driving him out street by street, they are.'

'Do you have to remind us how cold it is? Can't you find something cheerful to say? Hang on; is that Bo I can hear? At least he'll cheer us up.'

When Bo walked in, the room began to feel warmer. He emptied his pockets, dropped a small brown paper parcel on the table, and grinned.

'What's this?' Jenny asked, picking up the parcel and untying the string.

'Cinnamon. It's real nice in biscuits.'

When Jenny opened the packet the dry sticks tumbled out on the table. 'Here, smell that, Lou. That's nice. You and Sadie could have a go at baking some.'

'Mmm, it does smell nice,' she said, pushing her damp hankie up her sleeve and sniffing one of the little sticks.

'Alice said to ask if she can have some eggs for the cakes for the party,' Ruby said, scraping up the stalks from the dried fruit and handing the colander to Jenny.

'Does she say how much she'll be paying for them?'

'They're for a party for the officers at the camp.'

Bo lifted one eyebrow. 'The officers?'

'Captain O'Donal, and Captain Leary, I think. They came to dinner. Mrs Grey says it isn't really a party. It's a meeting with her and Mrs Prendergast.'

'That nosey old cow,' Jenny said. 'What does she want? Always sticking her nose in and looking down on everybody.'

'It's got to do with organising.'

'Aye, well, it would have.'

'Organising, entertainment and welfare.'

'Bet it's a dance and a kiddies' party,' Sadie said, getting up and taking Bo's coat. 'Bo and me can do that. Can't we, Bo? I saw Father O'Flynn the other day and told him we'd do a party for the children, if we could have a dance for us. You try and find out what they're planning, Ruby. You want to help, Lou? Oh, come on. It'll take your mind off things, and Frank wouldn't want you feeling in the dumps all the time, now would he?'

Jenny looked over at her daughter and then back to Bo. The night before, Nellie Lathom had collared her on her way home from the factory, pretending she was just coming out to close her front gate, but Jenny knew different. She'd asked her outright if Sadie was walking out with one of the black soldiers. Jenny had bitten back a sharp comment, and instead she'd said, 'Our Sadie's got lots of admirers, as you well know, Nellie.'

She smiled as she heard Bo making the girls laugh, cheering Lou up. If Sadie was taken with him who could blame her, when he was such a handsome young man: wide shoulders, lovely eyes and skin the colour of pale coffee. Jack Lathom was a nice lad, but he wasn't what anyone could call good-looking, and Sadie was no fool. 'He's just a friend, Ma,' she'd said, 'same as Jack. Me being his girl is all in her head. And don't go on about Jack and his uncle's garage: who knows where we'll all be next Christmas.'

She was right. And he worshipped her. You only had to look at him to see that. Nothing was too much trouble, and they would have really struggled without his help. Bo and the other lads had been a godsend, and with that pale skin, he could pass for an Italian.

'Well, if they're for Bo's captain,' she said, handing him a cup of tea, 'we'll have to see what we can do. What's he like, love?'

'Oh, Captain O'Donal's a nice enough guy. He's a northerner. Rumour is, his father was some big war hero. He means well, but lets the lieutenants push him around. Don't know much about the other guy.'

'How's young Con?' Granddad asked. 'Not seen him for a bit.'

'Con? He's fine. We all are. We got our mail from home yesterday, and Con's got a girl in town. He met her at a dance.'

'You didn't tell me,' Sadie said. 'What's she like?'

'I don't know. I was with you, at the movies. Say, do you want to go dancing this weekend? The guys said the folks at the dance were real friendly.'

'Does that mean he won't come here to see us?' Ruby asked, as her stomach suddenly jerked.

'Of course he will,' Granddad said. 'He'll want to help me and Michael work on the motorbike.'

'You'd best try and keep your hands out of sight,' Alice said. 'Missus won't like rough hands like that.'

The washing, particularly the scrubbing, had made the skin on Ruby's fingers crack. Over the weeks, the dry openings had become deeper and wider, and now rinsing the clothes in cold water made her fingers sting. The splits didn't bleed

200

and gradually their crinkled edges had widened into dry, little mouths.

They were waiting for Mrs Grey to ring the bell for them to take in the tea. Ruby looked up at the wooden box on the wall by the kitchen door. It had a row of ten holes, one for each of the rooms in the house. When someone rang the bell in a particular room, a black disc with the room number on it in white would drop down over the hole. When the bell in the sitting room rang, the disc with number two on it would drop over the second hole. Number one was the front door and three was the dining room. The rest were for the bedrooms, except for number ten: that was Doctor Grey's surgery. The discs made Ruby think of Beryl, a doll her father had bought her. Beryl was her favourite doll. She had yellow hair that could be combed into different styles and eyes that would close when she was put down to sleep. She hoped Auntie Ethel hadn't given her away.

'Come on, girl, wake up,' Alice said sharply, as the bell rang, and the number two dropped over the hole on the box. 'Get that tray, and don't expect me to stay and help serve the tea. You'll have to do it yourself.'

Ruby tried to hide her hands under the silver tea tray. Alice wasn't in a very good mood. She'd hated all the extra work caused by Mrs Grey's fundraising afternoons and had been hoping that Winifred, the eldest of her sister's four children, might be taken on to help in the house over Christmas, but when she'd asked, Mrs Grey said that she would have to cope with the help Ruby could give her.

Alice followed Ruby into the living room with a plate of sandwiches and the glass cake stand. When Doctor and Mrs Grey took tea, the tray was put on the table next to Mrs Grey's seat and she served herself and her husband. But today Ruby had to serve the guests, handing around the sandwiches, serving tea and waiting by the small table near the door to refill their cups and ask if they would like more to eat.

'It's a daft idea,' Alice had said, as they'd been finishing off the little sponge buns with mock cream and candied fruit. 'You could be helping me with the bedrooms. I need a willing girl to help with the housework, not someone who plays the piano and does a bit of waiting at table.'

'You haven't brought the coffee. Our American guests might want some,' Mrs Grey said, as Ruby put the silver tray on the little walnut table near the sitting-room door.

'Coffee wasn't asked for, madam,' Alice said.

'Well I'm asking now. Captain O'Donal and Captain Leary will be here in about half an hour. I suppose it will be better to leave the coffee until they arrive. Ruby, you can bring the coffee and some hot water in at the same time. When Mr and Mrs Prendergast arrive, offer to take their coats and then bring them straight through. I'll come out with you and welcome the American officers myself. If they have a driver; take him through to the kitchen. Alice, you can give him tea in there.'

'I brought through all the cakes and sandwiches, madam, and I was due to do the bedrooms...'

'I'm sure you can find something to give him. Give him what you and Mr Watts will be having.'

'Mr Watts is in town, madam.'

'Well, I'm sure you can find something, and then if you're busy, give him the newspaper to read.'

'Ruby can—'

'Ruby can't. She'll be serving tea.'

After the door had closed behind Alice, Ruby noticed Mrs Grey's shoulders sag.

The Prendergasts arrived a few minutes later and sat side by side facing Mrs Grey over the low table.

'Are we not to have music today?' Mr Prendergast asked, as Ruby handed him a cup of tea.

When he smiled, Mr Prendergast's wet eyes caught the sunlight, and as his eyelids drooped over his protruding eyes, Ruby was reminded of a gull's broken eggshells abandoned on the shingle.

'Shall I draw the curtains, madam?' she asked.

'No. Don't do that on my account, Diana, my dear,' Mr Prendergast said. 'It's been such a damp day. We shouldn't shut this little bit of sunlight out. Ruby and I will move this chair,' he said, handing Ruby the cushion from one of the easy chairs.

Ruby liked Mr Prendergast who, although he was a very important person, always remembered her name and often slipped her a shilling as she handed him his coat.

'Reginald and I used the time on the drive over to discuss what we might say to Captain O'Donal and his colleague,' Mrs Prendergast said, inspecting the tiny gold watch on her broad wrist. 'What time are you expecting them, dear? I thought we should get our heads together and remind ourselves of what we planned to say.'

'They should be here in about half an hour. Perhaps less.'

'I think,' Mr Prendergast said, taking out his pipe and tobacco pouch, 'from what Pamela has told me, your plan for dealing with the problem is a capital one.'

At the sight of her husband's pipe, Mrs Prendergast's smooth forehead puckered.

'Reginald feels we need to tread carefully,' she said, 'but we must make it clear what we expect.'

'Yes, indeed,' he said, clearing his throat and replacing his pipe and tobacco in his pocket. 'Is the good doctor not joining us?'

'No,' Mrs Grey said, taking another cigarette from the box on the table. 'He's very busy, I'm afraid, poor dear. He was called out to a confinement last night and to a death the night before. Poor Mr Goodier, did you know him? Pneumonia. A blessing, really. My mother calls it "the old man's friend". Humphrey is at the hospital today. A serious case of blood poisoning. A child, I believe. And there's talk of scarlet fever in town. So I don't expect him back until very late.'

'I know he has quite strong feelings... It's very delicate. Don't want to upset the Americans. Government fudged the issue, in my opinion. Dowler had the right idea. Good chap, Dowler. Sent notes to officers. Advice on how best to deal with relations with the black troops. Trouble is, can't make them available to the civilian population. Too sensitive. Might upset the Yanks. Mrs Roosevelt: very keen on the black soldier. Political factors, my dear. Very complicated.'

Mrs Grey nodded and handed the mother-of-

204

pearl cigarette box to Ruby to take over to Mr Prendergast.

'Dowler's notes would seem a good place to start,' she said.

'I took the liberty of explaining to Reginald, dear, that we both think we could use the notes as a guide. Very sensible it seems, with the army base being so very near.'

'Quite,' Mr Prendergast said, taking a cigarette from the open box.

Ruby was returning it to the table by Mrs Grey's side, when the living-room door was thrown open and Mr Rollo walked in.

'Oh, Rollo, it's you,' Mrs Grey said, getting to her feet. 'You're not well enough to be up, and I think I've just heard my other guests arrive.'

Mr Rollo, who was wearing a loose velvet dressing gown over silk pyjamas, took the cigarette box from Ruby and sat down next to Mrs Prendergast.

'I've been driven down by Alice. She's banging around up there. What does she find to do that makes so much noise?'

'Yes, I'm sure that was someone on the drive,' Mrs Grey said, looking nervously at her brother, who was swinging an embroidered slipper from a naked foot.

'Ruby, come with me. You too, Rollo, darling. You really aren't well enough to be out of bed.'

Ruby, who was sure there wasn't anyone outside, followed Mrs Grey and her brother.

'What are you plotting?' he asked his sister, as she closed the living-room door behind them.

In the hall, the shadows cast by the dull

afternoon light from the long windows made his face look older. His skin looked dry, almost scaly, and the way he stared at his sister reminded Ruby of the look in Monty's red-rimmed eye when he was about to peck at her leg.

'Don't be silly. I'm not plotting.'

'Well, why didn't you ask me to stay for a cup of tea?'

'You're not dressed for afternoon tea. Now go back to your room, darling. Please. For me?'

'Well, what about some coffee and some more cigarettes?' he said, but as he turned to go up the stairs, they heard the sound of Alice banging somewhere above them, and throwing back his head, exposing the long black hairs escaping from his open collar, Mr Rollo started to moan.

'Have pity, Diana,' he begged. 'Let me stay. Get Ruby to bring me a pot of coffee. I'll sit quietly. I promise.'

'Oh, for goodness' sake, Rollo. The coffee isn't ready. I'll send you a tray. You are ill, remember? There's the bell. My guests are here. Ruby, get the door.'

'Some cigarettes? Get me some, or I shall have to go back in the living room and get my own.'

'I'll send you some with the coffee. Please go. Ruby, the door, now!'

Mrs Grey took the two officers back with her into the living room, and as Ruby hurried to the kitchen to make the coffee, Alice appeared at the top of the stairs.

'Ruby, put the water on,' she called. 'I'll come down to make the coffee.'

When Ruby carried the tall silver coffee pot into

206

the guests, they were chatting about the weather. The afternoon light had almost gone, and before she served the sandwiches, she put on the table lamps, closed the curtains and poked the fire. As she lifted the tarry mass gently with the brass poker, the coal sighed and orange flames began to leap, adding to the room's soft yellow glow. Then she served the visitors tea and coffee, sandwiches and cakes, all the time listening, hoping to find out something about the planned dance that she could report back to Sadie and Lou.

'Tell me, Captain,' Mrs Grey said, as Ruby waited for Captain O'Donal to help himself to the paste sandwiches, 'how are your men settling in?'

'Oh, very well, ma'am. People have been very kind. They appreciate the welcome.'

'I'm so pleased to hear it. We wanted to discuss plans for Christmas,' she said, holding up her cup for Ruby to fill. 'We want the men to feel at home and we thought it would be best to try to coordinate our celebrations.'

'It's the little touches, don't you think, that can make the difference,' Mrs Prendergast said, waving away the sandwiches and selecting a cream-topped cake from the cake stand. 'Touches can mean so much and ... customs ... recognising our different customs is important.'

'There's the question of how the celebrations should be organised,' Mr Prendergast added. 'How best to organise the religious services and ... dances and such ... in a way that would make the men feel at home. All the men must be included, of course.'

'The men won't expect... They're used to

separate facilities...' Captain Leary said, turning to choose a cake. As he took a small cake, decorated with a sliver of candied peel, Ruby caught the fluted cake stand on the edge of the table. The noise startled Mrs Grey, who put down her cup.

'I think we can serve ourselves, Ruby,' she said. 'Will you pour a cup of coffee and ask Alice to take it up to Mr Rollo?'

Reluctantly, Ruby poured out the coffee, and as she closed the door, the conversation started again.

When she got to the kitchen, she was surprised to see Holt sitting opposite Dick and Alice at the table drinking tea. Under the soft kitchen lights, Holt's dark skin had a damson's sheen, and she noticed that he was shivering.

'They left him outside in the cold, so I brought him in,' Alice said. 'What's this?'

'Madam said you were to take it up to Mr Rollo.'

'Ill, he's supposed to be. Out at all hours. You get on with that washing-up, and then we can have a bite to eat.'

'Young chap, here, tells me he knows your grandpa,' Dick said, as Holt grinned at her across the table.

'He does,' Ruby smiled. 'Michael's helped him with his motorbike.'

'What they up to in there?' Dick asked, refilling Holt's cup and pouring one for her.

'It's all about parties for Christmas. I promised Sadie I'd listen and let her know what they was going to do, but Mrs Grey sent me out with the

208

coffee. So I don't know. They'd only just got started.'

'Going to be a grand Christmas. I've heard all the kiddies are going for a party at the camp,' Dick said.

'Is that at your place, Michael?' she asked.

'I ... I don't...' Holt struggled to imagine children in the damp collection of huts that made up the camp. 'I don't rightly know,' he said.

'Well, your captain is here, but I suppose it might be at the place the other chap comes from.'

'If they're going to be some time, I'll show Michael, here, my greenhouse. Get us from under your feet. He's been telling me all about growing cotton, and all sorts of things. Fascinating. His granddad was a gardener. Had a hundred men working under him.'

Late that same afternoon, as Con was heading back to the camp, he felt edgy and decided to drop off in the village.

'I need some cigarettes,' he told the truck driver. 'I'll hitch a ride back.'

Almost unwillingly, his legs took him from the village shop over the two railway bridges. He hoped Henry would be home and invite him in for a drink and a chat, but when he knocked at the door, the cottage was empty. He wandered on down the little lane. He'd reached the stone bridge when he saw Mrs Bland coming towards him, pulling a tree branch behind her. The branch didn't look very big, but the old lady, who was tugging it with one hand, looked out of breath.

'Oh, good afternoon,' she said. 'Con, isn't it?'

209

In the dusk, Con thought for a moment that he could see a child or a doll swinging limply from her free arm, but when she changed hands and adjusted the bundle, he could see it was the body of a dead rabbit dangling from the crook of her elbow.

'I wonder if I could prevail upon you to help me back to the cottage,' the old lady said. 'I'm afraid the branch is much harder to carry than I first estimated. I have been checking my traps, you see. Quite a poor haul, I'm afraid,' she said, handing over the branch and taking the dead creature by its ears, 'but I was fortunate enough to find some wood.'

'Does the stream have fish in it?' he asked, carrying the bough, which was ungainly rather than heavy, over the little bridge.

'Some of the smaller pools, possibly, but the stream as it goes by the cottages doesn't, I'm afraid. Although I'm sure it must have done. Sadly, it's very polluted. It's the cotton industry, you see. Originally, the stream would have been the main reason the factory was sited here. Water power and then steam, of course. Must look very small to you. Detroit, isn't it, where you come from? A majestic river. The first settlers must have been amazed, don't you think? Just imagine, the great river and then the lakes.'

'Do you want me to chop this up for you?' he asked. 'I can do it now, if you have an axe.'

'Well, that would be awfully kind, and then you must let me offer you some refreshments. I'm afraid it will be dark soon. Will you be able to see?'

'Oh, it won't take long, ma'am.'

Con put the meagre pile of wood in the coal bunker at the back of the tiny cottage.

'Come through,' Mrs Bland called, from the door of the poky wooden lean-to that served as her kitchen and held a sink, a cooker and two battered cupboards. 'I've made us a cup of tea. Would you like to stay and eat with me?' Inside the living room, the rabbit's corpse lolled on a rough wooden table between a dainty china tea set and a pile of carrots.

'No thank you, ma'am,' he said, looking at the soft creamy fur on the animal's chest and the tiny thread of blood hanging from its mouth. 'I'll be expected back at the camp. I stopped by in the village to buy some cigarettes.'

'It is rather chilly in here,' the old lady said, pushing up the sleeves on her worn coat and picking up one of the carrots. 'Still, the winters must be much colder in Detroit.'

'Yes, ma'am, but not so damp,' he said looking at the listless fire. 'The air there is drier, somehow.'

'It was the damp climate here that made this area ideal for cotton. Needs to be damp for the thread. Vital. The first mill owners built the mills by the water. Had to. They used it as a source of power. In those days, there wasn't a village here. The place would have been quite isolated. They needed workers, of course, and they solved that problem by using orphaned children from the workhouses. No one would have complained. They brought the children here. Appalling conditions. They slept under the looms. If the mill failed, the children were left to wander the countryside and starve. Cotton has a cruel history. The conditions in the Manchester slums shocked the world. Money makes men cruel, and smug,' Mrs Bland said, tugging open the table drawer and taking out a broad knife. 'Took their own families out to the clean Cheshire air,' she added, slicing off the rabbit's head with one blow, and with barely a flash of the blade, quickly unzipping the creature from its brindled fur. 'Pass me that bowl from the dresser would you, dear? But the people ... the working people of Lancashire, now they were a different breed. The American Civil War is a case in point. They felt a common fellowship with the slaves. In the face of the blockade, the Lancashire workers were very brave, stoical. Sent messages of support to Lincoln, even though they were starving, while their masters held bales of raw cotton in their warehouses, speculating on the increase in the price.'

Con sipped the pale tea and watched as Mrs Bland chopped at the peeled carrots, as if each represented the tender parts of a despised cotton master.

'My grandma was from the South,' he said. 'Moved north in her twenties. She was brought up on a plantation. Educated with the daughters of the owner until she was fourteen.'

'What happened then?' Mrs Bland asked, pulling the naked carcass towards her. 'Was she sent to the fields?'

'No,' he said, as the rabbit's inquisitive eye peered at him around the floral cream jug. 'Her family had always been indoor servants. In fact, she looked down on the field hands.'

212

Con eased his chair back, avoiding the gobbets of sleek, purple wetness splashing into the bowl at his elbow.

'Divide and rule,' Mrs Bland said, dropping the carrots into a blackened saucepan and hacking at the pink rabbit flesh.

As the sharp tang of blood and freshly exposed intestine rose from the enamel dish, he fingered the pack of cigarettes in his pocket and asked for permission to smoke. After a couple of deep inhalations, Con found the taste of tobacco in his throat had successfully masked the smell of decaying grass rising from the freshly exposed entrails. He couldn't help thinking that Grandma Eloise would not have approved of squat Mrs Bland with her uncombed hair and slovenly dress. His grandma, as daughter of the head footman, had modelled her own dress and manners on those of Miss Grace and Miss Susanna, the daughters of her employer, and she'd looked down on not only the field hands, but all the lower order of workers in the house as well.

'She became secretary to their mother and read to their grandfather, who was going blind. She read him the newspapers and his correspondence, but she also read literature to him. Her favourite writer was Shakespeare. She loved *Twelfth Night*. It was always performed in the house at Christmas time when she was a small child. All the household were allowed to watch, and she never forgot it. She read it to me as a little boy. Not that I understood it, but I loved the sound of her reading it, I suppose. I still read it to myself now. I imagine the characters on the stairs in the old mansion out in the middle of the cotton fields.'

'Are you sure you wouldn't care to stay and eat with me?' she asked, dropping lumps of the meat into the blackened saucepan.

'No thank you, ma'am,' he said. 'I'd best be on my way, but thank you for the tea and the history lesson.'

'As you can see,' she said, getting up from the table and wedging the pan on the smoking fire, 'I've a good library. Please feel free to avail yourself of my books. You might want to try another Shakespeare play. *Hamlet,* perhaps,' she said, nodding to the bookcases as she led the way to the front door.

'Thank you, ma'am, I'd like to. I only have the one book with me.'

'Well call any time,' she said, opening the door. 'All my books are unpacked now, and I think I should be able to find something that might interest you. It's strange isn't it, when you unpack things in a new house, how you discover a little treasure that had slipped your mind. I'd forgotten all about my Ophelia,' she said, pointing at the picture of a red-haired girl hanging by the front door. 'Who does she remind you of?'

'I don't rightly know, ma'am,' he said.

'Why, the little girl at the cottage up the lane. Mr Barton's granddaughter. She's going to be quite a beauty.'

CHAPTER NINE

The following Saturday night, Con climbed into the back of the truck and sat down next to Holt. The wrapping around the nylons he'd bought for Rita crackled inside his jacket. Holt handed him a cigarette.

'You goin' to the movies?' he asked.

'Naw. I'm meeting Rita.'

'You got a late pass?'

'Yep.'

'And you got protection?'

'Holt, you ain't my daddy.'

'This Rita... Wes says she's...'

'She's what?'

'Older than you, and...'

'Wes don't need to talk. He didn't exactly struggle...'

'Where is he?'

'Card game. Says he don't want to come to town. Got a letter from his girl, and gone all gooey-eyed.'

'Why don't you come to the movies with the rest of us? I'll save you a place in the queue.'

'Rita ... I don't know. I might do.'

'Bring her. You need to watch your back around town. I hear some guys got into a fight.'

'Yep, with some white guys. I know. They were GIs. I'll be fine. It's a real friendly place. What you goin' to see?'

'Don't know. Just wanted to get out. Somethin' happy.'

'You got bad news?' Con asked, gazing out at the shadowy outline of the terraced houses along the road.

'Naw. It's just... Well, I suppose getting Arleen's letters... It makes Paradise Valley seem an awful long way off.'

When the truck dropped them in town, Con made his way to the old barn of a pub near the dance hall where he'd arranged to meet Rita. He waded through the smoke-fogged room until he found her sitting with a crowd of girls. When she saw him, her chubby, yellow-stained cheeks flushed with a pinky glow.

'Oh, excuse me girls,' she giggled, draining her glass. 'My bloke's here.'

The five women at the table turned, taking in his athletic frame and mellow brown skin. A pale, thin girl with heavily made up eyes gazed up at him.

'He's gorgeous,' she said, addressing Rita.

The other women continued to gape, and Con shifted uneasily. Rita got up and slipped a proprietary arm through his. Holt was right; she was older than he was. In fact, she was almost nineteen. Almost, he told himself, as old as Sadie. The thing Con liked best about Rita, though she wasn't nearly as pretty as Sadie, was that she adored him. At least, he thought she did. She certainly didn't flirt like Sadie. The night he'd met her, Rita hadn't looked at another guy, and there were plenty – at least six guys to every girl. It was like that most nights in town.

They walked across the road to the dance hall, and he followed her between the rows of seats to the dance floor, squashing the occupants who were packed so closely together they were scarcely able to drink from their glasses.

Rita barely reached his shoulder, and as they danced, Con looked around the crowded floor. Holt's warning had made him feel nervous. There were rumours around the camp of white GIs hunting in packs, ready to beat up any black guy they saw. And the thing that made them real sore was a black guy with a white girl. There were plenty of white guys in town and plenty at the dance. As well as English soldiers on leave, there were French, Dutch, Norwegians, Danes and Canadians. The week before, there'd been a group of Polish guys, who'd bowed and clicked their heels when they'd asked for a dance, and the girls had loved it. Everyone had been real friendly. None of them worried about the black GIs. They were all glad the Americans were here. It was the white GIs who were the problem. Holt had been right; it was best to stay in a group. If you came across trouble in a group, you had a chance.

'Where's the rest of them tonight? They coming later?' he asked.

'The girls will be coming over in a bit. You met Jean last week at the house. Do you remember?'

Con smiled and shook his head. His memory was hazy. He could remember dancing with Rita and complaining to Wes about the beer. She'd taken them to a pub. Then they'd moved on. Every place they'd stopped, Wes pushed a drink into his hand; he hadn't wanted to say no and be thought a baby. After a while, the places had become a blur of faces and noise. The rest was a series of images: a wet street, a cold lamp post, Rita's laugh, an old man singing and then a rough, cold wall against his face. He remembered her room with stockings hanging from a line. And then Rita's mouth, her tongue slippery and enquiring, a stale, narrow bed and folds of pliant flesh. Later, as his head cleared, those same soft layers and her round, yellow face had repulsed him, and all he'd wanted to do was escape. The nylons were to tell her that he'd been drunk and he was sorry. Then he planned to leave, and when the guys asked, he would say she'd stood him up.

At first he was going to wait until the music stopped, but when the dance ended Rita moved in close, reaching up, pressing her soft, heavy breasts against him, curling her arms around his neck. Her skin was velvety and her hair smelt good. Then the band began to play again, and the next time the music stopped, her friends were waiting on the edge of the dance floor. He danced with all of them. Between dances, they giggled and flirted with him and the other soldiers who were crowding around, waiting for a turn to dance. There was an English guy called Sid who was on leave, a couple of Norwegian sailors and a large Canadian who knew Paradise Valley well. For the first time in days, Con felt happy. Then Rita dragged him away. She left him waiting for her in the busy entrance hall, struggling drunkenly to light his cigarette, and went off to powder her nose. He hadn't noticed the group of white GIs barge through the door, or how they'd suddenly stopped joking with

218

the woman selling tickets when Rita finally came back and he'd helped her on with her coat.

Outside, the night felt mild and damp, and her lips tasted warm and sticky. When he gave her the nylons, she squealed with delight, and they swayed along the street, until she collapsed, stumbling and laughing, against an iron gate.

'Come on,' she said. 'Let's go in here.'

The old churchyard gate squeaked, and Rita giggled as she led him between the gravestones and into the protective shadow of the trees. The sky was clear. In the starlight, Con could see couples huddled together against the buttressed walls. She pulled him towards a flat, white tombstone supported by four curved pillars and then perched on the side.

'We can't go back to mine. Two of the girls I share with are on the other shift to me. They'll be sleeping. It's nice here,' she said, lying back on the white stone. 'Look up there.'

Con climbed up next to her and gazed up at the stars. They began to pulse.

'I reckon they're swaying,' he said.

'I reckon you're drunk,' she laughed.

She rolled over and began to cover his face with kisses. In the pale-blue light, her face floated above him. Rita pressed her body into his, and Con slipped an exploring hand inside her coat. He heard the iron gate creak and saw the red tips of cigarettes bouncing in the darkness. Con smiled, imagining other couples from the dance hall sneaking around looking for a place. Under his fingers, Rita's heart thrummed. She gasped and her soft weight shifted. Then the space above

219

him filled with dark shapes. He smelt stale liquor. Rita whimpered and her warmth was suddenly replaced by the cold night air.

He heard someone growl, 'Whore.'

Con tried to sit up. He could see three dim forms against the patch of sky. Hands grabbed him and held him fast. He tried to move, but his arms were clamped to the coarse stone. He kicked. There was a yelp and fingers dug into his leg. Close by, someone swore. The voice was American. From the South. He shouted, called to Rita, but she didn't answer.

He heard footsteps. Then the same voice, low and angry, gasped, 'Filthy whore.'

'Catch her,' another voice above him ordered.

Then Rita whispered, 'Don't hurt me.'

'You don't scream, and you don't get hurt,' the same voice said. 'An' you, bastard, you shout an' I'll gut her an' then you.'

'Leave her alone,' Con shouted, straining to lift his head.

The first punch made the pleasant fuzziness in his head disappear. The second made his teeth judder. When Con struggled, cold fingers probed and pressed his windpipe. His body fought for air. His lungs tore and pumped. He twisted and pulled, but he was held fast.

'Reckon we should string him up as a warning to the rest,' another voice, excited and breathless with the effort of holding him, said.

'Got no rope,' a third slow, reasonable voice replied.

'Let's cut his balls off. Not bother any white whore then, will you, boy?' the first voice said.

Then a hand slammed his head into the stone, and above him, Con heard drunken laughter.

'He don't like that idea,' the slow voice drawled. 'He don't like that idea at all.'

Then, out of the darkness, a guy shouted, 'Hey, Yanks, leave him alone.'

The laughter stopped, and the grip on his limbs slackened. Con lay still, listening, hoping.

'You leave him, you great bullies,' a woman called. 'How many of you is there?'

They let go of his arms. His legs were freed. Fingers grabbed at his hair. When his face hit the white stone, Con bit his tongue, and as his own blood flooded his nose, he remembered the smell of the dismembered rabbit.

'This is an American problem, you folks,' the first voice said. 'We got no quarrel–'

'No it ain't, mate. You leave him alone and get lost. You come late to the bloody war, like you always do, and now you want all the say.'

Con rolled on to the floor and vomited. Above him, the graveyard was full of movement. The voices were mostly English.

'Rita, love, are you all right?' he heard her friend Shirley call. 'Have they hurt you?'

'No, but they've ripped my bloody stockings,' Rita said.

'You can leave her some money for some new nylons,' he heard Sid, the English soldier, shout. 'You earn enough, and we're sick of you throwing it around.'

'No thanks,' Rita yelled. 'I'll use gravy browning, rather than take money off these bastards.'

'We'll get you, boy. You remember that,' one of

221

the three GIs whispered in his ear, before following the other two towards the gate through the crowd of jeering couples.

'That's right, mate, clear off, and find your own women,' Sid yelled after them.

'Bet no bugger will have them,' he heard Shirley call.

Above him, clouds covered the stars. Around him, the crowd laughed and then jeered some more, as the GIs made their way out of the cemetery, and Con, who had wet himself, was glad of the darkness.

Ruby counted out five shillings on to the counterpane. Christmas was only two weeks away. She needed to buy presents and hoped that Bo would get her some tobacco for Granddad. She'd wanted to send Auntie Ethel and Uncle Walt a present, but Sadie had said they wouldn't expect it and to send them a card instead, telling them what a good time she was having.

It wasn't true. At first, she'd expected a letter every day, telling Granddad to take her back. She knew Jenny thought she wasn't going to stay, but now no one mentioned her going back to Everdeane. Now, Jenny counted on her to do the cleaning, and if she complained, she pointed out that girls of her age worked nine hours a day plus overtime in the factory. Ruby rolled over on the knobbly counterpane and chinked the coins in her hand. If she did get work at the factory, she'd have more money, regular money.

She didn't earn regular money working for Mrs Grey, and now she'd gone down with a chill, the fundraising teas had been cancelled. Ruby thought that she must have been feeling ill when the American officers came for tea. At the time she'd been disappointed that Mrs Grey, who usually praised her appearance, hadn't noticed that she'd made a special effort to look smart, wearing Sadie's cream sweater over her green-and-black tartan kilt, lengthened from the top using some strips of blackout curtain, but now she realised it was because Mrs Grey hadn't been feeling well. The problem was that without the money she earned playing for the fundraising teas, there was very little cash to hand over to Jenny.

Ruby sat up and slipped on her shoes. Everyone was at work, and before she left she put a note on the table for Jenny, telling her that she'd peeled the potatoes and they were soaking in a bowl of water. Then she took her coat and basket from behind the door. Today she was going to help Alice to get the house ready for Christmas. They were going to clean the living room, and if Mrs Grey was feeling better, they would probably get out the decorations. When she arrived at Doctor Grey's, as she walked up the drive and before she turned to follow the narrow path to the back door, Ruby always pretended that she was coming home. Today she imagined that she was on her way home from boarding school for Christmas, and that Dick – who would have been sent to meet her at the station – would be bringing her trunk in the car, after he'd delivered some life-saving medicine to the hospital. In this imaginary life, instead of being Ruby, she was Cordelia, Cordelia Grey, and her mother, Diana, would be waiting for her in the living room. Then Alice would bring them tea, and they would sit together, laughing and gossiping and telling each other their news. When she opened the kitchen door, Alice was standing at the sink beating something in a mixing bowl, and Dick was sitting at the table with a collection of screws and screwdrivers on a piece of newspaper.

'Missus wants a word,' he said. 'There was a right panic here earlier on. The girl who plays Mary has mumps and–'

'That Mrs Prendergast was here first thing,' Alice said. 'Said the teacher and Father O'Flynn were in a right state.'

'And Alice told me last week, you could say the part word for word.'

'When we was doing the brasses, you did the whole thing. So Dick says to the missus to ask you.'

'"The Magnificat",' Ruby said. 'It was part of it. I could remember it from school.'

'I said she had it off pat, didn't I?' Alice said. 'I thought it must be something like that.'

'Well, the missus couldn't understand how you could have, and Alice kept telling her you did.'

'They was sat there tryin' to think who they could get, but there was no one. All the children have parts, or are off with mumps,' said Alice.

'There's I don't know how many off with it. Some of them's right bad. Poor little things. They'll miss the party, and going to the Yanks' camp to see Father Christmas. They come for them in a truck last time, and you can't take sick kiddies in a truck. Perhaps they'll get their presents sent.'

'Shut up, Dick. I'm tryin' to tell her that the missus said she wants to see her. In the end, they decided you'd have to do it, even if you're not at the school. There was no one else. You'd best go and see her now.'

As she walked towards the living room, Ruby's stomach began to squirm and wriggle. Mrs Grey was sitting on the couch, her legs tucked under a hairy picnic rug. She looked rather pale and she wasn't wearing make-up.

'Ah, Ruby,' she said, putting down the cut-glass tumbler she'd been drinking from. 'Alice and Dick have assured me that you know the part of Mary. Miss Conway needs to hear you, but we are desperate. Do you think you could do it?' she asked, swishing the golden liquid around in her glass. 'I know you can perform before people. Do say you'll have a go.'

Ruby dug her nails into her hands and took a deep breath. 'I... Please, madam... I'm to ask if there'll be a payment.'

'What on earth do you mean?'

'I'm to say are there wages?'

'Oh really, Ruby,' Mrs Grey sighed, and put her hand to her head. 'This really is too bad. I'm trying to help. The Nativity play is in jeopardy. And all you can think of–'

When the door opened, Mrs Grey put down her glass. Ruby, who didn't dare turn around to see who it was, felt her ears begin to burn.

'May I go, madam?' she asked.

'No you may not.'

The room fell silent and she stared hard at the carpet. She heard someone move to the table

225

near the door and pour out a drink. Then Doctor Grey walked by her and sat in his usual chair. He lifted one eyebrow and sipped his drink.

'We don't get paid, Ruby. It's for our community. Most people would think it an honour. Humphrey, darling, will you fill my glass? I'm exhausted.'

'Then I think you should go and lie down, dear,' he said. 'Alcohol... Unless you have a sherry. That might help your appetite.'

'I don't want a sherry. I've had the most awful day. All the children in the Nativity play have mumps, and I had hoped Ruby could help us out, but she's holding me to ransom.'

'Ruby, will you excuse us for a moment? Run along to the kitchen and tell Alice that Mrs Grey will take lunch in her room. Doctor's orders, Diana.'

Ruby sat down at the kitchen table, attacked the pile of carrots with the vegetable knife and prayed that she wouldn't be sent home and told never to come back. She'd almost peeled the whole pile when the door opened. Doctor Grey sat down and picked up a carrot.

'Was it your idea,' he asked, considering the deformed vegetable thoughtfully, 'to ask for payment?'

'I was told to... Grandma Jenny said next time to ask if there was wages.'

'Ah. Well, in that case, I think you should do whatever Mrs Grey has asked you to do, and then report to me. We can't have Mrs Grey upset. When the play is over, I want you to come to me, and I'll pay for the hours it has taken.'

226

Then Doctor Grey squeezed her hand and left. Ruby picked up the twisted carrot and began to chop. When Alice returned from taking Mrs Grey's meal up to her room, the pile was almost done and Alice remarked that, from the amount of sniffing she was doing, Ruby might be coming down with a chill, or something, as well.

'So,' Sergeant Mayfield said, looking at Con who was perched on his bed. 'You men be careful. Watch out for each other. The guys who attacked Con were southerners. No surprise there. There's a rumour some of them are tryin' to organise a clan chapel and they've got some support.'

'Not in our town,' someone called from the back of the hut.

'Don't push it,' the sergeant replied. 'I know young Con here, and the rest of you, want to have a go at these guys, but we need to keep the officers on our side. We don't want to give them any call...'

There was some restless muttering from the men in the crowded hut, and Bo, who had been leaning against the wall, pushed himself up to his full height.

'Can't agree with you there, Sarge,' he said. 'The officers ain't ever goin' to be on our side. The way I see it, we got to look out for ourselves.'

'If there's trouble, they'll start to cut down the number of passes into town.'

'They're doin' that already,' Wes said. 'We used to go into town to the movies, but now there's less late passes. There's more an' more guys stuck here all the time.'

'You said it yourself, Sarge,' one of the southern

227

soldiers added. 'You told us last week a lot of the white officers, an' most are from the South, believe black men are natural cowards. It's why they don't want us for combat. If we let 'em git away with what they done to this guy... Well then they're goin' to think they was right.'

'All I'm saying, and I think Bo will back me up on this, is that it would be wrong to go out looking for trouble. Give me a week or so. I'll see what I can find out about passes. I'm tryin' to get us more facilities here. Basketball, baseball. I got them thinkin' about it, and Lieutenant Hart is on our side. Don't want anything to happen to mess that up. All I'm sayin' is keep in groups, and don't give 'em cause to point to you as the troublemakers.'

When the group began to break up, Holt sat down beside Con. 'You fancy getting out of here for the day?' he asked. 'Bo can get passes for us and for Wes. We're picking greenery to decorate the church. We tell them we're goin' out helping, doing stuff for the church, and they don't care how long we stay away.'

The next day was cold and sunny. The privet hedges were stiff with frost, and in the distance Con could see a sugaring of snow on the hills. When he'd woken up that morning, he'd been torn between the desire to get away from the camp's drab routine and the idea of spending the day with Bo and Sadie. But once he'd looked out at the sparkling weather, he couldn't wait to leave.

When they arrived at the cottage Sadie and Lou were waiting, together with Johnny Fin, who swung himself up on to the truck and grinned his gummy grin.

'Johnny's coming with us to help us find the best stuff,' Sadie said, handing up a bag and a pair of gardening shears. 'And to pick some for the pub – and some to sell, if I know 'im.'

Sadie and Lou were dressed in boiler suits and old tweed jackets. Con noticed that, despite her practical clothes, Sadie was wearing her lipstick and a pair of earrings.

'Hello Con, love,' she smiled. 'You don't look as bad as I expected.'

'He was real bad when he got back,' Bo said.

'You've not been to see us,' Lou said, sitting down next to Con. 'You'll have to come over at Christmas, won't he, Sadie? We need some help trimming up and Ruby's in the play at church, so you'll have to come to that and join in the carols.'

'Con remembered one of their voices,' Bo said. 'This guy had this real slow way of talkin' and he'd recognise his voice again. There's a lot of trouble in town. Some of our guys ran into this big blond sergeant called Hal. Our sarge asked around and he reckons he knows who the guy is. Been around here before.' Sadie, who had been lighting her cigarette, stopped and looked over at Johnny Fin who twitched violently, bumping into Con's still-tender ribs.

'Sound... sounds like the same bloke as used to sell black-market stuff round the pubs,' he said. 'Went down to the south...'

'The south... That's right,' Bo said. 'Well, he's back.'

'You know him?' Holt asked.

For a moment there was silence, and Sadie looked out at the passing landscape and shivered.

'Keep clear of him,' Johnny said. 'He can be an awkward sod.'

He directed them out of the village and away from the flat, open country they had driven through in their trucks. The lanes were steep and deserted, with only a scattering of farmhouses and cottages. To the west, they could see the coast. Inland, there were the mill chimneys each with streets cross-hatched around them and near the centre of the town a tall, white spire. When they climbed down from the truck, Johnny led the way along a steep, rutted path between the trees. At the top of the climb they could see the flat, open valley and the river swinging out in a long crescent towards the town. It was clear that their guide knew the wood well and he found them enough fresh greenery to fill the truck. Under Johnny's direction they worked methodically, cutting down the boughs of holly with the brightest berries, hacking down branches of evergreen and picking the mistletoe hidden in the knobbly oaks, but when they began bundling up the greenery to carry back along the narrow path, Johnny disappeared.

'I know where the old bugger will have gone,' Sadie said. 'Listen.' In the wood, in the cold air, they could hear the sound of sawing. 'He's after fetching some logs.'

Johnny was in a clearing, his jacket on the floor, his back and legs bent and his toes turned in. He was pushing at his saw, straining with the effort as the teeth sank deeper into the trunk. Bo and Holt took off their tunics and took a turn with the saw. Lou and Sadie held the rough hessian sacks, and Con helped Wes to collect the logs.

'See, I told you he was crafty,' Sadie laughed. 'I thought you'd brought these sacks for us to sit on and have our butties. You said you just wanted some holly.'

Johnny smiled, his eyes sapphire blue in the frosty sunlight. 'We can walk round t'other side, when we've done this. There's some sights the lads might like to see, and there's some rocks there we can sit on. They'll be in the sunshine.'

When they'd filled the sacks, they followed Johnny out of the wood and along the top of the rocky escarpment. Out to the west, near the horizon, they caught the shimmer of the sun on the sea. To the south, in the middle of the rolling pasture, there was a single hill, little more than a mound, with a castle poised on top and the river snaking around it. Con laughed and turned to the others. Their faces reflected his surprise at the storybook castle, barely three miles from the clattering mills.

'It's real beautiful,' he said.

'Aye, it's a bonny thing.'

They sat down on a muddle of flat grey stones, and Sadie handed out sandwiches and cold tea from a billycan.

'It's almost like spring,' Lou said.

'It'll not be, later,' Johnny said, munching his sandwich. 'I can smell snow.'

Con sniffed. The air was cold, clear, but there were no clouds.

'You could bring your girl with you to the play and stay for your tea,' Sadie said, ignoring Bo's warning look.

Con pressed his still-swollen lip. 'I don't see Rita no more,' he said.

'Well come for your tea, anyway. Oh, I almost forgot. I've got some whisky to put in the tea, if you're a bit cold.'

'I'll have some, lass,' Johnny said, holding out his tin mug. 'You come down to Henry's, lad, and I'll show you how to box, and next time...'

'Boxing wouldn't have helped none,' Bo said, getting up to give Sadie a hand collecting the waxed wrapping paper from their sandwiches. 'There was three of them against him. Come on, let's get this stuff back.'

When the others began to move away, Con stayed, looking at the castle in the sunshine.

'You okay love?' Sadie asked.

'It's so pretty here,' he said, 'when it stops raining.'

Ruby was looking out through the high classroom windows at the blue, cloudless sky. Miss Conway, who had already reduced most of the choir to tears at least once, crashed to the end of 'Silent Night' and began to shout. Pauline rolled her eyes, and Ruby grinned. She already knew her lines, where to stand and how to move, but the more time Miss Conway kept them at it, the more hours she could tell Doctor Grey she'd spent on the rehearsal.

When Miss Conway began to play the next carol, Pauline wandered over and propped her elbows on the windowsill next to Ruby's.

'It's not their fault,' she said. 'It's Miss Conway. She's playing much too high.'

232

They heard the jeep on the road before they saw it, and when the driver swung into the playground, they stood on tiptoe to see who would get out.

'That's Captain Leary,' Ruby said. 'I've seen him at Mrs Grey's.'

'He's nice.'

'The other one, Captain O'Donal, is nicer. He looks like Rhett Butler.'

Just then, Captain Leary looked up at the school windows, and the two girls ducked their heads below the sill. When they looked out again, Mrs Grey, dressed in a pale-blue fitted coat and a blue hat with a peacock feather, was standing next to the American.

'Do you think they're in love?' Pauline asked.

Ruby gazed at the couple in the middle of the playground and thought of the handsome, if rather short, Doctor Grey.

'They can't be,' she said. 'She's married to Doctor Grey.'

'That doesn't matter,' Pauline said knowledgably. 'Scarlett was in love with Ashley Wilkes, and he was married.'

They watched as the couple walked by the window, and Ruby had to admit that Captain Leary did look very smart in his uniform. They didn't notice that the singing had stopped, until Miss Conway joined them at the window.

'Ah, good,' she said. 'Captain Leary is here. The two of you can go and get our guests a cup of tea. They'll be in my office.'

The door to the office was only just ajar, but they could hear Mrs Grey laughing. Ruby was about to knock and ask if they would like tea

233

when everything went silent.

'They might be kissing,' Pauline whispered. 'My mum says she's no better than she should be. Folk say she's from London, and she leads poor Doctor Grey a right dance.'

As she edged nearer, Ruby was glad to see that Mrs Grey and the captain were standing on either side of the stout oak table.

'May I be frank?' the captain was saying. 'This isn't the army's idea. It's political. Can I offer you a cigarette?' he asked, walking around to her side of the table.

'Well, if we're being frank,' Mrs Grey said, accepting a cigarette, 'I would have thought they'd have been more suited to a warmer climate.'

'The trouble is, you see,' the captain said, lighting her cigarette, 'they were sent because there's a lot of angling for the black vote in the elections.'

Relieved that Pauline had been wrong about Mrs Grey and the captain, Ruby tapped on the door.

'Please, madam,' she said. 'Miss Conway said to ask if you would like tea.'

'Were they having a cuddle?' Pauline asked, when Ruby joined her by the chipped sink in the caretaker's room.

'No. They were talking,' Ruby said, watching Pauline trickle cold water into the old enamel kettle.

The small room smelt of paraffin and dust and held broken desks and an assortment of tools. Pauline lit a gas ring on the small stove by the door, opened the wooden cupboard standing next to it and bent down.

'What about? Did you hear? What was he saying? I think it's funny how they talk, don't you?'

Ruby bit her lip. She rubbed a finger in the fine powdery dust on the workbench and studied the rows of small wooden boxes hanging from the brick wall above it. She wasn't sure what she'd heard. It was something about the soldiers, but she hadn't really understood it.

Pauline reached into the cupboard and dragged out a brown teapot, two pale-green cups with matching saucers and a wooden tray with a picture of two bright-yellow birds painted on it. Then she got out a small milk jug, and taking off the cover – a circular cloth, held down with small red beads spaced evenly around the edge – she sniffed at the contents and swirled the liquid around. Finally, she added a matching sugar bowl to the tray and scraped the tiny amount of sugar sticking to the sides back down into the bowl.

'What are you doing, girls?' Miss Conway called from the classroom door. 'How long does it take to make a cup of tea? In here now, Pauline, please. Ruby, take in the tea and then come over to the hall, and be quick about it!'

'My mam's going to be mad if I'm not home soon,' Pauline said, sprinkling the tea leaves from a black-and-gold tea caddy into the pot.

Ruby couldn't knock at the partly open door because she had the tray in her hands. As she hesitated, deciding if it would be better to take the tray back to the caretaker's room and then to knock, or if she should put the tray down on the stone floor, she heard the captain's voice.

'...or limited access. One town, one colour. The

235

town nearest each camp limited to blacks or whites. The solution to the problems with the Christmas celebrations... Though, I suppose we can't ask him to limit attendance at church services. What do you think?'

Mrs Grey, who was sitting at the table, picked up her pen. 'So to recap,' she said. 'Separate entertainment. Advice, unofficially, through church groups and the WRVS, about the risk of disease, and local shopkeepers to be told not to encourage them... Ah, there you are,' she said, getting up from the table and opening the door wide. 'Good girl.'

Ruby put the tray down. 'Shall I pour, madam?' she asked.

'No, dear,' Mrs Grey said, giving Ruby one of her prettiest smiles. 'Off you go. Ruby is such a clever girl, Captain. Not only can she play and act beautifully, she can also magic cups of tea out of thin air. Thank you, Ruby. The captain and I will help ourselves.'

When Ruby left the school building, the fading light had turned the church into a greying hulk against the pale-gold sky. As she reached the yard the infants used as their playground, a truck pulled in through the gates. She could see Bo behind the wheel. She waved and slipped inside the hall.

'That was Ruby,' Sadie said. 'She could have stopped and given us a hand. Bet that miserable old bat of a teacher has her running errands.'

'Before you start handing that stuff down,' Johnny Fin said, as he and Con jumped down from the truck, 'let's get organised. Is it all going in the hall, Sadie?'

'No. Some's goin' in the church, for the crib and the altar, but most of it has to go in here. I hope nobody asks how we got it.'

'I'll say it was off a well-wisher.'

'An' who's that?'

'M-m-m-me,' he laughed. 'I-I-I cut it down, so it's from me.'

With Bo and Lou's help, Sadie dragged the branches of holly and greenery off the back of the truck into two piles.

'That lot's for the church,' she said. 'You can help yourself to some of it. The rest is for the hall, and we'll need the stepladders and some nails.'

'Steps is in the vestry,' Johnny said. 'I was using 'em during the week. Nails is there as well. If you lads come with me, we'll bring the steps and nails and we'll bring the Christmas tree in off the lorry. If you climb down, I'll pass some of this stuff, and Lou can help you to start carryin' it in.'

As Sadie struggled to get the branches of holly through the door, the children came pushing out.

'You packing up?' she asked.

'Yep, she's sent us home, at last,' Pauline said. 'She's got Ruby putting furniture back.'

When they staggered into the hall, Miss Conway looked up from the piano, where she was sorting through the sheet music.

'We've brought some greenery for trimming up,' Sadie said.

'Well, you can't do it now. I'm about to leave, and there's nobody to lock up.'

'That's all right, I'll do that,' she replied. 'I know how.'

237

'But I can't just leave the key with just anyone... Ah, here's Mrs Grey. I didn't realise you were staying to supervise the festive decorations, Diana.'

'I shan't be. What lovely greenery. Father O'Flynn is on his way over and he's agreed to stay and supervise. We've just finished our meeting. Here he is now with Captain Leary. I really must be going. Doctor Grey will be home shortly.'

'Can I offer you a lift, Diana?' Captain Leary asked. 'And Miss Conway, of course. I have to get back to camp, but I'd be happy to drop both you ladies off at your homes.'

'That would be most kind. I must admit, I'm feeling quite exhausted.'

'That's very kind of you, Captain,' Miss Conway said. 'I'll go and collect my things from my classroom.'

'It will be a pleasure, ma'am. We'll wait for you in the jeep. I'm sorry I have to leave, Father,' Captain Leary said. 'I could ask for a detail to be sent over to help with the heavy work.'

'No. Thank you for the thought, but as you can see, I have plenty of helpers to put the decorations up in the hall.'

'Indeed, Father. Thank you, again, for your generous invitation to my men. I'm sure your efforts will be appreciated, ladies,' he said, smiling at Lou and Sadie. 'My, you have been busy.'

'Oh, this is only part of it,' Sadie said. 'There's some to go up in the church as well.'

As Captain Leary and Mrs Grey turned to leave, the door opened. Bo and Holt staggered in carrying the stepladder, followed by Con and Johnny Fin with the fir tree Johnny had cut down for them. For a moment, the group hesitated, standing awkwardly with the ladder swaying above their heads. Then Bo nodded to the officer and he and Holt carried the heavy wooden ladder over to the wall. Captain Leary didn't wait for an explanation, or for a formal recognition of his status, and in the darkening room, they heard the sound of his jeep as he rode back along the road.

'Where's he from?' Bo asked.

'That's Captain Leary,' Father O'Flynn said.

'White camp,' Bo said, opening the steps and testing their stability.

'I told you, Father,' Sadie said, 'if we could have our dance, I'd get you all the greenery you wanted. You should see how much there is for the church, and Johnny's got a lot as well. No doubt, there'll be holly and mistletoe all over the pubs. Come on, let's get on with it. I've got all sorts of ideas and I've got some wire from Henry's shed. What we really need is some hooks. He claimed he didn't have any. Will you lads get the rest of the stuff out of the truck? Ruby, love, put them chairs down and help Lou with the blinds, and then we can put the lights on.'

'Sadie,' Father O'Flynn said, sitting down heavily on the piano stool. 'There might be problems ... about the dance. There might be difficulties about inviting the black troops...'

'What?'

'Mrs Grey tells me there have been concerns. The police and the authorities... There's been trouble in town, and it's not their custom... They – Captain Leary and Mrs Grey – they don't want them to be invited.'

'Whose church is it? You tell them you'll not–'

'Sadie, I'm your priest.'

'Sorry, Father, but–'

'I have the interests of all my parishioners to consider. The children are going to his camp, and it was suggested that his men come back here, as an appreciation–'

'Well they can, but so can the lads from–'

'No. They don't mix. It's how they are in their own country... There are very few contacts between black and white GIs.'

'It's not how we are.'

'They are our guests. The feeling is that we should ... fit in.'

'You're trying to fit in with the doctor's stuck-up wife and the Prendergasts. I bet they have something to do with it. There's some folk think the war's run for them. Never been so important. In charge of everything. The lads have helped in the village. Ask anybody.'

Ruby put down the stack of infants' chairs she was carrying and sat down on one of them next to the window. Her knees were trembling. She remembered that Mr Prendergast had said something about dealing with the black troops the day Captains Leary and O'Donal came to tea. She'd been excited about serving, getting everything right. Then later, when she'd tried to hear what they were planning about the dances, Mrs Grey had caught her and sent her away. At the time, she hadn't understood what she'd heard, although she knew all about what had happened with John Bardley's tractor and the MPs.

In the dark hall, her nose filled with the smell of

the dusty curtains, but in her imagination, Ruby was in the porch at Doctor Grey's. The meeting had finished, and the two American officers were leaving. Mrs Grey was smiling; her hair had turned to silver in the lamplight. As Captain Leary pulled on his gloves, he'd turned to her and said, 'Would you go tell my boy we're ready to go.' At first she hadn't understood, but then Mrs Grey had said sharply, 'Ruby go and get the captain's driver.' And then she'd realised that he'd meant Michael.

She pushed her body against the grubby curtains, hoping that Sadie wouldn't be angry and want to know why she hadn't told her what had been said at the tea party. When the door to the church hall banged open again it made her jump, and across the dark hall, she saw Bo and Con staggering in under an unstable pile of greenery.

'I thought you would have started already,' Bo said. 'Is there something wrong with the lights?'

No one answered. Then Sadie took hold of Con's arm and pulled him over to the piano stool where Father O'Flynn was sitting.

'No there isn't,' she said. 'Bo, put that light on. Look at him,' she said, turning Con's swollen face towards the priest.

'Sadie, you are to respect my cloth, if not me.'

'Never mind that. Look at him. That's your white soldiers, three of 'em, and he's just a kid. Well, you can forget your bloody greenery. Put it up yourself. Ruby, leave them tables and chairs. He can put them away himself as well. There'll be no dance. Not for you,' she said, looking over at Bo. 'That captain, he said thank you for inviting

241

his men, and they're white GIs. You've agreed with them. You're goin' to do what they say. It's not fair. They don't come to our shops and pubs and help our old folk chop firewood like these lads do.'

'Yes, I have made my decision, Sadie,' Father O'Flynn said. 'The white GIs will be invited by the church ... as Christians, as Catholics... The church has a responsibility. Pastoral care. Let me finish. The men have a right to worship at Christmas and be offered the friendship of fellow Christians. I will contact Father Basil. His church is the nearest to Captain Leary's camp, and if he agrees to invite the white GIs there... Now, do you have something to say to me?'

In the starkly lit hall, Sadie bowed her head, but when she spoke her voice still sounded angry.

'I'm sorry,' she said. 'I should have–'

'Yes, you should, and if I didn't need you to put up my greenery, I'd throw you out now. Still, I can think of a better penance. You can do the crib in the church, as well as decorate this place.'

'I'm sorry. I was... Will you get in trouble? The Prendergasts and Mrs Grey...'

'Probably so, probably so.'

'Well, thank you.'

'It's not for you, Miss Sadie, pretty though you are,' the old priest said, getting up from the stool and tweaking Sadie's flushed cheek between his fat fingers. 'It's for myself. That I can look at myself and tell the Lord I did what I thought was right. That the good captain heard only what he chose to hear is no fault of mine. Now, I'm away to my supper. My housekeeper will bring something for yourselves, and when you have done, I'll be at the

242

Railway Inn, waiting for you to buy me a drink or two to soothe my pride and steel me against the onslaught of the Prendergasts.'

CHAPTER TEN

Ruby adjusted the borrowed headscarf and opened the church door. She took her place at the end of the short row of penitents waiting for Confession, pushing the hem of her coat under her knees to spare her precious nylons from the kneeler's rough surface. As everyone in the small group shifted, edging along the bare wooden kneeler, the sound of each tiny movement tumbled forward, rolling and splashing through the empty church. The chancery light winked in the gloom, and the greenery looped around the feet of each of the saints caught in the glow of the votive candles.

After Sadie had cheeked Father O'Flynn, everyone helped to do her 'penance'. They'd worked in the hall until late on Saturday and gone back there on Sunday, spending most of the morning under the stage, dragging out the grimy, life-size plaster figures of the Holy Family and the shepherds from behind a pile of old scenery flats. It had been Con's idea to use one of them – a picture of a garden and a blue sky seen through a French window – as a backdrop for the crib. They'd carried it into the hall, where he'd sketched out the skyline of the town of Bethlehem against the blue sky and the stark domed houses of a Bethlehem street. A few days later, she'd helped Sadie fill them in, using white paint stolen from the camp. Now the flat, with the figures of the Holy Family and the shepherds in front of it, was behind a curtain in the alcove next to the confessional box, waiting to be unveiled on Christmas Eve.

To ease the pressure on her knees, Ruby tried leaning on the bench in front, taking the weight of her body on her arms and cautiously raising each knee in its turn. She sniffed at the unfamiliar scarf. It belonged to Jenny who'd given it her to wear when Father O'Flynn had insisted that, if she was to take the part of Mary in the Nativity play, she must come to Confession. Ruby liked the pattern of fruit and leaves, and the fine, loosely woven wool felt expensive, but the colours – yellow, rust and orange – didn't suit her and she pulled the edges down to cover her red hair.

Each person who came out of the confessional box clattered their way across the church to say their penance in the benches opposite. The first was an elderly man with a twisted ear, who whispered the familiar words of the Hail Mary, as if each prayer was a secret. When the next one – the plump woman who worked in the chemist – walked across, her movements set off an explosion that had barely stopped rumbling before she got up and headed for the door, leaving Ruby to wonder why she'd been given such a small penance.

The door of the confessional led into a small box. There was a square grille with a narrow ledge in front of it and a kneeler fixed to the floor. Ruby knelt down. At the other side, Father O'Flynn drew the curtain slightly open as a signal for her to begin. The box smelt of caramels and mould. Ruby adjusted the ends of her coat over her knees. When they'd learnt about Confession, she'd imagined that her soul was a dishcloth of coarse knitted cotton and her sins were splodges to be cleaned away. At school, the whole class had been taken to Confession on the first Friday of every month. Then, her sins were always about arguing with her mother, or being jealous of Mavis, who'd a lot of friends. Now, shut in the tiny airless box, Ruby searched her soul, but instead of definite splodge-shaped sins, the knitted cotton was grubby with use. Father O'Flynn asked how long it was since her last Confession, and in the church the kneelers thudded. She wondered if it was a sin to wish that, instead of being Ruby and living with Granddad and Jenny, she was Cordelia, and Doctor and Mrs Grey were her parents. Were dreams sins? In another dream, she was on the stage in the Nativity play, and when she looked down, there was Pearl and her father, dressed as they'd been when they'd gone out to the Christmas dance, smiling up at her. Did that count as vanity, or was it some sort of lie?

'Have you lost your temper, or said unkind things?' the priest asked.

'Why did he take my mum away?'

'It wasn't Our Lord who did that, child. It was just an accident. You must pray to Our Lord to give you strength. I'm sure your poor mother is watching over you. Offer up your suffering to Our Lord Jesus and to His mother.'

Back in the cold church, Ruby watched the

puffs of white breath escape from her fellow penitents and hoped that the priest was right. She hoped that Pearl was watching, but each day her memory of her mother, like the perfume on the clothes in her trunk, was fading.

The following afternoon, Ruby sat happily on a small wooden chair eating one of Pauline's sandwiches and watching the school clock track the hours to the beginning of the performance. Unlike Miss Conway and some of the choir, Ruby didn't suffer from performance nerves. Sitting by the pipes, with her blue cloak already pressed and hanging from a nail above the window, she was cocooned against the growing hysteria in the hall. It was a true state of grace: she'd got out of doing Doctor Grey's washing and had Pauline all to herself. On the other side of the room, the serious boy playing Joseph was having his false beard attached by his mother.

'Sit down there, Trevor,' his mother said, dropping a cardboard box on to one of the small tables. 'Miss Conway has asked me to use as little glue as possible. It's difficult to replace, and they are hoping to do *The Pirates of Penzance* before Lent. There are quite a few beards, but she's given me the most suitable. Goodness, it doesn't look very clean.'

Trevor folded his body into a tiny infants' chair, but when his mother shook out the beard, the stale make-up holding it together escaped, leaving the horrified woman clasping two ragged clumps of black horsehair. Behind the shelter of the blue cloak, Ruby and Pauline giggled and

246

shared the last sandwich.

'His mother wants him to be a priest,' Pauline whispered. 'She told my ma she goes to Mass every Friday to pray that he has a vocation, but he hasn't had the call yet. Anne thinks he'd be nice-looking without his glasses. She even sent him a note in class pretending to be me and asking him to take them off. He didn't, and now he goes red every time he sees me. I think that's why I'm the angel instead of Mary. Still, Anne is prettier and she has dark hair, and in the picture we have in our house, Mary's hair is dark, although it's not curly like Anne's.'

'No. It's because you have blonde hair,' Ruby said. 'Angels always have blonde hair.'

Pauline looked pleased and hitched her coat over her flimsy white tunic. 'I want my hair like Sadie's. I want it cut short and permed just like hers. Mum says I'm too young and I'll have to wait until I start work.' Pauline adjusted her tinsel halo and sighed. 'Sadie's that pretty. I saw her waiting for the bus with one of them black soldiers. Is he her boyfriend?'

'Mmm, Bo,' Ruby said, watching Trevor's mother furtively applying glue to her son's face.

'He's really handsome. Mum says all of 'em are that good with the kids. They're always playing with them on the rec. You work at Doctor Grey's, don't you? I don't fancy skivvying for folk. I'm going to work in a factory. A girl I know is starting at one next week making tents. It's really good money, but I don't know if they'll take someone my age on. Some places they want older, but I've asked her to find out for me.'

'Lou, Sadie's friend, she works there. It's good hours, but she says it's mucky work. It's the wax. It gets in their eyes. It makes their noses bleed, as well. So now, they only work on tents for half a day, and another shift works on them in the afternoon. Lou said they looked that daft, all of 'em coming home with their noses plugged. Hers was still bleeding that night.'

On the other side of the room, Trevor's mother was persuading him into his costume.

'He'll have to take his glasses off,' Pauline said fidgeting with her wings. Then, lifting the delicate things from their place on the table to hide her face, she whispered, 'Joseph wouldn't have worn glasses.'

The two girls studied Trevor, who was now dressed in an old dressing gown and had a tea towel on his head.

'Them black soldiers from the camp are coming to sing with the choir,' Pauline said. 'Miss Conway's not that pleased. I heard her say to Father O'Flynn that it was a waste of time teaching the little 'uns to sing, if they was goin' to do it. But he said they'd just do one of their own songs and "Silent Night", and the children could do the rest. And then they're goin' to give out presents at the end. Are you invited to the kids' Christmas do at the camp? I am. Me and Anne will be helping with the infants. You should ask if you can as well. I think she'll be coming, if she's well enough by then. She wanted to come and do this instead of you, but her mum said she couldn't, as it might have put her back. Her mum works at the same place as Sadie. Anne has to look after her little brother and sister and their neighbour's kiddie as well. Her and Anne's mother work opposite shifts, so they all have their teas together. Depending on whose mum is at work, they have them at Anne's, or Anne and the little ones go next door. I've been helping. All the kids have been ill, and I've already had mumps when I was four. I'm going to her house on Boxing Day. Her mum's making us a party.'

Jealousy nibbled at Ruby's stomach. Through the window, she could see parents arriving with the younger children. Johnny and the caretaker began carrying in long wooden benches for the audience to sit on, and the haven she'd been sharing with Pauline started to fill with excited infants. Then Trevor's mother beckoned to them to follow her to the back of the stage, where she helped Pauline fix her wings and tugged at the white veil on Ruby's head, until she was satisfied that it completely covered her hair. As the children began the first carol, they could see through a gap in the curtain that, with the exception of the chair occupied by Captain O'Donal, the seats reserved for dignitaries at the front of the hall were empty.

'Doctor Grey has probably been called out on an emergency,' Trevor's mother said, peering over Ruby's shoulder. 'Mrs Grey is still quite poorly, and the Prendergasts have pleaded war work.'

Then Father O'Flynn began the first Bible reading, Pauline and Ruby took their places on the stage and the old gentleman in charge of pulling back the curtain balanced on the balls of his feet and reached for the rope.

After the second reading, when Ruby followed

249

Joseph out in front of the curtain for their encounter with the innkeeper, she was pleased to see that Doctor Grey had arrived, but instead of Mrs Grey, the seat next to him was occupied by a lady who was expecting a baby and a couple of very elderly men with walking sticks were sitting in the Prendergasts' seats. The next scene was in the stable. As the crib was hurriedly set up and the straw scattered, she heard the GIs begin to sing a soft, melancholy song she didn't recognise. Everyone took their places among the straw. Instead of a baby in the crib there was a light bulb, but when the choir came to the end of the song and the curtains were about to be drawn back, the light symbolising the Holy Infant went out. As the old man working the curtains tottered and swayed, the caretaker, whose job it had been to set up the crib, frantically worked the switch, but no light came on. On the other side of the curtain, the noise began to build. Then suddenly Trevor darted forward and gave the bulb a sharp twist. Instantly, the crib was ablaze with light, the curtains were drawn back to reveal the tableau, the audience gasped and softly the GIs began to sing 'Silent Night'.

Con and Holt watched the performance from the back of the hall. Earlier, when the band of infant angels had left the classroom, they'd carried the boxes of candy bars and other treats in from the truck. When the guys at the camp heard that the priest had stood up for the black GIs, they'd all wanted to come and sing, or buy candy for the kids, and it was certain that the old priest wouldn't want for a free drink while the truck companies

250

were stationed nearby. The only person who didn't seem too happy was Captain O'Donal. He hadn't said as much but he looked uneasy, and they'd all noticed that things around the camp had become tighter: the huts were checked more carefully for inappropriate reading materials, card games were regularly broken up and gambling of any kind was punished. There'd always been black newspapers going around the camp, but O'Donal, if he'd known that copies were being handed around, hadn't taken too much interest. Now any articles from these papers were confiscated. Still, as more men moved in, it was harder to keep watch on all of them, and there was a new guy on his way whose job it would be to organise the promised leisure facilities.

Con recognised most of the readings and carols as those his father used at Christmas in his church in Paradise Valley, and if he'd closed his eyes, he could almost have been at home. The thing that had surprised him most was Ruby's confident performance. On the stage, in front of the audience, she'd become a different girl, and when the curtains opened on the final tableau, it was as though a painting of the Nativity had come to life in front of them. As the choir began to sing the people got to their feet and joined in, many of them weeping, hoping, he guessed, that by next Christmas the war would be over. Con felt the same way: he found it hard to remember the feeling of excitement that had driven him to enlist in the first place. In the early days, when he'd first joined up, he'd been desperate to become a soldier. A lot of the guys he'd met in training wanted the excitement of leaving the States, and he had as well, but most of all he'd wanted to fight for America, because his country was under attack. Now, after the trouble with the white GIs, he thought that even if they'd let him, he might be too scared to fight. He wanted to be the boy he'd been in Paradise Valley, and this time he'd have listened to his mother and gone to college. It wasn't something he could admit to anybody, not even to his parents. He felt for their letter in his pocket and swallowed hard.

When the carols and the readings had ended, the soldiers gave out the sweets and chocolate to the excited children, and although Ruby and Pauline thought they were a bit old for such treats, they queued up with the rest.

'I see that Mrs Grey's not here,' Jenny said, as she tucked the chocolate Ruby had been given into her bag. 'I've just heard him telling somebody that she's too ill to come, but Henry saw her going off in her brother's car. She'd not want to face these lads. That's what it will be, after her trying to get them stopped from coming here.'

'You was that good, Ruby,' Sadie said. 'Wasn't she, Ma?'

'Aye, very good.'

Ruby smiled and Granddad winked at her. 'Theatre's in the family,' he said. 'Isn't it, love?'

Ruby blushed. She was enjoying the attention, and although the money she was going to get was important, she couldn't help feeling pleased by the admiring glances and smiles from the people who'd been in the audience. Father O'Flynn had squeezed her arm, and even Miss Conway smiled. The only thing that spoilt it was that Mrs Grey wasn't there.

'I think it must have been what Mrs Prendergast told her,' she said.

'What do you mean?' Sadie asked, accepting a cigarette from Jenny.

'She said, in America... Well, they don't mix, and so they shouldn't here.'

'She didn't have to agree with her, now did she? Doctor Grey doesn't. He's here,' she said. 'He's over there chatting with some of the lads now. So why is she so set on it?'

Ruby didn't reply, but she knew that it was probably something to do with them being friends: Doctor Grey was away a lot, and organising the fundraising lunches and other things with the Prendergasts made her happy. Ruby could understand that. Mrs Grey was probably lonely; Mrs Prendergast was her friend, even though she was as old as Auntie Ethel and really bossy. She walked over to Pauline, who was helping her little brother on with his coat.

'I still take Bess out sometimes,' she said. 'I could bring her down to the rec again, or we could take her out for a walk... Next Sunday, I could–'

'I'm going to Anne's Sunday afternoon,' Pauline said, as the little boy tugged her towards the door. 'We're putting up their tree. I'll have to go. My mum's over there waiting for us.'

That evening there were shirts to soak. After tea, Sadie and Bo had gone into town, and then Jenny and Granddad left for the pub. But when the door closed behind them, instead of settling into a placid silence, the house felt uneasy. Ruby wandered between the dismal front room and the kitchen. Before Bo became Sadie's boyfriend, she would have gone across the lane and asked Mrs Lathom if she might have Bess for company. But now, when she asked if Bess could come and stay with her, Mrs Lathom made an excuse, although she still allowed her to take the spaniel out for walks. Then, as Ruby was peering into the mirror over the sink, trying to twist up her hair into a sleek roll, the hens began to squawk. She picked up the long-handled brush, turned off the light and went into the garden. The henhouse was locked and the birds were safe. But close by, among the fruit bushes, there was an almost imperceptible movement. Using the brush, she slashed at the leaves: a prowling fox might not get in the cabin, but it might put the hens off laying. Then she stood in the starlit garden and listened, until the hens began to settle. The air was damp, and once she was happy that she'd driven the fox away, she hurried back inside. For a moment, when she switched on the light, Ruby's brain refused to make sense of the black, formless thing crouched on the kitchenette. Then it turned towards her and spat. The animal, the largest, most evil-looking cat she had ever seen, held its ground, lashing out with its claws and hissing when she tried to dislodge it with the end of the brush. The creature was guarding the remnants of the chicken that she should have put away in the meat safe, and Ruby, who was poking at it furiously, didn't hear Mrs Bland at the door until she spoke.

'It's only me, dear,' the old lady said, edging through the door. 'I didn't mean to make you jump. I knocked at the front door, but no one

254

answered. I'm looking for– Ah, you're here, and you've made friends already,' she said to the cat, as it began to rip at the remaining meat. 'Is Ruby feeding you? How kind.'

'He got in. I left the door open... I thought it was a fox going after the hens. That chicken ... there was enough for tomorrow.'

'Oh dear. Poor Ruby. Please don't be distressed. Was that for your...? Timoshenko can be such a rascal. I'll go and get his basket. Then, if we can persuade him into it... Yes. That might be best.'

The cat ignored his mistress's concern for Ruby's welfare, and turning its back on them both, continued eating the chicken. When the old lady had gone, Ruby pulled Henry's old coat from the back door and made a grab for it. The startled animal thrashed and yowled, but she hung on, rolling him inside the coat and carrying the struggling bundle to Mrs Bland's cottage. Once he was released, Timoshenko took up position on the stairs, lashing and spitting furiously as his owner tried to scold him.

'I know you didn't mean it, but it was very wrong of you to take Ruby's supper. It's his experience of the bombing, I'm afraid. He's had to fend for himself for some time and his manners are not what they should be. I'm sure if we leave him for a while, he'll calm down.'

Mrs Bland insisted on cleaning up Ruby's scratches with her own herbal liniment and then made cocoa. The little room was chilly and the old lady was wearing a selection of worn jumpers under her old tweed jacket. As they sipped their cocoa, she put a record on the gramophone and began nodding in time with the wistful music.

'I've been meaning to ask if you would consider some cleaning. Have you some hours to spare? I need someone to help clean the books. You would need to be trained. They were bombed, and then the storage was less than satisfactory. They will need very careful treatment,' she said, picking up one of her grubby leather-bound books and brushing it as gently as if it were a child's sooty face. 'I'm afraid I can't pay you much.'

'I don't mind, but Jenny will expect... I have to pay my way. I'll be getting a job in a factory soon, but until then, I'd like to help.'

'Ah, you're someone who loves books.'

'Yes. I like reading. I've read all my dad's books.'

'Now, what would you like, I wonder? You must let me think about that, and I'll see what I can find that might interest you.'

Once the excitement of the Nativity play was over, Ruby began to look forward to the time she spent with Mrs Bland and her angry cat. The war meant that Granddad, Jenny and Sadie were working longer hours. Often they would be on different shifts and want to eat at different times. There was a build-up of American troops as well. That meant Bo and the other GIs were busy bringing in more equipment and didn't visit so much. The house was often empty, and when she had finished her work, she would sometimes go and help Mrs Bland with her books. The war also meant that food was harder to get, and in addition to the cooking, Ruby was also responsible for the shopping and queuing.

She would often shop on her way to Doctor Grey's, and then on her way home she would sometimes walk the long way round through the village again to check if there was a queue outside the Co-op or the butcher's. At least, that's what she told herself, but the walk also took her by the school at about the time Pauline would be on her way home. A few days after the Nativity play, as Ruby turned the corner by the chemist's, there was a queue of women waiting outside the butcher's. She hurried across the road.

'He's got pork,' the woman in front of her said. 'That's the rumour. Pork, recently killed.'

Ruby pushed her hands deep into her pockets and hunched her shoulders against the damp. More people joined the queue, but the line in front didn't move. Up ahead of her, she could see Aunt Maud. She hadn't spoken to her since the day she'd let it slip to Jenny that she and Granddad had called at Maud's house. Her granddad still sent his sister vegetables and fruit from his garden, but now he didn't risk taking the parcels himself. He was so scared of Jenny that – instead of handing the vegetables over to Ruby in the garden – he would whisper that there was something for 'our Maud' in the hedge by the gate and that she must leave it on Maud's doorstep on her way to Doctor Grey's.

'Not a word to Jenny now, love,' he would murmur, 'best to keep the peace.'

Alice and Dick would sometimes give her left-over food for 'poor Maud' as well. And today, with a woollen shawl over her head and wrapped tightly over a shabby black dress, Auntie Maud reminded

257

Ruby of the beggar women from the Marshalsea Prison in the book Mrs Bland had given her to read.

The shop window was empty, except for the statues of two smiling pigs, standing on their hind trotters and dressed in chef's outfits. Inside, the walls were tiled – white with a blue border. The waiting women chatted happily amongst themselves, pacifying their babies with the small home-made toys hanging from the hoods of the prams and keeping the toddlers occupied with small crusts of bread and promises of bacon for tea. The good-natured queue only began to turn restless when a well-dressed woman with bright-red lips hurried out of the shop, calling a cheery goodbye to the butcher. Her departure was followed by a ripple of discontent, as the women waiting in line took in the comfortable bulge under the snowy cloth covering her basket.

'It's not fair.'

'There'll be nowt left.'

'Should be ashamed of himself.'

'Wants reporting, he does.'

'I'll bet that's the pig's heart and liver gone, for sure.'

'More like a whole leg by the look of her basket.'

'Perhaps he'll be calling round there for a bit of leg later on.'

'How do you mean?'

'Well, probably he's given her one of his legs and she's promised to show him hers.'

The women began to chuckle. When she heard the laughter, Maud glanced up, nodded in Ruby's direction and then turned away.

'He can 'ave a look at mine any time for a nice bit of ham shank,' the toothless old lady next to Ruby said.

'Now then, Ethel,' a woman further down the queue shouted, 'what would your Albert say?'

Then the queue shuffled forwards up the worn stone steps and Ruby managed to squeeze inside the door. Mr Ashton, the butcher, was a large man of about fifty wearing a red striped apron. His sister, Agnes, a pale, humourless lady who wore thick spectacles, and a spotty boy called Fred were helping him to serve the customers. The queue moved slowly over the sawdust floor, until Ruby could see Maud in front of the marble-topped counter.

'What can I get for you today, Miss Barton?' the butcher asked.

'Sausages. Four, please.'

'You've enough points for some...'

'No. I fancy sausages, and some bones, if you have them, for the dog.'

The butcher nodded, and disappeared into the back of the shop. Ruby saw some of the women around her shift uneasily, while others lifted an eyebrow, but when the butcher appeared with a lumpy parcel and dropped it into the old lady's basket, there wasn't any disapproval in the looks that passed between them.

Ruby managed to get belly pork and some bacon and paid for it with part of the money Doctor Grey had given her for her performance in the Nativity play. As she walked home, planning what she could make with the pork and thinking of how

259

pleased everyone would be when they came in from work and smelt the bacon cooking inside the potato pie, she didn't see Johnny Fin pushing his bike along the road until he called to her.

'Dick's given me some spuds. I've been givin' him a lift with the car. There's too many for me. I swapped some of 'em. I was on my way to drop the rest off for Maud, but you can save me the trip, if you will.'

'She's just been in the butcher's. I'll try to catch her up,' Ruby said, taking the rough sack from Johnny.

'Tell her there's something in there for Joe as well.'

The old lady was opening the front door to the little terraced cottage, when Ruby caught up with her.

'This is from Johnny,' she said, handing the old lady the sack. 'It's potatoes and something for Uncle Joe.'

'It's you our Henry's got leaving stuff at my door, isn't it? You'll have to knock next time,' the old lady said.

'I will,' she nodded breathlessly, but Maud had already gone inside, letting the door slam behind her.

When Ruby got home, the kitchen smelt of spice and the doors to the kitchenette were hanging open.

'That you, Ruby?' Sadie called from the front room.

Sadie and Lou were sitting on the sofa, with Con squashed between them. Sadie's arm was in a sling. They were each holding one of the tumblers from the top shelf of the kitchenette filled with red liquid.

'What's happened?' Ruby asked.

'Accident with the machine. I've had to have stitches. And he give me an injection for the pain. I think it's wearing off. It doesn't half hurt.'

'She was lucky it didn't take her arm off,' Lou said, sipping the deep-red liquid from her glass.

'Not be able to work for a bit. Told me to go back and see 'im in two weeks. I don't want to miss two weeks' money.'

'Well, there's Christmas in between,' Lou said. 'So you'll not be that bad, and there'll be a bonus. Should be. That's what I heard from our neighbour.'

'I felt that faint I went round to Lou's, she walked back with me. Then Con turned up with a bottle of Buckie. At least, that's what it said it was on the label.'

Con smiled. 'It was for Henry. He told me—'

'Da won't mind. It's medicine. It's a tonic for me arm. Me and Lou need a tonic. Don't we, Lou? Want to try some, Ruby, love?' Sadie asked, waving the glass at her. 'Oh, come on. He's brought some spices and some more of those cinnamon sticks as well. He's been showin' us about some of their Christmas customs in America. And very nice they are.'

'You'll have to show Ruby,' Lou said, refilling their glasses. 'Come on, Con, don't be shy. She's such a nice girl,' she said, smiling at Con, who was steadying her hand, as she poured more of the dark liquid into Sadie's glass.

'Tell you what. I've got an idea,' Sadie said,

261

attempting to stand up. 'Ruby, put the radio on.'

'No. Jenny said I–'

'Oh, come on,' Sadie said, falling back on to the couch. 'We could have a dance.'

'Ruby, you,' Lou said, in a fit of giggles, 'should have more fun. Shouldn't she, Con? You'll have to learn to dance. If you learn, you could come out with us.'

'Lou, I don't think you should have any more,' Con said. 'You've got to go to work. She's on the late shift,' he said grinning at Ruby. 'I think you'd better make her something to eat.'

'I'm making potato pie and I got some bacon from the butcher's. There'll be enough for everybody.'

'See what I mean?' Lou said, trying to focus her eyes on Ruby. 'She's such a nice girl, but she should have more fun.'

'If we can't dance,' Sadie giggled, 'we'll just have to keep on trying that American custom young Con's been teaching us.'

'That injection the doctor gave her... I think it's reacted with the drink,' Con said. 'I think they'll both need to eat something.'

'Ooh, yes,' Lou said, joining in the giggling again. 'Now that's something else Ruby needs to be shown how to do. Tell her what you do at Christmas with the cinnamon sticks, Con. Tell her about what you do in America.'

'It's just that some of us, the youngsters...'

'No. Tell her properly.'

'It's when... Well, sometimes when we make biscuits with cinnamon – cinnamon biscuits for Christmas – well, sometimes we put the spice on our lips ... and kiss each other. It's just a game.'

'It's lovely. You'll like it,' Lou said. 'Go on, Con, put some on.'

Ruby watched Con put the cinnamon on his lips and took a deep breath. He stood close. She could feel his warmth and smell the spice. She squeezed her hands tightly and hoped he couldn't hear her heart banging.

'Go on, Ruby, look up,' Lou ordered.

When she did, she saw that he was smiling. And although she'd seen it done lots of times at the pictures, she couldn't remember if she should shut her eyes. He took her shoulders and bent down. When she lifted her face closer toward his, she was glad that she'd kept them open, because as his face came nearer, she could see his long, graceful lashes leisurely sweeping down over his eyes. Then she closed her eyes and felt his lips, soft, steady, pressing. He touched her mouth with his tongue. Ruby held her breath and tried not to move. She didn't want it to stop, ever. It felt holy. The smell of the spice filled her nose, and a taste – his taste – cold and sweet, filled her mouth.

CHAPTER ELEVEN

The city was fastened up, walled inside its own bitter fog. On the quayside, as he followed the line of trucks swinging in through the dock gates, Con inhaled the sour city-taste fused with the damp sea mist. The cranes on the dockside were still, but out on the river, the ships left blind and stranded by the fog had set up a lament. He climbed down from the cab, pulled up his collar and joined the huddles of men leaning against their cooling truck engines. At least he would get to stay outside the camp: late passes – five to midnight – were scarce. Lately, the only way to escape was to volunteer for duties at a village Christmas party or to sing for some church. And the joke was – according to Sarge Mayfield – it was the churches, some of them at least, that wanted to stop the black soldiers mixing with the locals. The other reason for rationing the passes was that, although the black and white GIs drank in different towns, the colonel was afraid of what could happen if they came across each other. And it was true that, in some of the villages they'd thought too small to be designated black or white, fights had been arranged.

He nodded to Wes and some of the other guys that he recognised.

'Word is we'll be here until morning,' Wes said, flicking his cigarette stub into a puddle on the cobbled quayside. 'They'll not risk bringing the ships in.'

'Guess not,' Con said, squatting down on his haunches and offering Wes another cigarette.

Even if the fog meant they stayed on the docks until morning, Con didn't really mind: now the ban on black newspapers had been tightened, meeting guys in other trucks was one of the only ways left of getting news from home.

'See that guy over there. The fat guy? He's from Paradise Valley. Name's Walter. He's only been

264

over here a couple of weeks.'

Con followed Wes over to the circle of men standing around an overweight GI.

'Got worse since August,' the fat man said. 'It's starting to hurt war production. If you ask me, they'd rather fight each other than Hitler. Labour relations are poor, and in a lot of the plants, it spills over into fighting between blacks and whites. Then it carries over on to the streets, particularly around the parks at weekend. It's not safe for families to go out there, even on Sundays. Aircraft plant at Willow Run's producing parts for... I know I shouldn't say... But, hell, we're all black folks here.' Walter looked around the group of men. 'There isn't no Nazis here. The plants are producing parts for B-24 Liberator bombers. They keep upping the production. Wanting more and more folk to work there, and folk from the South is coming in. Can't get that sort of pay down there. All the houses and apartments are full with workers, even an hour's car drive away. Little Washtenaw County's full. Trailer camps all over the place. Them places have no schools, policing or sanitation. The white folk ain't happy 'cos of all the blacks coming in.'

Although he wouldn't admit it, Con could understand why folks – black and white – should resent the increase of new workers coming in. The only people that would benefit were the shopkeepers. And the new black workers from the South would take lower pay. That didn't help the Detroit blacks none. The people who went to his father's church worked hard and didn't want trouble with their white neighbours.

'We got our own Nazis now,' Walter said. 'The Silver Shirts they call themselves. A lot of them is Poles. Detroit Poles. The Clan's mixed up with it – National Workers' League. Papers say it's a front for the Nazis. German Americans and these Silver Shirts. They say this war's not worth the life of one American boy, and they talk against the Jews and the black man. They reckon Jews hire black folks, so they can give 'em low wages.'

Con shifted uncomfortably and nudged Wes. 'You coming up town?' he asked. 'I went in this place with Holt last time. The food was good, and I think I can find it, even in the fog.'

'I was hoping Holt and Bo might show up. Do you know what they were sent on this morning?'

'No. They could do, I suppose, but there's no point in waiting, and I'm pretty hungry.'

They walked along a street leading away from the docks. On the clear blue day Con had visited the street-corner pub with Holt, as they'd crossed over one of the terraced streets, he'd caught sight of a ship sailing across the other end, so close that he'd felt as though he could have reached out and touched it. The pub was a tiny place with a bar in the main corridor and a series of small crowded rooms, each with a fire, a leather seat running along the walls and a push bell to call for service. Despite the choking fog, the pub was crowded. Most of the drinkers lived in the streets nearby, but because it was a port, the locals came from all over the world. Most of them were sailors or worked on the docks or in one of the warehouses along the quay. Con liked the place: it felt easier than the pubs around the camp that were all

266

white. They ordered food, bought pints of beer and found two seats next to the fire, alongside a group of Irishmen.

'You want a little drop to warm you, boys?' a small toothless man asked, handing them two small glasses of pale golden liquid from a tray on his table.

'That's very kind of you, sir,' Wes said. 'You must let me pay...'

'No, no. If you'll drink my health. I'm ninety today and my son has arrived to help me to celebrate. It is the first time I have seen him for many a day,' the little man said, nodding towards a man who looked almost as old as he did. 'My son Eoin has brought me a couple of bottles of a very singular drink.' The old man's son told them that he knew America well and had been to Detroit several times, and they chatted happily about the places he remembered until their food arrived.

'That was a mighty nice drink,' Con said, tucking into his meat pie. 'I think I can feel my feet again.'

'Would it be better than Buckie?' Wes asked innocently.

'Buckie?' Con repeated, his fork frozen in mid-air. 'How do you...?'

Wes grinned. 'Henry said that, when he came home...'

'Henry?'

When – under Lou's orders – Con was kissing Ruby, they'd heard the front gate open. Lou had grabbed bottle and glasses and dashed into the kitchen to hide them, but there'd been no hiding the fact that both she and Sadie were drunk, and that Ruby, although she hadn't drunk any of the Buckie, looked equally guilty. Luckily, when Henry and Sadie's mother walked into the cottage, all they'd been concerned about was Sadie's arm, and her worries about losing wages just before Christmas. Even when he discovered that the Buckie was all gone Henry hadn't complained, although his chest was very bad. This patient acceptance, in addition to the guilt he'd felt for his part in the drinking, meant that Con had been willing to pay almost twice as much to find Henry a replacement bottle.

'I got the Buckie for him because I felt sorry for the old guy. He said it was the only thing that helped when he was gassed, and he thought it might help him again. His chest is awful bad.'

'Does Henry know what was goin' on in his house – and what about Bo?'

'What?'

'Do they know about that story you told the girls? The one about the cinnamon sticks?'

'It ain't no story. Just because you didn't do it. We did in my neighbourhood. Does Bo know about Sadie and...?'

'No.'

'Then how do you?'

'Lou told me you said it was a custom. An American custom, you told her...'

'It was her and Sadie. They got drunk. I got the Buckie for Henry and went along to drop it off and...'

'You took advantage. That's what I heard. Now you're not going to tell me you protested. And you made out with little Ruby. Now you're not

268

telling me that she—'

'That was Lou's idea. We didn't make out. I just... She's only fifteen. Too young for me.'

'She's awful pretty.'

'I know, but she's just a kid. It wasn't my idea. Lou and Sadie just kept on, and by then... Well, we'd all had some of the stuff. It's real powerful. Does Bo... If she's told you, then Sadie might have...'

'You'd best hope not,' Wes grinned. 'I bet Sadie don't remember enough to tell him. Lou said you were all real gone.'

'Lou should learn to behave. She's a married woman. Anyway, I got him another bottle.'

'That was your guilty conscience. Here, get me another drink and I'll think about keeping my mouth shut. You'd best hope the girls and old Henry do the same.'

When Con came back with their drinks, one of the Irishmen had begun to sing and gradually the little bar filled with people listening to his rich baritone. One of them was a black guy wearing an RAF uniform. He smiled and nodded at the two GIs, and when the singing stopped, he came over to their table.

'Have you just arrived?' he asked.

'No. We're here collecting parts.'

'You been in Northern Ireland?' he asked, nodding at the Irishman singing.

'No. We came over from the States. Pardon me asking, but where...'

'I'm from Jamaica,' the man said with a smile. 'I came over to offer my services to the RAF. The uniform fools an awful lot of people. The name's

George, George McDonald. Would you like another drink?'

George settled down with them to chat and listen to the music. Con, whose own attempts to grow a moustache had resulted in little more than a vague shadow on his upper lip, gazed in admiration at George's neatly groomed moustache and short, slicked-down hair.

When the Irish baritone finished his song, he was replaced by a burly Irishwoman called Bernadette, who sang 'Hills of Connemara' in a sweet, girlish voice that didn't match her age or size. Now his stomach was full, Con felt mellow and comfortable in the crowded room. He stretched out his long legs, his eyes began to feel heavy and he tried to forget the uncomfortable night ahead in the back of a cold truck. At the end of the song, the old Irishman's son, Eoin, began topping up their glasses from a large brown bottle.

'Come along,' he said, handing a glass to George, 'we'll drink a toast to my father.'

As they waited, he moved around refilling glasses and offering drinks to the newcomers.

'Good evening. Will you two gentlemen have a drink? It's my father's birthday,' he called to someone towards the back of the crowded room.

Con turned, and saw that he was speaking to two white GIs; one was small and wiry, the other taller and flabby with greasy hair flopping in his eyes. Both men were swaying.

'It's lovely. It will warm you on a cold night,' the large lady singer called.

As the big floppy-haired guy reached out his hand, trying to focus on the tray of free drinks,

Con saw Bo and Holt standing in the doorway holding pints of beer. At first, the smaller GI sniggered at his friend's drunken attempts to reach the tray, but then his eyes locked on Con's.

'Naw thank you, ma'am,' he said, grabbing at the back of his friend's tunic. 'We don't drink with blacks where I come from.'

His words made the fat GI's concentration slip and he fell forward almost upsetting the drinks. Bo, who had been standing behind the two GIs, reached over and steadied the tray.

'Then maybe you should find yourself another place to drink,' he said, taking one of the glasses for himself.

The drinkers fell silent, and the packed room filled with the moan of the foghorns out on the river. Con felt his heart start to pound. He saw Wes tense, as though ready to spring out of his seat, and George, who had slipped his tobacco pouch back into his pocket, narrowed his eyes. Bo ignored the two white GIs, and lifting his glass to the Irish woman, he took a sip. Con could see that his face and tunic were damp from the foggy night, and that behind him, Holt was wiping his face with his cap.

'Steady now, lads,' the Irishman said, moving the tray as far away from the threatened danger as possible, 'we don't want no trouble in here.'

'There'll be none, sir,' Bo said. 'These gentlemen are leaving.'

Alerted by the sudden silence, the landlord peered round the door. 'All right, lads. What's goin' on?' he asked. 'Is that poteen I can see, Michael Clancy?'

271

'I was just offering my friends a small taste of Ireland. It is a drink brewed only on my family's land and has the most delicate of flavours. Won't you take a glass?' the old man asked.

'I'll ask you to put it away, if you please. I've my licence to think of – and you gents,' he said looking at the two GIs, 'there's room in the other parlour. You'll be comfortable in there.'

'I'll not drink out of a glass used by no black,' slurred the larger man.

The landlord's pink shiny face clouded. 'Your friend's had enough by the look of him, mate,' he said to the smaller GI. 'It might be best if you take him home.'

When the smaller soldier began to protest, two large barrel-chested men in the mufflers and caps Con had seen worn by dockers grabbed his friend by the arm.

'Off you go now, lads,' the landlord said, as the two GIs tottered obediently into the night.

When Bo and Holt had been introduced to George and the small glasses of spirit drunk, George took out his pipe and pouch again. 'You guys often get that sort of trouble?' he asked. 'I must say, I've had one or two problems with your chaps myself. Couldn't make them understand that I wasn't an American. I pointed out RAF on my uniform, but it didn't do any good, I'm afraid.'

'What about the RAF guys?' Bo asked.

'Oh well, you know. It's not official here. No colour bar, but most of them are surprised at first and a bit nervous to fly with me, until they get to know me. Here in the port is okay. More cosmopolitan, you see. Not like the rest of England.

Your guys, well that's different.'

The next morning the fog had lifted, but there were so many ships waiting to dock, that they were told it would be late afternoon by the time their trucks could be loaded.

'Guess we could have a walk around,' Holt said. 'Go up town, maybe there's time. Could have a drink and take in the sights. The way things are going with O'Donal, we might not get passes, even at Christmas.'

'Don't say that. I've promised Sadie, and she's awful low with her arm and everything,' Bo said. 'Henry says to tell you you're all welcome over Christmas, anytime. Just call by.'

'I reckon we should tell them we're not goin' out singing and bein' all happy, if they'll not give us passes,' Wes said.

'We've got to do somethin',' Holt agreed. 'But that just punishes the folks who've invited us.'

'Let's have a day off from all that today, guys,' Con said. 'Come on.'

The four of them wandered through the maze of terraced streets and into the centre of the city. In the daylight, they could see the evidence of the bombing. They lingered, fascinated by the destruction that until recently they'd only seen on newsreels.

'Let's try here,' Bo said, heading over to a large pub whose ornate marble frontage was pitted, but had a sign on the door that proudly announced: 'Business as usual'.

The interior gave no hint that the world outside was full of dust and broken buildings: every

273

marble, tiled and wooden surface gleamed. Behind the bar, the handpumps and glasses sparkled and a dance band played cheerfully on the radio. The barmaid – small, dark-haired and with a strange and hard to understand accent – asked what they would like.

Bo, who as always took the lead, made her smile, and as she poured their drinks, she asked where they had come from, and sympathised when he told her about their cold night on the dockside.

'Next time, come here,' she said. 'We got rooms. Better than a cold night out there.'

'It's quiet in here,' Bo said, handing around the pint glasses.

'Oh, it won't be long before it livens up,' she said. 'We've been ever so busy. The place is full of British Tommies. Waiting for ships, most of them. Here we are,' she said, as a group of British soldiers crowded through the door. 'What did I tell you?'

There was little conversation, until they all had drinks, but then a small, chubby sergeant nodded over to them.

'That tastes bloody good,' he said with a wink. 'We've been stuck on a bloody train all night in the middle of nowhere. Bloody fog.'

'What did I say?' the barmaid laughed. 'This lot will drink us dry.'

'You just come off one of the ships?' the sergeant asked.

'No,' Bo said, answering for all of them, 'we've come down from further north. We've been here since autumn. Driving. Trucking up and down to the port and the airfields, mostly. Waiting for the stuff to be unloaded.'

'You been held up by the fog as well?'

'Yes, since yesterday. You shipping out?'

'Don't know yet,' the sergeant replied, finishing his first pint at an impressive speed, 'where we're off to, or when. The city's full of soldiers. We all must be going somewhere.'

'Could be Africa,' a tall bespectacled private said.

'I reckon that's it.'

'They'd have given us tropical gear by now,' another private said, ordering a brandy.

'Come off it,' the sergeant laughed. 'We might be hanging round here for days. We'd bloody freeze to death.'

'There'll be some poor sods wandering about in tropical gear, and then they'll send us out there, instead,' another private grinned cheerfully. 'Then the other lot will end up goin' up to friggin' Norway or somewhere. Bloody army.'

'Just had embarkation leave,' the sergeant said. 'Then we were told this morning we'll be billeted round here until... God knows how long. Anyway, Monty's sorted that lot out, so I don't reckon North Africa's on.'

The barmaid had been right. The pub quickly filled with soldiers waiting for ships, and the landlord, a small man with a club foot who went by the name of Taffy, joined his daughter serving drinks. The four GIs sat at the end of the bar, watching the soldiers' antics and listening to the chatter.

'Looks like this lot are settled in for a heavy session,' Taffy said to Holt, when he bought their next round. 'They're making the best of it while

275

they can, and who can blame them?'

'Is there any place we can buy food?' Holt asked.

'You could try the British Restaurant round the corner,' he said. 'It's subsidised, but very tasty from all accounts. I'm clean out of grub, I'm afraid, and more's the pity with all the squaddies in town.'

'They're not bad places,' the chubby sergeant said. 'Set them up all over after the bombing, so as folk could get a bite.'

'That one was set up after we had the May bombing,' the barmaid said. 'I've heard it's very good.'

'Is that when all this damage happened round here?' Bo asked.

'Mostly. Though we've had more than our share. Not that you hear about it on the radio. It's all London on there.'

'There's a good reason for that,' the sergeant said. 'They don't want Jerry to know they're hitting our docks.'

'Over fourteen hundred killed and the cathedral hit,' the girl replied. 'Bloody Hitler. Come to hit the docks and ships, but he got the houses miles out of town as well.'

The British Restaurant, housed in part of a badly damaged department store, was packed with soldiers and bombed-out families. The food, potato stew and sponge pudding with a little jam, was basic but filling.

Bo lit a cigarette and glanced around the busy restaurant. One of the customers, a middle-aged black man dressed in smart civilian clothes, was sitting with a white woman of about the same age, wearing a coat with a light-coloured fur collar and a black hat. When he and the other guys walked in, the children had peered at them, but nobody was staring at the couple; they didn't cause much interest. The two old women sitting in the corner might have been whispering about them, but he couldn't be sure. Would it, he wondered, really be possible? Then, as if reading his thoughts, the black guy caught his eye and nodded, as if to say, if that was what he wanted, then yes, it was.

When Con went to collect their cups of tea, he had to wrestle with the teaspoon tied on to the counter with a string.

'Do people steal them?' he asked the woman in charge of the tea urn.

'No love, mind you, some might. It's the metal, you see, there's a shortage. Not many spoons around.'

The heavy food had made them all feel reluctant to move. When he'd finished his mug of weak tea, Bo yawned and shook his head.

'I ain't got Sadie a Christmas present yet. I wanted to get something real special that she'd not expect. I thought I might get somethin' in the city. Somethin' different. But all the shops ... well, I don't know.'

'How about a bottle of Buckie?' Wes said, wincing as Con landed a sharp kick to his ankle under the table.

'She don't like strong drink. That stuff's awful powerful. It's not for a lady. I wanted somethin' pretty.'

'You heard what they said. This place was the main department store, before it was hit,' Wes

277

said. 'If we could go to the PX like the white—'

'Well we can't.'

'George, the guy last night, he told me about this place, a pub. He wrote down the name. You can get anythin', if you've got the money. A guy hangs out there and he'll get you what you want.'

'A spiv?' Wes asked. 'How you goin' to find him?'

'Like I told you, I got the name. George said the guy was called Len and he has this walking stick with a handle like the head of a horse, and when a stranger walks in, if you ask if you can buy him a drink, he knows what you've come for, but he said don't go in a crowd, best to go alone. You guys stay here.'

'He might not have anythin'.'

'George said he knew for a fact he's got some French perfume.'

'I'll come with you,' Holt said.

'No.'

Ten minutes later Bo was back. Smiling broadly, he dropped a dark-blue box on the table and went to get another cup of tea.

'I reckon we went to the best pub,' he said, sitting down next to Con. 'The beer in that place was awful, and a couple of white GIs over at the dartboard looked real mean.'

'I told you I should have come with you,' Holt said, inspecting the dark-blue box. 'How could he get French perfume? You've bin cheated.'

'No I ain't. It's sealed up, I checked, and I recognise the package. Had a girlfriend use the same.'

'Bet you don't tell Sadie that,' Wes grinned. 'It's

278

looted from the bombed store, I bet.'

They retraced their steps out of the city centre, along streets full of grubby children, swinging on lamp posts with lengths of old rope and dragging home-made carts filled with bricks.

'I thought they'd have been evacuated out,' Holt said, as the children mobbed them for pennies and gum.

'They'll want to be home for Christmas, now the bombing's stopped,' Bo said.

In the next street there were more signs of bomb damage; some of the houses had been flattened, and all that remained of others was an unsupported wall or the broken carcass of a staircase. Half-bricks lay scattered in the road, and there was a smell of burning wood in the air. Unlike the other streets, this one was empty, except for the black man from the restaurant, his wife and two white GIs. The GIs – both little guys – were pushing him and shouting. Con watched Bo's face and waited. The man was holding two sheets of wood that flapped in his hands as he argued with the soldiers. Bo didn't move, until one of them, a thin, pasty-faced guy, knocked the wood out of the older man's hands and it skittered along the ground.

'I said for you to step off the sidewalk,' the other GI shouted, pushing his chest up against the black guy. 'Do you hear?'

It was hard to see why the guy didn't retaliate: he was older, but the GI who was doing the shouting was a little, runty red-haired guy he could have pushed over with one fist.

'You move out of the way when a white man

279

walks by. Do you hear?'

The woman picked up the wood, grabbed the black man's arm and tried to push by the soldiers, but the pasty one swore and spat at her.

In two strides, Bo was between the couple and the soldiers. He grabbed the pasty guy and punched him. The GI went down so easily, sitting down suddenly in the gutter with his legs out in front of him, that it was clear to Con that he must be drunk. The red-haired guy stared down at his buddy, as if he was finding it hard to understand why he'd suddenly sat down in the road. When he tried to pull his friend to his feet, he fell over himself, and it took both Con and Wes to get the two GIs on their feet again.

'Back off, buddy,' Holt said. 'These folk are English.'

'That don't make it right,' the pasty-faced GI said. 'This fuckin' country. Come on Louie, let's go. It stinks of blacks round here.'

'You watch it,' the red-haired GI called, as he and his friend stumbled away. 'The MPs are around ... and...'

The woman was crying, and the black man took out his handkerchief and dabbed at the spit on her coat.

'We saw the wood on our way into town, and Larry said it was just the sort of stuff he needed. Our little grandson has asked Father Christmas for a fort, you see. And you can't explain to a four-year-old about rationing. He's expecting his daddy, our son, back for Christmas as well. He's in the Merchant Navy, like Larry was. He's all of a tremble,' she said, taking hold of her husband's hand, 'and his pills are at home. He's only been out of hospital about a week. We just fancied a walk into town. I must get him back.'

'I hope it doesn't cause you any trouble,' Larry said, shaking Bo's hand. 'At one time I could have...'

'I'm just glad we happened by,' Bo said, as they walked with the couple down to the corner of the street. 'You folks should report it to your police. We're on our way to the docks,' he said, when they came to the crossroads, 'but we'll stay here and wait until you're safely on your way.'

'We don't get much trouble, not round here, anyway,' the woman said. 'Not the same as if we go outside the area. It's with it being a port. People have settled round here from all over. My family are from Portugal, originally. My dad was a saddle maker. He wasn't keen on Larry at first, but we've been married nearly thirty years. How are you finding it where you are?'

'Folks are mostly very friendly,' Bo said.

'Good. Pleased to see you over here, I expect. They think you're all good at singing and dancing, no doubt,' the woman smiled, 'but they'd not like it if you married their daughters.'

'Come on, Janey,' her husband said. 'She's concerned for our youngest, you see. Army, he picked. Didn't want to go to sea... Last letter home, he sounded a bit down, and she's concerned that folk where he is might not be too friendly.'

'I got a girl and they don't seem—'

'Not yet,' the woman said, 'you've not been here long enough, love, but when the novelty wears off...'

Once the couple were out of sight, Con and the others headed back to the trucks, passing the remains of shops and the empty spaces where houses had been. They'd walked a couple of blocks, when a group of five white GIs stepped out from a deserted patch of land and barred their way. Two of them were the guys who had been harassing the couple; the others were bigger, and to Con, they looked meaner and not so drunk. The tallest was about Bo's height, but heavier.

'Willy here tells me you saw fit to interfere when some old black was getting high and mighty,' he said.

There was no one around. The houses stood open to the chill grey air. Con glanced up and down the street. He thought that the river and the docks must be quite near, because he could smell the sea.

'Don't you even think about it, boy,' the second-tallest GI said, standing directly in front of him. 'You just keep coming.'

'You need a lesson,' the pasty GI said. 'It was the big guy that dropped me, Don. He was the one that was giving us lip.'

'If you got a problem with that, buddy,' Bo said, nodding to the largest man and walking on to the deserted ground, 'then let's sort it out.'

'Told you he was lippy,' the pasty GI said, as they all followed Bo on to the scrubby waste ground.

Don, the biggest guy, had already begun to unbutton his tunic. He moved slowly, although he wasn't as drunk as his buddies. The second-tallest GI, a thin guy with a blue shadow on his chin, took

282

Don's coat and grinned. Then Don wheeled around and made a grab for Bo's shirt, tugging him off balance, bringing his knee up sharply, but Bo was too fast and landed a heavy strike to the side of his face. When the larger man staggered, the circle of soldiers widened, and Con saw a knife blade flash. He leapt for the arm and the blade. He and the blue-chinned GI rolled on the floor. The guy was drunk and sweating furiously, but he was heavier than Con, and he wouldn't release the knife. Con's arms burned with the effort. Around them boots kicked up the dust and bodies rolled and fell. Then the GI under him flopped; his head rolled to one side and the knife fell out of his fingers. Con dived for it, but a boot kicked it away and he was grabbed and hauled to his feet. He saw the half-brick Wes had in his hand, and then the knife on the ground between his boots. Con snatched the handle, throwing it, watching it turning in the air, before it disappeared over a broken wall. Blood trickled from the motionless GI's head. Con sat down heavily beside him on the dusty ground. The guy was much smaller than he'd thought and not so old as he'd imagined. It began to rain. The wind was lifting the grubby curtains hanging through the windows of the empty houses. On the other side of the bombsite, ragged streamers of wallpaper flapped from the wall of a once-cherished parlour. The GIs, both black and white, were silent. Then two of the white GIs picked up the unconscious man, and without a word, both groups walked in opposite directions down the empty street.

The afternoon of Christmas Eve was dark and cold, but inside the cottage it was snug and cheerful. Although Sadie's arm was painful, she was in a good mood and sat on the couch listening to the radio and giving Ruby directions on how best to clip the little candleholders to the Christmas tree.

'I don't care how bad this arm is, I'm going to the pictures with Bo next time he gets a late pass, no matter how many pills I have to take to stop it throbbing. I'm not missing the new Bogey film for anything. Leave messing with that tree, Ruby, and come and help me with my nails. You can be my manicurist. Get that little stool and sit here in front of me. Be careful with the nail polish, though, it has to last for the duration.'

'I've not finished here yet,' Ruby said, trying to make the holders balance on the branches and the candles stand up straight.

'This is more important. I can't let everybody see me with chipped nails. I look bad enough as it is with this arm all wrapped up. Come and see if my hair's dry at the back. I can't reach to undo the hair clips. What time's Alice expecting you?'

'She said to be there by five at the latest. I don't think it will be dry,' she said, unrolling Sadie's butter-coloured hair from one of the metal clips.

'No. It's still damp. You'll have to leave it in, and I'll—'

'I can't do that. There'll be people calling round later for a Christmas drink. Tell you what, I'll sit on the stool with my back to the fire and you sit on the floor.'

Ruby left the little tree to squat unwillingly on the rag rug. She hated the job: it was fiddly and

284

time-consuming, and she'd too many things to do already. Sadie edged the stool nearer the fire, and supporting her bad arm with her knee, she gently pushed up the sleeve of her cardigan. The exposed flesh at the edge of the bandage looked angry, and Ruby could see that the swelling had spread out from the original wound. When she took her arm, Sadie winced. Under the bandage, the damaged limb looked swollen and the bruising had turned her fingers to a lurid shade of purple. Ruby dipped the tiny brush into the deep-red nail varnish and steadied a discoloured finger. Sadie closed her eyes and hummed softly to the music on the radio. Since she'd hurt her arm, Sadie had seen to it that Grandma Jenny's rules about the use of the radio and the amount of wood and coal that could be put on the fire didn't apply to her. It was possible for her to get Jenny to agree to anything she wanted, but the extra wood that Bo had sent over for them helped as well. He'd also sent them a leg of pork for Christmas dinner, but now it wasn't certain that he would be there to help them eat it: all four GIs were in trouble with the officers at the camp and hadn't been to the cottage for days.

Not that any of it worried Sadie as much as her loss of wages, and that she wasn't well enough to go out to any of the dances and parties with Lou. Ruby was sure that – if she'd had a boyfriend – she wouldn't have been as willing to go off to dances, just because he couldn't get passes out. She dipped the polish in the bottle and began on the next finger. Sadie's eyes were closed and her breathing shallow. Ruby sighed. And she wouldn't have been fretting to go dancing at the American club, when she knew that her boyfriend wouldn't even be allowed in.

Sadie opened her eyes and inspected her nails. 'Why don't you make us a brew and come and sit with me for a bit before you go?'

Ruby cut herself two slices of bread and filled the kettle. As she sat on one of the brass boxes to toast the bread, Sadie blew on her nails and sipped her tea.

'I wish we still lived in town,' she said. 'Christmas was much better when we lived in the pub. I loved it there at Christmas. It was always lively. Always something going on, but Christmas was best. It's that boring here. Always the same folk, and always wanting to know your business. Gets me down, it does.'

'I didn't know you'd lived in a pub,' Ruby said, easing the bread off the fork and turning it over.

'Mum was the landlady, and a good one. My dad, Arthur, he had a couple of pubs and a bookie's.'

'Did he die?'

'No. Got married. Muriel. Twenty-five. She has a little lad. Told Ma and me to get out. No papers. Nothing to say we could stop. Don't you go saying nothing to her about it. She doesn't like it broadcast. Have you told the Greys yet that you're finishing?'

Ruby shook her head and scraped the remnants of jam from the side of the jar. 'No. They've been good to me, and I like playing for the dances.'

'They'll not want you as much after Christmas, and the factory work's regular. You know how

286

much you'll have every week. Not frightened to spend, like you are now, in case she doesn't need you for a couple of weeks. Anyway, I thought you didn't like it there, after the way she was with the lads?'

'I think it was a misunderstanding.'

'Misunderstanding, my hat!'

Ruby skewered the second piece of bread and shrugged. 'No different than going to the camp or the American club.'

Sadie, who had been admiring her nails, looked up. 'How do you make that out?'

Ruby felt her cheeks redden. 'You and Lou go dancing with the white soldiers, and Bo and the others aren't allowed in there.'

'I've only been once, and that was to keep Lou company, and we was asked to go from work, as part of the war effort.'

'You should have said no. Does Bo know you went?'

'No. And don't you go sayin'. Anyway, it's not the same. They'll not change anything, just because me and Lou don't go to a dance, but Mrs Grey and the Prendergasts ... well, what they say goes round here.'

'Father O'Flynn didn't let it stop him, even though...'

'I thought you was in a hurry,' Sadie snapped, picking up her mirror and inspecting her neatly plucked eyebrows.

The Christmas Eve party at the Grey's was busy and lively. When Mrs Grey gave her a Christmas present, a handkerchief, embroidered with sprays

287

of heather, she felt it was a sign that the discord, caused by the Nativity play and Mrs Grey's differences with Father O'Flynn about the black soldiers, had been forgotten; although she noticed that the old priest hadn't been at any of the Christmas celebrations.

There were twelve people for dinner. When she arrived, Alice was already at work in the kitchen. Ruby helped with the preparations until seven, when she was called into the drawing room to play for the guests. After the meal, Mrs Grey and her guests danced to records and then they played parlour games, so she wasn't needed. She hoped that Alice would say she could go, but instead she had to help Dick with the washing-up and clearing the pots away. Later, Mr Rollo slipped out of the party and made them a drink with egg and brandy in it. Alice told him he was wasteful and that she would report him to madam, but she was laughing when she said it.

Mr Rollo often came into the kitchen; he said it was more entertaining than sitting with his sister's friends. Alice often grumbled about him, because he spent all day in bed and then left his room in such a mess. She and Mr Watts didn't believe he was ill and thought that a man of forty-five should be making his own way in the world. It was true that he was always hanging around in the house. Sometimes during the day, when they were cleaning, he'd come into the drawing room and get her to play for him. Alice complained that he was holding up the dusting, but he made her laugh and she always gave in. A few days before Christmas, he'd given Ruby some new songs and asked her to learn them for New Year's Eve. She'd said she couldn't, that she hadn't got the time, but Alice had said she should, because Mr Rollo wanted to sing them for Mrs Grey and she would be pleased.

After the Greys and their guests left for midnight Mass, Ruby helped Alice clear away. It was almost midnight when – giggling together at one of Mr Rollo's silly jokes – they finally pushed open the kitchen door and rolled in the old wooden trolley stacked high with dishes that still needed to be washed. Her granddad was sitting at the table, his narrow chest heaving. Alice fussed and scolded him for coming out on such a cold night, when he should have been in bed. Under Dick's instructions, he was given a dose of Friar's Balsam and warm water to drink, and once the pots were cleared away, Dick poured a small tot of rum for both of them to protect them against the damp on the journey home.

The next day – Christmas Day – both Sadie and Granddad were ill, and although Bo and the other GIs got passes to have their Christmas dinner at the cottage, they were due back at the camp by five.

'It's crazy,' Bo complained, struggling out of his rain-soaked coat. 'There's nothing for us to do in the camp today. I don't think we even have to leave early in the morning. It just gets the guys more frustrated for nothing.'

They decided to wait until after the Christmas dinner to open the presents stacked up around the tree. Johnny Fin was the last to arrive and added a welcome bottle-shaped parcel to the pile.

Even though Granddad's chest was bad, he came downstairs for Christmas dinner, and after a warm whisky and water, he was soon tucking in to the pork and roast potatoes.

'Well, here's hoping that it will be over by next Christmas,' Johnny said, when Bo had filled everyone's glasses.

'Not at all,' Granddad said, waving his knife in the air. 'It'll be 1945 before this lot's settled, mark my words. No offence, lads, I know you lot are helping to turn things around, and our boys are doing us proud, but look how long it's taking in Tunisia. Think how long it will be to take a heavily defended place like France.'

'France is gonna be easier,' Wes said. 'Tunisia's mountainous, troops have to advance beyond the air cover we can give them, but in France, we'd get to give better support.'

'Come on, Montgomery,' Jenny said. 'Stop being so gloomy and hand over your plate, if you want some more meat. We'll all be shakin' our heads this time next year an' wonderin' why it took us so long to get rid of that little jumped-up bugger.'

When Henry began to argue, Jenny gave his bony ribs a well-aimed nudge with her elbow and filled his plate with a succulent helping of meat.

'How long is that captain of yours goin' to keep this thing about passes up?' she asked. 'I mean, it wasn't like you were out drinking round here when this happened. It was because you was stuck in the fog. Did you tell him what they did to that chap and his wife?'

'Yep,' Holt said, accepting a dish of sprouts,

'but it didn't make no difference. The problem was, there was MPs waiting at the dock. With the fog the night before, most of the guys had taken some time out in town, and they was getting pretty itchy that it might hold everything up. Fog cleared earlier than they thought.'

'Well that wasn't your fault, now was it?'

'Well, quite a few of the guys had come back... Well, let's say they'd been havin' a good time.'

'It's not surprising, if they're not giving you any late passes. Wes, love, have you had enough? There's plenty. Hand me your plate. I mean to say, young men hanging around for no good reason.'

'It'll get worse,' Bo said. 'There's more white guys coming in every week. I was up at one of the bases yesterday, and the place was crowded with new guys. White guys fresh from home. Trucks and guys all over the place and nobody knew what was goin' on. More white guys means more trouble.'

'Not if they stay out of the town,' Sadie said. 'That was the idea. Keep the blacks and the whites apart. If they stay round the base and...'

'Shouldn't carry on like that. You're all in it together,' Johnny said. 'Anyway, I understand you gave the bugger a belting.'

Bo grinned. 'One of them pulled out a knife when they could see their man was getting the worse of it.'

'If Con hadn't jumped on him,' Sadie said, 'well, I dread to think what could have happened.'

'Didn't know it was you that saved the day,' Henry said.

Con look shyly down at his plate, but he was pleased with his part in the scuffle. He'd been terrified, but now he was glad that he'd played his part and the guys didn't see him as the baby any more.

Bo laughed. 'You can hardly blame that MP. When we walked on to the docks, we were covered in blood, both me and young Con. You should have seen that MP's face.'

'Did I tell you I saw Jack Johnson fight?' Johnny asked. 'Now, he was a fine figure of a man. Very skilled. It was in France. After he beat Tommy Burns, this was. He'd gone to live there. Beat Jim Jeffries as well. You have some fine boxers to look up to, young Bo, if you're thinking of taking it up.'

The shortage of dried fruit meant that the Christmas pudding contained a large quantity of grated carrot, but once the white sauce, flavoured with the last of the cinnamon, was poured liberally over the helpings, Jenny declared herself satisfied with the result.

The GIs had brought presents for them all. Ruby's was a scarf with matching gloves. They were made of the softest lambswool and in a very pretty shade of powder blue. But since their kiss, she'd been secretly hoping that she might get a present from Con, and she couldn't help feeling disappointed. She'd made woollen socks for each of the soldiers, to keep them warm in the trucks. And she'd made Johnny a pair of gloves with the tops of the fingers missing, so that he could work, but keep his hands warm. If Con had given her a present, she had something ready to give him in return; it was wrapped up and hidden under her mattress. She'd found it in town, on a stall selling books to raise funds for bombed-out families.

'You off colour?' Jenny asked, when they were washing up after the soldiers had gone. 'You catching Henry's cold?'

'No. I'm just tired after working last night and there's the Boxing Day dance and then the New Year's Eve party.'

Ruby took off her dress, curled up on her bed and closed her eyes. She tried to remember the kiss, tasting the cinnamon and feeling the pressure of his lips on hers. After a while, she rolled off the bed and took out the book she'd bought for Con; it was wrapped in a piece of wrapping paper she'd slipped out of the drawer downstairs. She put it on her bookshelf and sighed. She felt tired, but she was restless as well. She opened her mother's case. She hadn't tried any of Pearl's clothes on for some time, and now that her hips and breasts were beginning to fill out, she could see that some of the dresses might fit her. Ruby took out a short, slim-fitting dress she remembered Pearl wearing the first Christmas they'd spent at Everdeane. Her father had been working in one of the big hotels on the front: a beautiful white building that, from the prom, looked like an ocean liner. He'd got her mother some work there, singing in the cocktail lounge over the Christmas holiday. She'd worn the dress the first evening. It was heavy cream silk, fitted at the waist, with swan's down around the neckline and seed pearls on the bodice.

She took the dress into Sadie's room and put on the light. It fitted perfectly, and when she clipped Sadie's pearl hairslides in her hair to hold it off her face, the attractive woman looking back at her made her blush. She walked backwards away from the mirror to get a full-length view, but her black, low-heeled shoes were not delicate enough and spoilt the effect. Ruby opened Sadie's wardrobe. As she knelt down and pulled out a pair of pale leather sandals from the bottom drawer, her nose filled with the smell of the apples swaddled in tissue and stored inside. She was holding the delicate shoes in her hands, when the familiar metal click of the front gate made her jump and set her heart thumping. She sat on the floor and listened, afraid that it might be Sadie, who was walking Bo part of the way back to the camp, but it was only Johnny leaving. She knew that, when she came back down the lane, Sadie wouldn't be able to see the light through the blackout curtain, but she switched it off just the same and brought a candle from her room. Feeling guilty and excited, Ruby put on the shoes, pushed the mirrors back and then changed the angles, twisting and turning in front of them to see the swell of her hips and her slender legs. Then she slipped off the shoes, pulled the mirrors back into their place and unfastening her dress let it fall. For a moment, when she took the clips from her hair, Ruby caught the eye of her own image. Holding its attention, she shook out her curls, and slipping off her underslip, gazed at her naked body in the candlelight.

On the afternoon of New Year's Eve, the cottage was quiet. Granddad's cold had settled on his chest and he'd been in bed since Boxing Day. Sadie's arm hadn't improved either; she'd spent most of the time since Christmas Day moping around, so when Bo had sent a message to say he couldn't get a pass for New Year's Eve, she'd decided to stay in bed as well.

Ruby had spent part of the morning steaming the skirt of her black velvet dress to bring up the pile and sponging the collar and cuffs. She would have loved to have worn the cream dress, but in addition to playing, she had to help Alice serve the food and she was afraid the dress might get stained. With her usual dress drying in front of the fire, she dragged out the tin bath and tested the water in the boiler.

'Don't forget, no more than five inches,' Jenny said. 'Don't take too long. I might as well get in after you.'

When she arrived, the Greys' kitchen was busy. Alice was poking the breast of an enormous goose she had just taken from the oven.

'A present from a grateful patient, she says. Shot it on the marshes. Likely story, if you ask me. More like, that brother of hers got it on the black market. There are regulations. It should be the same for everybody. All these parties, and more guests tonight than ever, but when I asked if I could bring in my sister's girl, she wouldn't let me, and me and Dick haven't had a minute to ourselves over Christmas. Mr Rollo's been asking for you – something about the music.'

The drawing room was unlit, and she didn't see Mr Rollo until he sat up and smiled at her over the couch. His hair was rumpled, and she guessed he'd been sleeping. When he stood up a newspaper dropped to the floor.

'I want to run through the two songs with you, Ruby. I want you to play "Waltz of My Heart" first, and then... After I'd sent you the music, I changed my mind. I couldn't decide, but now I'm sure. So the second song will be "My Dearest Dear". I'd almost decided on something patriotic or festive, but no. I do love it, don't you? *Dancing Years* is my sister's favourite musical.'

'I haven't played it for ages. It isn't what you said.'

'My sister will love it, and I'm rather in the doghouse. Come on. Don't let me down. You'll pick it up. Here, I'll put the lights on.'

'The curtains. You've not–'

'You're becoming almost as strict as Alice, aren't you?' he said. 'Do you never break the rules?'

When she'd played the song through, her fingers began to remember the chords, and when he could see that she was ready, he sat down next to her and started to sing. He had quite a good tenor voice; not as rich as Bo's, but light and expressive.

'Now, should I sit next to you? I could sit down, as though I'm just going to play as well. Then once everyone has come through...'

'No one will be sat down,' she said. 'Madam said for us to move the chairs and rugs once we've served the dessert, and then there'll be room for dancing to the gramophone.'

'You're right. I'd forgotten. Well then, when we break for drinks, you'll be helping Dick. Then, once everyone's got a drink, I'll switch off the gramophone, you put down your tray and I'll take my place by the piano. Yes. I think I'll stand. Then I'll dedicate the songs to my sister. What do you think of my voice, in your professional opinion?'

'It's lovely, sir.'

'Do you think so?'

'Yes, sir.'

'We make a good team, don't we? Would you like to play for me more often?'

'I'd best close the curtains, sir.'

'You should use your talent,' he said, following her over to the window.

As she pulled the curtain cord, Ruby could feel him standing right behind her. His closeness in the darkening room made her breathing quicken. He slipped his arm around her waist and tried to kiss her neck, but she wriggled free, and treading heavily on his soft Turkish slipper, she headed for the door.

'I haven't dismissed you,' he said, sitting down unsteadily on the sofa. 'Put some coal on the fire and switch on the lights. Then you can go.'

No one noticed her return to the busy kitchen. The New Year dinner took everyone's attention, and when it was time for her to return to the drawing room and play for the newly arrived guests, she was relieved that Rollo was nowhere to be seen. He didn't reappear until it was almost time for the guests to go into dinner. He would normally have smiled and thanked her when she served his food, but tonight he was busy making the two young ladies seated on either side of him laugh. After the meal was served, she helped Dick to move the couches and chairs and roll up the rugs, and then helped to serve the drinks, and it was Dick who gave her the message that Mr

Rollo was ready for her to play. It went well, and at the end of the second song, Mrs Grey was dabbing her eyes.

At twelve, they heard the guests singing 'Auld Lang Syne'. Dick went out of the back door and came back in through the front, carrying a piece of coal for good luck, and everyone cheered. Then Doctor Grey brought through glasses of whisky for Dick and Alice and she had lemonade.

'You get off now, dear,' Alice said. 'Is your grandpa calling for you?'

'No, he's still poorly.'

'Oh, I'd forgotten, and Dick's just taken Doctor Grey's two aunts home in the car. You could have had a lift in the front. They're very nice old dears and wouldn't have objected.'

'I've got my torch. He only comes for me because he's been for a drink, but tonight he'll be at home.'

'Well, all the best, then,' Alice said. 'I'm off up to put water bottles in for them as is sleepin' over.'

Ruby went into the pantry to get her coat. When she came back, Mr Rollo was standing in the kitchen. She hesitated.

'I've come to see if you're cross with me,' he said. 'I hope we're still friends.'

Unsure what she should say, Ruby looked down at the kitchen table and hoped that Alice or Dick would come in.

'Thank you for playing for me,' he said, taking a ten-shilling note from his wallet. 'I know I behaved badly and I would like you to have this. My sister was really delighted with the songs.

Please take it. You deserve it. It's worth it to see my sister so happy. Am I forgiven? Look, I'm such a fool, but you are a pretty girl, you know, and I must confess that I'd had rather too much to drink at lunch. Nervous about singing, you see. Not a real performer, not like you.'

Ruby studied her hands and felt her cheeks turn red.

'Please,' he said, bending slightly to see her face. 'I'll feel such a lot better if you took the note. You are being so unkind, and it is New Year's Eve. Please say you'll forgive me.'

Ruby knew that he had been drinking and that he was really sorry. And Alice was always saying that he was a fool, but there was no real harm in him. But she didn't know what to say, so instead she nodded her head.

'Oh, does that mean you've forgiven me?' he said. 'Really? Then please smile. That's better. I can see you smiling, so now I know I'm forgiven. We made such a good team, didn't we? You played really well. Now please, take this note for your professional help.'

'Thank you, Mr Rollo,' she said.

'So, we'll say no more about it? You haven't complained to Alice, have you? You know how she frightens me.'

'No, sir,' Ruby laughed. 'I've not said anything.'

'Good girl. Well, good night and happy new year.'

'And to you, sir,' she said.

Outside, the garden was damp and silent. There was no moon or stars and the little beam from her torch barely penetrated the solid blackness. Ruby shivered, hitched the basket full of leftovers on to her arm and began to pick her way down the path. When she neared the front of the house, she could hear dance music still playing inside. Around her, raindrops from the sodden trees pattered on to the leaves beneath. She heard something shifting deep inside the shrubbery and imagined small creatures hurrying by, brushing against the damp leaves. Then out of the blackness, someone grabbed at her coat. Ruby tried to pull away, to scream. She dropped her basket, heard the contents thud on the gravel and hit out with her tiny, useless torch. Her hair was caught, trapped. He held her close, so close that she could feel the heat of his breath. He bit her lip. The pain made her eyes water, and she almost lost her footing. Her nails, nibbled and worn, were ineffective claws. He pulled at her dress. They struggled. She felt his fingers hard and cold against the inside of her thigh. Large hands wrenched and tore, making her stagger and fall. When she pushed him away, he punched her. She began to cry. He called her a tease, the jolt of the familiar voice held her for a moment: fear, choking and sharp as a fish bone, stopped her throat. Smothered in his shoulder, Ruby smelt pomade, felt the gravel beneath her legs and started to pray. Then, without warning, the bushes around them were alive with movement. As quickly as he'd appeared and grabbed her, Rollo let her go. She heard branches snap, and deep inside the shrub-bery something crashed and fell. Ruby crouched on the damp, pebbly ground holding her breath. In the darkness, she thought she heard Rover, the Greys' dog, growl and wondered if someone, hearing noises in the garden, had let him out of his kennel. When the noise stopped, a beam of weak light moved from side to side across the path in front of her. Then, through the stillness, she heard Johnny Fin whisper her name and she reached up towards his comforting beery smell.

CHAPTER TWELVE

Edged in under a swollen sky, the hens slopped through the muddy garden, and in the cottage the hours moved stiffly. To get the best of the dull unchanging light, Ruby worked on the wooden draining board; pressing close to the window, she used the bread knife to pare tissue-thin slivers of soap into a small glass fruit dish. When she'd scraped enough to fill a teaspoon, she added a spoon of precious white sugar. The mixture, a recipe for a poultice, was to be spread on to a piece of fine gauze and taped to Sadie's arm. She hoped it would have more effect than the bread poultice that Jenny had sworn by.

Sadie was curled up on the old settee, her unbandaged arm resting on a cushion, waiting for Ruby to make the poultice. The wound looked angry. The edges of the torn flesh were purple and raw; a substance as thin and lumpy as sour milk leaked from between the puckered folds. When Ruby came in and placed the gauze as gently as she could on her throbbing forearm, Sadie bit her lip and stared straight ahead, fixing her eyes on

Ruby. In profile, Ruby's face appeared distorted, her torn lip and bruised cheeks making the outline almost unrecognisable. It was over a week since Johnny had brought her home, and every night she'd heard the poor kid moving around in her room long after she should have been asleep.

After she'd rebandaged her arm, Ruby put the soiled wadding on the fire, pressing it down with the poker until it took hold. As the flames began to leap, Sadie watched their light turn Ruby's scabbed face into a repellent mask.

'Come and sit with me for a bit,' she said. 'I know, you can tell me the story of that book you're reading. Or I could tell you about the film we saw; it was ever so good.'

Ruby smiled and went to get her book from the mantelpiece, but then the gate latch clanked and she scuttled away.

'Ruby, don't go,' Sadie called, getting up from her seat as the kitchen door closed. 'It's only Michael. He'll have come to see Da. Stay and say hello.'

Ruby didn't get as far as the top of the stairs, before her granddad's bedroom door opened. The effort of dressing quickly had made him wheeze, and as he held on to the banister, she buttoned up his cardigan for him.

'It's Michael, Granddad. He'll have brought that cable you've been wanting,' she whispered, tucking the ends of his white muffler inside his collarless shirt. 'Flatten your hair down. It's standing up at the back.'

He nodded breathlessly and patted her arm, before edging his way down to the kitchen. Ruby followed him to the turn in the stairs and then sat with her head against the distempered wall, tucking her skirt over her legs to keep off the draught blowing in under the back door.

Since the GIs first visited the cottage, Michael and Granddad had spent weeks repairing an old motorbike. Now Granddad's chest was too bad for him to go outside, but it hadn't stopped them. Instead of working in the yard or in the Anderson shelter, he got Holt to bring the bits into the kitchen. Then, if Jenny wasn't there to stop them, they'd spend hours rubbing and polishing, until Granddad's breathing gave out. Like Granddad, Michael loved engines, and Granddad said he had a feel for them. She knew that was probably why he liked Holt the best: he didn't get tired of discussing motorbike engines, or listening to Granddad's tales about his time in the trenches in France. She supposed Michael enjoyed the stories because they were new to him.

Ruby waited on the stairs, listening to Sadie moving around, hearing the cups chink and the sound of Michael's boots on the flags as he carried the tray back into the front room for her. Then she tiptoed downstairs into the gloomy kitchen and put her ear close to the door.

'Thanks, Michael,' Sadie said. 'Just put the pot down on the hearth. How are things with you?'

'I'm fine,' he said. 'Here, let me pour the water into the pot. I got a letter from Arleen a couple of days ago. Is that enough water?'

'Yes, that's fine. I can manage to pour it out, but we'll let it brew first.'

Ruby perched on the edge of the kitchenette

303

and prised the living-room door open until she could see a sliver of light. Holt and Arleen had married just before he came to England and she lived with his parents, because they couldn't find a flat of their own.

'How is she?' Sadie asked.

'Things are getting worse. She's real fed up. There's not much room and her mother wants her to go back home, but I don't want her to, 'cos her brothers don't like me.'

'How's the rationing over there? Is it as bad as here?'

'No. I don't think so. There are petrol and meat shortages. Problem is, Arleen works in a department store, and it's running short on some things, and part of the money Arleen makes is commission on what she sells. She's thinking about munitions work to get more money. Her brothers and her mom don't like the idea.'

'I wouldn't mind trying munitions,' Sadie said. 'I suppose it depends what job you get. It's good money. They're strict about things like smoking. Have to be. They check you for fags and matches and any metal. You can't even have hairpins. Lou has this mate, and she said they have a long way to walk between buildings and a lot of it's underground.'

'That's not fooled Jerry, though,' Granddad said. 'They even know the colour they've painted the railings.'

The kitchen was getting darker, and Ruby could hear rain, sharp and hard, on the kitchen window. She shivered and hoped that Holt wouldn't stay for tea. Since the night at Doctor Grey's, she

304

didn't want to see any of the GIs – not even Con. She didn't want to see anyone. She knew Sadie would be disappointed that it wasn't Bo who had called, but Bo, Wes and Con were away a lot of the time now, driving trucks up and down to the ports and the airfields. Holt could still visit, because someone at the camp had found out he was good at mending things and now he stayed there most of the time to repair the engines. She rested her head against the frosted glass in the kitchenette and peered into the living room. Granddad and Holt were sitting at the table with their heads together.

'Da, can you do the curtains?' Sadie asked. 'This poultice Ruby's put on my arm is pulling.'

'Well, that's good,' he said. 'If you can feel it pulling, it means it's drawing the badness out of your arm. It's working.'

'I know, but it hurts like mad.'

'Well, off you go and get one of Jenny's headache tablets from upstairs. That should move it.'

Before Sadie could get out of the chair, Ruby was across the kitchen. She took the stairs two at a time and rushed headlong into the darkening bedroom. In the half-light, her foot struck something that clattered across the floor. Her stomach twisted and she scrambled for the blackout curtain and the light. On the floor, she could see Sadie's upended dish and wash jug. Since the attack, no matter how carefully she washed, her skin didn't feel clean. At first, she'd used an old bucket, carrying it up to her room, rubbing at the long gouges scored into her thighs, making them sting and bleed. Then one morning Sadie had caught her and brought in the pretty blue-and-white set from her washstand. Ruby picked up the jug and the dish, breathlessly fingering each surface, fearing a chip or crack. The soapy water inside was icy, and when she'd finished, she put them on the chair for safety and curled up on the bed.

She'd learnt to call what happened that night an accident. When Johnny brought her home, Jenny had been waiting up for her. He'd helped her over to Granddad's chair, and Jenny stood in front of her, wiping her hands on her apron and looking from her to Johnny and back again, but she hadn't said anything. They'd left her. At first, she'd heard angry voices in the kitchen, and then he'd brought the blanket from her bed, wrapped her up and given her brandy. She'd shaken so much the glass rattled on her teeth. After she'd finished it, Jenny bathed her face and told her she must say that she'd fallen over in the dark, and since then, it hadn't been mentioned.

Ruby rolled over and looked at the cottage on her rug. Before Con kissed her, when she'd looked at the rug, she'd imagined the soldier who'd given her the letter was coming home to his girl, Maggie Joy. After the kiss, Ruby had imagined that, instead of Maggie Joy, she was in the bedroom under the thatched roof, sitting in front of the mirror on the dressing table, listening for the sound of the front gate opening. Sometimes she wasn't listening, she was reading Con's letter, and when he came to the door it was a surprise. Then he'd take hold of her hand and tell her that he'd come to spend his last two days with her, before going off to war. Other times, she imagined that he was coming home for good. They would walk in the garden, looking at the lupins, and he would tell her he wanted to marry her and take her to America. But now, instead of imagining that gentle kiss, there were yellow teeth biting into her lip and filling her mouth and nose with their sour taste.

The next day Sadie was feeling better. After dinner she volunteered to walk into the village for the shopping, and Granddad, who'd been awake in the night with his cough, went for a nap. As Ruby was clearing the plates in the kitchen, she heard two quick rat-a-tat-tats on the front door. Guessing it must be Johnny Fin – who always did two quick raps on the knocker – she hurried to the front door wiping her hands on the tea towel. When she opened the door, Doctor Grey raised his trilby.

Doctor Grey's car – with Dick behind the wheel – was waiting by the gate, pulsating softly in its own small off-white cloud. She couldn't quite see if there was someone in the back seat of the car, because the hedge was in the way. She stood on tiptoe and thought that she could make out the top of a familiar cloche hat. Her stomach squeezed with excitement; she was glad that she'd spent the morning cleaning the brasses and had just dusted the crumbs from the table, but then Dick rolled the car forward and she could see that the back seat was empty: Doctor Grey was alone.

He followed her into the cottage, and putting his bag and a parcel on the table, drew her towards the window, turning her chin to the left and then the right. He asked about her injuries, where she had fallen and why. Ruby recited her well-practised tale. Doctor Grey raised an eyebrow, and when he asked if she'd been alone, she touched her lip and nodded. The parcel contained the tinned peaches, the present from Alice she'd dropped when Rollo had grabbed her, and some sheet music she'd left behind after one of the fundraising concerts.

'It's probably better,' he said, 'now you're getting older, to look for more permanent employment. In the factory, perhaps? It would be more patriotic,' he said, replacing his hat and moving towards the door. 'I'm sure Alice will be happy to give you a reference.'

Jenny found the tin of peaches still on the table when she and Sadie arrived home.

'Well the mill's not going to take you on looking like that,' she said. 'You should have said you wanted paying until you could work.'

Sadie handed the two bottles of stout she was carrying to Ruby and went to the looking glass over the dresser.

'Oh, Ma,' she said, rolling her eyes at Ruby through the mirror, 'it's not their fault she fell on the way home. And anyway, if you'd remembered to tell her to wait for Johnny, she might not–'

'I thought...' Ruby whispered, one of the bottles of stout slipping from her fingers and crashing to the floor. 'I thought... I didn't know he was coming... I'd have waited and...'

'Now look what you've done,' Jenny shouted. 'I've Henry struggling to breathe, and you ... and only my money. He told me she was only here for a few weeks, and now she's stopping for good.

And who's going to pay for that? Not him. Not her. Not you. I'm the only one as is working here.'

'What's goin' on?' Henry called between coughs.

'Are you happy now you've got him up?' Jenny hissed, rescuing the second bottle from Ruby's trembling fingers. 'Ruby, make yourself useful and go and see what he wants. Sadie, stop gawping at yourself and get a cloth and clean this mess up.'

'I'll get paid,' Sadie said, red blotches appearing on her neck as she turned to face her mother. 'When Jack Holloway was hurt—'

'You think you're so bloody cocky. Blokes get compensation if they're hurt 'cos they've families depending on them,' Jenny said, her hand shaking as she poured water from the kettle into a waiting pot. 'You'll not. You'll be depending on me, and don't forget it. Ruby, bloody shift yourself. Go and see what Henry wants.'

The day after the argument, Sadie hugged her. 'She's upset,' she said. 'She feels guilty. That night, New Year's Eve, Johnny had called to see Da and he was asleep. He'd said he'd call for you, but you'd have to wait until he'd finished at the pub, and she forgot to say. If you'd been with Johnny on the way home, you might not have fallen and then... Well, you were going to leave the Greys anyway. She shouldn't have let Johnny think it was his fault. That was mean. I reckon it's because they're not married, her and Henry. If anything happens, we'll be out. She's scared.'

Ruby nearly told her, nearly confessed about the lie, but if she'd spoken about it, that might

309

have made it more real. As the bruises faded and the cuts healed, there were times, when she was busy, that she would forget it had happened, except that it felt strange not going to the house any more, and she missed Mrs Grey and Alice. She tried to stay out of Jenny's way when she could and made a bit of money, once her face was presentable, cleaning books for Mrs Bland. The other thing that had changed was that she didn't like the dark, but Mrs Bland always waited at her door until she reached the cottage, and then she would call goodnight.

Although Mrs Bland's cottage was very cold and smelt strongly of her cat, Ruby gradually developed a liking for the old lady. Mrs Bland always treated her as though she were a visitor, even when she was paying her to do some cleaning. She would ask her opinions about the books she'd given her to read and she really listened to her answers. Tonight, she'd been invited just to visit, and they sat together knitting blankets for homeless families and listening to the news on the radio.

'I think we should celebrate such good news, Ruby, dear,' she said, at the end of the broadcast, and offered Ruby a liquorice toffee from a small paper bag. 'The Germans are going to be forced to use their Junker 52s to relieve their army outside Stalingrad. The front's eighty miles away now and halfway to Rostov. Hundreds shot down. It makes one feel so humble, does it not, and so proud.'

Mrs Bland's delight at the destruction of the encircled German army made her knitting even more holey than usual and added to the blanket's irregular shape.

'Now tell me what did you think of *Tess?* Did you enjoy it?'

'I couldn't,' Ruby said, concentrating on her knitting, 'understand why Alec d'Urberville was so unkind. He was supposed to be a gentleman and educated. How can you... How could she know? When someone is kind, and is ... well... How do you know? Men... I mean, people... If someone... I mean, how can you tell? How would you ever know? Or they might be like Angel...'

'No one ever really can look in another's heart, dear. You can sometimes watch and judge...'

'But when you can't. When someone seems nice, or harmless and then...'

'The important thing is that you don't lose faith in yourself. Life is hard, dear. A pretty young woman is vulnerable. Poor Tess had so little power over her own life. We women must fight to have control. We have the vote, and one thing this awful war might do is give us more sway. In the last war, women were able to show that they could do men's jobs, and now they are doing it again. Money, financial independence, is so important. In their relationships with men ... well that's more difficult. Many, most women, you could say, are economic and emotional slaves.'

'You mean because men get all the say at home? Granddad doesn't. Though he does rent the cottage. I suppose we would all have to go, if he said so. It's not the same as a real slave. We would be free to go, if we could find somewhere. Why do you think the black people stayed in the south? Why didn't they all go to the north? Con's grandma did. Do you remember, he said she was

311

an educated lady, but she still thought of the white family as her betters?'

On the opposite side of the weak, smoky fire, Mrs Bland sucked contentedly on her sweet and considered the question.

'There were threats and brutality, of course, but also the slave owners knew that the most successful way to control their slaves was by encouraging loyalty.' Mrs Bland stopped knitting and peered at Ruby over her glasses. 'Loyalty is a very powerful means of control,' she said. 'They used slaves to help in the houses. The women wet-nursed their white owners' babies, and house slaves were brought up as part of the family. Then, even when they were freed, some were still tied emotionally to the people who'd exploited them.'

'Like Con's grandmother?'

'Indeed.'

'From what Con and the others have said, where they live it's still not equal.'

'No. Competition for jobs has always been a factor, of course, but the black people,' Mrs Bland said, wrapping the discarded knitting around her legs, 'are treated differently, solely because of their colour. I think now there is a fear that after the war, when the black soldiers go home, they will want to change things. Here, when the men come back, they'll want their women back in the kitchen, as they did before, but many women will want to keep their freedom and financial independence; they'll be used to making decisions for themselves. Things will be different for the young. Young men like Con will want to change things for their people. Such a

312

charming young man, don't you think? Loves reading. Now, that's always a sign of a sensitive man. He's read this one,' she said, dislodging the cat that was sitting on the book and handing it to Ruby. 'You could too, and then you might ask him how he enjoyed it, the next time he calls to see your grandfather.'

It was almost a fortnight later before Ruby saw Con. He came to the cottage one evening just after tea to see her granddad, the collar of his overcoat pulled up over his ears.

'I've come to pick Henry up,' he said, grinning at her. 'We... We have a bit of business.'

Her granddad, whose chest was improving, had been nodding over his newspaper, but he was quickly on his feet and hurrying out to the kitchen.

'I'll be with you in a minute, lad,' he called.

'Are you on your own?'

'Jenny's working extra shifts and Sadie's at the pictures with Bo.'

'He said you'd hurt yourself. Are you okay?'

Ruby blushed and nodded, as an oath and the sound of a clattering came from the kitchen.

'I'd best go and see what he's up to,' she said.

Granddad had dragged out an old mac from under the stairs and was pulling on the boots he used in the garden.

'You're not going to the pub dressed like that.'

'Pub? Ah, well, no. Well, if Jenny asks.'

'It's cold out.'

'I'm wrapped up. This old mac's really warm. Now, we don't want Jenny to worry, and I'll probably be back before she is.'

313

'But where–?'

'Never mind about that.'

'It's not fire-watching...'

'Fire-watching? That's right. I've not been since before Christmas. I thought I'd see how they was–'

'Then why is Con–?'

'Now, don't you worry, Ruby, love,' he said, hurrying back into the living room and pulling his cap from the peg near the door. 'I'll be back in no time. Come on, young Con.'

In the living room, Con stamped his feet, warmed his hands on the fire and listened to the conversation in the kitchen with interest. He wasn't very clear about Henry's plans. He'd agreed to come along because recently, without a late pass to go into town, he'd found the local pubs fairly dull. The dances in the villages were fine, but not half as lively as the ones in town, and the cinema close to the camp was real small and got so full that sometimes the audience's cigarette smoke almost blotted out the screen.

He'd bumped into the two old guys a couple of days before on his way back to camp and joined them for a drink and a game of darts. In the afternoon the pub was empty, and Con had been pleased at the thought that he was away from camp without permission. The old guys always told lots of stories, and he didn't mind listening and going along with the tales.

When Henry was ready, they left the cottage. Con followed his directions to a white farmhouse standing in the middle of low-lying fields and parked up on an old farm track under a clump of poplar trees. Inside the cab, the old man's chest

and the borrowed truck's cooling engine murmured.

'You okay, Henry?' he asked.

'Aye, lad, just gettin' me breath. Johnny will be
here in a minute. Told him to meet us here. He'll
have been out with his gun shooting rabbits, or
trapping vermin for local farmers, or the odd bit
of poaching. Can turn his hand to anything.'

'Do you want a drink?'

'Oh, good lad. That'll help no end,' he said
taking the bottle of whisky. 'Eee that's good. Gets
right down the tubes, that does.'

A few days earlier, when he'd been sitting in the
pub listening to their stories, Johnny had told
him about the sugar smuggling. At first Con
hadn't taken much notice, but then they'd told
him how one of the men behind the smuggling
was this guy Prendergast, the same guy who'd
wanted the old priest to ban the black GIs from
the Christmas dances, the guy whose wife was
planning how she and some of the other rich folk
could turn local people against them. In the
warm pub, the plan hadn't sounded so crazy and
he'd promised he'd help.

In the moonlight, he could see the large black-
and-white house across the field. It had been
Johnny who'd discovered the smuggling on one
of his shooting trips. The way he told it, he'd seen
an unfamiliar van taking a corner too quickly,
and when the van turned into the drive and
speeded in the direction of the farm, it had
whetted his interest. He'd followed and watched
from behind a hedge, as the sacks were carried
from the van to the old stables. Johnny knew it

couldn't be feed, because they didn't have any horses. When the van drove away, he'd crept into the yard and found the stack of sugar under a tarpaulin in one of the old stalls.

Con shivered and took the whisky bottle back from Henry. Clouds slipped over the moon, leaving only a hint of silver in the sky. The field and the white house had gone. Near the cab, just outside in the blackness, he heard an unearthly cry and thought of Johnny and the animal traps. Then Henry's door was thrown open, and Johnny Fin climbed up beside him.

'We could drive in closer,' Johnny said. 'They're out at some big meeting. Him and his missus both go. Top dog round here, and he's makin' money hand over fist sellin' black-market sugar.'

Con drove the truck out on to the road and then down a pitted track that led to the house. As Johnny had said, it was in darkness.

'How can you be sure there's nobody home?'

'No car, and there's a meeting tonight. They're both on the committee, him and her. There's no help in the house. Only Derek Foley's missus and she only does the odd morning.'

'You got a spade?' Johnny asked, as he jumped down from the truck. 'They might have put the stuff under a pile of muck to hide it.'

'You didn't say about any muck,' Con said.

'Well, it was inside under a tarpaulin, but it's been moved. There's a pile of muck against the wall. It's old stuff, but I reckon that's where they've hidden it.'

They followed Johnny along the track and into the stable yard. The moon had disappeared

316

again. He couldn't see clearly, but followed the sound of Henry's wheezing and wondered how they would escape if anyone did arrive. The muck, partly protected from the weather by the stable's wall and overhanging roof, was heavy but dry. It didn't smell as bad as he'd feared, but he wasn't used to using a spade, and their digging disturbed a lot of creatures that skittered over his boots in the darkness. Then the full moon came out from behind the clouds and with Johnny's help, he got the hang of the digging.

'Wait a minute lads, we've hit something,' Johnny said, exploring the hole they'd cleared in the muck. 'Here we are,' he said, tugging out an old feed sack that had been used to cover the sugar. 'Look at this lot. Didn't I tell you? This lot will make us a pretty penny.'

'You're going to sell it?' Con asked, his voice sounding louder than he intended in the quiet night. 'But that's just as bad...'

'Not at all,' Henry said between coughs. 'He's tellin' folk what they should do. Makin' out he's somebody and all the time... Anyway, we'll not charge as much, and them that can't afford, will get it free.'

Con sighed; he shouldn't have come. When he'd heard what they were planning, Holt had warned him to stay out of it, but by then it was arranged, and he wasn't going to let the old guys think he was a coward.

Carrying the sugar to the truck was a problem. Henry had helped with the digging but he'd needed to stop every few minutes. By the time they'd loaded up the sacks with packets of sugar, the sound of his breathing filled up the still night. Con gazed around; there wasn't a sign of anyone at the house, but every moment he expected the door of the white house to open and someone to come running out. Henry insisted on carrying his share and got Con to lift the sacks on to his back for him. Then, bent almost in two, he made his way to the truck. Con and Johnny did two or three to each of Henry's one trip, but he refused to give in, and by the time they were finished, he was too breathless to climb into the truck without help.

'I think we deserve a drink on tonight's work, lads,' Johnny Fin said, when they'd thrown the last sack into the back of the truck. 'Yes, a couple of pints will go down nicely.'

The pub was quiet, and Con sat with the two older men in front of the fire. Henry looked pale and his breathing was still uneven. When he'd tried to smoke, he coughed so much he had to sit forward with his hands on his knees, gulping in the fuggy, warm air.

'I don't know about unloading that sugar, Henry,' Johnny said, winking at Con. 'I think I'll have to carry you home on me shoulders, like I did in France. Did he tell you about that, young Con? Five miles it must have been, over rough ground. Though it felt like bloody twenty. Infantry, you see. Right on the front line. You're with a better lot, believe you me. Never mind Bo sayin' you lads should be fighting. There's not a soldier alive as would want his boy to be on the front line.'

'Bo doesn't want anyone to think us cowards. None of us do. We want to fight. Well, except... I

318

don't know if I could, for real.'

'Ah, you'd be as good as the next man,' Henry said, recovering and taking a long drink of beer. 'It's the training that kicks in. Everybody's terrified. You'd be a madman not to be. When you look at it, war is always the same, working men killing each other. The leaders never get it in the guts, do they? Most of the time you're killing people you can't see. Not up close, anyway. Then it's just a job you've been trained to do, but sometimes... There was this one bloke. I think he was lost in the smoke or looking for his mate. It was a reaction. Like I said, the training takes over. Then we was trapped with the counter-attack, and he was there next to me on the ground, as close as you are to me now. This Jerry, about the same age we were. He can't have suffered. Must have gone instantly. He had segs on his hands and a picture in his pocket of his wife and kiddie. His gun ... well you could tell he took pride in it; looked after it, like a workman should with his tools.'

Johnny got up and went to the bar. Con was about to suggest that they had a game of darts, when he came hurrying back.

'You'd best be makin' your way to the camp, young Con. Bert's just heard the MPs are goin' in the pubs checkin' passes. That truck outside will attract attention. There's a rumour some of your lads and the white lads have been fighting. Big scrap's been arranged, so he heard.'

After Granddad and Con had left the cottage, Ruby was alone until Jenny arrived home pale and exhausted from her shift at the factory. As

319

she took off her headscarf and lit a cigarette, the hens began to squawk.

'Where's your granddad?' she asked.

'Con called for him earlier. I think... Well, he didn't really say. I think they went fire-watching.'

'Fire-watching?' Jenny said, grabbing her torch and heading for the door. 'Fire-watching, with his chest? I'll give 'im fire-watching.'

It was hard to make out the figures in the dark garden. Ruby stood next to Jenny and listened. Somewhere in the thick night, something moved. Ruby held her breath and wrapped her arms around her body. Jenny's torch – a quivery, uncertain orange – swept the garden, picking up two figures that were half concealed by the Anderson shelter. For a moment there was silence. Then they heard the rattle of Henry's familiar wheezing cough, followed by the clatter of the shelter door and Johnny and her granddad tittering together like schoolboys. The sound made her feel safe, and when Jenny walked back in the house and slammed the door, she decided to wait for them, planning to slip away upstairs once Jenny had begun her scolding. She was pulling her jumper over her fingers to keep them warm when she heard the sound of breaking glass. Ruby thought for a second that the two dafties had stepped on the cold frame, but Johnny's frightened yell sent her running up the garden. He put on his torch, guiding her along the path to where a body, rigid and cruciform, lay groaning pitifully. Ruby scrambled over her granddad, pulling out his pockets until she found the small pill bottle.

Gradually, as the pain gave way, they got Henry into the cottage. Once they were inside, they helped him out of his coat and into his armchair. Jenny, who was sitting at the table, didn't move, but went on eating her stew. Ruby poured brandy and warm water into a glass and held it to the old man's lips, as Johnny looked on anxiously, twisting his cap in his hands.

'We got wind of old Prendergast storing black-market sugar,' he said. 'Young Con offered to help us.'

'That's what you brought here, is it?' Jenny asked. 'Black-market sugar you've stolen from Prendergast?'

'Nowhere else to hide it. It's in the shelter. I'll move it on. I'll get someone tomorrow. But n-not tonight. Don't worry I'll k-keep it moving, until we've got customers. Leave it to me.'

'He was much better, almost ready to go back to work. All three of them – this one as well,' Jenny said, nodding towards Ruby, 'haven't been earning, but eating and under my feet all the time. I've had to work extra shifts. No other money coming in. Then, I come home tonight, and now look at him.'

'I don't think it was Con's fault,' Ruby said.

'Oh, you don't, miss? And how do you know? You can keep your nose out. You've caused enough trouble as it is.'

Jenny got up from the table and Granddad, whose colour was returning, waved Johnny to a seat.

'Now, I'll thank you to be on your way, Johnny Fin,' Jenny said, replacing the brandy bottle.

321

'You'll clear that sugar out by tomorrow. I don't care how. And don't call round for a while, and you can tell Con the same thing. We've more than enough problems, without inviting more.'

The next day Ruby put on her cream jumper and tartan skirt and went to the factory. She was shown into a small, dusty office. The manager, a plump man in shirtsleeves, studied her over some rolls of cloth.

'You'd normally come with a parent,' he said. 'I'd want to see that your parents have given you permission.'

Ruby explained that her mother was dead and that she lived with her granddad who was too ill to come with her.

'Irene, give her a form, will you?' he said.

When the middle-aged woman got up from behind a typewriter to hand her the form, Ruby noticed that, in addition to the usual desks and cupboards, the office also had two camp beds.

'You get him to sign that form, and then you can start,' he said. 'I'm going up to the spinning room now, so you can come and look round. You'll be working nine hours. That's the regulations for a girl your age, but there's overtime, but not fire-watching,' he said, nodding towards the camp beds. 'You're too young.'

He put the light on and led the way up a flight of wooden stairs. All the mill's windows were blacked out and no hint of the outside light came through. At the top of the steps, he pulled open a brown door. The noise, the incessant pounding, filled her body. She gasped with the shock of it, and her

322

mouth filled with a sticky heat. The man beckoned to a woman who edged towards them between the long rows of pumping machines, trundling a huge box on wheels behind her. She wore a short-sleeved blouse under a sleeveless wrap-around overall. Tendrils of hair escaped from under her turban and stuck to her damp face.

'This is Elsie – Mrs Rostron. She'll show you what to do. She's thinking of starting here, Elsie,' he said. 'I thought doffing. I know they're short-handed.'

Mrs Rostron took a rag out of her pocket and wiped her neck. 'She ever done this sort of work?'

'No. She'll want showing.'

Mrs Rostron wrinkled her forehead and walked out of the door, pulling the box full of bobbins behind her.

The next day, Granddad stayed in bed. For weeks now, the sky had been grey and sullen, each day moving drowsily through the half-light, and it was hard to remember a time when it hadn't been so dreary. Ruby waited until mid morning before she took up a tray with two cups of tea. Granddad was sitting up in bed, choosing seeds for the spring. Once he was sipping cheerfully at his tea, she told him about the factory and gave him the form.

'It's a nasty, rough place for a little lass,' he said. 'Jenny has a sharp tongue sometimes, I know. It was me that she should have taken it out on. I'm an old fool. Why don't you go back to work for Mrs Grey? You like it there, playing the piano, and it pays your way.'

Ruby shook her head. 'I'm grown-up now,' she

323

said, 'and Doctor Grey said it would be more patriotic to work at the factory. Jenny's having to pay for us all.'

Henry sighed. 'It should be me as is bringing in the money, not you. She's right, all I've done is make me chest worse, and she's takin' it out on you and poor Johnny.'

'And Con,' Ruby said. 'She told Johnny to tell him he's not welcome.'

'Well, if you're determined to do it. You can do one thing for me, though. Call in on Maud. I'll let Johnny know to leave some sugar for her, and you could pick her some veg, but don't let on. Perhaps you could have your baggin' there some days, for a bit of company. I'm not sure you'll take to some of them women at the factory. Some's all right, decent folk, but they tease the young 'uns.'

'Would she let me take her dog out? What sort is it?'

'Dog? Our Maud's not got a dog.'

'But she got bones for it at the butcher's.'

Granddad handed back the form and shook his head. 'They'd be for a stew for her and Joe. She's a proud woman, you see. She'd not want the rest of them to know she can't afford meat. It's fine tellin' us what rations we can have. With the war coming, there's more work about, but if you're too old or ill to work, you can't afford the prices anyway. No point tellin' the likes of Maud and Joe they can have good cuts of meat. They can't afford 'em, rations or not.'

Ruby didn't mind the women in the factory. The work – putting empty bobbins on the spinning machines and taking them off again when they were full – was hard, because there were so many machines in the room. She hated the noise and the thick, damp heat. At the end of each shift, she was glad to escape outside into the cold, smoky air. Then she wished the hours would slow down, until she had to go back to work again.

There wasn't anyone of her own age in the same room, and most days she and Elsie Rostron sat together to eat their food. Elsie had two sons, one in the army and one in the navy. Her daughter worked at the factory as well, but because she had young children, she didn't do many hours. Like most of the people at the mill, Elsie Rostron knew her granddad, and she also knew Alice and Dick.

'I saw Alice,' she said, during one of their tea breaks. 'She was asking after you. Asked if you was all right, after your accident. Said to tell you she felt terrible for letting you go that night. She wasn't sure what had happened. Said Doctor Grey didn't say much, except that you wasn't coming back. Her niece is working there now. Said it was funny, because she'd found the tin of peaches and your basket in the garden, but she couldn't understand, if you'd been hurt there, why you didn't go back in the house and tell her.'

Ruby couldn't think clearly. It was only a couple of weeks after she'd begun working in the spinning room, and her head still throbbed from the constant noise.

'I fell twice,' she said. The lie made her mouth dry, and she sipped greedily at the cold tea from her billycan. 'I slipped in the garden and ... my torch... I couldn't find it and I couldn't find my basket,' she said, feeling her face begin to burn as she struggled on. 'I slipped in the garden and... Then I was walking, and this truck came really close ... and I fell.'

'You was lucky. Though, couldn't you have gone in and borrowed a torch? I wouldn't have liked to walk all that way without one.'

The first week she'd begun working at the mill, Ruby had taken Maud and Joe some vegetables from Granddad's garden. She'd knocked at the door, and when Auntie Maud answered it, she'd asked her in. They'd sat in the little living room and talked about the factory. Maud told her how she and the other weavers used signals and lipreading to talk to each other and how, when the mills had closed for the men to check the boilers, they'd all gone away for a holiday by the sea. Ruby remembered people from different mill towns coming to the seaside and walking in big laughing crowds along the prom. Maud told her stories about the days out, and she found a photo of herself standing in front of one of the looms on the day some dignitaries came to inspect the factory. The photo showed Maud as a young woman, staring back unsmilingly at the camera with the looms pounding around her.

'How did you stand it?' Ruby asked. 'The noise and–'

'I would go back tomorrow, if they'd let me. I was one of their best weavers. Had more frames than anyone else,' Maud said, her face brightening. 'Never had any fault in the cloth I wove. I've heard there's all sorts coming out of there now as wouldn't have been passed when I was there.'

To avoid Mrs Rostron's questions, Ruby began having her dinner with Maud and Joe. She was afraid to take too many vegetables and only dared steal the odd egg, but she tried to help in other ways: each evening when she made her baggin' she'd slip in a little extra and invited Auntie Maud and Joe to help themselves, which they sometimes did, and she always took a twist of tea with her or some sugar. Some days she would play snap with Joe, or she would take an old newspaper, because one of his favourite things was drawing glasses and moustaches on the photographs. Other times Joe would be lying very still, hardly breathing at all. Maud would put a cold tea cloth on his head, and she would rub his hands and tell her 'Joe wasn't himself'.

One day when Joe looked quite poorly, Ruby called in again after work to see if he was better and found him sitting up happily playing dominoes with Johnny Fin.

'Maud said you might call,' he said, pulling up a chair for her near the board. 'Joe's started looking forward to you coming.'

When it was Joe's turn, Johnny called out for him what tiles he needed to put down. The games were quite slow, because Joe took a while to decide which dominoes to play. Ruby soon realised that Johnny could see Joe's tiles and often changed the order in which he put his own tiles down so that Joe would win. Each time he won, Uncle Joe got really excited and everyone had to clap and cheer for him.

'Is Jenny still mad?' Johnny asked, as they were

turning over the tiles at the end of a game.

When he mentioned Jenny's name, Maud, who had been reading the newspaper through her magnifying glass, made a disapproving noise and went into the scullery.

'There's no love lost there,' Johnny said, nodding in the direction of the scullery door. 'She thinks Henry is a fool for taking up with Jenny and that it'll end up with trouble. Maud thinks he'd be better off without her, and there's no point arguing.'

'Granddad's much better. He's hoping to be back at work by the end of the month. Should be getting milder by then, and the money from the sugar has come in handy.'

'Aye, well, once he's on the mend and back at work, perhaps it will all be forgotten.'

They played dominoes until the factory hooter made her jump and she noticed that the blackout curtains had been drawn.

'I'll be off,' she said. 'I'll try and catch a couple of the women. They live further down the road than our cottage.'

'No, stay,' Johnny said. 'Let's finish this game, and then I'll be going your way. I've got a bit of business with John Bardley.'

Outside coal smoke hung damply over the narrow streets. Ruby shivered and put her arm through Johnny's.

'How are you, Ruby, love?'

'I just… Well, I don't like to go out. I think he might…'

'Oh, I don't think you'll see him again.'

'Why…? You mustn't…'

328

'Oh, don't worry, my pet. Though it's what I'd like to do. N-n-no. Th-that sister of his has told... Well, it's come from Dick, really. They couldn't make out what had happened. I know they... Well, his sister, Mrs Grey, told them that he went out in the garden and heard somebody, and when he went to tackle them ... for t-trespassing ... they knocked him down and stole his wallet. I don't know if that's what he told her, or if she's made it up. Then Alice and Dick were foxed, you see. They thought it was funny that you fell and hurt yourself, and then the same night he gets attacked.'

'Alice said something like that to Mrs Rostron. I work with her. She said she couldn't see why I didn't go back in, if I'd fallen in the garden. I forgot the basket, you see. I lied. I said I fell in the garden and lost my torch, and then on the road a lorry came close to me and–'

'Never you mind. There'll be some other poor bugger to gossip about soon enough, and Alice has got her own family in at the house now, so she's suited. He's gone back to London where they came from. That's what Alice says. Got some job in supplies or something. Doctor's wife, she's put it about that he was ill, but that he's gone because he couldn't stand not doing his bit. Alice says Mrs Grey's really down now he's gone. So we'll not see him again. I hope I'll see you at Maud's. I'll not be seeing much of you at your grandpa's until Jenny's calmed down. She's all right, is Maud. Had a hard life, that's all.'

'I've got used to her now,' Ruby said, opening the cottage gate. 'I like her and Joe and Mrs Bland. Johnny, do you think Con will come back as well, once Jenny's calmed down?'

'Con? I suppose he might. Though he's a young chap and he'll have plenty of other things to keep him occupied. It was us that got him to help, you know. It wasn't anything to do with him, not really.'

At first, when he'd found out from Bo that he should stay away from the cottage, Con had been angry with Henry for getting him into trouble with the old lady, but later he'd decided it was probably for the best; Sadie was a flirt and he was anxious not to upset Bo. Then a couple of days after he'd been given Jenny's message, the promised new lieutenant arrived at the camp. He was very keen on baseball and he quickly found a site. The plan was to begin preparing the pitch as soon as the weather improved. The rest of the time, when he wasn't working, Con spent in the workshops learning all he could about the trucks, and when he did manage to get a pass, he went into town with the guys, dancing and drinking or to a movie. He tried to stay away from the battles with the white GIs, but it wasn't always easy.

Now it was spring, the damp huts were beginning to dry out and he'd grown accustomed to his new routine at the camp. He still went to the meetings, and Sergeant Mayfield was still trying to educate them. The talk that night was about General Andrew Jackson calling for black Louisiana volunteers to defend New Orleans. Con could see why he wanted them to understand their own history, but what was really worrying most of the guys were the rumours about what was happening back home and what the black papers were saying. These new concerns meant that a lot of the guys came as much to swap newspapers as to listen to Sarge Mayfield, who was in full flow.

'Jackson praised them for their courage, giving special mention to one of their commanders, Joseph Savory. There were two all-black battalions, three hundred in each, commanded by a black officer named Francis E. Dumas, who was a slave owner himself. But they weren't allowed to stay in the army, nor was there any public acclaim for their service...'

Con gazed out at the trees coming into bud. He reckoned Sergeant Mayfield was right about one thing: a lot of the trouble was because the army didn't like the idea of black GIs going back home and wanting to change things, once they'd seen how folk were treated outside their own country. He watched one of the guys from the South reading the newspaper, his lips moving slowly. He felt bad now to think that, when he'd been with southern guys in training and when they'd first come to the camp, he'd despised them for their lack of education; when he got home, he'd be a lot different.

The next day he went into the town with Holt. The sun was shining and the place was busy. As they wandered around the stalls on the flagged square in the centre of town, he was reminded of his mother and her fundraising for his father's church. The trees along the sidewalk were in blossom and the sun felt warm. The street climbed slightly uphill, and as Con gazed down, he saw Jenny puffing towards him. He didn't recognise the young woman with her at first, because the sun was in his eyes. Ruby grinned at him shyly. She was wearing a smart blue coat and had her hair curled differently. She looked real cute.

'It's a warm day,' Jenny said, dabbing her face. 'I'm that dry.'

'Can I get you a cup of tea? There's a stall over there and some benches and tables.'

'Well, that'd be very nice of you, lad,' she said, heading over to the wooden benches and tables set out under the trees.

Con bought tea for them and an extra one for Holt. 'I'm waiting for Michael, he's around here somewhere,' he said, waving his hand in the direction of the stalls and he smiled across at Ruby. 'I hardly recognised you,' he said. 'You look awful grown-up.'

'I'm working at the mill now,' Ruby said, her cheeks turning pink.

'Do you like it?'

'No, not really,' she said laughing, 'but the money's good. The work's boring, and I do get tired. I went round to Mrs Bland's to help her with her books last night and fell asleep in the chair. It was almost ten when she woke me up.'

'That's a good cup of tea and it's very welcome, I can tell you,' Jenny said, sipping the drink and patting her neck with her handkerchief. 'Ruby, love, I need to rest my legs. Will you nip and get my pills? I'll hang on here for Michael, and then I might feel more like a walk round the stalls. Try the chemist at the top by the library. Why don't you have a walk up with her, Con, and have a look round the stalls on your way back? There's

332

all sorts by the look of it, and it's all for a good cause. I think there's games as well as things to buy.'

'Is it okay if I walk up with you?' he asked.

'Of course it is,' Jenny said. 'Isn't it, Ruby?'

As he strolled along with Ruby, chatting about her granddad and life at the camp, Con watched the way the spring sunlight lit up her hair, and he couldn't help noticing the way the slim coat fitted her neat figure and the admiring looks she was getting from other guys who walked by them on the street.

'It's ages since you were at the cottage,' she said. 'I tried to explain to Jenny that it wasn't your fault, but she wouldn't listen, and if she knew the truth about the sugar, well both her and Granddad would fall out with Johnny. I knew he must be wrong when he said the sugar belonged to Mr Prendergast. I knew it couldn't be him. He's such an important man. I asked my Auntie Maud and she said that he hasn't owned that farm for a good few years. She's heard that the man who owned the sugar was from Liverpool. She said Granddad and Johnny should have known they didn't live there now. She said it was just typical of them to get such a daft idea.'

On another day, if someone else had told him, Con would have been real sore at the old guys for what they'd put him through, but today, with Ruby at his side, he just laughed.

'Well, I guess everybody got some cheap sugar and the guy lost out.'

'Look, this is the place,' she said, as they reached a small chemist shop next to a pub. 'You can wait out here if you want.'

'No, that's okay. I'll come inside with you.'

Con opened the door for her and stood aside as a large lady in a brown tweed suit bustled out calling good day to the assistant. Inside the little shop it was dark; every wall had a row of glass-fronted cupboards with large pear-shaped bottles filled with coloured liquid on top of them. The rich varnish on the cherrywood cases shone. The brass-handled doors sparkled and the powders, mixtures and pomades filled the air with a pleasant confusion of smells. A tall, stooped man with a rosy face and a pencil tied to the button-hole of his white overall came out from the back of the shop, blinking at them and smiling. Ruby asked if they had Doctor Cassell's tablets for blackout nerves, and he pushed one of his large pink ears forward and asked her to repeat what she'd said. When she asked for the pills again, the man nodded as if he'd understood, but then asked if they were for her dog or her cat. Con felt a chuckle begin to build in his chest and tried not to look at Ruby, who was explaining that she didn't have a pet, but a grandmother. The man mumbled something to himself and disappeared. Then he came back with a lady in a glowing white overall who asked Ruby what she wanted, and as Ruby explained, he pushed his large pink ear forward, nodding and smiling again, before asking the assistant what Ruby had said. The lady rolled a newspaper up into a cone and, putting the narrow end up to the man's ear, began shouting down it that Ruby wanted pills for her grandmother's nerves. Once he'd understood, he patted the assistant's hand and with an angelic smile handed Ruby a tiny box of pills.

They giggled almost all the way back to the little square, and Con realised that he felt happier than he had for weeks.

'Do you think she'll let me come and see you all sometime?' he asked.

'She might,' Ruby laughed, 'once she's had some of her nerve pills. She's still really mad at you and Johnny. Though, both me and Granddad said it wasn't your idea. I was a bit worried she might tell you off when we saw you, but her feet were that sore, she'd other things to think about.'

Con didn't want to go back. As they walked around the little stalls, he pretended more interest than he really felt in all the fundraising that was going on. He got Ruby to explain to him how he should pin the tail on the donkey, dawdled over the second-hand books on the Aid for Russia stall and insisted on watching the parade of children, dressed as characters from history, collecting money for the Build a Spitfire Fund. He put coins in all their tins and chatted to the children about their costumes. When the band struck up in the centre of the square and couples got up to dance, Con took Ruby's elbow.

Ruby blushed, but didn't refuse, and he was steering her towards the band when a white GI stood in their way.

'Not so fast, buddy,' he said. 'Where you goin' with this young lady?'

Ruby's blush turned to a deep red and she looked down at her hands. Con could feel his heart pounding. He looked over in the direction of the little stalls, glad that the crowd were around him. The GI had the same accent and the same brown eyes as the son of the Italian shoemaker from back home.

'Answer me, boy. What you doin' with this lady, here?' the guy drawled.

Around them, people were beginning to stare. 'Look,' Con said, 'I don't want any–'

'Say, honey,' the soldier said, pushing Con out of his way. 'You wanna dance?'

Ruby shook her head, but he grabbed her arm. Con could smell liquor on his breath, and when he pushed him away, the GI lost his footing and the Pin the Tail on the Donkey stall crashed to the floor. The drunken GI lay among the wreckage. On the other side of the stalls, another white GI and a dark-haired woman were watching them.

'You okay, Ruby?' Con asked, as the woman and the GI came around the stalls towards them.

'Come on, guy,' the white GI said, trying to get the drunken soldier to his feet.

'The MPs are coming,' the dark-haired woman said. 'Come on, love. We don't want trouble. Leave it to them.'

'Aw, let me handle this,' the GI replied and walked towards the MPs. 'It's okay, you guys,' he called. 'It was an accident. The guy just slipped,' he said, pointing to the drunken soldier who was getting up from the floor.

'Papers,' one of the MPs said, putting his hand out towards Con. 'You do this damage, boy?'

'It wasn't me.'

'Where's your papers?'

'It was an accident,' the white GI said. 'I told

336

you, the guy just slipped.'

'The black guy pushed me,' the drunken GI complained.

'You fell over, buddy. I was over there at the bookstall. I saw you.'

'I've asked to see this boy's papers. Now unless you want some trouble, you an' this lady had best just move along.'

Con unbuttoned his tunic pocket and handed over his pass.

'It wasn't his fault,' the GI protested again, as his girlfriend hurried him away.

'What you doin' here with this lady, boy?' the MP asked, throwing the pass on the floor.

The crowd around them began to mutter, and the white GI who had caused the trouble dusted himself off and staggered up to the main road. Con wasn't sure what to do, but he determined that whatever happened, he wasn't going to bend down in front of the two MPs and pick up the pass.

'It's okay, folks,' the MP said to the people watching, 'there's nothin' to see. We'll deal with this.'

'Pick up your pass, boy,' his buddy said.

'I'm not. I–'

'You what? You cheeking me?'

'Leave the lad alone,' someone in the crowd shouted.

'Now look what you've done,' the first MP said, pushing his face into Con's. 'You've upset these nice people. Now I'm goin' to have to arrest you.'

'No. Please,' Ruby said. 'It wasn't–'

The MP turned and smiled, as though he

337

hadn't noticed her before. 'Tell me, honey,' he said. 'What's a nice girl like you doin' with a black guy? Where I come from, nice girls don't associate with no blacks.'

'He's ... our friend,' Ruby said, close to tears. 'He's–'

'Leave them alone,' one of the women from the Pin the Tail on the Donkey stall called. 'It wasn't him. It was that drunken lout you let wander off. Go and sort him out, if you want to arrest somebody.'

'Go on, clear off, you're frightening the kiddies,' the man in charge of the Spitfire Fund shouted, as one of the little girls Con had given a penny to began to cry.

'We're just doin' our job, sir,' the first MP said, switching on his smile.

'Aye, well you've done it, and now you're upsetting folk.'

When the MPs turned to go, Con was shaking, but this time it wasn't fear that was making him tremble, but anger.

'Come on, you two,' Jenny said, pushing her way to the front of the crowd. 'I've got Michael to get me another cup of tea, before we walk round the stalls. Ruby, stop snivelling; he's not been hurt. I hope you'll come and see Henry the next time you get some time off, Con, love,' she said. 'You'd be very welcome; we've not seen you there for a while.'

CHAPTER THIRTEEN

The war meant there was little time for Con and Ruby to meet up, and the increasing scarcity of late passes made it even harder. The issue of the passes had made him and the rest of the guys at the camp very bitter: everyone knew that the white GIs got plenty more passes than the black guys did. As often as he dared, Con made up for his lack of passes by delaying his return to camp from the neighbouring bases: it didn't make up for the wrong he felt, but it helped to soothe his resentment. When Ruby was at home, he would call at the cottage and sit for a while in the steamy kitchen, watching her cook or mend, and listen to the radio, but on warmer days he would drag her away from her chores to walk under the new hazy-green canopy in the nearby woods. When there was no one at home at the cottage, he would call in at the pub, and when that was closed, he called on Mrs Bland and raided her library. One day he found the old lady unpacking books from a battered box and looking almost as spitting mad as her old cat.

'They asked for books to make a library for our soldiers. I was happy to contribute, but they've returned my donations – "too anti-war and pacifist in nature", apparently,' she said, kneeling by her unwelcome offerings.

'They look real nice,' Con said, reaching down

and ruffling the gilt-edged pages of one of the leather-bound tomes.

Appeased by his words, Mrs Bland looked up and smiled. 'You're a young man whose mind needs to be fed, your stomach as well, no doubt. Join me for some food. I have a stew, if you would care to share it. It is only plain vegetable and lentils, I'm afraid.'

They ate the stew out of large blue-and-white striped bowls at the bare wooden table, along with slices of rough, grey English bread, which they tore in pieces and soaked in the gravy to make it palatable. His grandma served her stew with corn bread that she made herself; Con smiled, as he thought how shocked she would have been at the sight of a white lady scooping up food with a spoon, without a tablecloth or napkin in sight.

'The anger you feel at your treatment,' Mrs Bland said, chasing the last piece of bread around her bowl. 'Don't let it burn uselessly inside you. Use your reading and your experiences to change things. The young men who come to your meetings at the camp need people to show them the way. Your sergeant is a wise man; learn from him. He knows how powerful knowledge can be. That's why they've rejected my books; writers are needed in times like these, as keepers of our ideas and dreams. If you take away access to ideas, you smother progress and freedom. Can I offer you a cup of tea, dear, and then we'll find something that might interest you?'

During that early spring, Ruby had learnt that the monotonous work – taking off and replacing the

340

bobbins on the spinning frames – meant that she didn't need to use her brain. Instead of being shut inside in the spinning room's heat and noise, as her hands picked up and replaced each bobbin, Ruby was by the river, or she was walking in the woods with Con, their feet disturbing the scent of last year's decaying leaves. The other thing she'd learnt was that the days at the factory fused together in her mind: it was hard to separate any of them out, except for Fridays. On Fridays, there was always a feeling of expectation; everyone was in a good mood, looking forward to the feeling of contentment a wage packet brought, even if it was only for a few hours. Not that there was much to buy, but at least if there was something in the shops on Friday – and you'd the points on your ration card – you had some money in your pocket to spend.

As they waited outside the office window, watching the figures moving about behind the frosted glass, the tacklers – mostly older men because of the war – shouted to the office manager that they were losing valuable drinking time, and he called back, saying that there was plenty of time and to take their money home to their wives first. It was the same jokes every week, until the little window was unbolted and they lined up to collect their money.

This week, when the window rattled up, it wasn't the manager standing there, dripping ash from his cigarette on to the wage packets, but Trevor, the boy who'd played Joseph in the Nativity play, dressed in the same grey sweater and wearing the same dark-blue tie he'd worn for school. The manager stood at his shoulder, joking with the men about his new assistant. When it was the weavers' turn to get their pay, some of them tried to flirt with him, telling him he was much better-looking than the manager, asking him his name and if he was courting, or telling him they hadn't a boyfriend, or that their husbands were away. The more they teased him, the more nervous he became. When it was Ruby's turn – her cheeks glowing – she gave her name, but Trevor didn't look up. Instead, he gulped and handed her the pay packet without a word.

She pushed the brown envelope in the pocket of her overall. Now that she was working – along with her granddad and Sadie – Ruby handed over her unopened pay packet to Jenny every Friday night. It was the same ritual every week. They had their meal, then Jenny got out the biscuit tin from the drawer in the sideboard and they handed over their pay. She opened her own packet first and then the others in their turn, handing each of them some of the money back. Ruby knew that both Sadie and Granddad spent most of their money every week, but she put part of hers with the ten-shilling note Uncle Walt had given her; with the rest, she would sometimes go along with Sadie and Lou to the little cinema near the camp, and other times to the church dance on Saturday.

'Edna Pye, that Trevor's mother, is friendly with Nellie Lathom, next door,' Sadie said the next evening, as they were getting ready for the dance. 'A couple of right old gossips they are. That Elsie Rostron is another one. They're always gossiping, the three of them. Nellie still doesn't speak to me,

342

unless she has to, even though Ma told her that I only said I'd write to her Jack to be friendly.'

'She still doesn't like me taking Bess out. If I go round, she makes excuses. I wouldn't care, but she doesn't take her out either,' Ruby said. 'She only lets her out on the field; Mrs Bland says it isn't enough exercise for a dog that size.'

'That's just stupid, it was nothing to do with you, or the flippin' dog. Anyway, you couldn't have kept on doing it now you're working. It's not like she's going to catch anything, is it? Though, I've heard that folk have been saying the lads from the camp have ... have a disease, and you shouldn't let them use your toilet. It's a story that's come from the doctor's wife, so they all think it must be true.'

Ruby, who'd been concentrating on the way Sadie was applying her make-up, glanced up and met her eyes in the mirror.

'I don't think Mrs Grey would say—'

'It was her that wanted to stop them coming to the dances,' Sadie said, getting up from her seat and struggling into her dress. 'Oh, look at this,' she said, turning towards Ruby and exposing a jagged purple line on the inside of her pale forearm. 'This is one of my summer frocks. I haven't had it on since my accident. Look how it shows.'

'You could try rubbing some make-up on it to make it fade.'

'I've hardly enough as it is. I haven't got enough to keep covering this up. Who's going to want to dance with me with this ugly thing on my arm?'

'Bo is,' Ruby said, as Sadie's face crumpled. 'Let's have a cup of tea. Then we'll have a look

343

for something else you could wear.'

Before she followed Sadie downstairs, Ruby went to her own room and opened Pearl's trunk. She selected a blouse in the softest lemon, with silk swirls embroidered on its gossamer-thin sleeves. Now it didn't feel as if she was giving part of Pearl away; instead, she felt that she was helping a friend – an equal.

'Here,' she said, draping the blouse over a chair in the kitchen. 'This was Mum's. It would go with the skirt you altered.'

Compared to the dances in town, the dance at the church hall was a very simple affair. Instead of a band of elderly musicians, the music was provided by records, but probably a more serious deficit was the lack of strong drink: during the refreshment interval, only tea and soft drinks were served from the little hatch off the hall, and instead of the bars in the town's dance halls, the dancers had to sip their drinks in the infant classroom, amongst the pictures of nursery rhymes. As a result of this shortcoming, most of the young women had to be content to dance with each other, until more potential partners began to arrive, after calling at one or more of the local pubs.

'Let's sit out for a bit,' Sadie said, leading Ruby over to a corner seat, where they could watch the other girls dancing in pairs. 'Can you see the girl over there in the blue – the big one with the red hair? She works with Lou. She says to Lou that her dad's thinking of complaining about all the black truck drivers on the road. Reckons all the lorries going down their road have stopped his hens layin'. She says that we should complain as

344

well, because it must have been one of them that hit you.'

'No it wasn't,' Ruby said. 'It wasn't any of the black GIs.'

'She asked Lou if you was badly hurt. When she said you was, she says that they must have been goin' over twenty, and we should complain and ask for compensation.'

'It wasn't any of the black GIs.'

'What sort of lorry was it, then?'

'I don't know; it was dark.'

'Well, how do you know? If it was a lorry in the dark... How do you know who...? All the Yank drivers are black... Oh look, here's Bo and the lads. You want to say, if it wasn't one of them. They're getting the blame for it.'

The room filled up with young British soldiers home on leave and the black GIs who'd been lucky enough to get one of the treasured late passes. One of the soldiers asked Ruby to dance, allowing her to escape Sadie and her questions. Between partners, Ruby found a seat by the hatch to the tiny kitchen, where a couple of ladies were getting out the teacups ready for the refreshment break. When the ancient tea urn began to snort, one of them put her head through the hatch and waved to Father O'Flynn, who, once the record had ended, got up from his customary seat near the door and announced that refreshments were about to be served.

Normally the dancers would line up at the serving hatch, before taking their drinks through to the infant classroom where they would squat on the tiny chairs and chat, but when the queue

345

began to form, Wes sat down at the piano and began to play. The music made the hall's floor quiver and the tea urn bounce. Bo and Sadie began to dance. He took hold of her hand and their feet moved together in perfect time to the piano. When they saw how well they could dance, spinning around with such skill, the rest of the dancers forgot about collecting drinks and crowded around cheering and clapping.

No one noticed the door to the infant classroom open, or saw the two women dressed in WRVS uniforms standing in the doorway, until Father O'Flynn – who'd been puffing happily at his pipe and tapping his feet to the music – motioned to Wes to stop playing. Ruby saw the priest usher Mrs Grey and Mrs Prendergast back into the classroom, followed by one of the women from the kitchen, carrying a silver tray containing three cups and a plate of biscuits. Then the dancers began collecting their cups of tea from the kitchen hatch, but instead of following the priest and his guests with their drinks, they stood around the piano, listening to Wes, who was now playing more softly.

Con brought Ruby a cup of tea and they wandered over to a quiet space near the infants' classroom. They were watching some of the GIs showing the others new dance moves, when they heard a voice through the open door: it was Father O'Flynn.

'...I'm happy to invite all the GIs here. I've told you that before, but I will not...'

Then, as Wes began another dance tune, the priest's angry voice became jumbled in with the music and the excited chatter of the dancers, until the piece ended and Mrs Grey's shrill reply filled the silent hall.

'The danger is, you're encouraging the type of behaviour we've just witnessed. You can't encourage our young women to treat these ... men as equals. If you tell them to be friendly ... the danger is you're leading them into trouble...'

Con looked for Bo, but he couldn't see him or Sadie in the crowd. The music and the laughter had been forgotten and, alerted by the sudden quiet and lack of customers, the women manning the tea urn poked their heads out to see what was going on. Then Mrs Prendergast's voice sliced through the fuggy air.

'I've seen them in the town whistling after girls. And, because of the way people like you encourage them to think, these young women feel they must be polite. An Englishman wouldn't do that in the street. And their drinking. I was in town the other evening and two of the louts almost pushed me over.'

'They'd have had to be in a bloody truck to do that,' one of the squaddies sniggered.

Hoping to hear more, the dancers edged closer to the open door, where they were joined by the ladies from the kitchen. Then suddenly Father O'Flynn's bulky shadow fell over the picture of Jack and the Beanstalk hanging on the classroom door. At this signal, the two women bustled back into the kitchen and the dancers clustered into smaller shuffling groups, lighting cigarettes, feigning interest in each other's conversation, or in their cooling cups of tea.

'I think we have had this discussion before,' the priest said. 'And I have the young people to... If I can show you ladies out.'

As Mrs Grey followed the priest across the room, Con left Ruby's side and approached her.

'Excuse me for addressing you directly, ma'am,' he said, 'but I couldn't help overhearing your conversation...'

'Ah, may I introduce you,' Father O'Flynn said. 'This young man is Con, a member of the Quartermaster Truck Company. As you see, we have a number of friends here from the camp. Mrs Grey and Mrs Prendergast are here. The main reason for their visit, I understand, is to invite some of the young ladies here to a dance at the camp.'

'Not ... not the same place,' Mrs Grey said, ignoring Con.

'It would be awful hard for us to invite anyone to our camp, ma'am,' Con said. 'You see, the facilities are too poor for us to ask guests. I hope you don't think I'm being rude, but I wanted to put the record right. You see, as I said, I couldn't help overhearing that you ladies have some concerns. Well to be honest, we have some concerns of our own. We're guests in your country, and don't want to give offence. As the other lady said, we enjoy going out into town, but I can assure you ma'am, our behaviour to the girls we meet is respectful. Sure, we joke and we whistle, but so do the English soldiers. We're just doing our best to be sociable and fit in. My father is a minister, and I wouldn't want to shame him or my uniform with my behaviour. I'm sure the rest of the guys are the same.

'To tell you the truth, it isn't that we are having such a good time. We try to help when we can and we sing when we're asked to. In fact, we're making the best of being here. Don't get me wrong, we wanted to come and help out our country. We're all fighting for the same thing. It's what we all believe in, isn't it?'

Con, and the rest of the youngsters, looked at the two women. In the stillness, all that could be heard was the chinking of teacups, as the two ladies who'd been serving the tea busied themselves clearing away any crockery that was within easy hearing distance of the group in the middle of the hall.

If it were not for the pounding of his heart, Con would have believed that the words had been spoken by someone else. As the silence expanded, he began to wonder if it was a dream and he would wake in the back of a truck again, with Wes's smelly feet in his face. Then he felt Ruby slip her coarse, warm fingers around his, and Mrs Grey recovered her anger.

'I'm really surprised that you allow this behaviour,' she said, addressing herself to Father O'Flynn. 'I shall be asking my husband to speak to Captain O'Donal...'

'And to the abbot,' Mrs Prendergast added, taking her friend's arm as they headed for the door.

'Does this mean we can't go to the dance at the camp?' the big red-haired girl called after them, but her question was lost in the sound of excited chatter and Father O'Flynn's appeals for silence. Once the chattering had settled, the old priest, as

349

he always did, ended the refreshment break with a prayer, followed by an exhortation to the dancers to attend the Sunday Mass, in order to secure their admission both to everlasting life, and to future dances.

By Monday morning everyone at the mill had heard about the incident. It was hardly an hour into their shift before Ruby saw Mrs Rostron and one of the other women gossiping between the lines of machines. They turned away quickly, but she'd already learnt enough lip-reading to pick up the words 'dance' and 'black GIs'.

As she collected a truck of empty bobbins, Trevor pushed open the door. He blushed when he saw her and tried to speak. Ruby pointed to the stairway and followed him out on to the relatively quiet landing.

'I've been sent to find out what docket numbers are on the order that's being done in here.'

'You've been sent to the wrong building,' Ruby said. 'It's the weaving shed on the other side of the yard you need.'

'I've been over there,' he said, biting his lip. 'They told me to come up here. In the office they said I'd got to be quick, because they can't start work unless they have the right docket.'

'The folk in the shed were having you on,' Ruby said. 'They don't want to start work, that's all. While you're running around, they'll be stood in there gossiping and having a laugh. They do it with all the young ones – send you on daft jobs. Go back and look for the little glass office, just behind the big doors at the end. You need the tall curly-haired chap in there. Just give the numbers to him and he'll give you the ones they've already done to take back.'

'How long have you been working here?'

'Since just after Christmas. Did you only start last week?'

'Yes, bookkeeping and wages clerk.'

'Don't worry about it. The novelty will soon wear off, and they'll find somebody else to torment,' Ruby said, as the door swung open and Mrs Rostron peered out.

'Never mind canoodling,' she said. 'We're waiting for that truck in here.'

Now that the days were getting longer, Ruby helped her granddad in the garden. Since his illness, he'd found the digging harder and would often sit on an old bench against the house wall, resting between bouts of gardening.

'Them's coming through grand now,' he said, nodding towards a row of cabbages showing their pearly green heads above the soil. 'Nice time of year this. The beans is doin' nicely as well. Jenny likes a few beans. She'll be pleased with them.'

Ruby rested her head against the cottage's rough white wall. She liked this part of the day, sitting with a bowl of vegetables to peel for the next day's meal or just looking at the garden and listening to the birds, until it was time to help Jenny with the tea. Glancing at her granddad on the bench beside her, she noted how the neck of his collarless shirt – now at least two sizes too big – sagged around his scrawny neck, and how the belt on his gardening trousers was pulled in by two extra notches. In the weeks after the theft of the black-market sugar, Ruby had carried buckets of coal upstairs to feed the bedroom fire. It was then, listening for each struggling breath, that she'd begun to fear that he might die, and now – like a faithful old dog – that same wordless dread nudged her awake each morning.

Leaving Granddad contentedly smoking a Player's, she went to help Jenny. The evening before, the remaining scraps from the lamb Bo had brought them at the weekend had been used to flavour the stew of carrot and potatoes that was now simmering in the oven by the fire.

'This looks thin,' Jenny said, poking at the contents of the pot.

'It smells good, though,' Ruby said, 'I could smell it when I walked in, and I'm that hungry. Shall I set the table? I think I heard the gate. I bet it's Sadie.'

'You'll have to wait a bit. She can help you sort out tomorrow's tea first.'

Sadie put her gas mask on the draining board and began to untie the scarf she wore turban-style around her head.

'Peel them two onions for me, love,' her mother said, dropping two sad-looking onions on the draining board next to the oilcloth-covered box. Sadie wrinkled her nose and dug a fingernail into the blackened vegetables.

'These onions are that soft,' she said, wiping her fingers on her overalls and moving her stylish gas-mask box away from the offending vegetables. 'They smell horrible as well.'

'What's the matter with you?' Jenny asked.

'I've just seen Lou up the lane. She heard this

mornin', her Frank's brother-in-law, you remember, Lydia's husband?'

'The one with two little girls?'

'That's right. His convoy was attacked and he's missing.'

'Oh, them poor kiddies.'

'Lou says she can't stand to think of it,' Sadie said, picking up one of the onions. 'Lydia must be out of her mind with worry.'

'What about Frank?' Ruby asked.

'Oh, he's not on the same ship. They've never gone on the same one for that reason,' Sadie said, slicing one of the onions in half. 'These will hardly be worth cooking, Ma.'

'It's either that, or it'll just have to be cheese and potatoes, and there's not much cheese, so I'd do your best. Slice them potatoes thin, Ruby. I was thinkin' of layers and crispin' the potatoes on top.'

'Well there's not much here, and if there's not much cheese why don't we have a pie instead?'

'I've done the potatoes thin, but they'd do just as well in a pie.'

Jenny wiped her hands on her apron and opened the door of the kitchenette. 'I was goin' to make jam window pie tonight as a treat, with that stew not being so tasty. You'll have to go easy with this flour, Ruby,' she said, handing Ruby the large blue-and-white striped flour jar. 'You know what they say, "flour costs ships" and, if we're havin' cheese and potato pie tomorrow, you'd best let me roll the pastry out. I can get it thinner than you.'

The meal was spoilt not by the stew, which was saved by the addition of plenty of mint and some sage, but by Sadie's sad news.

'Frank's always said their safety was low down on the list. He told Lou that when they're attacked and they're at their stations, the ship sometimes rolls and they lose their lifeboats...'

'Thought Frank said it was gettin' better?' Granddad said. 'More aircraft, supposed to be. Gap narrowing where there was no protection, and radio officers getting more information?'

'It's just the same if they're hit, the rest still have to go on, and then it's up to the navy to look for them. Lou and me was supposed to be goin' out on Friday as well. Now she's talkin' about tryin' to get time off to go and see Lydia. I don't think they'll let her, but she says she doesn't fancy coming out anyway.'

'Let's talk about something a bit more cheerful,' Jenny said, getting up from the table and taking the jam pie from the oven.

'Oh, that looks grand, Jenny, love,' Granddad said, as the smell of blackberry jam filled the room. 'Jam window pie.'

'Let's hope so,' she laughed. 'I had to swap the rest of the eggs for this jam.'

'If Lou wants to do something for Lydia's little girls,' Ruby said, 'why doesn't she bring them up here for a break? They'd get fed, and we could take them to the seaside. Con said he wants to take us to the seaside for the day.'

'When did he say that?'

'After the dance, when they dropped us off. Said we could all go in one of the lorries. We'll be goin' on a Sunday, so we could take some of the little ones from the school.'

'He'll need passes. Bo said they–'

'He said he was goin' to see them about it, and tell them it's not fair.'

'It's one thing puttin' them two stuck-up women in their place,' Jenny said, topping the helpings of pie with mock cream, 'it's a different thing to tell them at the camp.'

'They were talking about it at work,' Ruby said. 'I heard them.'

'There's all sorts of gossip goin' about,' Sadie said, catching Ruby's eye. 'I reckon her and that Prendergast woman are starting a lot of it, and folk are daft enough to believe it, 'cos of who it comes from. She said she was goin' to report Con to them at the camp; if she does, he might not get any passes at all, and they might take it out on the rest of them.'

'I thought it was brave,' Ruby said. 'He was only saying to Mrs Grey what he thought, and it wasn't rude. He was polite.'

'Well, you've changed your tune,' Jenny said. 'It's only a couple of months ago you thought the sun shone out of her backside. If she has complained, I bet I can guess whose side they'll take, and it'll not be his.'

Con had hoped to see the new lieutenant alone, but when he opened the door, instead of the new guy, it was one of the other lieutenants and Captain O'Donal who were waiting to see him. It was clear that the confrontation at the dance was on their minds, and he got the usual lecture about being visitors in the country and respecting the way the British did things. As he listened to the lecture, Con fixed his eyes on the maps and copies of orders pinned on the wall behind O'Donal's head. Unlike the shabby huts that made up the rest of the camp, the administration building was a neat wooden construction that he guessed had been purpose-built, and from what he could see, it didn't leak.

'Are you listening to the captain, soldier?' the lieutenant yelled.

'Yes, sir,' Con barked.

The sudden holler made Captain O'Donal's eyes flicker, and when Con asked for permission to speak, the captain glanced uneasily at the lieutenant, before nodding and shifting forward in his chair. The lieutenant, unlike O'Donal, was a southerner and a regular soldier, and like most southerners in his position, bitterly resented his posting to an all-black unit.

'From what I understand, sir,' Con said, addressing himself to the captain, 'the British don't have laws about whites and blacks mixing...'

'That's enough,' the lieutenant roared. 'We'll not have a lecture from an uppity...'

It was little more than a beat, but was enough time for O'Donal's colour to rise, and for the lieutenant to gobble down the word.

'What happened, then?' Wes asked the next day, as they were grooming the baseball pitch.

'I was dismissed,' he said, remembering his heart's involuntary leap, as he flicked his gaze from the senior officer and looked straight into the lieutenant's pale-grey eyes, knowing that the swallowed insult would lay hard and dry for a

356

long time in his gullet.

'Didn't get the chance to ask for any pass, or ask about the seaside.'

Sarge Mayfield, who'd wandered down to the pitch, shook his head. 'He wouldn't have given you one anyway. If you'd come to me, I'd have told you that. The seaside towns are all for white R&R. We could perhaps get a truck and take these kiddies to see *Bambi*, or somethin' in town. You won't get a pass to go to the seaside, no matter how many kids you want to take. Let me go to O'Donal. I'll have to get him on his own.'

'He's runnin' scared of some of the more experienced lieutenants,' Wes said, leaning on his rake. 'That's always been the problem. That lieutenant is dumb, but he's regular army.'

Mayfield grinned. 'It's true what they say about you young northern boys, you sure are somethin' else, but take care: the guy is old South and he's not goin' to take that off you. You faced him down, and he'll be after your hide.'

'He wants so bad to go to the seaside, Sarge,' Wes grinned.

'Are you helpin' or are you talkin'?' Con asked, scowling at him.

Wes loved teasing Con about Ruby, and tempting him to admit he'd lied about his own age to get into the army.

'Tell you what, that film *Bambi* sounds like a good idea,' Wes said, moving out of reach. 'Con will like that.'

Con tried to grab him, but Wes yelled and jumped clear as Con made a dive for his feet. Then he kept him at bay with the end of the fork, and they dodged and chased around the pitch, until they were both breathless and Sergeant Mayfield called them to order.

One hot June afternoon, shortly after his interview with O'Donal, Con went to the cottage. As he closed the little gate, Henry came down the path to meet him.

'I've got a surprise for you,' he said. 'Our Ruby said you might be coming by today. She's at work, but she'll be here in about an hour. Come on round the back and I'll show you.'

Con followed him along the old brick path and around the side of the cottage.

'Now what do you think about that?' he asked.

At the edge of the yard, there was a large tin bath half full of water and next to it a small patch of sand.

'If you can't go to the seaside,' Henry said with a smile, 'the seaside has to come to you. Sit down. They should be deckchairs, really,' he said, patting the faded upholstered seat of one of the two dining chairs standing on the patch of sand, 'but these will have to do. Take your boots and socks off and have a paddle. I'll not be a minute.'

Both the tub and the sand were protected from the lane by the side of the house, and it was a hot day. Con sat down on one of the familiar hard-backed chairs; he untied his boots and pulled off his socks, telling himself it was really to please the old man. When Henry reappeared, he was carrying a couple of beer glasses.

'I've got the bottles cooling in the tub,' he said, bending over to pull at a piece of parcel string

358

attached to the neck of a beer bottle. 'Mind you, they'd probably have been just as cold left in the pantry.'

The old man fished out the bottle, and after pouring the tepid beer into their glasses, he sat down with a contented sigh.

'Grand this, isn't it? When we've had these, we can have a paddle. In a way, I'm glad this trip of yours didn't come off. Might have unsettled our Ruby; she's only just got used to it here. She was living with her mother's family in Blackpool. They have a boarding house. It was where she was born, Blackpool. I'd hoped that her aunt and uncle would have taken her in for good. She's a handy girl, and Walt and Ethel are both in their sixties. They never had any kiddies of their own. I'd hoped that if they took to her she'd get the business, once anything 'appened to them. She was undone when they wanted her to leave. It was the only home she'd ever known, what with her parents travelling so much. Though, it would have been nice for the kiddies, just the same. There'll be some round here that's never been to the seaside, not since the war's been on, anyway.'

'It's kind of you to do this, Henry,' Con said. 'This beer tastes pretty good after a hot day.'

'My pleasure, lad. Go on, enjoy yourself, feel this nice bit of sand in your toes. I'm looking forward to havin' a bit of a paddle as well,' he added, taking off his slippers and socks and waving a veiny foot in the direction of the water. 'Should have put a bit of salt in it.'

Con closed his eyes, and Henry lifted his old, wrinkly face to the late-afternoon sun. They were still happily squidging their toes in the sand and sipping their beers, when Ruby walked around the corner of the cottage, followed by a tall boy in glasses.

'Granddad, what's going on?' she laughed. 'What are you doing?'

'Me and Con is at the seaside,' he said, his knobbly hands resting on the front of his grubby railway shirt. 'Since they'll not let him go there, we're havin' it here. Go and get you and your young friend a chair and come and join us.'

'Where's the sand come from?'

Henry sat up and looked sheepishly at their visitor. 'It's from one of the fire buckets at the church. I'll be takin' it back, when me and Johnny go on duty later. Now then, young man,' he said, smiling at Trevor, who was staring with undisguised fascination at the pink undersides of Con's feet. 'Can we interest you in a paddle?'

'No, he's not stopping. This is Trevor, who played Joseph in the play,' Ruby said, taking off her headscarf and brushing away the stray cotton threads that were trapped underneath. 'I told you, he's working in the office at the factory.'

'Oh aye, Mrs Pye's lad.'

'I'm taking him round to see Mrs Bland in a minute. We saw her going over to Bardley's. She'll have gone for some milk for the cat. She's some books that he wants to look at.'

'Nice to meet you, lad, and how do you like it at the factory?'

'Folk keep teasing him,' Ruby said, smoothing down her hair and pulling out the cotton waste from her curls.

'Let the lad answer for himself.'

The boy was dressed in a pair of shapeless trousers that were too short and tight for him. He was clearly nervous and when he spoke, his voice was high and childlike.

'I'm working in the office, bookkeeping,' he said, 'but I want to do something for the war effort. I want to enlist when I'm old enough, but my eyesight's against me.'

'Aye, well 'appen it'll be over before then,' Henry said. 'This here is Con, by the way. He's like you, can't wait to go. Both of you should listen to your elders and hope that, now we've broken through them dams, our Lancasters will make short work of the rest of the buggers.'

'If Con wants to wriggle his toes in some sand,' Ruby said, 'then I'll take him down the field to the river, once I've taken Trevor to Mrs Bland's. I'll be back in a minute.'

'I never thought about the river,' Henry said, looking around critically for the first time at his efforts to create a seaside environment for Con.

'It was kind of your grandpa, to try and make up for not going to the sea,' Con said later, as he and Ruby walked across the field to the river.

'I wondered why he was asking if I'd brought some seashells with me from my Auntie Ethel's,' she said, leading the way across the field to the bend in the river.

She strolled along the water's edge, where the mud deposited by the winter floods had been dried by the unseasonably hot weather into a substance that resembled sand. Then untying her hair, she pulled out the last of the tiny threads of cotton and let them fall into the water. Con sat down on the edge of the grassy bank, watching the sunlight sparkle off her curls and light up the fiery copper in her hair.

'One day I would like to take you to the seaside,' he said.

'Just me?' she asked, squinting back at him curiously, and pushing her hands in the pockets of her brown wrap-around overall.

'Just you,' he said.

Later that evening, when Con had left for the camp and the shadows in the garden began to lengthen, it was so hot that they ate their meal – lamb and new potatoes – cold.

'I hardly feel like eating, never mind cooking,' Jenny said, rubbing her distorted ankles. 'It was that hot in the factory. I could have done with you leaving that tub of water, Henry. It would have been nice to soak me feet in.'

'Most of it's gone on the veg,' he said. 'The ground is that parched. They need plenty of water this weather.'

'Some ice cream would be nice,' Sadie said. 'I could just fancy some. I'm going to get in the bath and wash my hair, though I don't know why I'm bothering. Might as well, I suppose. Bo's gone to Manchester in one of the biggest lorries they've got. He'll be back too late to go out, and Lou's going to Liverpool tomorrow, so she's not coming out.'

'I'll do your nails for you after tea,' Ruby said. 'I'll show you how to do shell stitch on the bottom of your underskirt as well, if you like.'

'Oh, government's banned embroidery on underwear, don't forget. We might get arrested if you do,' Sadie said, pouring herself another cup of tea.

'It's only on stuff in the shops though, isn't it?' Ruby asked.

'No, love,' Jenny giggled. 'Haven't you heard? They're going round inspecting everybody's knickers now, so you'd best watch out.'

'I'll help you clear up that sand if you want, Granddad. How are you going to get it back to the church?'

'Oh, there's no rush about getting it back, Ruby, love. There's plenty there, though it would be handy if you can help me sweep it up. It shouldn't be too bad; it's on some old sacking. I only said I was getting it back today when that young lad was there.'

'What young lad?' Jenny asked.

'Young Trevor Pye. Our Ruby brought him round to get some books off the book woman.'

'Trevor Pye?'

'Yes, I told you he'd started at the factory.'

'That'll not go down well, him coming here. His mother'll not be keen on that,' Sadie said. 'She's not keen on the black GIs, almost as bad as her across the road. She'll think you're leading him astray.'

'He's all right. They really pick on him at work. Yesterday, when he was taking the dockets round, one of the tacklers sent him looking for a long stand, and when he got back to the office, he got told off for taking too much time handing the dockets out. It's a right shame.'

'Well, he is a bit mard,' Jenny said, getting up from the table and collecting the pots.

'No wonder, with his mother,' Sadie said. 'Do you know what the latest is? Do you remember the doctor's brother? No, it was his wife's brother. You must have seen him; the one they said was ill and couldn't work? Then all of a sudden just after New Year, he went. Well her, that Mrs Pye – and she reckons it's come from Alice – has told someone at work that he caught one of the black soldiers cuddling a girl in the garden, and when he challenged him and told them to clear off, the bloke beat him up and the girl took his wallet. Now he's trying to get the Yanks to compensate him, and they're saying that's why the lads can't have late passes, 'cos they can't be trusted. I said that it couldn't be true 'cos Ruby was workin' there over Christmas and New Year and she would have heard about it, and I've asked Bo, and he said he's not heard anything either.'

'I thought you was havin' a bath,' Jenny said sharply. 'If you're going to wash your hair, you'd best get it done. I'm going to sit outside, now it's getting cooler, and Ruby, if you're helping Henry, you'd both best make a move, before it gets too dark to see.'

Ruby was glad to escape. For the next hour she helped Henry to get the sand back into a sack, and then insisted on sweeping the yard clear of the excess.

'She's a good lass,' he said, sitting on the old wooden bench next to Jenny.

Jenny, who had her feet in a bowl of water, lifted her eyes up to the darkening blue sky above

364

them. 'Can you hear that?' she asked, as the dull drone of a heavy transport plane filled the quiet garden.

'It's one of ours,' Henry said, puffing on his cigarette. 'If you ask me, it was a mistake to invent them. Better off without them, that's what I say. I ask you, what good are they to the working man?'

'Oh, that's better,' Sadie said, coming out of the back door and joining her mother and Henry on the bench. 'I've left the bath for you, Ruby,' she called, 'if you want to get in.' She sighed and took the cigarette Jenny offered her. 'I keep thinking of Bo. It's that hot in these lorries. He says the big ones are the worse. It's that hot, they're getting ill with it on these long trips.'

The thick evening heat made the blackout almost unbearable, and it was nearly eleven before they reluctantly went indoors. In her stifling bedroom, Ruby sat on her white coverlet and cooled her feet on the linoleum. Sadie's story about Rollo whirred around in her head, almost chasing away the walk by the river and Con's promise to take her to the seaside. She curled up and closed her eyes.

'Just you,' she whispered into the blackness. 'Just you,' she said, until her breathing slowed and the incantation summoned a dream.

She was wearing a dress with a sweetheart neckline and a tie belt that fluttered in the sea breeze. It was made out of the dress material – navy cotton decorated with white flowers – she'd seen in Coupé's window. Their feet were bare and left a pattern of footprints on the newly washed sand. For as far as she could see, the shoreline was empty. Con took her hand. Ruby smiled, and was imagining him bending down to kiss her, when a noise forced her back to the hot, dark bedroom. The sound – a crack, somewhere in the darkness – came again, and she heard Bess and the dogs at the farm begin to bark. Ruby sat up and pulled aside the blackout curtain. Over the trees, in the direction of the neighbouring village and the army camp, there was a sudden burst of light, a crackle of explosions and then silence. She heard Grand-dad stir, the bed springs creaked and he padded over to the window. In the dark, the cracks and rattles sputtered fitfully. Along the lane, the dogs barked, and Sadie's excited feet pattered across the landing.

'Are you awake, Ruby?' she hissed. 'Get up as quickly as you can. The Germans have landed.'

CHAPTER FOURTEEN

Bo spent most of that burning June day in the cab of a heavy transporter, driving between the port at Liverpool and Manchester. He started the day in a good frame of mind – even though he knew he wouldn't be back in time to see Sadie. The journey was a familiar one, and he took pride in his ability to handle the heavy equipment transporter on the narrow twisting lanes between the two cities. By midday the heat inside the cab was almost intolerable. Bo thought it curious that back home in the States he'd been used to the summer heat, but here, in England, he was finding it hard to stand. He wondered if it might be the sudden contrast between the cool spring days and the intense heat that had flared out of nowhere in the middle of June. Whatever it was, he was not enjoying the ride. It took power to shift the heavy gears, and from mid morning, once the sun was full up, it felt as if there was little air inside the cab, and the sweat was already trickling down his back. By midday, as he reached the outskirts of Manchester, his eyes burned with the effort of staring at the stark, bright road. Bo couldn't remember a time when he'd ever been so thirsty, and once the tank wrecker was unloaded, he was sure he'd drink the Red Cross Station dry.

'I'm sorry, soldier,' the plump Texan at the Red Cross Station said. 'It's whites only.'

Afterwards, Bo thought that it must have been his desperation for soda pop and doughnuts that had made him so amenable. He didn't shout or holler. Instead, he explained calmly that he'd been on the road since dawn and was unlikely to get back to his camp until dark, but the fat girl just shrugged her shoulders.

'We've been told it's whites only here,' she said.

Her reply made the two white GIs already eating doughnuts shift uncomfortably and study their plates, as though the plans for the invasion of Europe were written there.

'Aw, come on, honey,' a white soldier who was waiting behind him protested. 'Give the guy a break. It's as hot as hell out there, and the guy's a long way from home.'

It was no use, and it was only when the white

soldier followed him out, offering him his own K-rations, that his anger overwhelmed his desperate thirst. He drove on, passing deserted roads of terraced houses, seething from the treatment he'd received and hoping to find a shop – any place that would sell him a cold drink. At the corner of one street, two children were squatting on the pavement, drinking a bright-orange liquid out of a bottle. He pulled over and climbed down. The little boys with scabby knees and patched shirts got up, looking wide-eyed at the enormous transporter in the tiny street.

'Hey, kid,' he called, 'where can I get a drink around here?'

'Henty's shop,' the taller boy said, pointing down a side street.

'Will you go and get me one?' he asked, 'and some bread, if they have any.'

The children scampered off, and Bo stood in the shade of the truck, lit a cigarette and fumed at his own cowardice, comparing his spineless performance with that of young Con, who'd stood up to the two women, and been bawled out by O'Donal for his trouble. How relieved he was that none of the guys had seen him climb meekly back into his truck and drive away. When the children came back, they brought a little gang, who clamoured to be allowed on board the truck and begged for gum. The wonder in the children's eyes at the colossal beast he was in charge of cheered him, and by the time he'd finished his drink, there was an admiring crowd of locals to wave him off. He was in a better mood as he headed for the airbase, but the warm sugary drink had done little to slake his thirst. As he waited at the guardhouse on the perimeter, he could see a detail of black soldiers working on the edge of the runway in the blinding sun.

'Where can I get a drink and a bite to eat around here?' he asked.

'Not on the base,' one of them replied. 'They'll not serve no black man on here. You should know that.'

'But it's real hot...'

'Rules is rules,' another of the men said. 'You just as black on a hot day as on a cold one.'

'Once you get inside,' the first man called, 'see that shed, over by the hangar? We go over there. There's a water tap outside, you can use that.'

When his papers had been cleared and he'd parked up, Bo headed over to the shed and waited with four of the work crew, who were filling cans and bottles from the tap.

'The white guys in the hangar, the ones that's workin' on the planes, they okay,' the first guy said. 'They'll get us stuff from the PX, and they don't mind us using their facilities, so long as none of the officers see us. We got a sergeant, but he's black an' he don't mind, as long as the work gets done. Come inside out of the heat.'

Bo filled the pop bottle he'd bought in the town and followed the men inside. The hut smelt warm and dusty; the walls were lined with bits of metal and broken tools. The men, all from the South, took their places on a collection of battered metal chairs around a wooden table, covered with a piece of red oilcloth. They told him that, since they'd arrived in England, it had been their job to work on the construction and then the maintenance of the airfield. They asked him about the truck, and as the chat went around the table, Bo basked in the men's respect for his ability to handle the heavy equipment and his technical knowledge of the engine.

'You guys heard how the Tigers do?' Bo asked, handing round a pack of cigarettes.

'Lost both games of a double header to St Louis Browns, 6–3 5–4. You from Detroit?' one of the men asked, handing Bo a slice of bread and offering him a tin of ham from his knapsack.

'Sure am,' Bo replied, drinking the tepid water from the pop bottle.

'You heard about the rioting?'

'I heard some rumours about trouble at the factories. We get some newspapers at the camp. They don't like us havin' the black ones.'

'It's worse than the trouble in the factories, this time,' a thin-faced man sitting next to him said. 'Happened at Belle Island at the weekend. Reckon there was thousands involved. Some reckon it was 'cos the place was so crowded that caused it. Black and white out there trying to cool off.'

'I heard a fight at Eastwood Park started it off,' a plump man said. 'White sailors chasing some black kid.'

'No. It was 'cos the place was crowded,' another man said. 'Squabbles broke out over picnic ovens and such, and pushing in queues. It was real busy. Buses full, boats full, cars stalling on the bridge and crowds of folk walking across tryin' to get home. Then there was a fight. It's right; it was an argument between white and black, but it wasn't

370

a black kid they beat up. They, these sailors, saw the whites was gettin' the worst of it and joined in. Then hundreds of white folk waiting at the mainland entrance to the bridge started beatin' on any black that come by.'

'Anyways,' the first man said, offering Bo another slice of bread, 'there was hundreds hurt, and when the police arrived, they began beating on the black guys and rounded 'em up. Makes you think we should be back home protecting our own people, don't it?'

When the men left to go back to work, Bo dozed fitfully in a chair, but the news from Detroit hung on to his mind. Before heading back to collect his orders, he wandered for a while around the deserted hangar. Then, instead of returning with the transporter as he'd expected, the depot sergeant pointed him to a truck full of supplies for a base near the coast. Filling all the bottles and cans he could find, Bo climbed back in the truck and swung out of the gates, calculating that it would be late evening before he would get back to camp. As the afternoon wore on, he hoped that the heat would ease and once on the open road towards the coast there might be a cool breeze, but on the long road north the air was still and the heat only pressed harder. When he licked his lips his moustache tasted of salt, and no matter how much of the warm water he drank, his mouth stayed dry. He knew there was little chance of the offer of a cool drink at the base where he was heading; the only available water was the faucet used for washing down the trucks. By four o'clock, as he was passing through a small market town, he decided to call at the store to buy himself some fruit and a cool drink; this would mean he wouldn't have to ask the smirking guys on guard duty for anything. He drew up outside the grocery store and climbed down.

After the bright sunlight, it took him several moments to adjust to the shop's dark interior. As his eyes began to focus Bo could see that, unlike the shops in the villages around the camp, this shop was well supplied with fresh vegetables and smelt invitingly of cheese and smoked ham. Alerted by the tinkling doorbell, the woman behind the counter and her lone customer, a plump young woman in a floral dress, looked up from their conversation to see who the new arrival was. When the young woman grabbed her basket, Bo took hold of the door's brass handle and held it open.

'Good day, ma'am,' Bo said politely, as she hurried out of the shop.

When he closed the door again, the woman behind the till had gone. Guessing that she must have slipped out through the door at the back of the shop, Bo looked around at the well-scrubbed counter and the rows of little drawers that ran along the wall at the back of it. Taking in the tinned food stacked high on the shelves, he hoped that he might find some treat to take back for Sadie. He heard the door open again and turned around, expecting to see the same woman, but instead two men stood shoulder to shoulder behind the counter. One of the men was around sixty, and the other a much younger man of about twenty-four or five. From their strong resemblance

– watery blue eyes, ruddy complexion and matching pendulous lips – Bo guessed that they must be father and son.

'Good day,' he said. 'Can I buy some food and something to drink?'

'No you can't,' the older man said. 'We haven't got any for sale.'

'Pardon me, sir,' Bo said, pointing to the large wheel of cheese sitting on the bleached wood counter in front of the men, 'isn't that cheese?'

'We haven't got any for sale,' the man repeated, 'or bread.'

'It's all spoken for,' the younger man added. 'We're closing, so you'd best be on your way.'

'Well, can I buy something to drink?'

'We only keep stuff for local folk here,' the older man said. 'We want to shut the shop now, and we don't want no trouble, and my lad's asked you once to go.'

Bo climbed back in his cab and sat for a while under the shade of a tree, sipping tepid water from the pop bottle. It was almost half past five and the street was empty, but the open sign still hung on the door of the little shop. He had been surprised rather than angered by the shopkeeper's reaction: he was used to being met with curiosity when he called in the small country shops, but he'd been greeted with genuine friendliness as well. He poured the last of the water over his head, and was wiping the water and sweat from his neck, when two small boys appeared in front of the truck. Bo smiled and reached for a pack of gum: children were always the same, always begging for gum or chocolate.

When the first stone hit the truck door it hardly registered, but the second one struck his arm. Bo drove away, leaving behind him the two little boys whooping triumphantly outside the pretty half-timbered store.

He made good time to the camp. As he waited in the idling truck outside the guardhouse for his papers to be checked, Bo began to hope that he might make it back in time to have a glass of beer in a friendly pub, before he was expected back to camp. He knew that the rest of the guys – except those lucky enough to have passes – would probably be playing or watching baseball and he wondered if any of the other Detroit boys had heard the same rumours. The guard strolled back over and spat on the floor by the truck.

'You gotta take it through. It's not to be unloaded. Not today, anyways,' he said, staring into the middle distance. 'You can sleep in the cab, or underneath it, and get a lift back where you come from in the morning.'

Bo knew it was pointless to ask for food or water from these guys: any request for help would raise nothing more than a sneer. He drove into the camp, the image of a pint of straw-coloured beer slowly fading away. Then his luck changed; another truck was leaving in less than an hour with emergency supplies needed for a base near Liverpool.

'If you ask me,' the guy said, 'they just move this stuff around to keep us busy. I swear to you, that stuff is the same I brought up from the docks there not two days ago.'

With Bo's willing help, the truck was fully

loaded in less than half an hour, and by the time the sun was going down, they were close to the town. The driver went off his route to get him near home, dropping him off in sight of the row of tall poplar trees and the church spire near the camp. As he jumped down from the truck, Bo could almost taste the sharp straw-coloured beer on his tongue. To avoid the camp, he decided to take a small track that came out at a junction near the edge of the village. He'd only been in the low-beamed pub at the crossroads once before, but when he heard voices inside, he quickly tried to tidy himself up and headed for the bar.

'Time's been called,' the barmaid said, nodding towards the white towels covering the pumps.

'I'll take a bottled beer,' he said.

'Not here, you won't,' she replied, dunking a glass tankard in the sink, 'towels are up, it's after time.'

'Come on, Rose,' one of the English soldiers leaning on the bar said. 'The poor bloke's gasping. Let him have a pint.'

'It's not up to me,' the barmaid said, taking the handles of four empty glass tankards in each hand and drawing them towards her across the wooden bar. 'I'm just doing my job.'

'Hey, Fred,' the soldier called to a thickset man in a white shirt. 'Let's have a pint for this lad. He's gaspin', poor bloke, and I'll have another half while you're at it.'

'Over here, Bo,' one of the guys from the camp called, peering at him from the other side of the bar. 'Come on, over here.'

Bo dipped his head and looked under the rows

375

of glasses hanging above the bar. He could see about eleven or twelve guys around the dartboard, including Con, Wes and Holt, all in walking-out dress.

'How come you all got passes?' he asked.

'Mayfield went to the new lieutenant; that cracker lieutenant is goin' to be real sore when he finds out,' Wes called. 'Come through. We've got a pint you can have. We bought a double round before the bar closed.'

Bo shook his head; he didn't want a beer they'd bought to extend their night out, any more than he wanted a beer prised out of the hard-eyed barmaid by a well-meaning squaddie. He wanted to walk up to the bar and buy his own beer, as any man would do who'd driven through the heat of the day.

'I want a drink,' he insisted. 'I'll have a light beer from the shelf behind you, ma'am.'

'I've told you, it's after time,' the barmaid said.

'I'm asking for a bottle of beer. I've been driving all day. All you need do is reach out...' he said, his sweat-stiffened shirt growing damp again.

'Now then, lad,' the landlord said, putting another tray of glasses on the bar, 'we don't want trouble.'

'I don't want trouble either, sir. I am thirsty and all I want is a drink.'

'Come on, you miserable old sod,' a blonde girl hanging on the soldier's arm said.

'Aye, come on, Fred. It was only a minute after time,' a girl dressed in ATS uniform standing next to her agreed, giving the landlord a playful wink.

'There's a bloody war on,' another red-faced English soldier shouted. 'Get them towels off the bloody pumps and fill us all up.'

'If I have any more of this,' the landlord said, his sweaty face turning from pink to a purplish red, 'I'll clear...'

The rest of his threat was drowned out by shouts from the crowded bar, as optimistic customers pressed forward, hoping to get their glasses refilled, and in the crush, Bo felt someone push an open bottle of beer into his hand. He lifted it to his lips, but when the barmaid saw him she shrieked, and the landlord made a grab for it. He was a big man but overweight. Bo held him off easily with his free hand, while to the applause of the crowd at the bar, he raised the bottle to his lips.

Holt, who'd been watching the argument from across the bar, glanced around regretfully at the still-untouched glasses of beer.

'Let's go,' he said, tugging at Con's sleeve. 'Let's get Bo out of here.'

Holt and the others stood at the door of the vault, as drinkers drawn by the raised voices pushed along the narrow corridor in response to a rumour that the bar really was going to open again. At the same time, some of the other customers – older people and courting couples – who had been sitting in the maze of smaller, quieter rooms off the same corridor, were calling out goodnight to each other and easing their way in the opposite direction toward the front door. Eventually, the whole group of GIs made their way out of the vault and were pressed against the wall, waiting for a gap in the crush, when the pub door suddenly crashed open. Two MPs stood in the open doorway; one of them was a small, plump guy some of the GIs recognised from the patrols in the local town. The other was a tall swarthy-skinned guy they didn't know.

'Passes,' the small MP said, nodding towards the black soldiers and holding out his hand.

The tall MP pressed through the jostling drinkers towards the noisy bar. When Bo turned around, the MP stood in his way.

'Where's your pass, boy, an' why you out incorrectly dressed?' he demanded, as the second MP arrived, followed by Holt and the rest of the GIs.

The rowdy drinkers around them fell silent. Some of the locals who'd been laughing and cheering began to leave, but most of the soldiers and their girls hung around the bar finishing their drinks.

'I said, where's your pass, boy?' the taller MP said again, pushing Bo in the chest. 'And you tell me why you're out incorrectly dressed.'

'We goin' to have to arrest you,' his partner said.

'Leave the bloke alone. All he wanted was a bloody drink,' the ATS girl at the bar called.

'Aye, clear off,' a soldier standing further down the bar shouted.

As the two MPs edged closer together, Con noticed the barmaid sliding empty glasses from the bar top into the safety of the sink.

'These guys are–' the taller MP began to explain.

'Never mind what they are, mate,' a burly English sergeant called. 'They're just havin' a drink and botherin' nobody. So bugger off. Who called you, anyway?'

378

'It weren't me,' the landlord said, bustling behind the bar with a tray of glasses. 'All I want to do is to close up.'

'There you are then, lads,' the sergeant said, smiling confidently at the two MPs. 'Why don't you let us all finish our drinks, and then these chaps can get back to the camp without causing you any trouble?'

When the remaining crowd of locals murmured their agreement, the outnumbered MPs retreated, closing the front door behind them. Wes and the rest of the guys retrieved their abandoned drinks from the table near the dartboard and joined the squaddies and their girls at the bar, swapping stories and jokes.

'I just wanted a drink of my own,' Bo said, reluctantly accepting the half-glass of beer Wes offered.

'The landlord's not a bad guy,' Holt said, topping up Bo's glass with some of his own beer. 'He don't know you. You don't drink in here.'

'Well at least we got to finish our beers,' Wes said, 'though he's not goin' to open up again.'

'Hey, you guys heard the rumours?' Bo asked.

'You mean the trouble in Beaumont? In Texas?' Holt asked. 'I heard it was supposed to be Axis agents started it.'

'No. This only just happened. Heard about it at the airbase.'

'What you heard?'

'Detroit. Riots. Black folks bein' killed. Not in the factories. Eastwood Park.'

Holt put down his empty glass. 'Who you got it off?'

379

'At the airfield, today. Some guys working there. It might not be so. It's just a rumour. Somethin' about crowds on the bridge comin' back from Belle Island.'

'Sarge Mayfield might know,' Holt said. 'You ready? We'd best be goin', anyways. Like Wes said, the landlord's not goin' to open again.'

When he saw that his unwanted guests were ready to move, the landlord hurried out from behind the bar. The GIs heard him unbolt the front door and made their way out along the corridor, followed by the rest of the young locals who'd finished their drinks. Bo was one of the last to leave, carrying the half-empty bottle of beer he'd been given and had abandoned on a table near the bar. Outside, the air was still at blood heat. The group of girls and soldiers dawdled by the shuttered pub, reluctant to go home to their airless bedrooms. Bo drank the last of the bottled beer, and was listening to one of the soldiers telling a drunken tale, when he saw a jeep roll to a halt by the roadside. The tall MP got out; his white helmet bobbed towards them through the thickening twilight. The group began to break up, and when the other GIs moved off, Bo tried to follow them, but the MP barred his way.

'Have you been demanding beer, boy? You been cheekin' these good people? I'm going to have to arrest you.'

'Leave him alone,' one of the women called. 'What do you want to arrest him for?'

'You've been told there was no trouble,' the English sergeant shouted. 'There'll be no arrests tonight.'

Bo felt the MP's stale breath in his face and ran his thumb around the neck of the empty bottle.

'You want me?' he snarled, taking the bottle by the neck. 'You take me.'

'Back off, boy.'

Bo sensed the gun in the MP's hand before he saw it.

'I ain't scared of you,' he said. 'I'm sick of bein' scared.'

'He's going to shoot,' a woman in the crowd gasped.

Bo felt arms fold around his neck, and someone whispered, 'Come on, Bo.'

'Don't shoot, use your stick,' the smaller MP shouted over the whine of the jeep's engine. 'There's too many of them, come on.'

Bo shook the arm away and took another step towards the MP. In the fading light, the jeep wheeled around in the road, and the tall MP jumped in beside his partner.

'Come on, Bo. Put the bottle down. Let's go. They'll be back with more guys,' Wes said, as the jeep drove off and the crowd began to cheer.

'Here you are, lads,' the ATS girl said, handing opened bottles of beer to Bo and Wes. 'Have these.'

They thanked her and took the bottles. Then the whole group began walking down the main road in the direction of the camp. Bo and Wes strolled along some distance behind the rest of the GIs, followed by Con and Holt and then by the English soldiers and the local girls, walking along the pavement. For the first few yards, Bo and the other guys were silent, taking in the confrontation with the MPs, but the happy mood of the following group soon overtook them, and when the squaddies cheered at the sound of a bottle bursting on the windscreen of a passing jeep, they joined in.

'Hey, watch out, they're coming back,' one of the girls called, as they heard the sound of brakes in the semi-darkness.

'Reinforcements,' Bo said.

The jeep headed back towards them and pulled up sharply on the opposite side of the road. As the engine died, a second jeep arrived from the same direction. This was followed by three more from the other end of the village. All three were filled with MPs. One jeep screeched to a halt by the side of the black soldiers and the other two blocked the road into the village and the camp.

For a moment there was silence. All that could be heard was the tick of expanding metal. Bo could see around twenty white helmets looking out at him. He took a sip of his beer, savouring the coolness and marvelling at the surprising sweetness of the taste that flooded his mouth. Then he bent down, settling the bottle gently on the edge of the kerb; he straightened, waiting for a reaction. He didn't wait long. The tall MP and the little fat guy got out of their vehicle.

'He's the guy,' one of them called as they headed towards him.

Then he felt something fly by the side of his head. The fat guy yelled, slumped to the ground and his buddie reached down to help him. He didn't hear the second missile until there was a soft thud and the tall MP groaned. He saw the doors of the jeep open and the other two men go over to help their injured buddies. As the injured MPs were helped into the jeep, he heard feet, boots pounding. When the first MP got to him, Bo threw a punch; the guy wasn't ready and he slumped to his knees. The first real blow was a fist that hit the side of his head. He saw small circles of light spark in the gloom and heard the crowd behind him shouting, protesting that it wasn't a fair fight. Around him, the road filled with men, struggling, punching and wrestling. Bottles exploded near him, but then he heard a heavier thud.

'He's a knife,' he heard an MP near him shout. 'Fire! Fire!'

There was another shout, a threat. Then an explosion in the deepening shadows and he heard an engine being revved. He saw the first jeep with the injured MPs inside speed away. The screech of the wheels set a vibration, a pulsing in his ear. Behind him, Bo heard scuttering feet as the crowd ran for cover.

Then the rest of the jeeps screeched off one by one down the street. The noise of their tyres sent a judder through his skull and he tried to lift his head from the road. He tried to crawl, feeling, groping towards the sidewalk, searching for his half-filled bottle, but the kerb was littered with broken glass.

'Anyone shot?' Holt called. 'Bo, you okay?' he asked helping him to his feet.

'I'm okay. Just some ... stinging ... in my gut...'

'Is anyone else hurt? Who's that?' Holt asked, as they heard someone moaning in the darkness.

'Help me with this guy,' Wes said. 'You all right, buddy? You bleeding? Someone get his arm, we got to get him back to camp.'

'No. I'm okay,' the GI said. 'I just got a knock to the head.'

The camp was barely two blocks away. By the time they arrived, over a hundred GIs, alerted by the sound of gunfire, had gathered around the gates.

'Get the gates closed,' someone shouted. 'The MPs are shooting black guys. Get the guns. They'll be coming back.'

'We need to defend ourselves,' another voice called. 'Get the guns.'

Bo hardly noticed the uproar. On any other day, he would have been the guy they turned to; he'd be the guy who'd know what to do. Now he was tired. The stinging in his lower abdomen had turned into a pain; he reached down and felt wetness. All day he'd been hot, much too hot, but now he shivered. In the pushing crowd, he almost lost his footing and took hold of Con's sleeve.

'Detroit,' he said.

When Con arrived back at the hut, Holt and some of the other guys, stripped to their vests and undershorts in the heat, were waiting for news.

'Sarge Mayfield got them to take him to hospital,' he said, peeling off his blood-soaked shirt. 'The cracker lieutenant wasn't going to, but we argued with him. Bo... He's real bad.'

'What's happening out there?' Holt asked. 'You see Wes?'

Con shook his head. 'He helped me with Bo; then he left. There was a real row goin' on near the gates.'

'I know. We were there,' Holt said, 'but I didn't see Wes. They promised they'd have those MPs under guard by midnight, but that's because the guys wouldn't back down. Most of us are ready to face off the MPs. Mayfield know any more about Detroit?' he asked, handing Con a cigarette.

'No, he didn't know anything, but there's all kinds of stories goin' around. Some heard that a black woman and her baby got thrown in the river. Some say the police turned on the black folks, and when more of them tried to make their way on to Belle Island to see what was goin' on, the police barricaded the bridge. A big fight broke out on the bridge, police cars got burnt and folk dragged out of their cars...'

Con sat on his bed and inhaled the cigarette smoke, hoping to drive the metallic smell of Bo's blood from his nostrils.

'Arleen and her folks ... that's where they'd go... It's hot, they go to Belle Island. She loves it out there.'

Con looked over at Holt. 'We don't know for sure,' he said. 'My folks go there too. My mom takes the children from the church. We ain't gonna find out more tonight.'

The hut fell silent. There was little air, and the blackout made the heat all the more oppressive.

'I think we're crazy to stay here,' Holt said. 'Some of the other guys went out lookin' for MPs. We should have gone out with them and hunted them down.'

'It's not what Sarge Mayfield thinks.'

'He don't have folks there, like we do. He's not heard what's gone on at home, in Detroit.'

Outside the hut, Con heard sudden bursts of running feet and somewhere deep inside the camp angry, frightened voices. Then he heard Wes close by, and the door burst open.

'Come on,' Wes shouted, 'get yourselves a rifle. The guys have forced the gunroom open, come on.'

Con followed Wes and Holt to the gun store, where terrified men were grabbing guns and ammunition.

'What we gonna do?' he asked.

'We got to fight them off,' Wes said. 'We got no choice. We got to defend the camp. They've gone for more guys. Word is they've a machine gun. We've got to fight, or they'll kill us.'

'Fight them off? No,' Holt said. 'You saw what they did to Bo. You heard what's happened in Detroit. We've had enough.'

'That's right,' one of the other GIs shouted. 'I'm with you buddy; let's go huntin' MPs.'

'Sarge Mayfield said the colonel would see that the MPs would get what's coming,' the guy next to Con said.

'Any guy not willing to fight is on their side,' one of the GIs handing out the rifles shouted.

The camp was as alive as in the middle of the day. Con followed Holt and some of the other guys who were fixed on getting out of the camp down between the huts to the main gate. They backed into the shadows and waited.

'Keep with the rest of them; make your way

386

over and round the back of the trucks,' Holt whispered.

'Where's Wes?'

'He's staying,' Holt replied. 'They think they can fight them off and defend the camp.'

Holt moved ahead of him down to the main street. The road was quiet, and they took up positions, using the garden walls of the terraced houses for cover. They heard the jeeps coming, and as the lights picked them out, the MPs fired. The bullets ricocheted from the walls; splinters of brick and mortar pattered down, and Con wished he'd grabbed a helmet. The group of soldiers moved, and he followed, hugging the walls, firing at the speeding jeeps. As he crouched by a rough wall next to a glowing-white doorstep, Con heard the front door open. A pair of slippers edged out, and he smelt pipe tobacco.

'Whatever's happening, lad?' he heard a quivery, old voice ask.

'Go back inside, sir,' Con whispered. 'There's goin' to be plenty of shooting.'

'I can hear that already, son. Who's doin' it? Is it fifth columnists?'

'No, sir, it's the MPs. Go back inside, sir, and keep away from the windows.'

The slippered feet receded, and the door closed. Con looked into the darkness. He couldn't hear Holt and the others. He hurried forward. A bullet exploded close to his head, showering him with fragments of coarse grit from a windowsill. Rifles spluttered and crackled on both sides of the street. He wasn't sure who was ahead of him – MPs or his own buddies. Then the shooting stop-

387

ped, the still air was punctuated with groans, a machine gun opened up and Con heard the thud of boots on the empty street. Uncertain what to do next, he took cover by a wall. From where he lay at its base, he could feel the warmth of the bricks close to his face. He waited, hoping to hear Holt call his name. He was on a street that ran parallel to the main road. At the next corner, the intersecting street led back to the main road. Halfway down, Con could see figures flitting across the centre of the street. He wasn't sure who they were or which way he should go. He got to his knees, listening hard. Then the machine gun on the main road opened up again, making the flags under his knees shudder. Barely two houses in front of him, a guy ran out, criss-crossing the road, and firing as he ran. Con got to his feet and followed, the sound of the machine gun coming closer as he neared the main road. When he reached the guy, he was flattened against the side of the end house. Con slipped in beside him, the cinders in the back alley crunching under his boots. He heard a movement along the street, and when he peered out, two guys were limping towards them. The guy who'd been firing motioned to him to wait until they were alongside before breaking cover. One of the GIs was okay, but the other was groaning.

'They've blocked the street,' the GI said, adjusting the wounded man's arm over his own shoulder. 'We got to double back. Can you get his other arm?'

Con helped to take the wounded man's weight. They moved out, going back along the street to the intersection, where they came across another group taking cover by a wall.

'He needs a doctor,' Con said.

'Get him out of the fighting,' one of them said. 'Make your way over to the churchyard. He'll be safe there. We can see the road from here, and if they come this way, we can hold them off until you get to the cover of the trees.'

'Do you think you could carry him?' the injured GI's buddy asked. 'I want to go back to find my other buddy. I think he was hit, and the rest of the guys I was with got pinned down.'

'I guess so,' Con said, 'if you help lift him on my back.'

They waited until there was a break in the firing and then they lifted the injured man across Con's shoulders.

'I'll take him to the priest's house,' he called after the GI, who was already heading back towards the fighting.

'Don't take him there,' one of the other guys said, getting ready to cover him as he moved out, 'if they see they're hitting us hard, they might send in more reinforcements.'

'He's injured,' Con said, balancing the weight of the slighter man on his shoulders, 'and they'll send for them anyway.'

'Sure they will,' another voice from the darkness replied. 'That's why we got to get as many of the bastards as we can, now.'

Con moved out from between the streets of closely packed houses. He'd crossed the lane before firing began again and the guys moved off. He found that balancing the injured man on his

389

back was easier than he'd expected and made good progress towards the churchyard, using the trees overhanging the larger gardens for shelter. He'd almost reached the inky bulk of the church, when a jeep hurtled around the bend. The guy on his back made it impossible for him to run, and when the jeep screeched to a halt beside him, he was relieved to hear Captain O'Donal's voice.

'Bring that injured man over here, soldier,' he called. 'I have Sergeant Mayfield with me.'

The captain walked toward him and helped to steady the injured man, who grunted as he was eased from Con's shoulder.

'You're the man who brought in the injured soldier, earlier?'

'Yes sir. How is—?'

'Bo's dead,' Sergeant Mayfield said, getting out from the jeep and interrupting his senior officer.

'Yes,' the captain agreed. 'I'm afraid he is.'

'How are you injured, son?' Sergeant Mayfield asked the GI Con had been carrying.

'It's my leg, sir. I caught a bullet in my leg.'

Con helped them ease the injured soldier inside the jeep and watched it speed away. Then he crouched by the church door; his throat felt tight and his hands and chest were still sticky with Bo's blood. He could hear the occasional burst of rifle fire coming from the terraced streets around the main road and the ping of bullets striking the hard surface of a road or wall. He wanted a smoke, but didn't dare light a match. He wanted to find his buddies, but didn't know where to start. Most of all, he wanted to go back to the pub, and this time, when Bo argued with the MP, he would hold on to him harder and force him to leave.

The next time the shooting stopped, he decided to head back towards the camp, moving carefully, using the hedges and the wall for cover. In the distance, a jeep was taking the lane's twisting bends far too quickly. He wondered if it was O'Donal and Mayfield collecting the wounded. He retraced his steps to the alleyway where he'd met the injured soldier. The tips of two cigarettes waved in the darkness. One of the guys he'd been with earlier stepped out.

'Is he okay?' he asked.

'O'Donal and Sergeant Mayfield took him to the hospital.'

'The officers agreed to let O'Donal and the sergeant go out earlier to check if the MPs had injured any of our guys. Mayfield insisted. They shook on it. Did he say how many of our guys is injured?'

'No, but one of my buddies, Bo, is dead. The MPs shot him on the road on the way back from the pub.'

Con eased himself into a crouching position by the wall, a lighter flared, and he could see there were at least four other men in the alley.

'Should we go back?' he asked.

'You crazy?' the first guy said, tucking his lighter back in his pocket. 'You hear what they're doing in Detroit? There's MP battalions from Fort Custer shootin' black folks. What do you think they gonna do with us?'

'I hear they got white GIs out on the streets in Paradise Valley shootin' women and kids, draggin' them out of cars,' another GI said. 'Hospital's full.'

'Hold up,' the first GI said, as two shapes broke out of the shadows.

Two new GIs slipped down beside them breathing heavily.

'More of their guys have arrived,' one of them said. 'More MPs. They pulled up at the camp in an armoured car and two jeeps with machine guns fixed to the top.'

'We got to split up, make ourselves scarce for a while,' the first GI said. 'I've a girl, lives just outside of town. I'm going there. Can you guys find somewhere you can hide out? Or head into the fields and wait up. You go back now, they'll shoot you for sure.'

CHAPTER FIFTEEN

Ruby was woken by a noise – a sharp clattering – outside her window. She reached out and nudged at the blackout curtain. It was daylight, somewhere between five and six o'clock. She yawned: it had been three before the shooting had finally stopped and she was foggy with lack of sleep. When something struck the pane a second time, she scrambled to her knees and pressed her face to the glass. She peered down; the garden was empty. Then Con walked out from the shelter of the building and tossed a tiny stone up at her window.

Using the handrails to take her weight, Ruby moved noiselessly down the uncarpeted stairs and carefully drew the bolt on the kitchen door. Con was waiting on the bench, his elbows on his knees, his shoulders and hair encrusted with crystals of morning dew.

'We heard shooting,' she said.

'It was the MPs. It was like a war.'

'Who were they shooting at? Granddad said it sounded like there was a machine gun.'

'At us,' he said, staring across the garden at the familiar rows of vegetables. 'At the black soldiers. They were out to kill as many as they could.'

'Come on,' she said, gently taking hold of his sodden sleeve. 'Let's go inside.'

'I got to hide my gun,' Con said, pulling the half-hidden weapon from under the bench with his foot and making its barrel scrape along the flags. 'We broke into the gun store, fought back. It was dark and you couldn't tell who was killing who.' He looked up at Ruby, his eyes raw and bloodshot. 'The other guys said it was best to hide until things calmed down. I don't know if it's safe to go back.'

'You'll be safe here. I'll put that under the pigeon cabin,' she said, and ran back inside, her naked feet slapping on the damp stones.

She reappeared with her shoes and sat down beside him, forcing her feet into the cracked leather. Then she lifted the gun, wrapping her pale arms around it. As Con watched, she carried it through the vegetables, the dew from their leaves streaking the twill overall that served as her dressing gown and soaking the washed-out night-dress she wore underneath.

'Let's go in, but you'd best take your boots off,'

she said, pulling off her own wet shoes. 'They should be fast asleep. We were up most of the night. Thought the Germans had landed. You go up. You know which is my room. I'll bring you a brew and something to eat.'

The last time he'd visited the little room, Con hadn't noticed how bare it was: there had been an open trunk, glittery dresses scattered over the floor and Lou's crinkly cardboard wedding cake sitting forlornly on the bed. That was little more than six months ago, when England still felt real strange. It was Lou's wedding. There'd been some upset over the cake, and he'd come to collect it because he'd been sweet on Sadie. They'd heard Ruby sobbing; he'd comforted her and thought she was just a sad, little kid.

'There's meat and cheese and some pickle,' she said, putting a plate on the floor and handing him a mug of tea. 'I daren't start cooking; it might wake them all up.'

As she knelt on the floor, he could see the delicate pink blush of her body beneath the damp nightdress. He looked away, concentrating on the shelves of the battered bookcase.

'I'll go downstairs... You need to sleep.'

She placed her finger to her lips, frowned and whispered, 'You'll not. Take your jacket off and get in that bed. You look awful. Come on. Do as you're told. Don't worry. Once Granddad's awake, I'll ask him to find a better place for the gun. He'll know what we should do.'

Con took a bite from the thick sandwich. 'I can sleep on the floor.'

'You'll not. You'll do as you're told. I'll go

downstairs. I'll sit up. I'll read, until, I hear him moving about.'

Con made a mock salute. 'Stay a while, until I've eaten my food,' he said, pulling the counterpane from the bed and slipping it around her shoulders. 'Here. You'll need this if you're going downstairs.'

'I'll sit here on the floor, until you've had your tea. It's all right to talk, if we're quiet. I've closed their door, and Sadie's. They're all well away. It was a right carry-on last night. Mrs Bland arrived with that flippin' cat in its basket and this old gun her father had in the last war. She gave it to Granddad to shoot the Germans with, but the bullets weren't the right ones for it. We were sure it was the Germans that had landed. Then Mrs Lathom arrived with Bess. I don't know which poor Bess was most frightened of, the noise or the cat. Mrs Bland and Mrs Lathom both wanted to go in the shelter, but Jenny said there was no point, because the siren hadn't gone, and if the Germans had come, there would have been a siren, because they would have been dropped from planes. Mrs Lathom was in a right state. She said the Germans was that crafty they'd probably come in ships. She kept on saying that they might have sailed up the Ribble and given everybody the slip, and the more Granddad tried to reason with her, the worse she got. What really happened?'

There was no reply, and when she whispered his name, he didn't move. She took the sandwich from his hand and crept over to her chair. Snuggled inside the counterpane, she watched his long curling lashes twitch, and as the daylight slid under the dishevelled blackout curtain, she tracked a perfect triangle of sunlight over the pillow and across to the gently beating pulse in his throat. When the hens began to wake, Ruby cursed the cockerel's boasting, but she need not have worried: neither Monty's bragging nor Henry's shuffling footsteps on the stairs woke him. Then she crept out, shutting her bedroom door as gently as she could on the exhausted soldier, and hurried down to the kitchen.

'Tha'd best get back upstairs and warn Jenny and Sadie,' Granddad said, when she'd explained about the gun. 'We don't want them waking the lad.'

The four of them ate their breakfast in silence, and when Henry disappeared, warning that they shouldn't open the door to anyone, they crept about making pots of tea and telling each other what might have happened.

'Where's the gun now?' Jenny asked, when Henry returned.

'It's best not to ask me,' Henry said, pouring more water on to the already weakened tea.

'What do you mean?'

'You don't ask, and I'll not say. That's the best thing.'

'But what if he comes down and wants it?'

'Then I'll tell him where it is.'

'And what if you've gone out?'

'I'll not have.'

'What about Johnny?'

'What about him?'

'Well, he's expecting you to meet him. I thought you said–'

396

'He'll not bother if I'm not there.'

'Well, what if they come looking for it?'

'Who?'

'The Americans.'

'I don't know anything about it, and neither do you.'

'You'll get yourself into trouble.'

'Well, I might.'

'And the rest of us.'

'Oh, for goodness' sake, Ma,' Sadie said.

'I was only saying,' her mother said, banging the teapot down on the table and taking out a cigarette.

'Give us one, Ma. I keep wondering about Bo. He'd have been in Manchester. Said he'd most likely have to stay. I told him to do his best to get back, with Lou not being here for me to go out with. Mind you,' she said, puffing on the cigarette, 'if he had come back, he'd have come here. Still, if they were shooting, he might not have. He might have gone to see what was happening. Did Con say it was just here at the camp? What if he heard the shooting and thought it best to stay away and he's stayed out all night? Or what if it wasn't just here, what if it was all over and one of their MPs has got him? He might not have known, and if they flagged him down... I think we should waken Con. Like Mum says, what if the Yanks come...'

'We'll tell them he's not here,' Ruby said. 'Con would have told me if Bo was there, and if Bo had been outside the camp with Con, he'd have come with him. Like you said, he wasn't at the camp.'

'Well what if they do come and if they want to

look round?'

'They'll not be able to,' Henry said. 'They're not our police.'

'They might come with–'

'I think that's Con,' Ruby said. 'I think I can hear him.'

'Then let your granddad go and see,' Jenny said.

When Henry opened the bedroom door, the dejected GI was sitting on the edge of the bed.

'This is a rum do and no mistake,' Henry said. 'Our Ruby says it was your own side as was firing on you.'

Con looked at his hands and then up at the old man. 'Yes, sir, that was about it. I'm awful sorry to have–'

'No, lad. I'm glad you came to us.'

Con stood up and – swallowing hard – tried again to break the terrible news. 'I'm awful sorry I have to–'

'No, lad, don't you worry about us,' Henry said, pushing open the curtain and pointing towards the river. 'Now, come here, and I'll show you. I've wrapped that gun in some oiled cloth and moved it into an old rabbit hole on the bank. Just down there, you see. See down there; it's just down there where the river bends. It'll be safe there. You have to lie down on the banking to see the hole. I've pushed the bugger down as far as me arm would reach.'

Henry turned and smiled, his eyes shining with excitement, and the news of Bo's death shrivelled on Con's tongue.

'Come on, now, don't look so downhearted.

398

What you need is some breakfast,' the old man said, patting him on the shoulder. 'Then, if I was you, I'd try and get a bit more sleep. I'll keep them women out of your way as long as I can, but they'll want to know all the whys and wherefores. Well, at least Bo would have been well out of it by all accounts. He told us he was going out Manchester way, and they'd probably either keep him there overnight or send him further on. Not at all pleased about that, Sadie wasn't. Had words they did, but it was all for the best, after all. Though she's still moidered about him. Do you know what's happened to the rest of 'em?'

Con turned to the window and looked out at the morning sunlight. 'I don't rightly know, sir,' he said.

Ruby had begged to be allowed to stay at home, and Sadie wanted to stay as well, in case Bo came to find her, but Granddad said it might look funny if none of them turned up for work. In the end, they'd left Granddad and Jenny to take care of Con. It was the best thing to do: they didn't want anyone coming to the cottage and finding him there. On her way to the factory, Ruby called in on Mrs Lathom: it was Granddad's idea, just in case Nellie took it into her head to call at the cottage to find out what they'd heard about the shootings. When she'd knocked on the door, Mrs Lathom had been so glad the Germans hadn't arrived, she'd even agreed to let her take Bess out for a walk the next day.

Although she'd been very late for work, the shooting had caused so much upset to the mill's routine that Ruby was able to creep into the spinning room and busy herself, dragging trucks up and down between the winding frames, before anyone realised that she'd been missing. Peering between the spinning bobbins, she'd tried to read the lips of the women, hoping for any mention of the missing soldiers, and at dinnertime she sat against the stone wall in the mill yard with Mrs Rostron, listening to the chatter.

'I heard there was at least forty of 'em shot, and they was beating the rest of them poor lads with clubs,' a weaver said.

'I know a woman in the carding room who lives opposite the camp,' Jack, one of the tacklers, told them. 'She said they'd hardly slept, and there was machine-gun bullets in her wall this morning. Her husband dug one out for the little lad.'

'Somebody said they've guards all over, and nobody can get near the camp. Some folk are locked out of their own houses,' Mrs Rostron said. 'I wonder what'll 'appen. Folk's right worried. Some of them as had husbands on night shift must have been terrified. They'll not be lettin' 'em out to dances and such for a good while after this.'

By late afternoon, the women moved leadenly between the machines, wiping the sweat from their chins. Ruby was dreaming of escaping, of rushing home and finding Con there, when Mrs Rostron touched her arm and motioned over to the door where the manager – panting and grim-faced – was waiting. He beckoned to her to follow him down the stairs. Ruby, her stomach tingling, expected to see a policeman waiting by the office door to tell her that Con had been discovered and

400

her granddad was in jail. It wasn't a policeman but a child she didn't know with a hastily scribbled note from Maud, telling her that Uncle Joe was ill.

As she hurried down the street, old folk were perched like dusty sparrows on rickety stools and dining-room chairs enjoying the sunshine. Maud's door stood open. Inside, Auntie Maud – her severe knot of hair unravelled – knelt by Joe's bed. His white face looked up at her over Maud's shoulder, a metal spoon fixed lengthways between his teeth.

'I'm sorry to have got you from work,' Maud said, sitting back on her heels. 'I couldn't wait any longer. I need his medicine and I've nobody else as can get it. I daren't leave him, and my neighbours are either working or old folk. Go as quick as you can, lass. He's really bad this time.'

'The doctor,' Ruby said. 'I'll–'

Maud shook her head. 'He's been twice already, yesterday and last night. If he was to come, he'd want to know if the medicine had worked.' Maud got up and went over to the dresser. 'There was so much you see ... so much medicine. My neighbour's lad went for me. I got the pills, as he normally has, but there was these powders. They have to be got from the chemist. He makes them up special and...' Maud handed her a half-crown. 'Give him the paper and tell him to give you what that will pay for.'

Ruby took the paper and the money and glanced at the clock, guiltily wishing that the same neighbour's child could be asked to go for the medicine again. There were no children in the street, and she hurried over the railway bridge, pulling off her scarf and mopping her neck as she went.

The chemist's shop was cool. The assistant took the paper, and then using the highly polished cupboards for support, hobbled into the back of the shop. A number of times Ruby caught her breath, as the woman, her pace awkward and uncertain, almost lost her footing. After a few minutes the chemist's assistant, whose fresh doll-like complexion contrasted strangely with her slow and painful movements, eased her way back into the shop.

'There's not much call for these powders,' she said, holding firmly on to the edge of the counter. 'It will take some time.'

Across the road, Ruby could see a queue outside the Co-op and she decided to investigate. After the dark interior of the chemist's, the bright sunlight made her squint; she didn't notice Jenny among the line of women waiting patiently under the green-and-white awning, until she waved to her from the middle of the queue.

'Johnny Fin will be upset when he hears about poor Joe,' Jenny said. 'When he came round to see what had happened to Henry,' she whispered, 'he nearly gave us both heart attacks. We didn't know he was there until he knocked.'

Through the open Co-op door, Ruby could see the shop assistants licking their pencils and adding up long strips of numbers with the dampened lead. On the opposite counter she could see the sugar, already weighed carefully into rations, and next to it a large wooden tub of flour with a ladle hanging on the side. Sometimes there was a huge golden mound of butter set on a slab of marble, but today it was missing, along with the bacon and ham wrapped in white stockinet. Today the line of women were hoping that the small packets of starch stacked next to the till – limited to one per customer – would last out until their turn came. When Jenny had tucked her prize in her basket, they walked over to the chemist's.

'We was just telling Johnny about what had happened – the lad was still asleep – when two blokes on bikes came knocking at the door, wanting glasses of water. We thought it was the Yanks,' she said, taking Ruby's arm as they crossed the road. 'Anyway, Johnny's gone to see if he can find the priest, ask his advice. Then he's coming back, and once it gets dark, he'll take the lad to a place he knows. It's not safe for him to stop with us.'

'He could have my room.'

'No he can't. We can't have him with us,' Jenny said, checking her reflection in the chemist's window and adjusting her hat. 'He's best going back, if you ask me. It's not like he could move around and nobody spot him.'

'Well nobody's looked until now.'

'Best thing is for Johnny to get the priest to go back with him to the camp. He's only a young lad; they'll not harm him, if he explains. Come on, let's get this stuff and be off back.'

'Maud hasn't the money for the medicine,' Ruby said. 'She said just to get what I could for two and six, but there's a lot more he needs. I was going to ask if I could pay tomorrow.'

'How?'

'I have a bit saved. I was going to use it. If you stay out here...'

Jenny tutted and opened her purse. 'Here. I

want it back, mind. Maud wouldn't thank you for taking my money, whatever it was for.'

The heat made it difficult for Jenny to walk quickly. 'I wouldn't have come out, not today, but sitting there was making me all of a dither. Off you go and take her that stuff,' she said, when they reached the end of the street where Maud lived. 'I'd say that Johnny would come and see how Joe was, but he's going to be too busy. We'll expect you when we see you.'

Ruby watched Jenny walk towards the little bridge, wishing she could go home in her place. She'd spent all day imagining that she was sitting with Con in the living room at the cottage, dreaming of how he might hold her hand under the table and how, once it was dark and Granddad and Jenny were dozing, they'd go outside and sit in the garden.

On Maud's street, the well-scrubbed doorsteps were empty; the old people had taken their chairs and gone inside, but many of the doors were still open, and she could smell cooking. In the cottage, the air smelt heavy and stale. Maud was still sitting by Joe's bed where Ruby had left her. Joe was quiet now. The metal spoon had gone, and he looked as though he could be sleeping. Ruby began to hope that she might not be needed after all. A neighbour, sitting on a wooden stool in front of the fireplace, turned to look at her.

'Lass is back with thy medicine,' the old woman croaked.

'There was enough for all of it,' Ruby said, putting the parcel on the table.

Auntie Maud looked round, but didn't reply

and bent forwards stroking Joe's fat hand.

The neighbour, a woman of about eighty, wore a mob cap over her hair. When she stood up, she was as broad as she was tall and dressed in a long shapeless dress covered by a greasy apron.

'I'll be off to make his tea,' she said, tapping her clay pipe on the side of the empty fireplace. 'There's a pie in the meat safe, enough for you both. You see she gets some sleep,' she said to Ruby. 'She's never had those clothes off for two days. She'll be ill herself.' The woman shuffled to the door, and then pushing her pipe back into her mouth, looked over at Maud. 'Remember,' she said, 'urine straight from the chamber pot is the best thing for a compress. Works every time, and send out for some common ale. There's no better tonic. I'll be round in the morning, but knock on the fireback,' she said, nodding towards the fireplace, neatly laid with twists of newspaper and a few sticks, 'if you need me in the night.'

The pie consisted mainly of carrot and potato inside a crisp pastry case. When they had eaten, Ruby got up to make a cup of tea. There was nothing in the meat safe, except an inch of sour milk at the bottom of a jug.

Auntie Maud sipped her black tea. 'There's beef tea on the stone slab in the pantry,' she said. 'That's the coolest place. There's a tea towel on top of the bowl. Warm it, but not too hot, and put some bits of bread in it, cut small. If he doesn't wake, don't wake him. He's exhausted. Wake me if he fits. He might get upset if he opens his eyes and sees you. He might not know who you are. Read to him if he wakes and he's quiet. He likes to hear the news,' she said, nodding towards the newspaper on the end of the table. 'If he does fit, put a spoon in his mouth and come for me.' Then Maud got up, took her cup to the sink and washed her face. 'I'll say goodnight, then,' she said.

'Is there anything ... jobs...? Shall I do the washing?' Ruby asked, pointing to the pile of sheets on the floor near the scullery door.

'You could put them to soak in the sink,' she said, walking wearily to the stairs, 'but don't leave him, and if you go in the scullery or the pantry, leave the door open, so as you can see 'im. He's to be watched all the time.'

Ruby explored the cupboards, looking for a stock of tinned meat or dried fruit, but found nothing but a flour jar, barely half full, and an open packet of tea. As night fell, she thought of Con and wondered where Johnny had taken him. When she looked up, Joe had opened his eyes and was staring at her with a quiet interest. His eyes followed her over to the pantry, and watched with unblinking concentration as she warmed the beef tea in a pan. He sucked each little cube of bread, and when they were all gone, he sipped the rest of the dark liquid from the spoon she held carefully to his mouth. Then he settled back on his pillows and gave her his full attention as she read out the latest news reports, births, weddings and deaths, followed by all the advertisements and notices, including a church bazaar in aid of war orphans. Eventually Joe fell into a doze, and it was just before six o'clock when she heard Maud moving around in the room above. She came down the stairs as the clock chimed the hour, her hair back again in its tight bun.

There was no mention of breakfast, and after a cup of black tea, Maud took her up to the sparse back bedroom and pulled up the blind.

'It's going to be a bonny day again,' she said. 'You get to sleep now. There's nobody to disturb you. I'll not call you unless... Well, he's probably on the mend. I know you meant well, but I'll not take charity. I'll pay for the medicine.'

'I thought it was best...' Ruby said. 'If the doctor said he needed...'

'Aye, you're probably right. I can see that. Did you read to him?'

'Yes,' Ruby laughed, 'for about three hours. I read most of the paper.'

'He'll know if I read the same things as you have,' Maud said, her stern features softening. 'He'll shake his head if he's heard something before.'

Ruby took off her skirt and blouse and slipped her shoes under the narrow bed. The sun was casting fingers of pale light across the shared courtyard at the back of the cottages. She curled up under the thin sheet, listening to the sound of footsteps and the irregular scrape and thud, as the wooden doors to the three communal toilets opened and closed.

Con hadn't slept much. Johnny had waited until it was dark before he'd led him to a hut that was a short walk from the cottage and close to the river. He'd left him some food and bedding, but when the door was closed and he was alone, the hut felt airless and the smell of engine oil and dust filled his throat. He'd spent most of the night among the trees, flinching at each sound, until the squeaking of the bats and the owl's wild hunting cries became familiar. Once it was daybreak, Con went back and hid for a while inside the hut, squinting out through the split wooden boards, expecting at any minute to be discovered, until it had occurred to him that the hut might be the first place that anyone might look. Then he'd slipped outside again, taking the remaining food with him.

For part of the day Con hid out in the trees, keeping the hut in sight, hoping that Ruby might come and find him or that Johnny might arrive with Father O'Flynn. The growing heat made him thirsty and he stole down to the river, kneeling on the bank, dipping his cupped hands through the sparkling surface and slurping in the cool water, hoping that Johnny would bring him a cup, or maybe even some bottled beer. He was about to lower his head, to douse his face in the river, when flashes of green light on the water caught his attention. Con sat up, scanning the opposite bank nervously. He peered in the river again; every time he looked into the ripples, all he could see was clear water and the stones at the bottom. Then each time, just before he became convinced that it was his imagination, there was a flickering in the water again. Con lay down, hanging over the river, determined not to blink. It was almost a full minute before he saw them: a shoal of small silver fish, their scales caught for a fraction of a second in the sunlight.

He was still there, stretched out on the grass

watching the fish, when Ruby came along the opposite bank with Bess, and his shocked expression at the sound of the dog's excited bark made her grin. As he got to his feet, Bess splashed through the river towards him, and she took off her shoes and waded in after the dog.

'I thought you'd be in the hut. There's no news,' she said, putting the basket of food on the ground. 'Granddad said to tell you that he's tried to find out what's happened to Wes and Holt, but they have the camp under guard. There's nobody allowed in or out. Sadie thinks Bo might have been arrested on the road. She thinks he would have been back by now.'

Con sat down heavily on the grass, and Bess, taking this as an indication that he was ready to play, wagged her tail and beamed with delight. He nuzzled her head, letting the dog lick his face and then tussled with her, rolling over on the short, mossy grass.

'Everybody round here heard the shooting, and when it got out that it was the Americans shooting their own, they all took your side. They think it's not right.'

She sat down, wrapping her hands around her knees. Con threw a stick for Bess, and when Ruby tried to look at him, his extravagant lashes swept down avoiding her gaze.

'I reckon the army is right. We must be pretty stupid, leaving our families to fight their war,' he said, his long fingers tugging angrily at the grass. 'Fighting for democracy; it's a pointless war for us.'

She wanted to take his hand, but she was too

shy, and for a while they sat side by side, listening to the soft, comforting water.

'Look over there,' Ruby said, pointing to a spot where the water ran smoothly off a line of stones. 'Can you see? Over there in the middle? It looks that smooth. It reminds me of the glycerine my mum used when she made icing. It looked like that, when you poured it out. Clear, but thick like oil.'

Con turned and smiled at her. 'My grandma used to make all kinds of things out of icing, things for cakes, for birthdays. She learnt it when she was young and she taught my mom. Mom can make anything you want: cradles for a christening cake; a cake with Cinderella's coach on the top; a whole Easter egg out of sugar with a cute little cut-out scene inside. She does all kinds. Before I came away, she made me a cake with the names of people wishing me well around the side – friends and people from the church. It was real pretty. She iced a flag on the top and made two sugar hearts that stood right in the middle.'

'You could have brought them with you.'

'You can't do that, sugar hearts break real easy.'

'All that sugar would have come in handy.'

His face exploded into a smile. 'I'm glad you came by,' he said. 'Nobody else would have thought of that. Come on, let's walk. I'm goin' crazy just waiting around.'

'I've got something as will cheer you up,' she said.

'Has Henry sent me some beer?'

'He has, as a matter of fact. Said to tell you to stand it in the river,' she said, gently easing the

410

dark-brown bottles from under the basket's cover. Con could smell the soap on her skin, and the great hollow feeling he'd carried since he left home grew deeper. Then, as they would have on any other day, he took her hand and they walked through the wood. As they wandered along, Bess trotted behind them and then scampered along in front, before turning around to dart back down to the water. When she was busy investigating an interesting scent by the river's edge, they hid. Once she looked up and discovered that she was alone, Bess put her nose to the ground and quickly discovered their hiding place. On the bend of the river, she startled a fishing heron, and as the great bird lifted up, she chased back up through the trees shaking the drops of water from her coat over them, making them laugh. Ruby danced away from him, brushing the drops from her pale lavender dress. Her loveliness stung his heart, and when she saw his laughter fade, she walked back towards him.

'What's the matter?' she asked.

Con bit his lip and smiled. Her beauty made him nervous. He'd grown used to the girls from the town who always took the lead. He wasn't used to making the first move, and he didn't want to scare her.

'Mrs Bland was right,' he said. 'You're just as pretty as the girl in her picture.'

She walked away, and for a moment he thought she was angry, but when she turned around, her face was the softest, delicate pink.

'We could go away,' she said. 'If Father O'Flynn takes you back, they might not let you out. If it's as they say, al the black GIs are being kept in the camp, and there are guards at the gates. We could go to Liverpool. Bo told Sadie that there was a black man and his... He said people are used to seeing black people. Bo saw them...'

'Ruby,' he said, 'about Bo... I...'

When he tried to speak, to tell her, she reached up, solemnly drawing him to her, and kissed his mouth.

'I'll keep you safe,' she said.

Sadie had been willing the shift to end and left her machine long before the hooter sounded.

'If anyone asks, tell 'em I'm not feeling too good,' she said to the woman on the next lathe. The woman nodded; she could see that Sadie didn't look herself.

By the time the rest of the workers were trailing out into the late-afternoon sunshine, Sadie was already waiting for a bus.

'Don't normally see you at this stop,' one of the men in the queue said.

'I've to collect somebody from the dentist's,' she lied. 'She's havin' a tooth out. She was bad last time. It was the gas.'

As the rest of the queue settled into telling stories of their own tooth extractions, Sadie stared down the empty road. She'd hoped that Bo would turn up at the cottage, but now she was sure that he must have been taken back to the camp. No one at the factory had seen a truck driven by any of the black GIs since the shooting, and the rumour was that they were all under guard. In the end Sadie decided that, instead of waiting for news, she'd go and see for herself. She'd have called at Lou's and they'd have gone to the camp together, but Lou was still in Liverpool. If Con wasn't hiding down by the river, Ruby might have gone with her, and if she'd told Ma she was going, she would have insisted on coming; she didn't want that.

When she got down from the bus, the road was quiet and there was no sign that anything had happened, but as she neared the camp she saw a group of six or seven women standing around a man in blue overalls.

'You can see 'em clear as anything,' he said, pointing up at the wall of a small white cottage. 'Bullets flying all night. See, there's two there. See, just by the window. My missus was that scared. Landlord at that pub just up there, they told him to get inside and stay put, said there was going to be a battle. One chap was shot here. See,' he said, pointing to a dark stain on the pavement. 'Gunned down,' he said, taking a tobacco pouch from his pocket. 'Their blood's a different colour to ours, more of a purple than a red.'

One of the women who'd been listening burst into tears. She was comforted by one of the other girls, who put an arm around her shoulder and led her away. Sadie and the rest of them followed, walking down the main street towards the camp. All of the women were about her age, but they were all smartly dressed. Sadie looked down at her own greasy overalls and wished that she'd gone home first and put on something nice. One of them, a tall girl of her own age, caught up with her.

'Have you come looking for someone?' she asked.

'Yes. I didn't think he was here that night. I thought he'd been out with his lorry, but I think he must have got back before the trouble, because I haven't heard from him since.'

'They have them all inside; there's no passes,' the tall girl said. 'We've all come to try and find out, but they'll not tell us anything.'

'There are white MPs on the gate,' the woman who'd comforted the tearful girl said, 'and you know what they're like. They'll not take notes or messages for us, or let us see anyone in charge.'

'Have you come with your friend, or have you both got young men at the camp?' Sadie asked.

'Oh, this is my sister, Lilly. She's been that worried I said I'd come with her. We didn't know what was wrong. It was her birthday...'

'I couldn't understand it,' Lilly said, wiping her eyes. 'I'd only seen him the night before. He took me to my bus stop and told me he'd be there by four. We waited tea for him. I knew there must be something; he wouldn't have missed my... Then last night, my dad heard this rumour in the pub, and I had to come and find out what had happened.'

'Like that chap said, there's been some killed,' her sister added, 'but they'll not admit it.'

The women stood on the corner of the street leading to the camp. About halfway down, a jeep was parked across the road; four white-helmeted MPs lolled inside. Sadie walked towards them. The man in the front passenger seat was resting his feet on the top of the door.

'I want to go into the camp,' she said. 'I want to see the commanding officer.'

The MP sneered and glanced over his shoulder at the two broad, well-fed men in the back of the jeep.

'Git back up the road,' he said softly.

Sadie felt her heart begin to thud. The plump-cheeked men were all about her age; she looked directly at the one who had spoken.

'I want to find out if my young man is all right.'

'Git back up the road, whore,' he said a little louder, swinging his feet down and leaning back in his seat. 'Git back up that road.'

The young man's pale-lashed eyes held hers. The hatred in his voice made it hard for her to sound calm. 'We heard ... shooting... I want to find—'

'Ain't none of them boys comin' out no more,' the MP said, spitting into the road by her feet and wiping his mouth on the back of his hand. 'Tramps like you will have to make your money somewhere else. No white GI will touch you, even for free. Now git,' he said, turning to look up the road, as though she'd already followed his orders.

Up in her room, Ruby put the bunch of meadowsweet and ox-eye daisies she had picked by the river in an old jug she'd found under the sink. When she'd left him, Con had smiled a sad smile and shook his head, but she was sure if they could get to Liverpool, they would be safe. She put the flowers on her windowsill and sat down on the bed. She knew that it might take her a couple of days to plan, get everything together, but when she'd done that, it would be easier to persuade Con they could do it. She imagined walking across country in the summer twilight; if they stuck to the small lanes – it might take some time – she was sure they could reach Liverpool before dawn. Then she thought it might be better to catch a train – if they could find a quiet, out-of-the-way station. When they got near the city, they would be safe: no one there would know that Con had run away from the camp. She wondered if she should take some of Henry's clothes for Con to change into. Once they were in Liverpool, if they headed for the docks, he would probably be taken for a local – a dockworker or a seaman. Then ... she tried to think what would happen next, but the excitement began to make the blood thrum in her ears, and she gave up trying to plan what would happen in Liverpool and picked up the dark cup-shaped bird's nest she kept on her windowsill, turning the thing slowly in her hands. Granddad had found it for her only a few weeks after she'd arrived at the cottage. It was a meticulous construction of moss and grass, finished with lichen and tiny flecks of bark and held together with spiders' webs. It was a perfect little house. Ruby was still gazing at the nest when Jenny pushed open the door.

'How long are you going to be trimming your room up?' she asked, her sharp tone making Ruby almost drop her precious nest. 'There's the table to be set and food to be made and goodness knows where our Sadie is. She should have been home an hour ago.'

No one ate much that evening; instead, they sat in silence, as Sadie told them the unsettling story of her visit to the camp. Then Jenny put Sadie to bed with a glass of milk and brandy, and Ruby cleared away the uneaten food. The evening was still warm, and after she'd washed the pots, she joined her granddad in the garden, gently teasing weeds from between the closely packed young vegetables, inhaling their new green scent mixed with the smell of rich, warm earth. A blackbird peeked at her, darting forward to grab a scurrying insect, before smartly stepping away again out of reach.

'Just look at that cheeky fella,' Granddad said, resting on his hoe. 'It's no good you lookin' at me like that. I know who's been pinchin' all my ripe raspberries. It's you, tha little bugger. It's thee. Grabbin' the lot, he's been. It's all right singing away in the hedge, I know what tha's up to, me lad.'

They worked on in silence, until it was almost too dark to see the weeds. Then Granddad put away the hoe and sat down on the old seat. Ruby sat down next to him, her back against the warm, irregular stones of the cottage wall.

'Poor lass,' he said. 'It were a bad do were that. They'd no call to speak to her that way. No call at all. She should have let her mother or me go with her. I'll have a word with Father O'Flynn when I see him; I'll tell him what was said. He'll want to know. He'll take it up with the officers, I would think. A bad job that, and no mistake. No call for it. The black man, he's like us, like the working classes,' Granddad said, lighting a cigar-

417

ette and covering its tip in the palm of his hand. 'All right, we're not slaves, but not far off, if you ask me. We do have a vote...'

'Not all of us don't,' Jenny said, settling on the bench beside him. 'Youngsters don't, and they're fighting and doin' war work.'

'It'll not be like after the last lot. It'll not just go back to normal. Nationalisation: common ownership of the railways and the mines...'

'You're allus calling the miners.'

'Well I'm not now. Railwaymen, blokes like me, we're like the miners, and we've had enough. How's lass?'

'I've given her one of my pills and she's nodded off. Ruby, before you go to bed, will you look out any scraps of cloth big enough to make some little dresses and such for Lou's nieces? Sadie's that upset; I was thinking she should stay at home to-morrow. She could start cutting out. It would give her something to occupy her mind. Then, if Father O'Flynn does happen to call, and he's going up to the camp about the lad, he might as well know what happened to Sadie. He might want to tackle them about that as well.'

'Well, let her stay at home by all means,' Granddad said, 'but I don't know about Father O'Flynn. Johnny's heard he's back tomorrow, but it's not certain. Young Con will be glad if he is. We're hoping he might be here tomorrow, but it might be the end of the week, and we didn't want to leave it that long. It's better for the lad to go back than for them to find him hiding.'

Ruby let out her breath slowly and decided that there wasn't any time left for planning. Then she

418

looked out over the dusky garden and smiled. Plans, her father had always said, got in the way: they stopped you spotting the chances when they came.

It was late in the evening before they left the garden and went to bed. The blackout and the hot summer night made sleep almost impossible. Ruby lay on top of the thin sheet; tonight would be her last in the cottage. Once Con heard what had happened to Sadie, she guessed he'd definitely decide it was best that they leave for Liverpool. She'd set off for work as usual, hiding some clothes and food in the basket, together with the ten-shilling note Uncle Walt had given her and the money she'd managed to save from her wages. They'd have to wait, hide in the hut and set off in the twilight. Then they'd walk, keep on walking all night, and be in Liverpool by morning. Once they were there, she would keep him safe for the whole war.

Ruby couldn't remember falling asleep, but when she woke the sun was beginning to warm her bedroom. She sat up and rubbed her eyes. There wasn't a clock in the room, but she was sure that it must be late morning. Granddad hadn't woken her and she would be late for work. When she scrambled out of bed and opened the door, she could hear Johnny's voice downstairs. She tried to listen, and although she couldn't make out his words, the tone made her tremble. She pulled on the lavender cotton dress she'd worn the day before and hurried down the stairs. Granddad was standing in the kitchen, his thin sinewy arms holding on to the sides of the sink.

Ruby's throat dried. She willed him to stay there, telling herself that if he didn't turn around, it would mean nothing had happened to Con.

At the sound of her step he raised his head, first staring at her through his shaving mirror, before turning to speak to her. His eyes were red and his voice, hoarse with tears, was barely a whisper. She crept nearer to hear him.

'It's Joe,' he said. 'It's our poor, sweet little Joe. He's gone. Last night.'

Ruby's legs failed and she clung to her grand-dad. He patted her hair and comforted her, mistaking her relief for sorrow.

'Na then, na then,' he said. 'Don't take on so.'

She moved unsteadily into the living room. Jenny and Sadie were sitting on opposite sides of the fireplace with a pile of cloth between them on the floor.

'Are you all right, Ruby, love?' Jenny asked. 'I've got your sewing-box out. Are you sure Sadie can use anything in here? You forgot to look yourself last night, but never mind that now. Johnny, pour her a cup of tea, will you.'

Johnny Fin, who was sitting at the table, patted her hand, poured her a cup of tea and began explaining how Joe had collapsed suddenly just before bedtime, but she wasn't listening. When Jenny told her she must eat and to get herself some bread and jam, she went willingly to the kitchen. She put on her shoes and walked out into the yard. The seat of the bench was damp with dew. It was a bright morning; a soft breeze rippled the leaves on the fruit trees, and across the lane, the grass in Bardley's meadow was a sea of shifting green.

Ruby wandered to the gate and tried to clear her head. The number of people in the cottage was going to make it harder for her to slip her clothes and money in her basket without someone noticing. She wasn't sure how long they were all going to stay and if Jenny or Granddad would send her on messages. As she looked over at the quiet fields, she planned her escape: after breakfast, she'd go upstairs, change out of her crumpled lavender dress, put on her working clothes, pack her basket in her room and then leave by the back door, but instead of going to work, where she might be sent for or told to come home again, she would go to the hut and wait with Con until it was safe to leave. They would all think she was rushing off because she was late for work. Now it was decided she felt calm. She went back into the kitchen to cut a slice of bread and heard raised voices coming from the living room: Jenny and Granddad were arguing.

'We can't all stay off work all day,' Jenny said. 'You've lost that much money, what with your chest, and I can't leave Sadie. What if we need you to come to see these Yanks? You might have to take time off then. I'll not have my girl spoken to like that.'

'I-I...' Johnny Fin began.

'No, Johnny, you can't go,' Sadie said, her voice high and fretful. 'You're going to see Father O'Flynn, and he'll be back today. Twelve o'clock train, most likely.'

'Well, I'm not letting Ruby go,' Granddad said defiantly. 'A laying out is no place for a child.'

'She can call on her way to work,' Jenny said,

and to signal that the discussion was at an end, she opened Ruby's sewing-box. 'Here, Sadie, love,' she said, taking out a garment and giving it the sort of violent shake that Ruby suspected that she would have loved to have given Granddad, 'this looks as though it might do.'

Ruby saw a flash of blue fabric and recognised the dress she'd worn on New Year's Eve. She shuddered: that night when Johnny had brought her home, she'd rolled up the torn dress and stuffed it inside her workbox. Then each time she'd opened the heavy lid, Ruby had pushed the ripped dress in deeper, until it was swallowed up by the rest of her mending.

'Maud is my sister,' Granddad said, his face flushed with anger.

'I know, and Ruby's her niece. She can call and give your condolences on her way to work and say you'll call round later. If you go, you'll stay. That will mean you'll not go into work today, and you'd more than likely come back too sozzled to go to work tomorrow as well. Ruby could tell Maud you'll be seeing Father O'Flynn. She'll think it's just about the arrangements. You could mention it to him when he comes, once we've told him about Con and what happened to Sadie.'

'And ask him to find out what's happening to Bo and the other lads,' Sadie added.

'I know you, Henry. I know what'll be next. You'll be saying next you're havin' to pay for this funeral, and not enough money coming in to feed us.'

The thought of having to pay for Joe's funeral had made Jenny even angrier, and when she shook the dress again, a ten-shilling note fluttered out from the pocket, coming to rest on the rug at her feet.

'Where's this from?' she asked. 'Ruby, where's this note from?'

For a moment, as everyone's eyes rested on the note, Ruby's nose filled with the smell of Rollo's desperate body.

'It was from Mr Rollo,' she whispered. 'On New Year's Eve. I'd forgotten about it. It was in the kitchen before—'

'And why did he give you a ten-bob note?'

'He tried to ... to kiss me. He gave it me... He was drunk. He said he was sorry and didn't want his sister to know. He asked me not to tell her. And then after...'

'New Year's Eve is when they said he was attacked by a black soldier who was cuddling a lass in the garden. He was knocked out,' Sadie said. 'That's what's behind all this trouble; why folk have turned against the lads at the camp.'

'No, they haven't, and anyway...'

'Was it Con?'

'No. There was nobody there. No,' she said shaking her head.

'How could that have anything to do with our Ruby?' Granddad said. 'Whatever the rumours, they've nothing to do with her. New Year's Eve was the night I was ill and Johnny went to fetch her. She fell on the way...'

'It's not the lass's fault,' Johnny said. 'I ... I ...'

'There was nobody there. Con wasn't there, and it wasn't your fault either, Johnny. She just made you think it was... Nobody told me... I didn't know to wait for you. Granddad was ill, and I set off. I had my torch. I thought I'd be all right... She forgot to tell me to wait. Then to cover up for forgetting she told you that...'

'That's enough,' Jenny roared, snapping the lid of the sewing-box closed. 'It's you as took this money. You must have encouraged him, been too friendly. Thinkin' you're an equal, because you played the piano for 'em ... and then come home crying saying you'd been attacked... Makin' us feel...'

'He's old enough to kn-n-know... An educated m-m-man,' Johnny spluttered. 'Not fit to wipe that ... that child's shoes. And neither are y-y-you.'

After Ruby had left Con on that previous afternoon he had walked back to the squat little hut. He'd sat for a while, the sensation of her fierce kisses on his mouth and her promises to escape with him chasing through his brain. When she'd been in his arms he'd believed it was possible, but now what had happened at the camp, and the picture of Bo's rigid body on a gurney, pushed the dream away. He got up – felt in his empty pockets for a cigarette – and told himself that in his position Bo wouldn't have hesitated. Bo wouldn't have lost his nerve, but he wasn't Bo: he hadn't even been brave enough to tell Henry that his friend was dead. The memory hurt. He wandered outside. The hut was on the edge of Bardley's fields, and Con sat down disconsolately among the strong, new grass, hoping that Johnny would remember to bring him some more cigarettes. When a skylark rose suddenly in front of him, he

424

watched the valiant little bird's almost vertical climb. As he sat back on his heels, the creature rose higher, before hovering, a fixed point far above his head. The tiny bird's song filled the late-afternoon sky, and then it tumbled, parachuting to the ground, leaving behind it a pure moment of silence. Kneeling in the empty field, Con felt his chest fill with the bird's defiant song, as though the display had been just for him.

When Johnny arrived, there were no cigarettes or any books for him to read.

'I've heard the old girl with the books is off somewhere,' he said. 'Gone visiting and the place is shut up.'

Johnny gave him half the cigarettes he had left from his last packet and told him that – with luck – the priest would be back that day, or the next day at the latest. When he left, Con settled down, looking at the clear night sky through the hut door. He didn't mind the isolation; but he missed having something to read, something that would help him chase away the images of Bo that had begun to appear at the edge of his vision. Instead, he thought of Ruby, trying to recreate the moment when she'd been in his arms, but as his eyes closed, all he could recall was her moving away through the long shafts of sunlight.

The next time he woke, he could hear voices; the sun was up, and as he peered through the gaps in the hut's side, he could see three fishermen walking by, leaving a trail of cigarette smoke that taunted him. He got up and went out into the sunny morning. The grass on the riverbank was damp, but underneath the trees the earth was soft and dry. Con settled back against a tree and ran through a selection of imaginary books and possible daydreams. Since he was a little boy, he'd always lived inside his head. He didn't know if everyone did this, but he'd often found that life on the outside wasn't as good as in dreams and books. He closed his eyes again. In his dream, Ruby was walking towards him through the fields. As her dress moved, he could see her form from waist to hipline and the freckles, a sprinkling of gold dust, on her arms. He wasn't sure how long he'd slept, but when he opened his eyes, she was kneeling on the ground next to him shaking his shoulder.

'You should be more careful,' she said. 'I could have been anybody.'

Her hair was unpinned and rumpled, tumbling around her shoulders. Her eyes shone and a single teardrop had escaped on to a pale lash.

'Is everything okay?'

She studied the ground in front of her and then shook her head. 'It's... One of the family has died, and everything was upset and... I overslept and then everybody was there. I was going to make them think I'd gone to work... Have my breakfast and slip out with some clothes in my basket... Then Jenny started falling out with everybody, so I've just come as I am. I've not brought you any...'

'I've plenty of food. Johnny brought me some... Have you eaten?'

'No. The row started before I got a chance to have anything. I am a bit hungry.'

She sat down on the riverbank, and when Con disappeared inside the hut, Ruby splashed her face and hair with water from the river. She was trying to press out the worst of the crumples from her lavender dress, when Con came back carrying a basket with bread, cheese and beer. He sat down next to her, wedging the bottles of beer into the mud and stones, and she told him about Joe's death.

'I can go back after,' she said. 'I'll get some things. We can't go until it's dark, anyway.'

Con had settled the bottles in the shallow water, and when he turned around to hand her some bread and cheese, he noticed for the first time that she was wearing the same dress, and she wasn't wearing lipstick. He could see there was a delicate pattern of blue veins on her eyelids, and the shadows under her eyes were almost the same shade of lavender as her dress. He encouraged her to eat and then he took her hand, and they walked along by the river. At first Con felt a new unease between them and he wondered if she was regretting her promise to come with him, but then she found a blackbird's nest and showed him how to put a leaf over the baby birds' beaks so that they would open their mouths. The squirming chicks and their insistent little beaks made them both smile, and they sauntered on, as easy and happy together as they'd been before, with only the sound of the bumblebees and birds for company. When she slipped off her shoes and waded in the river he followed, and then they rambled back, Ruby collecting wild flowers along the way, until they reached the place where he'd left the bottles of beer cooling in the reeds. They sat for a while watching the bobbing moorhens, hoping to spot their nests on the opposite bank, and listening to the coots squabbling. Ruby had the flowers she'd collected in her lap and began making the daisies into a chain.

'Oh look,' she said, glancing up from her work. 'Look, dragonflies.'

As though to order, the creatures lifted gracefully up, allowing their wings to glisten in the clear light.

'That green,' she said, 'it's just the colour of one of my mother's dresses. I'll have to go back, before we go tonight. I'll need at least two of them. I could get a job playing in a pub. Bert won't let me play there, 'cos he says I'm not old enough, but in Liverpool...'

'Have you said anything to Henry? I've been thinking. I need to talk to him. Johnny said the priest would be back and... Well, Liverpool. He might not want you to come.'

'You can't go on your own. You don't know the way.'

'If the priest doesn't come, it might be better, if instead of us... It might be better if I go with Henry. He could get me on a train. A goods train, going to the city or the docks. He works on the railway. He'd know how to do it.'

'No. You'll need me to help you. You might not get a job, not at first. I've got another idea. You gave me the idea, you and Mrs Bland. I'll be able to earn money. Wait there. Close your eyes. Don't turn round, until I say.'

Ruby ran off in the direction of the trees. Con could hear her moving around, rustling the leaves. He fished the second bottle of beer out of

428

the stream and waited.

'Are you ready?' she called. 'You can turn round now.'

It was as though a beautiful painting had come to life. The soft green shadows caressed her naked back, and her long red hair, sweeping down almost to the swell of her buttocks, was patterned with golden coins of light. Ruby – her dress rolled down to her hips – wearing nothing else but her crown of daisies, gazed at him over the curve of her naked shoulder. He stood up, overturning the half-empty bottle on the grass, but before he could speak, she slipped away among the sun-flecked leaves.

'There'll be theatres in Liverpool,' she called. 'They'll pay good money. Mum would do it, when we were short. I thought about the picture on Mrs Bland's wall,' she said, reappearing in the lavender dress, the daisy crown askew on her rumpled hair. 'You know the one by the door? You said Ophelia looked like me, but that would be no good 'cos they'd have to have some kind of tank to float me in. So in this one, I'm Titania, Queen of the Fairies. Did you guess? I think it's a famous picture. My dad had postcards with the picture on. It gave me the idea for doing other paintings. Venus is one I thought of. Mum and some of the other girls did statues from history; I could do paintings.'

'You are beautiful,' Con said, his voice shaking. 'But you can't...'

'It always pulls them in. The takings were always good. That's why they used to do it, when the money went down, and it always worked.'

'You can't. Men...'

'You can't see them,' Ruby said, her excitement fading, 'they can't get near ... touch... My dad would wait for her. You could...'

'No. It's not... It's not what you should be doing... It's taking advantage of...'

'I'm being taken advantage of now,' she said, looking up at him and shading her eyes. "Exploited", Mrs Bland calls it. At least this is ... artistic and... Why is it worse than working in a hot, mucky factory?' she asked, pulling off her daisy crown. 'We'll need money, a place. When the war's over we might want to travel.'

'No. We couldn't. We couldn't live in the world as it is. It's a dream,' Con said, kissing the top of her head. 'Ruby, honey, running away wouldn't solve anything. I can't go. I don't come from here, Ruby. I'm going to wait for the priest, like Johnny said. O'Donal's okay. If they take me back and... I want to go back to my own country. When the war's over, there'll be a battle over there. The trouble here, now, it will carry on. Some of the white GIs will take that fear back home. They see the way it is over here, and they're afraid that the black soldiers will go home and, because of the way they've been treated here, they'll start looking, questioning the way things are in their own country. They're afraid we'll want more, and someone's got to be there to stand up and say what's right and what really happened here.'

'We can go back together.'

'We can't. I can't have a white girlfriend. There'd be no sort of life for us there: friends, family, jobs. There'd be nothing for us. There'd be no place for you. A white woman with a black man is hated more than the black man himself. If you love someone, you'd want to protect her from that.'

'Then stay here. The folk here don't think like that.'

'They'll learn to think of me as inferior. Plenty of folks are willing to teach them, and it would never be my country.'

'When Bo came back from Liverpool, he said... The couple you met. He wants to stay with Sadie, I know. Bo wouldn't...'

'Bo's dead.'

'What?'

'He's dead, Ruby. The MPs killed him. I'm sorry, I should have told you. That morning, after we fought back, when Henry asked about Bo, I couldn't tell him. I should have, I know. It's felt real strange. When I've been sitting in the hut on my own, and when I'm walking out here with you, the camp and what happened there isn't real. But now I've got to go back.'

Con lifted up her chin and stroked her face, tracing the long pale curve of her lips.

'I thought you'd want to stay,' she said. 'That we'd be like Sadie and Bo.'

'I need to go back.'

'They'll send you to prison. Or kill you.'

'No. Not if the priest comes with me and explains, and I admit I lied about my age. Johnny reckons—'

'He might be wrong.'

Con stroked her cheek, but as he bent his head to feel the warmth of her hair on his skin, he heard the sharp metallic click of a rifle.

431

'Run,' he whispered, pushing her away from him. 'Run, and don't look back. Run!'

Hal had only seen one lynching; it was 1926 in Mississippi, and then he hadn't seen the whole of it. He was fourteen and working on his Uncle George's farm. By the time he'd got there, the guy had been beaten up pretty bad. He'd lost an eye and an ear. They'd got a rope, and as the body went up in the air and danced, the crowd cheered. He was young, strong, not more than seventeen or eighteen, but he'd died quick and spoilt half the fun. It disappointed a lot of the folk who'd come for the show; they'd started cursing and throwing empty liquor bottles at the body. When they'd got bored of that, the corpse was brought down and the rope cut in small pieces and sold for five dollars each. His Uncle George said it was a tradition, and as it was his first lynching, he'd bought him a piece for luck. Then the boys and some of the men kicked the body around for a bit, until it wasn't clear that it had ever been a man. In the end, all that was left were lumps of black flesh in the dirt for the crows and the dogs to nibble on.

As soon as he'd heard that they were sending black troops to England, he knew it was asking for trouble. He'd been right. He'd tried to warn the locals. At first, when Sadie avoided him, he'd thought it was because she was sore at him for not writing like he'd promised, but then he saw her in town with the dead black guy. It made him real sore, but he and his buddies had some good times uptown, hunting out black GIs and making

432

sure they knew their place. When he'd found out one of the dead guy's buddies was still on the loose, Hal was sure he knew where to look and persuaded one of the MP patrols to let him come with them. He'd told them he knew where the guy was likely to be, and he'd been right.

The cottage was empty when they'd arrived, but an old woman in one of the cottages on the lane knew where they should look.

'You'll not find him in there,' she'd called over her hedge, 'if it's that black soldier you're looking for. He's off with the younger one, Ruby; no more than sixteen, she is. No better than they should be, either of them. The older one set her hat at my lad, but I saw her off. Then these black soldiers arrived. They'd not been here five minutes when I caught the younger one, young Ruby, with two of them. Henry, him who lives in the white cottage, Mr Barton, she's his son's child. Will, Will Barton he is. He's another one as is no good. Went off playing the piano in bars and picked up with a singer. That's Pearl, her mother, so you can't be surprised, really. Well, I went round this day, and she was coming down the stairs as bold as brass with two of 'em. They said something about coming to collect a cake, but it was clear what was goin' on. This one you're looking for, they say it was him as was with her, Ruby, in the doctor's garden, and when this young man tried to chase them off, he knocked him out cold, and then they took his wallet. I'm glad they've all been locked up in that camp. You should keep 'em there for good. Decent women can't go out. Try up the river. He's started calling for her, and they go off up there. She took my dog out the other day and brought her back wet through, so I reckon you might find them along the bank somewhere.'

He'd thanked the old woman, smiled politely and patted the dog. Then, as the rest of the guys were climbing over the stone wall and heading down towards the water, he took the rope from the jeep, just in case.

Ruby tried to make her legs go faster. When she reached the wall and scrambled over, the lane was empty. At first she thought about running across the fields to Bardley's farm for help, but then decided to head for the cottage. At least Sadie was there, and if Granddad was still with Maud, she could go and get him and send Sadie to the farm.

Just after the little stone bridge, the road kinked slightly and she could see the MPs' jeep drawn up outside the cottages. She couldn't understand what had happened: if they'd come to the cottage, why hadn't Granddad and Sadie tried to stop them or warned Con? The front door was locked, and no face came to the window when she called Sadie's name. The back door was bolted, but she banged on it anyway. Then her legs crumpled, folding under her, and she sat on the flags by the door. In the empty yard, the air around her rang with the screeching of the wagons' wheels from the shunting yards, followed by the clattering of points. These familiar sounds masked the chink of the front gate opening and the thud of boots on the brick path.

At first, Sergeant Mayfield thought the barefoot girl in the yard was hurt, but when Ruby got him to understand that it was Con who was in danger, he took her with him to the front of the cottage where Captain O'Donal was waiting in a jeep. Ruby was still explaining about the GIs and begging them to follow her back to the river, when Granddad arrived with Johnny and Father O'Flynn. Granddad knew a quick way to get from the farm track down to the hut, and they sped off leaving her behind.

CHAPTER SIXTEEN

It was later, when Granddad came up to her room and showed her the photo of Bo wearing the zoot suit he'd been so proud of, that Ruby realised Captain O'Donal and Sergeant Mayfield hadn't been looking for Con; the reason for their visit had been to see Sadie. Ruby curled up on her bed, and Granddad sat in the old cane chair and promised he'd stayed until he was sure Con was safe. When they heard the back door open, and Sadie called out that she'd been to Lou's to borrow a pattern for a kiddie's dress, Granddad told her to stay in her room. Ruby listened to his footsteps moving slowly down the stairs, and when Sadie began to scream, she covered her ears.

The next day Sadie didn't come out of her room. Ruby had asked Jenny if she could go and sit with her, but she'd shaken her head and picked up her sewing. Granddad hadn't looked up, but sat in his chair, hands clasped, staring into the pale flames of the smoky fire, refusing to tell her anything, except that Con was safe and that he'd been put in Captain O'Donal's jeep and taken to the hospital.

As if in sympathy, the warm sunny weather was replaced by unrelenting rain. In the evening, Ruby sat in her room staring out over the dripping garden. She wanted to see Con, but Granddad said that he was under arrest and he wouldn't be allowed to see anyone. Then the next morning, after Granddad and Jenny had left for work, she found Sadie sitting in the living room. She went to hug her but no warm cheek met hers.

'You must have known for days,' she whispered, her voice scraped and raw.

Ruby shook her head and crept into the kitchen, bringing tea and bread with honey.

'Con must have known. Why didn't he tell us?'

'I don't know. He said he didn't know how to.'

Sadie turned her face away, and when Sergeant Mayfield arrived later that day, shaking the water from his raincoat and telling them that Con had left the hospital, Sadie's sallow face had twisted with envy.

'Can I see him now?' Ruby asked.

'He's under guard.'

'When he comes back to the camp?'

Sergeant Mayfield stared into the cup of tea she'd made for him and shook his head. 'He won't come back to camp. Con's to be transferred to a US military jail, and then be shipped back to the US and out of the army.'

After the sergeant left she'd cried, but Sadie didn't sympathise.

'At least he's alive,' she said, 'and in a few months he could write, and when the war's over – who knows.'

The next time Sergeant Mayfield called, it was to return the books that Mrs Bland had lent to Con, and Ruby took him to meet the old lady.

'My goodness, ma'am,' he said, gazing around the bookshelves in the tiny room, 'this is a truly wonderful collection.'

'You must avail yourself as often as you like, Sergeant Mayfield,' Mrs Bland said. 'I'm delighted to meet a fellow bibliophile, and I know how much you have contributed to Con's education.'

Sergeant Mayfield looked up from the book he was examining. 'Do you think we were right, ma'am? All that Con really wanted when he came out here was adventure. He wanted to be a soldier and fight in Europe.'

'But you wouldn't have left the young man in ignorance of his own situation and that of his people and of how to make sense of his experience here? Sergeant, your example gave him a model, a template; you showed him how important it was to teach others what you know. Books must be read, and the reader then must decide for themselves what to do with that knowledge.'

'Yes, ma'am, I guess so.'

Ruby turned the pages of the books that Con had been reading. She'd imagined that they would be novels, but instead she found that most of the tissue-thin pages were covered with tight lines of text she found difficult to read. She examined the spines.

'What's a Jacobin?' she asked.

'I think you, too, Ruby, would benefit from a more challenging diet,' Mrs Bland said, 'and when I come back, I'll draw up a list. Some history, possibly, to back up the classics you've enjoyed.'

The next evening after work, she went with her granddad to Auntie Maud's to say prayers for Uncle Joe. When they arrived, Johnny was already there with Bert Lyons, who'd brought a couple of bottles of whisky from the pub, along with glasses, trays and extra teacups. Ruby helped him set out the trays in the scullery and boiled the kettle ready for the tea. From the window, she could see that the door of one of the toilets in the yard had been replaced by a large Union Jack.

'We took the petty door off to lay poor Joe out,' Bert said, following her gaze. 'Table wasn't big enough. It's just the job, propped on trestles from the pub and covered with a sheet. Folk quite often borrow the flag for a laying out, but usually to cover the coffin, if the bloke's been in the army. We use it at the pub to cover the tables for prize-giving for the bowling league and such. We've taken Maud's table next door, until after the funeral. She was concerned folk would be put out, when they found we'd taken the door off the petty. I told her there was still two they could use, but she wasn't happy. Then Johnny came up with the idea of using the flag, since it was big enough to cover the door hole, and like he says, if you're in there, you'll get plenty of warning. Tha'll not be startled, as folk will have to salute, an' that'll give um time to say, if it's occupied.'

The coffin took up most of the space in the living room. Although it was still daylight outside, the curtains had been drawn and the room was lit by candles. Auntie Maud sat by Joe's head. When the neighbours began to arrive, they each went up to speak to her and to pat Joe's folded hands. Then they took a seat along the wall, accepting a cup of tea from Ruby's tray, or a glass of whisky from Bert's. By the time Father O' Flynn arrived to say prayers, the house was full. Johnny opened the door, in order that the people in the street outside could join in the responses to the rosary.

Ruby had expected to see Jenny and Sadie with the rest of the mourners, but they didn't arrive. Next day, the day of the funeral, Jenny left for work as usual, leaving Sadie in bed and Grand-dad's breakfast on the table. The church was crowded, the organ played softly and she and Granddad walked behind the coffin with Maud. Outside in the churchyard, Father O'Flynn swung the incense, and when Joe was lowered into the earth, Maud closed her eyes. Bert had prepared a ham tea in the pub. Her granddad and Maud sat together, and in the late afternoon when everyone began leaving, they stood side by side and shook hands with the mourners as they left.

'You and Auntie Maud head off back home, Ruby love,' Granddad said. 'I'll just need to settle up with Bert. Johnny's coming with us; I need a hand to get that door back on its hinges and to carry the table in from next door.'

Outside the sky was a clear, deep blue. Auntie Maud and Johnny walked in front of her arm in arm; their funeral clothes – her dress the colour of dry shingle and his black suit – looked incongruous in the dazzling light. The curtains were still drawn in Maud's little house, and in the half-light the dress became ghostly. As she'd walked through the door, Maud had given a little cry; the table and chairs were back in their places, the two wooden trestles stood against the wall with the flag folded neatly on top of them, and when they pulled back the curtains, the sunshine crept over the newly starched tablecloth and the freshly mopped floor. Maud sat down heavily in her usual place by the table and gazed around the room. Johnny hovered by the door, peering out at the street looking for Granddad, and Ruby sat down opposite her auntie. She would have liked to take her hand, but instead she asked if she should make a pot of tea. Then, as if waking from a dream, Maud got up and went upstairs.

'She'll have gone to change out of her good things,' Johnny said, and went to put the kettle on.

By the time Granddad arrived, the tea was ready. Maud, dressed in her everyday skirt and blouse, came down and poured out some tea for each of them in some pretty cups that Ruby hadn't seen before; then Granddad added a tot of whisky and they drank a toast to Joe.

A few days after Joe's funeral, Sergeant Mayfield arrived at the cottage one evening with a book under his arm.

'I wanted to return this to Mrs Bland,' he said, 'but there isn't anyone at home.'

'She's away at her sister's,' Ruby said, wiping her hands on her apron. 'I'll give it to her if you like. We don't know when she's coming back. She could be away some time; she took the cat with her.'

'I was glad of the loan. I'm pretty short of reading materials, except for back numbers of some newspapers.'

The house was quiet. Jenny and Sadie were at work, and she and Granddad were sitting in the garden. The sergeant joined them on the bench. He sat for a while smoking with Granddad and talked about his home in the South, describing the cotton fields and the smell of honeysuckle on summer mornings.

'I have a message for you all from Con,' he said.

'Have you seen him?'

'No. I got the message off a friend. I'm to tell you that he knows how much he owes Henry and Johnny and your priest and that he'll never forget you all. I wanted to come and tell you. I'll be getting my orders any day now.'

'You're going as well?' Henry asked.

Sergeant Mayfield smiled and drew the cigarette smoke deep into his lungs. 'There's been big changes at the camp, though I'm not sure any of the MPs will be punished. Some of them were moved out, but I'm pretty certain that will be the end of it. The rest of our guys, the ones involved, got moved out straight away. Some were sent to other camps and some will be given jail. Holt was arrested, and Wes was moved out a few days ago. I don't know where. Don't know where I'll be sent either, but if I were to guess, I'd say the south, someplace near the coast or an airbase. The word is most of the guys – even those who'll be given jail

– won't serve the whole of their sentences. They'll be released, once everything dies down, perhaps in a year or so, we don't really know.'

'What about Con?'

'I guess he'll be on a ship home by now. They didn't rightly know what to do with him. Once in the US, he'll be discharged and sent to a correctional facility in New York. I understand that's because he lied about his age when he enlisted. I know he found... I know all the men found the folks round here opened their eyes. We didn't expect such a welcome.'

Granddad sent Ruby inside to get the bottle of Irish whiskey left over from Frank and Lou's wedding. He and the sergeant drank a toast to Bo and to the end of the war. Then they walked with him to the gate, and as she watched his jeep disappear into the twilight, Ruby knew she had lost another link to Con.

'Do you think Con will write?' she asked Granddad, as she helped him check the hens.

'I don't know, love, it might not be allowed. Best not to count on it too much.'

When Ruby came home from work the next day, a young brindled spaniel trotted along the front-garden path to meet her.

'Somebody tied the poor little bugger up to the rails,' Granddad said, appearing around the side of the cottage. 'Take him in through the front, Ruby, our Monty isn't too suited. I thought we could do with a dog. From next Monday, I'll have linesman duties. I'll be on me own, walking up and down the line, and he'll be company. Won't you, lad?' Granddad said, following them into the house and easing himself into his armchair. The dog, as if understanding what was needed, immediately sat down at his feet and allowed his ears to be tickled. 'I've called him Brag. Same as my dad's old dog. He'll need a bowl and a dish for his water. See if you can find him a biscuit or two, will you, or a nice bone. What do you say to that, Brag me lad?'

Ruby went into the kitchen and opened the biscuit tin. Before Jenny found the money in her dress pocket and Granddad heard about Rollo and the attack, he wouldn't have dared to bring a dog home, no matter how badly it had been treated. At the sight of a strange dog in the cottage, Jenny would have been furious and ordered him to get rid of it, but now Grandma Jenny didn't scold him as she used to. Other things had changed as well: now he didn't hide the fact that he gave Maud vegetables from the garden, and now he went to the pub with Johnny whenever he liked. At first, she'd felt glad that Granddad was angry with Jenny for the way she'd deceived him. Jenny had been mean to her and to Johnny and she deserved it. For a while, she'd enjoyed the relief from Jenny's sharp tongue, but Granddad needed someone to keep him in check, and now the cottage felt strange without Jenny scolding everyone.

'Is that all you could find?' Granddad said, when she returned with two broken biscuits. 'We'll have to do better than that, laddie, won't we? I'll need you to help me, Ruby. He'll need taking out, looking after, walking and such, on the days he doesn't come with me. This breed needs plenty of exercise.'

On his first night, Brag kept them awake with his whining. When Ruby came down next morning he'd piddled in the kitchen, but as Granddad pointed out in Brag's defence, the puddle was by the back door. Sadie showed little interest in the new member of the family, except to bawl at him to be quiet, and Jenny ignored him completely, behaving as though there wasn't an animal under the table at breakfast, begging for crusts and wagging its tail.

On the second night when he began to cry, Ruby carried him upstairs to her room, where he settled contentedly at the foot of her bed. After tea she took him for a walk by the river; she'd been down there only once since Con's arrest, and that had been to find her shoes. Now, glad to escape the silent house, Ruby followed the paths she'd wandered with Con, remembering as she walked by each tree the things they'd talked about and how pretty everything had looked when they'd been there together. As Brag sniffed and investigated his new territory, she stretched out on the soft grass, trying to imagine the feel of Con's tunic under her head and the buttery, spicy smell of his skin in the hot sun. When the dog returned, he gave her face an impatient, sloppy lick that made her giggle. She got up, and followed his waggy tail through the wood. Brag was foraging under a tree not far from the hut when he found it; the rope was heavy with rain. Ruby picked it up. It coiled around her arm and soaked her fingers as – tracing the twists and spirals they would have put around his neck – she said a silent prayer that Con was safe.

When they got back, her granddad was sitting on the bench against the cottage wall, swatting and cursing at the frantic midges around his head. In the garden, the plants drooped, pressed down by the weight of a threatening storm, and over in the west, the sky was the colour of rabbit fur.

'I reckon there's rain on the way,' he said. 'Good thing too. Garden could do with a good deggin' and this heat isn't healthy.'

'It was even hot by the river,' Ruby said. 'Look at the dog, how he's panting. I'll take him in and get him a drink.'

'I'd not go in yet, lass,' he said, patting the dog. 'There's been a bit of upset. It's Sadie; she's joined up. Papers have come through. I suspected as much, and 'appen it's best. Her mother's upset. Only to be expected.'

'When?'

'Couple of weeks, I would think.'

The couple of weeks stretched to almost six before Sadie's travel pass arrived. On the night before Sadie left, Ruby knocked on her door.

'I know you like it,' she said, handing her two tablets of fern soap wrapped in tissue paper.

'Thanks,' Sadie said, turning away and slipping them into her case. 'Thanks very much.'

'Are you going out? Last night of freedom, before you join up.'

'Out? Where to?' Sadie asked, fastening the clasp on her small brown suitcase and taking out a cigarette. 'If you went out, you'd notice there's no one as will even dance with any of us who had a black boyfriend. Not the white GIs, anyway. If I were you, I'd start thinking of moving out as well, once you're old enough.'

It was true that since Con had been arrested, Ruby didn't bother to go out. In fact, all she longed for was to sleep. Sleeping was her escape. In her dreams Con was still there, sitting next to her by the river, and sometimes for a moment, she could hear the rippling water and almost reach out and touch him.

The next day Granddad insisted that they all go into town to see Sadie off. The day was blustery; white clouds blew across the sky, each in turn covering and then revealing the sun.

'I'll treat you to a cup of tea in the Kardomah,' he said, as they followed him, clutching on to their hats and holding down their skirts at the corner of each street. Sadie wore a sober navy jacket over a pale-blue dress, her hair pinned up in a neat roll under a shiny straw hat in the same shade of blue. The café was busy, but the waitress found them a place, a high-backed booth near the window. Ruby sat next to her granddad, and looked down the length of the narrow room towards the counter. The hot water hissed in the shiny urns, and the glass cases, that in better times would have held cream cakes, displayed a dejected collection of biscuits and slices of dry-looking tea bread. When the waitress left, Granddad tried to make them laugh, telling jokes about his own training days that they'd all heard him tell before. The tea was served from a silver teapot, along with extra hot water in a white jug that matched the cups and saucers.

Jenny refilled their cups and they drank in silence. In the weeks since Bo's death, the long hours of shift work meant that Ruby had spent very little time with Sadie or her mother; now, sitting opposite the two women, she could see how they'd both changed: Sadie was no longer the cheerful girl who would have giggled and made fun of Henry's stories, and Jenny appeared to have grown smaller, her once-round cheeks now deflated and crinkled under their coating of rouge. She saw Granddad check his pocket watch, and when they'd finished their tea, no one suggested refilling the pot with the hot water for another cup.

They walked two by two along the pavement, Sadie with Jenny in front of them arm in arm. At the station, as they waited for Granddad to get the platform tickets, Ruby gave Sadie a bag of sweets for the journey. For an instant, the old Sadie grinned at her from under the staid little hat.

'Ruby, the things Mum said about New Year's Eve, it's because she knows it was her fault. She was scared that when Henry found out what had happened he would tell her to go, that's what was at the back of it.'

Then Granddad called to them from the barrier and the moment had gone. The station was busy and he led the way to the far end of the platform where the train was waiting.

'Do you remember the last time you were here?' Granddad asked, when Jenny had climbed on board to help Sadie find a seat. 'There was a young soldier gave us a letter for his girl. I wonder if she ever got it.'

When the train moved off, they waved until it disappeared, looking as any family might do who were sending a daughter off into the services. As

447

they walked back down the main platform towards the barrier, Granddad gave Jenny his hankie and patted her shoulder. Walking along behind them, Ruby saw that the young woman she'd become – reflected repeatedly through the windows of the station's waiting rooms and bar – had begun to smile.

In the evening, Granddad didn't go to meet Johnny. Instead, they settled down to listen to the radio as they used to do. The next day, the breeze had dropped and the temperature began to climb. The heat and the long hours made everyone at the factory short-tempered, but in the evenings, Jenny and Granddad were content to sit on the old bench, enjoying the cool air and watching the sun slip out of sight. Over the weeks, the riot was gradually forgotten; now the gossip at the factory wasn't about the doings at the camp, but the suspected cheating in the weaving sheds.

'I've heard they're making cloth for RAF officers in the big factory,' Mrs Rostron said, one dinnertime as they were sitting in the yard. 'The docket with the order says fifty yards, but fifty-two is wove. Now who's that for? Who's getting that? It's not right. Does young Trevor Pye know what's happening to it? He's been over there a lot these last couple of weeks.'

'Trevor? I don't think so,' Ruby said, wiping her neck with her hankie.

'Well, it's lovely quality. It being for the officers, it will have to be. They want reporting, if you ask me. There's some as is getting rich from this war, while the rest of us can hardly clothe ourselves.'

At the end of her shift, the air outside in the

dusty street felt almost as hot as in the spinning room. The main road was quiet; the only vehicle Ruby saw was a jeep, driven by a white GI, who made its wheels spin as he turned sharply into the lane. She crossed the road. At the bridge she stood for a while, looking down at the weak trickle of water, remembering the satisfying gurgle of the river that had flowed there just a few weeks before. It was as though it had never existed; it was as though both the people and the things she'd shared with Con were moving, changing, leaving her.

Inside the cottage it was cool. Ruby washed her face at the kitchen sink and poured a glass of water. The living room was in shadow, except where a book lay in a patch of sunlight at the back of the front door. Con's copy of *Twelfth Night* was crumpled and the edges curled. Inside the grubby cover he'd written: 'For Ruby'. She remembered the jeep she'd seen turning into the lane; not all the white GIs were the same: Con had told them of northern GIs who didn't object to drinking from a glass that had been used by a black soldier and would sit with the black GIs in the pub. She went to the gate and looked down the empty lane, wishing the soldier would come back and she could give him a message for Con.

Ruby took the book up to her room. In the last weeks she'd spent hours sitting there, staring at the cottage on her rug, pretending that she was Maggie Joy and that the next day the long-awaited letter would arrive. She stroked the book, knowing it once belonged to his grandma and how much it had meant to him. She turned each page, sniffing, inhaling, searching for a sign. The scrap of paper was hidden between the pages of notes at the back of the book. It was small and could have once been used as a bookmark. The scrap wasn't new; it felt soft, pliant, as though it had been kept in the book for a long time. It wasn't signed, but Ruby knew Con's neat, almost girlish writing.

'By the time you get this, I'll be on my way home in disgrace. Ruby, I'm glad I hid out and had some time with you. I'm not going to forget you and I'm going to miss you for a long time.'

She didn't hear Jenny arrive home and begin peeling the vegetables in the kitchen, and she didn't hear her granddad, until he called up to her that her tea was ready. Then she slipped the book under her pillow and hurried downstairs.

'Were you asleep, Ruby, love?' he asked, handing her a plate of tinned meat and salad. 'Your eyes look heavy.'

Jenny and Granddad sat side by side at the table. It was this new friendliness between them, and her fear that she might disturb it, that made her keep the book a secret. Instead, she blamed her lack of appetite on the weather, and Granddad happily relieved her of her unwanted Spam. She would have told Sadie, but now Sadie wrote only brief notes to them about her new life at the training camp and her new friends.

When tea was over and the washing-up had been done, Ruby escaped up to her room, pleading a headache. In some ways, now the waiting and the hoping were over, it was as though she was moving backwards, back to the time after her mother had died and back to feeling the dull, hungry ache for something she'd lost. She sat on her bed and looked out to the west and the sea. At Everdeane, no one talked about her mother; after she'd died, it was as though she'd never existed. The same thing was happening now: now Con and the other soldiers had gone, everything was changing and they would soon be forgotten. At Everdeane, she'd been afraid that she might begin to forget Pearl as well. Then, the first evening she took her mother's place waiting on the guests in the dining room, Ruby wore the gymslip she'd always worn to school, when Pearl was alive and everything was ordinary and safe. After the funeral Auntie Ethel had said she must earn her keep by looking after the guests. That first time she'd put her gymslip on under her apron it made her feel better. Each time she wore it, when she felt the familiar touch of the coarse fabric pleats against her leg, Pearl was there, serving the guests at the next table and smiling over at her. Ruby took out the lilac dress she'd worn by the river. Then wrapping Con's book inside it, she put them both in the suitcase with Pearl's dresses.

In the following weeks the weather became cooler, and the fruit in the garden grew plump. One Saturday, Ruby and Jenny spent most of the afternoon picking the ripe blackcurrants for jam.

'I'll take this lot inside,' Jenny said. 'Then I'm going to pop down to Lou's with the things our Sadie's sent for her little niece's birthday. We can top and tail this lot tonight after tea, before it's time for *The Man in Black* on the radio. Will you take the washing in when you've done? It'll be dry by then.'

It took Ruby the next hour to pick the rest of the berries. Leaving her granddad digging in the vegetable patch, she took them into the scullery and put them in buckets to steep. Then she went upstairs to change her stained clothes, before bringing in the washing. She was combing her hair, shaking out the stray blackcurrant leaves that had been caught in her curls, when she heard her granddad yell and the cockerel's angry squawk. Ruby looked down from her window, but all she could see was the abandoned spade, its twinkling blade spinning on the ground, and Monty flapping angrily beside it. She thought that it must be a stray dog or a cat in the garden. When Brag, who'd been locked in the living room, began to bark, she knew that whatever was causing the excitement must be at the front of the cottage or in the lane. Ruby hurried through to Sadie's old room, bending down by the low window to look over the front garden. At first she thought it was an argument, that he was seeing off the spiv by the gate, grabbing the man, knocking his hat off and sending his battered suitcase flying. Then she heard Granddad shout again, and this time she could make out the words.

'It's my boy!' Granddad was shouting. 'It's my boy!'

Ruby began running, leaving rugs skittering behind her, leaping the stairs' steps and dashing through the living room, almost falling over Brag, as the excited dog chased her down the path to the gate. She put her arms around them, hugging them both, father and son.

When Jenny turned the corner, she heard the stupid dog yapping and slowed her pace, watching the little group: Ruby, Henry and the threadbare spiv by the gate. She hadn't seen Will Barton before, but she guessed who the shabby new arrival must be, and with the first spots of autumn rain chilling her face, she walked up the lane towards them.

ACKNOWLEDGEMENTS

With thanks to my agent, Jane Conway-Gordon as well as Susie Dunlop and all her staff at Allison & Busby. My thanks to the staff at Lancashire libraries for their unfailing helpfulness; the cheerful ladies of the Westhoughton Writing Group for their reminiscences and encouragement, and I would particularly like to thank Sheila Clift for her wisdom and friendship. Finally, I would like to thank my husband, Chris, for his relentless supply of brews and sporadic meal production.

AUTHOR'S NOTE

The idea for *Ruby's War* began with the reminiscences of older members of my family and their friends about their experiences in WWII. These included not only the deprivations, the long hours and the comradeship, but also their first experiences of meeting men and women from other parts of the world. One incident that was always spoken of softly and with sadness was the US forces' treatment of the African-American soldiers stationed at a nearby military camp.

Part of the process of writing my novel has been to filter both the geography and history of this area of the Northwest through my imagination. This is a work of fiction, but I have used some of the details from the article 'The Mutiny at Bamber Bridge' by Dr Ken Werrell to frame the action in part of my story. I have also used the Detroit race riots that took place a few days earlier as a motivation for the uprising. This is a theory suggested by Graham Smith in his book *When Jim Crow Met John Bull.*

For those looking for purely historical fact about these incidents and the period, I suggest the following books and articles in the bibliography as starting points.

BIBLIOGRAPHY

BOOKS

Birtill, George, *The War and After* (Chorley: 1976)

Brown, Richard and Millgate, Helen D., *Mr Brown's War: A Diary of the Second World War* (Stroud: 2003)

Edgerton, Robert B., *Hidden Heroism: Black Soldiers in America's Wars* (Colorado: 2001)

Freethy, Ron, *Lancashire 1939–1945: The Secret War* (Newbury: 2005)

– – *Lancashire v Hitler: Civilians at War* (Newbury: 2006)

– – *Lancashire 1939–45: Working for Victory* (Newbury: 2007)

Garfield, Simon, *We Are At War: The Diaries of Five Ordinary People in Extraordinary Times* (London: 2005)

Hopwood, Edwin, *A History of the Lancashire Cotton Industry and the Amalgamated Weavers' Association* (Manchester: 1969)

Langford, Joan M., *The History of Farington Cotton Mill*, (Leyland: 2003)

Latty, Yvonne, *We Were There* (New York: 2004)

Motley, Mary P., *The Invisible Soldier: The Experience of the Black Soldier – World War II* (Detroit: 1975)

Shogun, Robert and Craig, Tom, *The Detroit Race Riot: A Study in Violence* (Philadelphia: 1964)

Singleton, John, *Lancashire on the Scrapheap: Cotton Industry 1945–1970* (Oxford: 1991)

Smith, Graham, *When Jim Crow Met John Bull* (London: 1987)

Valery, Anne, *Talking About the War: 1939–45: A Personal View of the War in Britain* (London: 1991)

ARTICLES

Rose, Sonya O., 'Girls and GIs: Race, Sex and Diplomacy in Second World War Britain', *The International History Review*, 19/1 (1997), 146–160

Schofield, M. M., 'The Slave Trade from Lancashire and Cheshire Ports Outside Liverpool, *Historic Society of Lancashire and Cheshire*, 126 (1976), 30–72

Werrell, K., 'Crime in WWII: The Mutiny at Bamber Bridge', *After the Battle* 22 (1978), 1–11

And, of course, the Internet...

The publishers hope that this book has given you enjoyable reading. Large Print Books are especially designed to be as easy to see and hold as possible. If you wish a complete list of our books please ask at your local library or write directly to:

Magna Large Print Books
Magna House, Long Preston,
Skipton, North Yorkshire.
BD23 4ND

This Large Print Book for the partially sighted, who cannot read normal print, is published under the auspices of

THE ULVERSCROFT FOUNDATION